THE SHROUD OF
HEAVEN

A NICK KISMET ADVENTURE

SEAN ELLIS

Gryphonwood

The Shroud of Heaven
Copyright © 2009, 2015 by Sean Ellis
Cover by J Kent Holloway
Published by Gryphonwood Press
www.gryphonwoodpress.com

ISBN: 978-1-940095-35-6

For Connor and Campbell, the future of adventure.

BOOKS BY SEAN ELLIS

Mira Raiden Adventures
Ascendant
Descendant

The Nick Kismet Thrillers
The Shroud of Heaven
Into the Black
Fortune Favors
The Devil You Know (novella)

The Adventures of Dodge Dalton
In the Shadow of Falcon's Wings
At the Outpost of Fate
On the High Road to Oblivion

Chess Team/Jack Sigler Thrillers
(with Jeremy Robinson)
Callsign: King
Underworld
Blackout
Prime
Savage

The Jade Ihara Adventures
Oracle (with David Wood)
Changeling (with David Wood-forthcoming)

Other Works
Dark Trinity - Ascendant
Magic Mirror
WarGod (with Steven Savile)
Hell Ship (with David Wood)
Flood Rising (with Jeremy Robinson)

PROLOGUE THE CHAINS OF GOD

January 1991

The Chinook abruptly lurched, gaining fifteen meters of altitude in a heartbeat, only to plunge back down an instant later. The pilot, an insectoid-looking figure in his bulbous headgear and night vision goggles, tilted his head sideways as if to grin at the helpless passengers clinging to nylon web straps in the rear of the helicopter.

"Sorry, mates. Telephone lines."

Nick Kismet nodded indifferently, though his stomach was still pitching from the sudden maneuver. Some of the Gurkhas were not as adept at hiding their momentary nausea; the one he knew only as Sergeant Higgins looked positively green despite the liberal coating of camouflage paint that concealed his face. Of course, in the monochrome display of the PV-7 night vision device affixed to his Kevlar helmet, everything looked green.

The swooping flight of the CH47 seemed an appropriate metaphor for Kismet's life recently. Still trying to overcome the temporary shock of the mobilization orders—a not entirely unexpected event given the escalation of tensions on the Arabian peninsula—he had been further thrown off guard by the strange mission thrust upon him less than a week after his arrival at CENTCOM in Riyadh. Unable to adequately process all of that information, he elected to simply ride it out until things made a little more sense. It was the same philosophy that would, he hoped, get him through this roller coaster insertion.

The flight was probably routine for the pilots. Kismet knew that American Special Forces and British SAS soldiers had already been dropped into enemy-held territory to gather information. As an officer in the US Army Department of Intelligence, albeit a lowly Second Lieutenant and a reservist at that, he was aware of the covert missions that were laying the foundation for the impending assault designed to drive the fourth largest army in the world from their entrenchments in Kuwait. That he would find himself a part of such an operation, much less one that would penetrate deep beyond Iraq's border, was a scenario too ludicrous to even consider. Nevertheless, here he was.

The sergeant swallowed queasily and flashed him an insincere thumbs up. Kismet nodded again.

The Gurkhas signified yet another indecipherable factor in the clandestine mission. He did not know a great deal about the men or their combat division; it was his understanding that they were a sort of foreign legion for the British, originating in Nepal and modeled after the fierce warrior tribe that was their namesake. They were indeed a cosmopolitan bunch, evincing a full spectrum of racial characteristics. Higgins, one of two Caucasian soldiers in the squad, was a Kiwi—originally a citizen of New Zealand.

Though their sand-colored uniforms had been sterilized—no indication of nationality, unit or rank—he had recognized them by virtue of their *kukri* knives. The large chopping knife with a broad, boomerang-shaped blade was their signature weapon. According to their tradition, each recruit was initiated into the elite corps through a bloody ritual in which he was required to behead a young bullock with a single stroke of his *kukri*. A few bits of presumably outdated trivia, however, represented the full extent of Kismet's knowledge about the Gurkhas. *Not much intelligence for an intelligence officer*, he thought sourly.

The presence of soldiers of the United Kingdom of Great Britain was a riddle at least partially explained. According to his commanding officer, the information leading to the mission had been channeled through British resources, and despite the fact that Kismet, an American officer, had been singled out for special attention, the British would continue to manage the particulars of the insertion. But that did not satisfactorily explain CENTCOM's decision to send this particular unit.

Though legendary for their fierceness, the Gurkha warriors were not an ideal choice for covert insertions. Those assignments, at least where Her Majesty's armed forces were concerned, typically went to the men of the SAS—Special Air Service—who trained extensively for everything from anti-terrorism to hostage rescue to long-range reconnaissance. He could think of only one compelling reason for the commander in charge of the mission to choose men who were not natural citizens of the British commonwealth, but rather rogues and expatriates: They were expendable. Kismet wondered if he fell into that category as well.

What little he had been told had not inspired him to confidence in the success, much less the importance, of their mission. He knew only that it involved the possible defection of a high-value target; someone who might be a member of Saddam Hussein's inner circle of advisors. After reading the operation order, a bare bones overview of what he would be expected to accomplish, Kismet had immediately become suspicious. His first impulse was that the supposed defection was an elaborate ruse designed to test the capabilities of coalition forces in penetrating Iraqi air defenses. Despite assurances otherwise, he remained skeptical.

The Chinook continued through the desert night, following the nap of the earth to avoid detection by radar, jinking and swooping when necessary to dodge phone lines and possible SAM sites. There was little for the passengers to see through the small portals on either side of the ungainly looking aircraft. Even with the aid of night vision goggles, the desert was a featureless wasteland. Each *wadi*—the dry gullies that cut randomly across the dunes—looked very much like the next, but one of them concealed the man he had been sent to meet.

In the earpiece of his headset, Kismet heard the pilots continue their exchange of information, calling out the obstacles that lay in their path as they became visible. He knew they were nearing their destination because the co-pilot regularly updated their ETA. The countdown was now a matter of mere minutes.

"City lights," observed the flight officer, pointing over the pilot's shoulder. He consulted a military map specifically designed for use with night vision gear. "That's Nasiriyah."

"Close as I want to get."

"I have a visual of the target," the co-pilot announced. His voice dropped to an incredulous murmur. "Bloody wanker's having a fag."

Kismet absent-mindedly translated the idiomatic expression. Somewhere out in the desert, the man they were supposed to meet was smoking a cigarette. In the display of the night vision devices used by the flight crew, the pencil-thin ember would flash beacon-bright as the man drew smoke into his lungs, even from a distance of several hundred meters.

One of the Gurkhas tisked. "He should know better. Must be an officer."

Kismet laughed, grateful for their humor. He was the highest-ranked person onboard and well aware of the age-old rivalry between enlisted men and officers, but he took no offense at the veiled jab. This close to the objective, with his adrenaline spiking, he needed the distraction. Nervously, he checked his gear one last time.

The mission called for the team to be dropped near a rendezvous point established by the Iraqi defector. This would give them an opportunity to reconnoiter the area, just in case it was a trap. The Gurkhas would then dig in, securing a temporary forward operating base, while Kismet made contact with the defector. They expected their mission to last no more than forty-eight hours, but even that short time span required each man to carry several liters of drinking water, along with all of their combat gear and body armor. In addition to his ruck, Kismet carried a stubby CAR15, the carbine version of the M16A2 assault rifle, and his personal side arm, a Beretta M9 automatic pistol. Most of the Gurkhas carried American M203s—M16s equipped with integrated 40 millimeter grenade launchers under the rifle barrel—but two of the men were packing fully automatic Minimi light machine guns. Kismet noted that the latter pair would not be carrying their own water, a fair trade for the additional weight of a thousand rounds of ammunition apiece, stored in drum magazines and cloth bandoliers. Ideally, they would not have to expend a single round. If everything went according to plan, they would be returning to Saudi airspace with only their water supply depleted.

The Chinook dropped quickly to the desert floor, bouncing the passengers violently one final time. The Gurkhas immediately burst into action, pitching canvas bags out into the sand as the aft ramp slowly descended. Their movements seemed practiced, belying the tension that Kismet knew each man must be silently enduring. After swiftly disembarking, the small group of soldiers huddled close to the ground as the twin rotors of the Chinook whipped up a sandstorm. A few heartbeats later, the helicopter vanished into the night.

Higgins removed his NOD and gazed skyward, fixing the North Star with a fingertip. He extended his other arm at a ninety-degree angle. "Our guy's that way. Wong, Renke, dig us a nice little den. Lieutenant, I guess you're leading the way."

Kismet was thrown by the Kiwi sergeant's pronunciation—"Leftenant"—and gaped dumbly at the other man for several awkward seconds. "Sorry," he finally mumbled, hefting the CAR15 and turning in the direction Higgins had indicated. "Let's go."

They stayed low to the ground, pausing at the dune crests to survey the landscape for signs of the enemy. Visual contact with the defector—still puffing away on his cigarette, or perhaps chain-smoking one after another—was reestablished almost immediately. They were less than two hundred meters from the man's location.

"I don't see anyone else," Kismet murmured. "No vehicles either."

"How the hell did he get out here?" Higgins wondered aloud. "Flying bloody carpet?"

Kismet stifled a chuckle. "Maybe." He turned to the sergeant. "I guess this is it. I'm counting on you guys to watch my back."

The Gurkha nodded, but Kismet was not overwhelmed with confidence. Nevertheless he crept forward, topped the dune and scooted down the other side, moving unaccompanied toward the sole Iraqi. If it was a trap, he alone would face that peril. Even if the Gurkhas brought their firepower to bear, there was little hope of his surviving the first moments of a hostile encounter.

As he drew closer, he was able to make out the facial features of the defector. The bland countenance seemed pale beneath his thick black brow, as if the man had somehow managed to avoid direct exposure to the sun during his life on the cusp of the Arabian desert. Only the nervous quivering of the cigarette at his lips bore testimony that his bloodless hue had more to do with anxiety than pigmentation. In the green-tinted display of his night optics, Kismet noted that the man's pupils were tiny white dots. The incessant lighting and smoking of cigarettes had compromised the waiting defector's ability to see naturally in the dark, verifying the earlier observation made by the Chinook pilot. Either the man was too inexperienced in matters of survival to know better, or he simply didn't care.

Kismet paused, scanning the surrounding desert for any indication of an ambush party in concealment.

Nothing. If the defector was bait for a trap, then it was a well-covered snare. He edged forward, circling around the smoking man, and approached from his left side. When no more than ten meters separated them, he rose from his cautious crawl and pushed his goggles out of the way.

There was no way to avoid startling the oblivious defector, but he tried to minimize the shock by softly clearing his throat. The Iraqi man turned his head slowly, almost absent-mindedly, before reacting exactly as Kismet feared he would. Yet, as the man flailed backwards, waving his hands defensively, Kismet's apprehension that he had walked into a trap eased considerably. The defector had not groped for a concealed weapon or called out in alarm; no hidden accomplices had leapt to the man's aid. Kismet waited motionless for his contact to recover.

"Is salaam aleekum." *Peace be upon you.*

The softly spoken greeting did not seem to soothe the frightened man, but he heard the muttered, traditional reply: "Wa aleekum is-salaam." *And upon you be peace.*

"Well that's a good sign," Kismet muttered in English. His grasp of Arabic was not as strong as he would have liked. A lifetime of world travel with his father had immersed him repeatedly in foreign language environments, but he considered himself fluent only in the Romance languages.

However, despite the fact that his self-directed words were barely audible, the defector suddenly brightened. "You are Mr. Kismet?" he asked in halting English.

Kismet blinked. In his pre-mission briefing, he had been given precious little information about how the rendezvous would proceed. There had been no arrangement made for passwords and counter-signs. His commander was unable even to supply a name for the defector, much less any sort of safeguarding procedures. The last thing he had anticipated was for the Iraqi man to know his name. He switched off his night vision goggles and swung them up, away from his face. "That's right."

"Il-Hamdulillaah," breathed the man. "God be praised. I feared that you would not be coming. I am Samir Al-Azir."

He sensed that the man expected to be recognized, but the name triggered no memories. He smiled and gave the man a knowing nod, hoping nothing would happen to further expose his ignorance. "We should probably get moving."

Samir seemed further relieved at the suggestion, as if suddenly remembering why he was lurking in the cold desert night. He flipped his cigarette onto the sand. "Yes, yes. Follow me."

Before he could protest, Samir turned and began climbing the dune. Dumbly, Kismet started after the Iraqi. At the top of the rise, he signaled the waiting Gurkhas by extending his arms out to either side, as though waiting to be searched. The unusual gesture was a previously established signal, indicating to his comrades that he was not being taken along under duress. If Samir noticed, he said nothing.

Based on his recollection of aerial reconnaissance photographs of the area, Kismet knew that the nearest road was more than a kilometer from their present location. That roadway was a featureless track snaking across the desert to provide access to the semi-permanent Bedouin communities, and more importantly, to expedite the deployment of troops in the event of a war. With that war now looming large, the likelihood of armed forces moving along the highway was greatly increased. He did not find Samir's eagerness to approach that destination encouraging, but what he saw as they crested yet another dune a few moments later increased his anxiety tenfold. Barely visible across the intervening distance was the unmistakable silhouette of a vehicle waiting beside the highway.

It took another ten minutes of struggling over the uneven terrain to reach the parked sedan, long enough for him to ascertain that the battered, silver Mercedes was unoccupied. "Where are we going, Samir?"

The defector flashed a grin over his shoulder, but Kismet could see the other man's concern etched in deep lines across his forehead. "Not far. The tell is nearby."

Tell? There were many ways of interpreting the word, none of which made sense in the context. He frowned, but did not press for more information. Instead, he opened the rear driver side door of the sedan and carefully slipped inside. Samir's pale face registered confusion at Kismet's decision to sit behind instead of beside him, but he said nothing as he turned the key and eased the car onto the paved road.

Kismet rested the CAR15 on the seat beside him, shifting the waist pack of his load-bearing vest to avoid sitting on it. That the Army-issue equipment had not been designed for use in the cramped interior of a passenger vehicle was only one factor owing to his choice of the rear seat. Sitting in the back represented an attempt, however insignificant, to take a measure of control over the situation. He was completely at Samir's mercy. Even if the defector meant him no harm, there would be no effective way for Kismet to respond in the event of a sudden crisis. From the back seat at least, should the worst case scenario play out, he would be able to encourage the Iraqi to heed his suggestions by holding the business end of his sidearm to the base of the other man's skull.

True to his word, Samir drove the car only a few kilometers along the highway before once more pulling off into the sand. Kismet hastened from the confining interior of the sedan, and began scanning the dunes for any sign of enemy forces. They appeared to be alone in the night. Samir lit another cigarette then motioned for Kismet to follow as he headed into the desert.

The path chosen by the Iraqi defector led north across a section of flat land where bare rock struggled up through the ubiquitous layer of sand. Kismet gradually became aware that they were descending into a low valley sculpted by centuries of wind and, perhaps in a forgotten age, water. In the otherworldly green display of his goggles, he saw clear evidence of previous foot traffic along their course; not simply a scattering of prints, but a line of disruption indicating the passage of several people. He hefted the CAR15, his thumb poised on the fire selector and his finger on the outside of the trigger guard, but resisted the impulse to spin strategies for dealing with a hostile encounter. He would likely be outnumbered and outgunned in such a situation, so there was little to be gained by worrying. Samir, however, seemed to relax, as if each step brought him closer to a place of refuge. Their destination soon became apparent.

From the outside, it did not look like a cave, merely a bruise in the surface of a vertical rock face which might simply have been the product of an ancient boulder collision. Only on closer inspection could Kismet perceive the depth of the cut in the rock and the fact that the stone surface was not stone at all, but weathered bricks of baked clay laid one atop another. It was not a cave, but a structure built by men in the middle of the desert and almost completely hidden beneath the dunes. Samir ducked through the narrow slit without hesitation. An almost blinding flare in the midst of Kismet's night vision display indicated a light source within. He switched the goggles off and swiveled them out of the way, then crouched down and followed blindly.

The passage beyond was narrow. His shoulders scraped against brick on either side as he descended along a crumbling staircase. The steps, like the structure itself, were clearly the work of human artifice, but their condition suggested centuries of both use and neglect. They were in an ancient place.

At the foot of the stairwell, he saw the source of the light. As his guide stepped forward into a large antechamber, he could clearly make out the flickering of several randomly placed oil lamps. It was not until he moved out from the narrow recess, however, that Kismet realized they were not alone.

Before he could bring his carbine up, or even identify a target, Samir hastened in front of him, arms extended. "No, no, Mr. Kismet. This is my family."

Kismet exhaled sharply and lowered the weapon. In the undulating lamp-light he made out several human shapes: an elegantly dressed woman, her head covered by a colorful scarf; a teenage boy who seemed a younger, thinner version of Samir; and several more indistinguishable lumps, hidden beneath blankets on the floor. In all, there appeared to be a dozen people camped out in the hidden structure, possibly representing three generations of Samir's clan.

"Family," echoed Kismet, the significance of the revelation sinking in. "No one said anything about your family."

Samir looked shocked. "I could not leave them. When it is learned what I have done, they would be made to suffer. Such is the way with President Hussein."

Kismet felt a moment of self-loathing for having questioned the matter. "That's not what I meant. It's just…well, we didn't develop a contingency for exfiltrating more than one person. There won't be room on the helo for all of us."

Samir's expression fell, prompting Kismet to hastily augment his statement. "What I mean is, we'll have to make some changes to the plan."

The Iraqi seemed pleased at the promise and brightened once more. "Allah is great."

"Yeah," muttered Kismet, loosening the chin strap on his helmet as he surveyed the room a second time. "Say, you didn't all come here in that one car?"

Samir grinned. "No. There is also a truck."

"Any more surprises?"

"No more surprises." His voice dropped to a conspiratorial whisper. "Do you wish to see it?"

Kismet sensed the defector was no longer talking about the truck, and that whatever he was referring to would indeed be a surprise, but the only way to know for certain was to play along. "Sure."

Samir launched into motion again, but did not move toward the stairwell as Kismet expected. Instead, he crossed the antechamber, picked up one of the lamps, and headed toward an arched entryway on the opposite side.

"The truck is here? Inside this—whatever it is?"

"These are the ruins of Tall al Muqayyar. We are very near to what you in the West call Ur of the Chaldees. It was the birthplace of Ibraiim; Abraham, the father of Ismail. Our nation takes its name from this place: Uruk. It is the birthplace of civilization."

"You don't say." He thought Samir sounded like a tour guide. He had studied enough source material about Iraq to recognize the truth of Samir's words, but ancient ruins held little appeal; he preferred the company of the living. "We are under the ground though?"

"The sands come and go. The ruins have been excavated several times since their discovery almost two centuries ago, but the sand always returns. In this instance, I have used the sand to conceal the main entrance to the ruin." He gestured with the lamp, throwing a wavering yellow glow into the shroud of darkness. Beyond the antechamber was a larger room, its ultimate width and breadth beyond the scope of Kismet's unaided eyesight. He resisted the impulse to swivel the goggles down, electing instead to wait for Samir's lamp to expose the room's secrets. As the Iraqi strode purposefully forward, his light cut a swath through the darkness in the middle of the chamber. After only a few steps, the bare floor disappeared beneath an increasingly dense accumulation of desert sand.

The lamp's rays soon revealed a vehicle in the buried chamber— what looked to Kismet like a deuce and a half, or 2.5-ton truck—its rear cargo area covered by a low slung canvas tarpaulin. The truck appeared to be a cast-off military vehicle, broken, repaired and mongrelized to the extent that its origins were unrecognizable. Beyond the truck, the sand rose up in a vast dune, completely blocking what must have served as the main entrance to the ruin. Samir placed his lamp on the rear bumper of the truck, but hesitated there.

Kismet tried to peer into the tent-like enclosure, but saw nothing in the shadows. "Well?"

"Forgive me. I am a coward. President Hussein says it is not the hand of Allah—that it is a Zionist trick—but he does not touch it. No sane man dares touch it."

"The hand of Allah?" Again Kismet sensed that he was expected to know more than he did. He decided to end the charade. "I'm sorry, Samir, but I have no clue what you're talking about. I've never heard of you and I haven't the faintest idea why you think I'd care about what's in that truck."

His declaration hit Samir like a blow. The Iraqi staggered back, his hands moving nervously. "You-you are not Kismet."

"I am Nick Kismet. Pretty sure I'm the only one." Given the unique circumstances surrounding the choosing of his name, he felt safe in the assertion.

"But then you must know. You of all people would know…"

Kismet shrugged. "They didn't tell me much about the mission, Samir. I didn't even know that you were the person I'd be meeting."

He could tell the revelation troubled Samir, but the Iraqi began nodding slowly, as if to clear his head. "I believe I understand. When you have seen it, everything will become clear."

Kismet stared once more into the cargo area of the truck. His thoughts began to spin out of control. Just what was the secret Samir was delivering to him? *The hand of Allah?* Had the defector snatched one of Saddam's much-rumored nuclear weapons? Almost trembling with eagerness, Kismet laid the CAR15 on the deck and pulled himself into the truck.

He had to crouch down under the low hanging tarpaulin, but once inside, his ability to see in the darkness began to improve. He could discern that the cargo bay was empty save for a lone object in the center, secured to a wooden pallet by a single nylon rope that zigzagged back and forth across the bed of the vehicle. Whatever lay beneath that web was further concealed by a heavy blanket of dark material, but he could make out a vaguely familiar silhouette. It didn't look like any kind of nuclear warhead.

Samir held his light close to the opening. "I would advise you not to touch it, but of course, you would know more about this than I."

Kismet stared in disbelief at the veiled bundle. He recognized the outline of the object only because it looked exactly the way it had in a motion picture he had enjoyed countless times as a child. "What the…is this some kind of joke?"

Samir's eyes seemed to dance eagerly in the flicker of lamplight.

"Does this not buy freedom for my family and I?"

Kismet spun to face the Iraqi. "If this really is what you want me to believe it is, then how in hell did you get it?"

"President Hussein has long feared that if the Zionists—the Israelis—learned that we possessed it, they would not hesitate to use any means necessary to take it back. And once they possessed it, they would be emboldened to make war with all Arabs. Yet he hesitated to destroy it—what if it truly is the work of Allah? But now with America ready to invade, he can wait no longer. If it is from Allah, then Allah must decide how to save it, or so President Hussein says. He ordered me to have it destroyed. Of course I was supervised, but I managed to switch it with a decoy. It was very costly. I had to find enough gold to fool the others, but I did. And when the chance arose, I sent for you."

Sent for me? He blinked furiously, trying to process what Samir was telling him. "Hold it a second." He gestured emphatically at the object. "What I meant was, how did this end up in Iraq? I thought it was in Ethiopia. Or Egypt." *Or some US Army warehouse*, he didn't add.

Samir pondered for a moment, then laughed. He shook his head. "None of those rumors are true. When those who ruled this land before—the Babylonians—sacked Jerusalem two thousand six hundred years ago, they took as spoil all the treasures of the Jews. This also was captured, but King Nebuchadnezzar wisely spread the rumor that it had been taken away by Jewish refugees before their temple fell. As the holiest of the Jewish treasures, it was a trophy of victory over God himself, and the Babylonians hid it in the deepest part of the Esagila—the temple of Marduk. When the Jews returned to their land after the Persian Empire conquered the Babylonians, it never occurred to them to ask for it back. They did not know it was there, and in time, it was forgotten by all.

"Even the first archaeologists to excavate the temple did not find the secret chamber where it lay, but when President Hussein decided to rebuild the glory of Babylon, his engineers—and I was part of that group—did find it."

Kismet shook his head incredulously, his mind racing. Samir had requested him—personally. How had the defector learned about him? And why had the Iraqi believed he would know, or even care, about some three-thousand-year-old relic? He rubbed the bridge of his nose, trying to banish the rampant speculations in order to form a strategy. "All right, this complicates things further. If we're going to get this out—" he gestured at the covered artifact, "—and everyone else, then we're going to need at least three helos and probably a shitload of close air support." He looked thoughtfully at the truck. "Either that or drive out. Think we could make it to Syria in this?"

Samir frowned. "You would risk bringing it so close to Zionist forces? Their agents would know of it the moment we crossed the border. I would think you, of all people, would want to conceal this from the Israelis."

Once again, Kismet got the feeling that Samir was dialed into some secret and erroneous source of information about him. He decided it was time to disabuse the Iraqi of those notions. Twisting around on the flatbed deck, he hopped backward onto the sand-covered floor to stand face to face with the other man. "Listen, Samir. My orders are to get you out—you. I am willing to risk my life to carry out those orders. I am willing to risk my life to help your family as well. But I am not about to put my life on the line for a... For some movie prop. If you insist on trying to get that thing back to friendly turf, then we are going to use the safest possible route, and if that means we drive through downtown Tel Aviv, well then I just don't give a shit."

Samir gaped in disbelief, but before he could even begin to frame a reply, a faint hissing sound distracted both men. Kismet turned toward the source of the noise and saw sand sliding down the face of the dune wall. His reaction was late by a fraction of a second.

He reached for the CAR15, but it was not where he expected, depending from its sling on his shoulder. Suddenly, the sand barrier erupted in a flurry of bodies and movement. Human shapes burst from the dune wall like reanimated corpses summoned from their graves. Remembering that his carbine lay on the deck of the truck, Kismet reached instead for the M9 holstered on his hip, but there was no time. One of the figures reared up before him and something hard and heavy crashed into his jaw. As he staggered back, the sound of Samir's cries of alarm dissolved into a ringing noise that seemed to originate inside his skull. Hands swarmed over him, stripping away his pistol and restraining his arms. He hovered at the edge of consciousness, vaguely aware that his wrists were being pressed together behind his back, secured with a hard plastic zip-tie. He struggled both against the shackles that bound his hands and the darkness that was overwhelming him, but in the end both battles were in vain.

Kismet awoke with a start, reflexively trying to raise his hands to shield himself from the object that filled his blurry gaze; someone had peeled back his right eyelid and was tapping the sclera of that eye with a fingertip. His hands did not respond, still securely bound behind his back, but the ferocity of his reaction was enough to remove him from the immediate threat.

He now saw the instigator of his torment, a lean lupine individual wearing desert battle dress fatigues similar to his own. The man's Caucasian features and dishwater blond hair suggested that he was a Westerner, but Kismet did not get the impression that his antagonist was there in order to rescue him. The man flashed a humorless smile, then turned to one of his comrades. The words he spoke sounded familiar, but Kismet didn't recognize the language. It might have been Hebrew, but with his head still swimming from the assault, he couldn't be sure.

The wolfish man leaned close again, thrusting something against his jaw. The object was frigid but yielding—an instant cold compress. "I told him he is lucky he didn't kill you," the man volunteered in English.

Kismet couldn't fathom why. He thought about Samir's words. "Israelis?" he croaked.

The man chuckled, again without a trace of humor. "Do you think you can stand?"

"Not without help," he replied, honestly.

Grasping the front straps of Kismet's combat harness, the man shifted his weight backward, lifting him from his supine position. Pain radiated from Kismet's bruised jaw and stabbed through his head. Bright sparks of light swam in his field of vision and for a moment, Kismet feared he would lose consciousness again. The man continued to hold him erect as his legs buckled, his head swooning, until the fog gradually receded. The ice pack slipped away from his cheek, but remained tucked in the space between his neck and the stiff collar of his flak jacket.

He saw that he was once more in the antechamber where he had first encountered Samir's family. They were all there, including the defector himself, lined up against one wall of the room in a classic hostage pose: kneeling with fingers laced together behind their heads. Some of them, mostly the children, were weeping and ululating. Half a dozen men in desert-pattern uniforms were spread throughout the room, each wielding a small submachine gun. Kismet easily recognized their arsenal: Heckler & Koch MP5Ks, the first choice of hostage rescue and commando teams worldwide. Unlike the man who held his load straps however, the rest of the combat force wore camouflage mesh screens over their heads, obscuring their faces, and soft boonie hats that matched their fatigues. One of the men also had Kismet's carbine slung over a shoulder.

He returned his gaze to the man before him. "You didn't answer my question."

His captor, judging that Kismet now stood on his own, relaxed his grip on the LBE straps. He maintained his silence a moment longer, reaching out to grasp the hilt of the Ka-Bar knife which hung from an inverted sheath on the front of Kismet's harness. As he drew the blade, Kismet shifted his eyes downward, surreptitiously checking the rest of his equipment. He immediately saw that, in addition to the knife, his other defensive weapon, the M9 Beretta pistol, had been removed from its holster. There was no sign of his helmet or night vision goggles, but every other piece of gear he carried seemed to have been left alone.

"Since I have no doubt that you and I will eventually meet again, and since it will not benefit you in any way, I will give you my name." He spoke with a faint accent that Kismet couldn't pin down.

The man circled behind him, deftly cutting through the zip-tie with the razor-sharp combat blade. As Kismet's hands broke free, the man resumed talking. "I am Ulrich Hauser. And lest you take the wrong impression, I am not a member of the Bundeswehr, or any other recognized army. I am not, I might add, an Israeli. Be thankful for that."

Kismet did not question why this distinction was important, but took note of it; Samir had made a similar statement. He turned his head, following as Hauser continued his orbit, but resisted the impulse to massage his wrists, letting his hands hang loosely at his hips. "Should I take from your comments that you're not going to kill us?"

Hauser returned to his starting point directly in front of Kismet. He held the Ka-Bar contemplatively between them for a moment, then slipped the naked blade into his own belt. At that instant, for no apparent reason, Kismet felt raw adrenaline dumping into his bloodstream, a premonition of something terrible about to happen, perhaps already beginning.

Hauser took the CAR15 from his accomplice and turned toward the line of hostages. It seemed to Kismet that he was moving in slow motion, but that was simply a trick of hyper-awareness. He didn't even have time to open his mouth in protest.

The carbine erupted in a spray of fire and noise. Hauser moved it from side to side, hosing Samir and his family with an unceasing torrent of 5.56 millimeter ammunition. Kismet felt hot bile flash into his throat and he involuntarily jerked toward Hauser, hands reaching for the gun even though he knew it was too late. Three of Hauser's men intercepted him, locking their fists around his biceps. He knew the air must be filled with the screams of the dying but all he could hear was the endless roar of gunfire. A chaotic pattern of gore and pocked brick now decorated the wall of the chamber, a carpet of corpses spread out beneath, yet Hauser did not relent until the last round was fired. Only when the final brass cartridge was ejected, landing with an barely audible tinkling sound in the eerie silence of the aftermath, did Hauser raise the barrel of the weapon.

Kismet's mouth worked, trying to form words, but there was only rage and futility in his throat. Hauser faced him now, his lips drawn back in a fierce grimace, his eyes dancing hungrily. Without warning, he thrust the gun sideways at Kismet, who reflexively caught it, his left hand grabbing the stock while his right fingers wrapped around the shortened barrel of the carbine. He felt the sting of hot metal scorching his skin but did not release the now-impotent weapon.

"Why?" he whispered, finding at least that single word. It seemed inadequate, but it was all he could manage.

Before Hauser could reply, if he intended to at all, a voice called out from the far end of the antechamber where it passed into the main area. The words were in the same unrecognizable language, but the commando leader understood. Nodding, he fired back a quick response in the same tongue, then addressed his sole remaining captive.

"This prize is not for you, Kismet. Not now."

The short declaration was not at all what Kismet was expecting.

"What the hell are you talking about? You did all this for...for that thing?" He gestured toward the main chamber where he had last seen the truck and its mysterious, ancient cargo.

"One day, you will understand what we have done, and why it had to be done." Despite his earlier, almost gleeful reaction to his act of violence, Hauser now seemed more subdued. He turned without another word and began striding toward the exit. His men followed, keeping wary eyes on the one man who did not belong to their number.

Kismet glanced down at the CAR15 in his hands, feeling the throb of pain in his right palm. Blue smoke continued to waft from the barrel and the air was heavy with the smell of burned cordite. He knew without looking that Hauser had shot off every round in the magazine, rendering the weapon temporarily useless, but there was something Hauser either did not know or had forgotten about. In two clip-on pouches, one on either side of his combat belt, Kismet carried spare magazines. He tried to estimate exactly how long it would take him to eject the spent clip, tear open the clasp on the ammo pocket, extract a spare and jam it into the magazine well. Two seconds?

Time enough for the cautious commandos to take preemptive measures; their weapons were already loaded.

As he weighed his options, the last of the men exited the antechamber, leaving him alone with the dead. He moved toward the passageway, walking slowly enough that he did not alarm the gunmen.

The commandos had made short work of the sand barrier Samir had used to cover the main entrance. The far end of the ruin was exposed to the chilly desert night, illuminated now only by the stars. Their work finished, the assault team began climbing into the rear of the truck. Hauser lingered behind them, catching his eye once more. "Do not fear, Kismet. It will be kept safe until the world is ready."

"Safe?" he echoed hollowly. "With you? You're a fucking psychopath."

Hauser hopped onto the rear bumper and pulled himself half inside the truck. He then turned to Kismet and grinned, shifting his head back slightly, like a werewolf ready to howl. Kismet shook his head to clear the image. "Who are you?"

"I've given you my name," Hauser replied, elevating his voice to be heard as the diesel engine rumbled to life. "Anything else I could say would only serve to confuse you. However, this much I will reveal: We are the chains of God, sealing Pandora's box for the preservation of mankind. We are Prometheus, guiding the destiny of the world until humanity is ready to ascend Olympus."

The words sounded like a mantra; a pledge learned by rote. The truck lurched into gear, spinning its wheels for a moment before finding purchase in the loose sand. Hauser steadied himself, then shouted over the din. "Do not try to follow us, Kismet. I have done what I can to spare you, but I will take no responsibility for the fortunes of war."

Something Hauser had said earlier now echoed in his mind. *I told him he is lucky he didn't kill you.*

"Why?" he shouted as the vehicle moved away from the chamber. "Why didn't you kill me?"

Hauser broke into unrestrained laughter; his first honest display of emotion. "Kismet, if I killed you, your mother would have my head."

If Hauser had anything more to say, it was lost as the truck moved away, threading the narrow alley between brick structures and sand dunes. Kismet took a step after them, then stopped as rage built in his chest and arms.

He pressed the button to eject the spent magazine from the carbine, then slammed a fresh clip into the weapon, slapping it with a mechanically practiced action to guarantee that the first round would not jam. He released the bolt, advancing a cartridge into the firing chamber, then raised it to shoulder height and sighted down the stubby barrel at the receding truck. Even as his finger flexed on the trigger, he knew the shot would be a futile gesture. He might get lucky and actually hit one of the escaping killers, but the odds were not good. With a defeated sigh, he lowered the gun and backed into the now deserted ruins. The oil lamps placed by Samir and his family continued to illuminate the abattoir that was the antechamber.

The sulfur odor of gunpowder lingered in the air, but there was a new scent added to the mix—the unmistakable stench of death. He had been in the presence of the dying and recently passed, but nothing like this. He had never seen healthy, vibrant individuals so violently ripped away from the world. It took a deliberate effort for him to search the memories of his combat skills training in order to determine his next action.

Like an automaton plugged into a new program, he lurched into action, systematically moving down the row of shattered bodies. The 5.56 millimeter green-tip ball ammunition had not ripped their flesh apart as larger and softer lead rounds might. Instead, the bullets had stabbed neat little holes clear through the victims, lacerating intestines and vital organs, wreaking internal damage with less outward trauma than might have been expected.

Samir and the woman Kismet assumed to be his wife had both expired from their wounds, but two of the younger children and one older male still drew ragged breaths. One of the children, a girl, clung to consciousness, whimpering when he turned her over to inspect the wounds. It was enough to throw him out of his almost mechanical routine, and he felt hot tears streaking down his face. He drew out one of two Syrettes of morphine hanging from a breakaway chain around his neck and quickly injected the contents into the girl's thigh. Her agonized moans soon gave way to shallow breathing.

He knew the morphine would probably kill her, but that would merely hasten the inevitable and with less anguish. None of those who still drew breath would survive the night. Perhaps with the care of skilled surgeons in a state of the art trauma center, the hand of the Reaper might be stayed, but here in the desert with only Kismet's basic first-aid skills and even more rudimentary first-aid kit, it was foolish to entertain hope. He cradled her in his arms and waited for the inevitable silence that would follow her final gasp.

"Bloody hell."

The low whisper from behind startled Kismet, but he did not let it show. Instead he turned his head slowly and saw Sergeant Higgins and two of the Gurkhas. Higgins was standing exactly where Hauser had been at the moment of the massacre, and was surveying both the carnage and the scattering of 5.56 millimeter brass casings on the floor. Higgins was solemn. "Did you do this, sir?"

Unable to find his voice, Kismet shook his head.

Higgins nodded slowly. "That's good enough for me, mate." His words carried the implication that Kismet's denial might not be sufficient for the others who would eventually ask the same question. The Gurkha continued. "We've got to move out, sir. Something has happened. About half an hour ago, the northern sky—by that I mean the sky over Baghdad—lit up like the end of the world. I think it's finally started."

Kismet eased the mortally wounded child to the floor and stood. "How did you get here?"

"We ran, didn't we?" Higgins managed a triumphant grin. "More like walked fast. We followed your tracks to the road. After that, it was trusting luck that we were going the right way and that you hadn't gone too far."

"Luck." Kismet looked around the chamber, at last spying his helmet and night vision goggles. "Let's get moving. We're going to need the devil's own luck to get through this."

They filed back up the staircase with Kismet leading the way. A fourth Gurkha waited at the entrance to the ruin, a guard left behind by Higgins. With a nod to the sergeant, he fell in with the rest as they marched single file back up to the roadway.

In the still desert night, Kismet could make out the sound of a distant vehicle engine, perhaps more than one. It might simply have been the sound of Hauser's captured truck stealing away with the prize, but they couldn't afford to make that assumption. They were deep in enemy territory.

One of the Gurkhas approached Samir's sedan cautiously, peering through the windows. Higgins turned to Kismet. "At least we won't have to walk back."

The soldier tried the door handle.

Do not try to follow…

Kismet threw off his paralysis and started toward the car. "Get away from there…"

The Mercedes suddenly split in two, lifting off the ground in an eruption of orange fire and black smoke. The shock wave slapped Kismet and the others to the ground and sucked the air from their lungs. He felt a heavy weight strike him in the chest—something warm and yielding—and reflexively pushed it away.

It took only a moment or two for the stunned group of soldiers to recover. Higgins, the most senior among the squad, sprang to his feet, sweeping left and right with his weapon. "What the fuck was that?"

The Gurkha sergeant was screaming, but Kismet could barely hear through the ringing in his ears. They had all been close to the blast, but none as close as the soldier who had triggered it.

"Singh!"

Kismet followed the line of Higgins' shocked gaze and saw what was left of Corporal Sanjay Singh of the 6th Queen Elizabeth's Own Gurkha Rifles.

The blast had knocked him away from the detonation site a fraction of a second ahead of the flames. The live ordnance in his equipment vest had been triggered by the shock wave, but his flak jacket had directed the force of those secondary explosions away from his torso. Nevertheless, despite escaping the force of fire, Singh's skeleton had been pulverized within by the release of energy, and his remains were now an almost-shapeless mass of smoking fabric and flesh near Kismet's feet. Kismet saw the streaks of blood on his own BDU blouse and felt his gorge rise a second time.

Another of the Gurkhas, the machine-gunner Private Mutabe, was down, his left arm opened to the bone by a slashing fragment of metal. The fourth soldier knelt beside the wounded African and fished out his Syrette, injecting him with a dose of morphine to dull the pain.

"Jesus Christ," scowled Higgins, stomping closer to where Kismet stood, reeling. "What the fuck was that?"

"Car bomb," murmured Kismet, feeling a fool for stating the obvious. "They booby trapped it. He tried to warn me."

"They? Who the fuck are they?" And then, phrasing it so it sounded like a curse, the sergeant added: "Sir."

"I don't know." Kismet's answer was inaudible.

"Well we're fucked good now, sir." He jerked a thumb at the column of smoke that spilled up into the night sky. "That's going to bring everyone within fifty klicks right down on top of us, and in case you hadn't noticed, we're down to three."

"I noticed," Kismet muttered. He turned away from Singh's corpse, fixing the sergeant in his gaze, scouring his memory for the leadership skills he had been taught but never applied. When he spoke again, it was more forcefully. "I noticed, sergeant. Now get your shit together and let's get moving. Those two can buddy up. You and I will carry Singh."

He felt like a fraud for saying it, for using a command voice; he had never commanded men before. And as he watched Higgins' face quivering with barely contained rage, he wondered if he had made a mistake. Higgins would blame him for this. He was the officer, the mission leader, and responsible for the lives of his subordinates.

An image of Hauser leering like a coyote flashed in his mind. *No,* he decided. *I didn't do this.* Hauser had murdered Samir and his innocent children. Hauser's men had rigged the car to blow.

You and I will eventually meet again…

In that instant, he knew that he would endure. For the sake of revenge, if nothing else, he would survive.

Perhaps Higgins saw that light of resolve igniting in Kismet's eyes. Or maybe it was simply the product of his years of military discipline. Whatever the case, the Gurkha's expression softened. He took a step toward Kismet, then knelt beside the shattered form of Singh. When he stood, he held the fallen man's *kukri.*

Gripping the back edge of the broad blade between his thumb and forefinger, he extended the hilt toward Kismet. "When we lay him to rest, I'll want this for his widow. Until then…"

Kismet accepted the knife, acutely aware of the honor Higgins was paying him. He held the blade out, contemplating its balance and the visible keenness of its edge. He then did something that flew in the face of his training. Bringing himself to attention, he saluted the sergeant.

Higgins stiffened respectfully and returned the salute, holding it until Kismet lowered his hand.

"Sergeant, I promise you that we'll give it to her together."

You and I will eventually meet again…

And that's the day I'll cut your heart out, you sick bastard.

But something else Hauser had said gnawed at him. It was a deeper mystery that he would have to solve before exacting his revenge, a conundrum that would supply impetus to his resolve to survive.

Both Samir and Hauser had known that it would be he, Nick Kismet, coming to supervise the defection. Both men had believed that Kismet would have a particular interest in the ancient—perhaps even holy—treasure unearthed in the ruins of Babylon. But Hauser had added one more dimension to the enigma.

Kismet, if I killed you, your mother would have my head.

Nick Kismet had never known his mother. The woman that had borne him into the world had vanished forever from his life mere moments after completing her labor. No memory or trace of her had remained to prove she ever existed, save for a healthy male child of indeterminate heritage, and a single word, written in the blood of her womb, in a language nearly forgotten; a word that translated alternately as luck, destiny and fate.

A word that had become his name.

Miracle

May 1995

Between heaven and earth, a veil…

She came to the waters once a year, not on Christmas or Easter or any of the days reserved for Saints and their feasts, but always on the same day: the second Sunday of May.

Pierre Chiron had once asked his wife what significance that date held but her answer had been vague and insincere. He had not thought to press the issue then. It was on the occasion of her second pilgrimage, and he could not have imagined that her annual tradition would endure through so many turnings of the calendar. Though he did not share her faith, he had always secretly believed she would receive her miracle. Surely it was only a matter of bad timing. Later, when the years of her barrenness stretched out for more than a decade—when the best doctors in France, then Switzerland, and eventually New York pronounced over and again the same sentence with the same requisite apology—Chiron could not find it in his heart to ask again or to call into question her earlier response. By that time there were other questions hungry for answers.

Once, after too many glasses of Bordeaux, he had shaped his smoldering ire into words. "How can you continue to beg this God of yours for a miracle when he repeatedly denies you?" *How can you continue to believe?*

He was not angry with her, of course, and her answer absorbed all of his fire, tacitly excusing his outburst. "There is a veil between heaven and earth. We cannot always see clearly the will of the Divine. It may be that He is still testing me to see if my faith is strong enough to deserve such a reward."

He did not want to relent in accusing her God for withholding the blessing of a child from this woman, his devout servant, while any common street whore, too lost in the delirium of a heroin fix to remember or care to employ a condom, might be graced with another bastard child, but her quiet certitude disarmed him, as it always did.

"Sarah, the wife of Abraham, was ninety years old when she

conceived Isaac," she had said, quietly repeating what she surely must have told herself every day. "Hannah, the mother of Samuel, wept openly before God for years, and He listened. I pray only that He will find me as worthy as those women."

"Well," he had harumphed, trying to step back from his argument without conceding the point. "If it takes until we are ninety years old, then I shall do my part and keep trying every night."

Collette had kept trying as well, praying every day in the Basilique du Sacré Coeur and visiting the Massabielle Grotto at Lourdes once every year in May. She was fifty-six years old now. From a biological standpoint, there was no longer any reason to continue trying. Her menstrual blood had ceased to flow and most of the symptoms associated with the change of life had already abated. *Perhaps not as old as ancient Sarah*, he thought, *but it will nevertheless take a miracle to give me a child.*

Millions came to Lourdes every year looking for miracles, and many went away believing they had found them. The history of the place, insofar as the believers were concerned, was rich with divine acts of provenance. The first such blessing had occurred in 1858 when two young sisters had experienced a visitation while gathering firewood in a cave on the banks of the Gave River, just west of the garrison town of Lourdes. In the years that followed, one of the women continued to experience the presence of the Divine, at one point miraculously locating a spring, the waters of which possessed healing powers, at least for the faithful. It was to this holy place in the southwest Hautes-Pyrenees that Collette made her annual journey looking for just such a miracle.

Pierre Chiron did not believe in miracles.

He always stayed behind when she went to the Shrine, not at home in Paris, but at a hotel in the nearby city. He knew from experience that she would be gone all day, and upon returning shortly after dusk, she would be eager to put her faith to work. Chiron had come to think of the yearly pilgrimage as a sort of holiday. If the weather was accommodating, he would lie by the pool and read a bestseller from cover to cover. When conditions were inclement, he would take a walking tour, safe beneath the capacious dome of his umbrella, darting from one café to the next until his veins were almost humming with caffeine and sugar. On such days, his stimulant-induced insomnia permitted Collette to repeatedly test whether her prayers would be answered.

Today was such a day, but Chiron no longer cared to hyper-stimulate his nervous system. He was getting old and missed sleep was now something he regretted. He nursed his café au lait rather than gulping it down, and lingered at his table, idly browsing through the morning edition of the *Courrier International*. Even at that, he ran out of coffee before he was ready to leave. Sighing, he folded the paper under his arm and stepped out into the rain. In defiance of Collette's God, he left his umbrella furled, letting the angry raindrops pelt his face and thinning hair. He was blinking rapidly to clear his vision when a limousine pulled alongside.

He started momentarily. The vehicle had appeared almost as if by magic. He shook his head, trying to rid himself of such deluded musings, and continued walking. The limousine kept pace with him, creeping along in the street less than a meter away.

When he was certain that the presence of the oversized car was no coincidence, he stopped, turned and peered at the tinted glass. A dark line appeared across his reflection and descended slowly as the window was lowered. Then he recognized the face gazing at him and instantly regretted his initial irritation.

"Bonjour, Pierre."

"Madame?" He fumbled for words. "This is a great honor."

The woman smiled wryly. "Get in."

The driver of the vehicle, a large man whose barrel chest strained the seams of his immaculate black uniform, circled around to open the door for Chiron, who climbed in without hesitation and laid his umbrella on the spacious floor. The limousine eased forward, cruising slowly along the narrow streets, but for Chiron, the world beyond the darkened interior of the vehicle had ceased to exist.

The woman scrutinized him for several moments as he settled into the plush interior, and Chiron stared back, his blood roaring with an unexpected surge of adrenaline. Though they had never met, he had no doubts concerning her identity. He recognized her by reputation alone. *Like Sophia Loren, only more so*, he had been told. The whispered, anonymous rumors were not very specific on the latter point, but he had developed his own interpretation, which he now found to be slightly in error. She indeed bore a striking resemblance to the Italian-born movie star, although considerably younger. And yet there was something in her that was like nothing he had ever seen in that actress, or for that matter in any woman: *a fire of purpose... No*, he thought. *It's rage. But at what?* It was not altogether unattractive. Chiron did not even realize that he had put all thoughts of his wife's struggle and his own divinely directed ire out of his head.

Thankfully, the woman's simmering wrath did not seem directed at him. Despite the fire behind her eyes, she gave him a reserved smile, then reached into a cabinet alongside the broad seat. "Cognac?"

Normally, he would not have dreamed of drinking so early in the day, but he surprised himself by accepting the offer. The warm brandy soothed his anxious nerves, allowing him to breathe and speak with more ease. "As I said, madame. You have paid me a great honor. I had not expected to meet you in person."

"It was convenient," she replied, explaining nothing. "I expect you have been eager to learn the status of your...shall we say, application?"

"After six months, I had come to accept the worst—"

"These things take time, Pierre. Six months is not even a tick on the clock of the universe. Besides, our enemies continue to multiply and ever seek to infiltrate our ranks. Our vetting process must be thorough."

"Then I...I don't understand why—"

"You may consider this a final interview, Pierre."

He gulped and suddenly even the cognac wasn't enough to calm his nerves. "I see."

"Tell me," she continued, as if his anxiety was irrelevant. "Have you determined the identity of your sponsor?"

He grimaced. "I'm sorry, I know I'm not supposed to have that information, but I could not resist trying to figure it out. I believe it is one of two men in the Ministry of—"

"It's not whom you imagine it to be," she said with a hint of dismissive irony. Then she told him.

"*Mon dieu!* He is one of you?" He had never met the person she named, a noted inventor and marine explorer, though he had corresponded with the man a few years previously in an effort to end atomic testing in the South Pacific.

"I did not say that, and you would be wise not to fuel such a rumor. Suffice it to say, he brought you to our attention—whether directly or indirectly, I cannot reveal."

Chiron raised the snifter to his lips once more, only to realize in dismay that he had already drained its contents. "Then I am doubly honored."

"We will speak no more of how this honors you." There was an edge to her voice. "Ours is not some gentlemen's drinking club where we sit around and congratulate each other on achievements of avarice and notoriety. Our goals are lofty, our purpose transcendent. You bring to our cause something of extraordinary import. All of us contribute something essential, or else no invitation is extended. You cannot buy your way in or know the right people; you must *be* the right person."

Her oration in no way diminished Chiron's sense of accomplishment, but he withheld further banalities. "And what do I have that will serve your cause?"

"Our cause," she reproved, but with a smile. "That is no great mystery, Pierre. Before you took your current post, you were the foremost scientific advisor to the French government. You still have a certain degree of influence in an area that is currently of great concern. We need you to do something, a very small something, but of considerable importance to an ongoing experiment."

"Yes?"

She shifted in her seat, banking her inner fire as the discussion became more business-like. Outside, the world was a blur of green; they were well beyond the city, cruising through the countryside. "On the fifth of September, the French Army will detonate a device in the Fangataufa atoll testing grounds."

Before her words could sink in, Chiron felt his heart lurch in his chest. "I cannot prevent that," he said hastily. "God knows I have tried."

"You misapprehend. The test must go forward on schedule, no matter what other forces conspire to postpone or cancel it, and they will try. We require only that you alter the order of the tests."

"Alter...I don't understand."

"The September fifth test must be conducted underground, in the Mururoa proving grounds. The Fangataufa test may take place on the second of October, the date originally set aside for Mururoa. Additionally, you must modify the yield specifications for the first test. The device must not exceed ten kilotons."

Now he understood her earlier declaration. This was indeed no platform for social climbing. He was not even a member of their ranks and already they were demanding sacrifice, a sacrifice that stood in opposition to everything he had worked for. "Madame, I fear that you have overestimated my influence. I have already petitioned President Chirac to suspend these tests he has planned. My advice was not heeded. Our new president insists on reminding the world that France is also a global power. Why do you think anyone will listen now if I make this demand?"

"We trust that you can make a persuasive argument to accommodate our request. What you say is at your discretion. It is not a significant deviation from the schedule, but the time and location are critical to an experiment we will be conducting at the observatory."

"Observatory?"

"You would know it by a different name." She told him.

He could not hide his surprise. "How can an event on the other side of the world influence your experiment in Paris?"

"That will become clear in time. There are many levels to our cause, and you are yet on the verge of the outermost ring. Do not mistake my presence here as an initiation. That will come when we see how you…" Her eyes lost focus and her voice trailed off, as she gazed past him out the rear window of the limousine. Curious, Chiron turned to see what had distracted her.

A motorcycle had appeared behind them and was racing to close the intervening distance. It did not seem a noteworthy development, but the woman continued to stare at the approaching vehicle as if trying to assess the significance of its presence. She toggled a switch on the armrest, activating the intercom.

Her words were unrecognizable, but after a second, the chauffeur's voice scratched from the speaker, likewise incomprehensible. *It's true*, was Chiron's first thought. *They have their own language.*

The limousine immediately charged forward, racing into a turn with a roar of horsepower. The tires slipped on the wet macadam, shrieking in protest as the heavy vehicle fish-tailed, only to become silent as the road straightened and control was once more asserted. The motorcycle fell back momentarily, caught by surprise and unable to match the other vehicle's power, but the rider lowered himself behind the abbreviated windscreen and surged forward.

"Is he chasing us?" inquired Chiron, still not grasping the situation.

"I told you our enemies were multiplying," replied the woman through clenched teeth.

The concern evident in her expression hit Chiron like a slap. *My God, we're in danger.*

With the prey alerted, the hunter now forsook subterfuge, taking full advantage of the motorcycle's superior maneuverability to close the gap whenever the road forced the chauffeur to apply the brakes. Chiron could now clearly see their pursuer. The aerodynamic motorcycle had been painted a glossy black to cover any telltale markings. It was impossible even to be certain of the vehicle's manufacture, but Chiron was a fan of speedway racing and instantly recognized it as a Caviga 125 Roadster. The rider's black leathers and helmet were not so easy to unriddle, but his driving skill suggested that he too was more than a little familiar with the dangerous sport.

The limousine was forced to slow as it entered a hairpin turn, the beginnings of a switchback that carved its way into the Pyrenees. The motorcycle shot forward and the rider lifted his left hand from the grip and drew an oblong object—*a gun*, thought Chiron. *Of course it's a gun*—from a holster on his hip. As the gap shrank to nothing, the rider laid the long barrel of his weapon across his rigidly straight right arm and sighted on the back window of the limousine.

Chiron ducked instinctively, but not before he saw a pinpoint of flame at the tip of the weapon. He knew the gun had been fired but heard no report; the limousine's insulation effectively squelched all outside noise. What he did hear however—a harsh, surprised gasp from his companion—froze his blood.

This cannot be. The glass must be bulletproof.

He looked over at the woman, confirming his worst fear to be true. She sat in stunned disbelief, her right hand clapped over her left shoulder but unable to staunch the scarlet flow that stained her white jacket.

She's wearing white, he thought. *Why didn't I notice that before?*

There was a sharp cracking sound, and he saw a neat hole, smaller than the thickness of a pencil, appear in the partition behind her head. The bullet had passed through both the rear window and the barrier separating the inner compartments. Even Chiron, who knew very little about small arms, was familiar with the concept of armor-piercing bullets. Impulsively, he threw himself forward, pushed the woman down onto the floor and covered her with his body.

The adrenaline that had surged through him at the initial meeting was now gone. The instinctive urge to flee or fight had departed, just when circumstances dictated he ought to have needed it most. Instead, there was only a surreal calm, as if he were a spectator watching a scene from a movie. There was no horror, only a curiosity about what would happen next.

Another Teflon-coated projectile perforated the window and continued through the partition with a harsh crack. Chiron immediately felt something change; the limousine was slowing. Even without looking he knew what had happened. The round, blindly fired through the mirrored glass by the motorcyclist, had struck the chauffeur. Something about the way the vehicle meandered toward the edge of the road told Chiron that the wound had been fatal.

The car careened from the road with deceptive slowness, as if it might at any moment stop, allowing its passengers to get out and stretch their legs. Chiron braced himself between the opposed seats and hugged the woman close as the large car left the paved road and crashed down an abrupt slope. Despite his preparations, he was thrown violently about the interior of the vehicle as it bounced chaotically down the hill. It was difficult to ascertain the moment at which the limousine stopped moving, but there was a final intense heave forward that lifted him off the prone woman and slammed him into the fractured partition.

Chiron felt no pain, though he knew the hammering he had taken must have resulted in, if nothing else, at least a mass of bruises. He lay stunned for a moment in the crook of the upholstered seat. The car was tilted forward at a forty-five degree angle, skewing his sense of balance like a trick in a carnival funhouse. He pulled himself toward the edge of the seat and looked down at his female companion.

"We've got to get out of here," he rasped, surprised at the sound of his own voice in the sudden silence.

She nodded, but seemed to be having trouble righting herself. Chiron reached toward her, then changed his mind and focused instead on disengaging the door handle. The door fell open, revealing a rain-soaked, but familiar landscape. Just outside the door flowed a body of water, and in the distance, he could see an overhanging wall of rock.

The grotto, he thought dumbly, cursing himself for having paid no attention to the route chosen by the chauffeur. An instant later, he realized what good fortune had provided them: If they could reach the mass of people, which even now was looking up from their prayers and ablutions in order to gaze on this unfolding spectacle, the assassin would not dare to follow.

There was a tortured squeal of metal behind him and Chiron turned to find a man clad in dark riding gear peering in through the opposite door. The cyclist had removed his black helmet, but the gun remained, now held in his right hand.

The assassin looked like a man about to transform into a savage beast. He sneered, thin lips pulling away to reveal teeth that seemed too large—*the better to eat you with*, Chiron thought, manically—and his eyes blazed with barely restrained fury. He glanced at the scientist first, appraising his value as a target and potential threat, then turned his fiery gaze upon the woman and began speaking.

It was a short declaration uttered, Chiron supposed, in the same strange tongue the woman had used earlier with the chauffeur. That their killer shared the mysterious form of speech with the woman ought to have been troubling to him, but somehow it seemed only a minor concern. He did not need to be fluent in their language to comprehend what the man had said. It was unquestionably a gloating pronouncement of victory: a death sentence. As if to underscore this supposition, the man extended the gun toward the woman and aimed down the barrel so that they were looking into each other's eyes.

A sudden flash of light filled the interior of the wrecked limousine. The gunman flinched involuntarily, blinded by the brilliant burst. The muzzle of the gun wavered as he blinked furiously to clear away the retinal fireworks.

A flash camera, thought Chiron. *Someone is here to save us.*

But any well-intentioned passerby with a camera would be ill-equipped to deal with a vicious, armed killer. That Good Samaritan would simply be added to the list of victims when the assassin's eyesight recovered. Chiron knew he had to act.

He thought about trying to leap at the man and attempting to wrestle the gun away, but dismissed the idea instantly. He was no fighter, and would have only the vaguest idea of what to do with the gun in the unlikely event that he succeeded in capturing it. Then his eyes fell upon the one weapon he was familiar with, not for close-quarters combat but rather battling the elements.

Without thinking, he snatched the umbrella off the floor and gripped its hook-shaped handle in both hands. The gunman must have seen the movement in his peripheral vision because the end of his weapon shifted toward Chiron, but the French scientist had the advantage. He thrust the metal tip of the umbrella up at the man's face.

Whether due to good aim or sheer luck, his attack struck home, extinguishing the fierce glow in the man's left eye. The lupine assassin's head snapped back and the cane handle was ripped from Chiron's grasp. The gun fell away as his hands flew up to his face to wrap around the shaft of the object that had reduced his eyesight by half, and he unleashed a bestial cry of pain and rage as he tore it free.

In a moment of unreal clarity, Chiron saw that the tip of the umbrella was now stained red and clumps of tissue were clinging to the metal point like bits of paper plucked up off the grass by a groundskeeper. The wounded assassin continued to cover his ravaged eye with one hand, but the remaining orb was bright with intensity of purpose. He scanned the interior, looking for his lost weapon, then gazed past his victims at the approaching throng of devotees drawn away from the healing waters by the commotion. His attention returned to Chiron.

"Well done." His voice quavered slightly but was otherwise restrained. "But you now find yourself on the wrong side of this war. Ask her and she will tell you what sort of enemy you have made today."

Dismissing Chiron, he turned to the woman and made another brief utterance in their shared tongue. She continued to hold her wounded shoulder, but her eyes were triumphant. When she spoke, it was in French, doubtless for the benefit of her companion, and though her comment was cliché, the sentiment rallied Chiron. "Go to hell."

The assassin chortled as he pulled back through the doorframe and vanished from sight. Chiron slumped in relief, and then roused himself to thank their savior. He turned to the door he had opened but there was no one there. Certainly no one with a camera, close enough to have activated the blinding flash that had distracted the assassin from his lethal task. The closest person—a young man running toward them—was still a hundred meters away.

That's odd, he thought. *Was it only lightning?*

"Pierre, listen to me." The woman's voice remained defiant, but he could hear a faint hiss of anguish in her gasping breaths. "This man would not have acted alone. He is a soldier, not a general. But I do not know who gave the order, nor whom to trust."

"You can trust me," Chiron replied, instantly feeling foolish for his eager promise.

She chuckled through the pain. "You are more right than you'll ever know. Alas, this will likely be our only meeting."

"I don't understand."

"The timing of this crisis is unfortunate for you, Pierre. It would have been a great privilege to offer you a seat at our table, but now I must implore you to forget everything."

"Forget?"

"Trust no one, Pierre. If someone tries to persuade you that the danger has passed, then you will know that the enemy is close at hand. Only in ignorance will you find safety."

Chiron sighed, comprehending the wisdom of her strategy, but nevertheless felt a pang of loss. *So close.* "And the tests? The atomic tests?"

Her eyes darted sideways, then fixed his stare once more. "The tests must proceed as I described."

He nodded earnestly. "It will be so, madame. And will you be safe?"

"I'll manage." She looked aside once more, her gaze shifting to the open doorframe behind Chiron. "There is one more thing, Pierre. A personal favor."

"Name it."

"Soon, you will cross paths with a young man. He is very special to me."

"I will welcome him as I would my own son." Even as he spoke the words, the irony of the statement rang in Chiron's ears.

"Thank you, Pierre. But he must never know of this conversation, nor anything about the group. He will find those answers in due time."

"How will I recognize this young man?"

"Oh, I don't believe you will have any difficulty. Your

rendezvous will seem like an act of fate."

"Are you injured?" shouted a voice in French. "What happened?"

He turned and saw the man he had earlier spied now drawing even with the wreck of the limousine. The newcomer wore casual clothes, a navy blue polo shirt with khaki chinos, but Chiron saw none of the expected accouterments of a devotee; no gold chain around his neck, no crucifix. The man was a tourist, marking this place off a list in a guidebook rather than seeking a blessing from the Divine. Somehow, the scientist found that encouraging. The young man was the vanguard of a small army of Good Samaritans, leaving their devotions at the grotto in order to render assistance to the victims of the accident.

Chiron did not know how to answer the latter question, so he addressed the former. "Yes. For God's sake, call the medics." He then turned back to the woman. "Everything is going to be fine..."

The words died on his lips. The woman was gone.

Chiron pulled himself across the seat and thrust his head through the opposite doorway, but there was no sign of his host. She had vanished as completely as the assassin before her. Only the crimson-tipped umbrella remained to give evidence that the encounter was not merely a delusion. Stunned by the disappearing act, he fell back into the seat, a wave of nausea creeping over him.

The tourist stuck his head inside and made eye contact with Pierre. "Help is on the way. I'm going to check on the driver."

The man then splashed into the shallow water surrounding the front end of the vehicle and forced open the driver's door. Chiron found himself wondering if the chauffeur had likewise evaporated, but a shocked exhalation from the young rescuer affirmed that such was not the case.

The young man reappeared before Chiron, his eyes now accusatory. "That man has been shot, murdered. What happened here?"

Chiron opened his mouth to reply without really knowing what he was going to say. He stared back at the tourist, trying to formulate a plausible fiction to conceal a truth he barely understood. "I'll wait for the gendarmes to arrive before I tell the story," he said finally, forcing his eyes away from the young man.

He could feel the young man's eyes boring into him. There was a familiar fire in that gaze, yet it wasn't until he looked away that recognition dawned.

It was convenient…

I should have seen it right away, thought Chiron.

He looked back into the other man's eyes. "Pardon, monsieur, but what is your name?"

"My name?" The tourist seemed rightly surprised by the question, but answered nonetheless. "I'm Nick Kismet."

"Kismet?" Chiron savored the word. "That's an unusual name. You are not French?"

"I'm an American."

"But the name is something else; Arabic, if I'm not mistaken." He gazed at the young, masculine face, astonished at the similarity of features. "But you do not appear to be an Arab."

"Right on both counts." The young man remained aloof, evidently suspicious of the stranger who shared a car with a gunshot victim and now seemed so interested in his name. "It's a long story."

"I imagine so. Still, it is a unique name. A powerful word. I believe it means luck or destiny. Or fate."

It was convenient…an act of fate.

Kismet nodded hesitantly, but said nothing.

Chiron managed a thin smile. "Well, I hope you will count this meeting an instance of good luck. My name is Pierre Chiron, and I am the director of the Global Heritage Commission of the United Nations Educational, Scientific, and Cultural Organization. If there's anything I can do to assist you during your stay in my country, please do not hesitate to ask. I have a feeling I can be of great assistance to you."

He knew by the sudden gleam in the young man's eyes that he would have to make good on his offer in ways he could scarcely imagine.

Six days shy of four months from the occasion of Collette Chiron's annual pilgrimage to the Grotto of Lourdes, a small borehole in the basalt gut rock of the Mururoa atoll vomited forth an eruption of force and fire. Though modest by the standards of modern destructive power, equivalent only to about eight thousand metric tons of TNT, the explosion nevertheless rocked that remote corner of the world.

Ten thousand miles away, Pierre Chiron stood at the foot of the structure he now thought of as *"le observatoire"*. He had arrived ninety minutes ahead of the projected time for the test and lingered for three hours beyond that pivotal moment. Yet he saw no indication of activity, nothing to suggest that an experiment was being monitored in the observatory, nor any sign that the atomic test in the South Pacific had exerted an influence here, on the other side of the globe. At last admitting defeat, Chiron left, pausing only long enough to take a picture for a tourist couple posing gaily in front of the monument, blissfully unaware of its dual purpose.

In the four months since the incident in the Haute-Pyrenees, Chiron had received no further contact from the woman or any of her agents. He had however developed a close friendship with the young man with the unusual name, fulfilling the second of two promises made that fateful day. Now, with the underground detonation of an atomic device at Mururoa, both pledges had been satisfied. He remained curious to see what fruit each of those disparate branches would bear.

The second test, an airburst over Fangataufa on the second of October, was judged a success by both the military scientists overseeing the project and the nationalist politicians intent on flexing the French military muscle in the face of NATO and the United States. Because he was paying attention on a different level, Chiron's observations were less sanguine.

Almost immediately following the Fangataufa test, Mount St. Helens, an active volcano in the Pacific Northwest region of the United States, began to resonate with tremors. In New Zealand, Mount Puapehu entered into a period of intense eruptive activity, as did Mount Merapi in Java. One week after the test, Mount Hosshu, dormant for over two hundred and fifty years, rumbled to life in Japan.

Over the next few months, Chiron saw fingers of force reaching out from the test sites to distant locations around the world, a series of unprecedented volcanic and seismic events coinciding with the atomic detonations. His observations led to more research, which in turn revealed an astonishing link between the weapons tests and geological activity, but he shared his findings with no one. He knew others were also watching and had perhaps been doing so for decades.

Meanwhile, a cluster of cells began to thrive and multiply in the warm and dark embrace of Collette Chiron's womb. It would yet be two months before she and her husband would discover that what grew there was no miracle.

She would make just one more journey to Lourdes, but her supplications would once more go unanswered.

PART ONE

REFLECTION

ONE

May 2003
Between heaven and earth, a veil.

It was an illusion—more accurately a mirage—and Nick Kismet was not fooled. Nevertheless, his eyes were drawn to the shimmering curtain of superheated air rising from the earth, pooling in mid-air like the surface of a vast lake somehow turned on its side. The Airbus A320 speared onward into the heart of the distortion and the convection waves magically receded.

Spring was now half done and already the desert days had become brutally hot. At sunrise, temperatures of nearly ninety degrees Fahrenheit were reported; by midday, the mercury would reach well into the triple-digit range. And yet, with the fall of night, the day's heat would radiate back into space to plunge temperatures in the austere environment to the opposite extreme. Indeed, it was a place of extremes.

That's why they call it the desert, Kismet thought darkly.

He hated this place, hated the arid nothingness and the severe temperatures and the scouring sandstorms. He loathed the constant thirst, the ever-present smell of scorched iron, and the way his clothes felt like sandpaper against his skin. Yet, there was much more to his contempt than recognition of the physical hardships imposed by the harsh conditions.

This was the place where he had almost died.

The desert extremes did not adequately represent the totality of the environment. As the plane sailed onward through the roiling air mass, shedding altitude and cruising speed on approach to its destination, Kismet began to see more green in the brown landscape below. The Tigris River was a barely visible ribbon, glinting in the sun, but its benevolent effects, courtesy of an ancient network of irrigation canals, were visible all around the city. From a distance, it was hard to believe that this place was still a war zone.

The aircraft began to vibrate as it struck pockets of disturbed atmosphere. The turbulence was not unlike slamming into potholes on a paved road, and as the plane made a particularly violent drop,

Kismet was grateful for his seat belt. He overheard snatches of conversation from some of his fellow passengers, mostly relief workers from UNICEF and other international agencies, wondering if the plane was taking ground fire.

He smiled humorlessly at the notion. If the civilian aircraft was indeed under attack from anti-aircraft artillery batteries, or even small arms fire, there would be no time to wonder. The plane would simply break up in the air over the city. Yet it was only right that the volunteers be concerned. For most, this endeavor would represent the greatest peril they would ever face—stepping willingly into one of the most violent places on earth in order to do nothing but good—and they certainly had every right to be apprehensive. If he did not share their trepidation, it was only because for him, this would not be such a singular event. As the soldiers with whom he had once served were fond of saying: "Been there, done that."

It had been twelve years and three months, give or take a few days, since Kismet's first journey into the desert. He had not come quite so far north that time, but in some ways he had gone much further. Yet that crucible of violence, from which he had escaped using only his wits and the devil's own luck, was not what he would remember most about his experience in the desert. War, even on such a personal, visceral level, was not the element which had forged him like steel and set him upon the path he now followed. Something else had happened that night in the desert, something he still could not fully explain. Somewhere in the world however, there was at least one person who did know, and Kismet had sworn to find that man. When he did, he would demand an answer to his questions and settle a very special account—a debt payable in blood.

He had been on that path for more than a decade, finding little in the way of solid information, but had never lost hope. In all that time however, his quest had not returned him to the desert sands where he had been reborn. It had taken another war to bring him back here.

He was not returning as a soldier to battle a modern enemy, but rather as a protector of ancient wonders. The second Gulf War—designated Operation: Iraqi Freedom—was not over. Not officially, as the objectives of the war plan had yet to be fully realized, and not literally. Not by a long shot. Men were still fighting and dying in nearly every corner of the country. Sporadic resistance continued to break out, both from organized groups still loyal to the fallen regime and from enraged citizens, striking out blindly at the foreigners who had come unbidden and shattered their world. In many cases, that violence had been directed at objects rather than at people. Several days of looting had followed the collapse of the regime, mostly from government offices, but also from hospitals, banks and museums. It was the latter area of need that had prompted Kismet's return to the desert.

As the city grew closer, the pilot put the plane into a shallow dive, shedding altitude rapidly. The engines whined with exertion, but Kismet knew they were actually giving up airspeed, slowing down in preparation for landing. He nevertheless got the feeling that the pilot was in a hurry to get his aircraft on the ground. The jet would never be more vulnerable to attack than when on final approach. The landing gear came down with a thump, and he sat back in his chair, knowing that while the flight was almost over, the journey was only just beginning.

Kismet took his place in the queue of passengers poised to disembark. He found it slightly amusing that he was nearly at the head of the line. That never happened when he traveled. Always a stickler for obeying the flight crew's directive to remain seated until the plane stopped moving, he usually found himself fighting to get out of the cramped row and into the aisle. Evidently no one on this flight was eager to leave the aircraft, their last link with a world that was, if not completely civilized, then at least recognizable.

He noticed one group of Red Cross workers who, like himself, were not put off by their arrival in the war zone. They moved with calm assurance toward the exit, shouldering their gear as if they were simply reporting for another day at work. It was not their collective demeanor that drew his attention however, but rather the face of their leader, a red-haired woman who pushed past him with a confident stride that could only be earned through years of experience in dangerous areas. She caught his appraising glance and returned it with a contemptuous curl of her lips. On a face less lovely, it would have been a sneer.

Must be French, he thought, answering her with a wink.

The heat of the day was beginning to fill the cabin, rapidly displacing the cool air-conditioned environment. The effect was welcome, buffering the passengers against the furnace blast that awaited them on the tarmac. Kismet squinted involuntarily as he stepped out onto the gantry, and then quickly descended. The recently re-christened Baghdad International Airport had not exactly been designed with a view to making travelers feel welcome, but an overwhelming presence of armored vehicles made it seem downright inhospitable. Like his fellow passengers, he was eager to be inside where there was at least the illusion of safety.

A small knot of grim-faced soldiers waited at the foot of the descending staircase. They were young—*just boys*, thought Kismet, remembering a time when he had been one of them—but their weapons added a gravity to their presence that somehow obviated the need for maturity. Kismet recognized the M4 carbines—the latest incarnation of the venerable M16 assault rifle—and the M136 AT-4 missile launch tubes slung over several shoulders. Despite their almost juvenile countenances, to a man they all had an aged appearance, as if the desert sun had bleached away the flush of youth.

"This way," directed one of the men, a staff sergeant and leader of the squad. His voice was tight, without a trace of pleasantness. He was not there to play welcoming committee. Kismet nodded and headed in the direction of the soldier's brusque gesture.

He reached the relative shade of the terminal, passing more soldiers but also men and women in civilian clothes. Armbands differentiated relief workers and agents of the UN, while cameras and sound equipment were the badge of the journalist, but all of the civilians, like the soldiers before them, wore flak jackets and Kevlar helmets. Kismet had been issued similar protective equipment, but it was packed away in the large duffel bag slung over his shoulder. He debated donning the equipment, but decided he could survive a few more steps without the precautionary armor.

"Monsieur Kismet?"

Despite the buzz of noise circulating through the terminal, Kismet distinctly heard his name and began looking for the person who had spoken. The voice had been feminine and accented—French, he determined, based on nothing more than the choice of honorific and the lapsed pronunciation of the last syllable: "Kis-may." He stopped moving, waiting for the caller to present herself.

A petite figure stepped forward, her hair and facial features concealed by a black combat helmet. Her stature was such that he found himself looking down at the top of her headgear. He ducked to get a better look at her face. "Je suis Nick Kismet," he replied, correcting her pronunciation.

She looked up at him, blinking as if in incomprehension. "*Bonjour, monsieur.* This way please."

She turned away before Kismet could commit her features to memory, but his initial impression was one of haughtiness. *Twice in one day*, he thought, shaking his head. *What is it with me and French women?*

He knew that his generalization was not quite fair. She had done nothing to earn such an accusation. He was simply projecting the leftover ire from his encounter with the woman on the plane.

He had seen enough to know that his guide was an attractive woman, with the sort of angular features common to European runway models. Though only a stray lock of her dark hair had been visible, sneaking out across her right cheek, it stood in stark contrast to her pale skin, as did her immaculate crimson lipstick. Perhaps her expression was not so much one of arrogance as an unconscious declaration that she did not belong in this place. Shaking his head, he followed after her receding form.

He had gone only two steps when a familiar cry rolled through the crowd. "Incoming!"

He reacted without thinking, echoing the message at the top of his voice though unaware that he was doing so, and launched himself forward. There was no hesitation; this was a lesson learned so deeply as to almost become instinctual. The woman was just starting to respond when Kismet grabbed her arm, pulled her down and covered her with his torso. As an afterthought, he held the duffel bag over his head, reasoning that the armor equipment inside would afford a degree of protection from whatever was about to happen.

With adrenaline coursing through his veins, Kismet could not accurately judge the flow of time. It seemed that several minutes had passed without anything else happening. The only sounds he could hear were the extraordinarily loud percussions of his own heartbeat.

And then the earth moved.

The blast felt like a slap from God, yet Kismet knew he was experiencing only the outer edge of the shockwave: a bubble of displaced air pushed away from the detonation. In the same instant, the roar of the explosion washed over him. There was a deafening rush of noise that brought with it a shower of sand particles and shattered clay bricks.

Through the ringing inside his head, he could distinguish the staccato pops of gunfire. The soldiers were mounting a counterattack against the perceived source of the threat. Kismet doubted the young infantrymen knew where to direct their fire. Most were probably shooting at anything that moved, but in the omnidirectional hailstorm of metal-jacketed ball ammunition, the odds did not favor the unseen enemy. He risked a look.

The wall of the terminal had taken a direct hit, leaving an enormous wound in the brick structure. Through the hole and the thick curtain of smoke and dust, Kismet could see the battle in progress, the young soldiers alternately firing and advancing across the tarmac toward the outer perimeter of the airport, several hundred meters away. The aircraft which had brought him across the desert sands sat impotent and vulnerable, only a stone's throw from the blast radius.

Adrenaline was still distorting his perception of time, giving him a strange clarity of thought. He became aware of the news crews, rushing forward as if invincible in order to capture scenes of the battle on videotape. Their eagerness seemed ghoulish, but Kismet knew that in their own way, they were as dedicated as the soldiers fighting the battle on both sides. The journalists were true believers in the cause of history. If that explained their enthusiasm, it did not entirely excuse them. Most of the world's problems could be laid at the feet of the true believers.

The focus of the battle seemed to shift, and Kismet saw a white finger of vapor reaching out across the paved runway. *RPG*, he thought. A rocket-propelled grenade.

Even as the munition was released it gave away the location of its user, and in a heartbeat, the place from which it had originated became the primary target for the soldiers. But no amount of retaliatory fire could alter the trajectory of the grenade as it streaked toward the terminal. Kismet covered his unnamed companion once more, waiting for the inevitable explosive climax.

The RPG streaked past the nose of the idle jet, missing it by less than ten meters, and slammed into the wall of the terminal, just to the left of the first impact. The orderly matrix of bricks blew apart in a rough circle, showering the interior of the building with deadly fragments. Kismet saw several people struck, some seriously, by the debris. Closer to the blast, a section of the wall that had initially survived intact now teetered inward and collapsed as a single massive entity onto a group of huddling relief workers and soldiers.

Disdaining his own safety, Kismet sprang erect and darted across the terminal. Chaos had replaced the orderliness of the greeting area. Shrapnel and brick splinters were everywhere, and some who had survived with only minor injuries, or perhaps none at all, now rushed back and forth across the terminal in search of safety. Most simply remained flat on the ground, awaiting the next blast that might finish them all.

A number of figures struggled from the outer edge of the collapsed wall. Kismet caught a glimpse of red hair and instantly recognized the woman from the plane. Her expression remained purposeful as she turned back toward the devastated tableau, immediately plunging her hands into the debris to effect the rescue of her comrades. He was at her side a moment later, lending the strength of his legs and back to the effort of lifting the wall. This time, she did not spurn his presence.

Working together, they shifted a section of wall nearly two meters square, partially revealing two motionless forms: a US soldier and one of the Red Cross workers. Kismet dug at a scattering of bricks that still pinned the legs of the latter individual, enough so that the woman was able to slip her hands beneath the fallen aid worker's shoulders in order to drag him to safety.

Kismet blinked in disbelief. The woman, ostensibly dedicated to bringing relief to victims of the war, had helped rescue a single individual—her own friend—before fleeing the disaster area. Shaking off his incredulity, he plunged into the ruin once more, pushing aside large chunks of the wall to reveal other victims in dust-streaked camouflage. Another section of the wall, twice as large as the piece he had helped move, had fallen inward, crushing several more unlucky souls. It seemed unlikely that anyone could have endured its massive collapse, but Kismet had witnessed survival stories far more improbable.

He was closer now to the perimeter of the terminal, and able to follow the battle raging outside on the tarmac. The infantrymen were advancing toward the position from which the grenades had been launched, filling the air with bursts of gunfire. He couldn't tell if they were taking fire but the soldiers were staying low in order to present as small a target as possible. Kismet gave the situation a cursory glance, but kept his focus on driving wedge-shaped pieces of debris under the outermost lip of the fallen wall, forcibly raising it, if only by microscopic increments.

Abruptly, the pitch of the skirmish seemed to change. Kismet looked up from his task, anxious that yet another RPG had been unleashed. Instead of a grenade however, he saw something far more destructive racing toward his position.

In that instant he realized that the grenade attack had simply been a diversion, a feint designed to engage the troops and draw them away from the terminal. The advance had opened a gap in their flank, allowing a single vehicle to break through the outer secure perimeter of the airport, onto the tarmac. At the same instant, gunfire—Kismet recognized the distinctive report of the AK-47—from no less than three separate locations began showering the exposed soldiers, compelling them to dive for cover and effectively preventing them from firing on that lone automobile. Kismet knew instantly the purpose behind the driver's suicidal attempt to reach the terminal and recognized just as surely that none of the men on the tarmac would be able to stop it. When that car, or rather car bomb, reached the idle jetliner, the battle would be over for everyone. The soldiers on the runway and every soul in the exposed terminal building would be caught in the ensuing firestorm.

With a deftness acquired through weeks of training—and like bicycle riding, never quite forgotten—Kismet snatched a long object from the shoulder of a fallen trooper, removed the safety pin and rolled the cylinder onto his shoulder. The AT-4 anti-tank weapon was only slightly different than the LAW 80 he had learned to use a decade earlier, and a brief glance at the instructions printed on the side of the tube was all he needed to prepare the launcher for firing. A tilt of his head brought the target into view in the peep-sight.

"Backblast clear!" He glanced quickly to his rear, checking to make sure that anyone close enough to have heard his shouted warning was hastening away from the area, then thumbed the red trigger button.

The launch tube filled with fire as the solid propellant rocket motor blasted the 80 millimeter high-explosive warhead across the tarmac. A cone-shaped inferno blossomed behind Kismet—the rocket's backblast—and an ear-splitting hiss filled the enclosed terminal building as the missile broke the sound barrier.

The car was less than fifty meters from the jet, close enough, Kismet knew, to ignite the fuel in its wing tanks if enough explosives had been packed into the station wagon. The vehicle was a fast-moving target, difficult to strike even in the best of circumstances. To make matters worse, he knew that in the unlikely event of a direct hit, the anti-tank missile would trigger the car bomb, accomplishing the very thing he sought to prevent. All of those factors had flashed through his mind in the instant he fixed his sights not on the advancing vehicle but on a stationary spot on the runway directly in its path.

The warhead slammed into the paved surface before Kismet could relax his finger, and gouged a large crater in the soft asphalt a mere whisper ahead of the car's arrival. What the missile lacked in pyrotechnic splendor, it made up for in raw kinetic energy. The shockwave swept underneath the station wagon, lifting its front end off the runway and tossing the entire vehicle backward like a sheet of paper in a windstorm.

In that instant, the car detonated in a brilliant supernova. The chassis swelled like an overripe fruit then burst apart in a spray of metal fragments, some still recognizable as automobile components. The shockwave from the secondary explosion radiated outward in a near perfect sphere of force to hammer against the defenseless plane. The wings shuddered and the airframe twisted and popped as a wall of air, hard as steel and moving at the speed of sound, slammed into the fuselage. The jet shifted sideways, pushed by the invisible hand of the blast, and its tires left long streaks of rubber on the runway. An instant later a wheel from the car crashed into the stabilizer fin, followed by a spray of shrapnel that tore into the aluminum skin of the aircraft, peeling back the thin sheets. The port wing gave an agonized groan as a long crack began traveling its length. Kismet saw jet fuel weeping from the underside of the damaged wing and closed his eyes, waiting for the inevitable. The explosion that followed was not what he was expecting.

"Are you insane?"

Despite all the fury of gunshots and explosions, that strident exclamation was the harshest noise he had heard since arriving. He turned slowly to find, not surprisingly, the copper-haired woman who had preceded him into the terminal.

"Did you even think to look behind you?" she continued, her

scream of fury like fingernails on a chalkboard. Kismet noted absently that the woman was speaking English, fluently judging by the few words he had heard, but faintly accented.

Yep, French.

He countered her ferocious mien with one of calm dispassion. "I checked. It was clear."

"You almost incinerated us."

Kismet understood her distress and tried to be sympathetic. To a non-combatant, the plume of fire erupting from the launch tube must have seemed quite threatening. But he had checked before triggering the device. Moreover, his decision to angle the shot into the tarmac meant that most of the rocket's exhaust had been directed upward, over the head of anyone unlucky enough to be caught in the backfire zone.

Outside, the last fragments of debris from the suicide bomb vehicle clattered to the ground. The plane now bore significant scars from the encounter, but could conceivably fly again with extensive repair. Aside from the sole occupant of the vehicle, there appeared to be no casualties directly resulting from the terrorist act.

Beyond the battered aircraft, the tide of the ongoing gun battle had shifted once again. The attacking force, anticipating only success, had suffered a morale-shattering defeat. Their return fire trickled to nothing as they abandoned their positions and retreated toward the city. As Kismet gazed across the tarmac, he saw a squad of olive drab military vehicles charge across the open expanse in pursuit.

The red-haired woman remained in front of him, seething with misplaced anger, but said nothing more. Kismet blinked at her, then attempted a compromise. "I'm sorry I frightened you, but you weren't really in any danger. Not from this at least." He proffered the spent missile tube like an olive branch.

The woman made a guttural noise that might have been a curse then thrust her hands at his face before spinning on her heel and stalking away.

He lowered the missile launcher, shaking his head in disbelief, and pitched his voice so that there would be no mistaking his ire. "You're welcome."

TWO

As the battle shifted away from the airport, those inside the terminal building began to emerge from their defensive cocoons. Many of the non-combatants, desperately needing something to do in order to restore their dignity following the terrifying incident, raced to assist Kismet in the effort of lifting the fallen section of wall or began administering first aid to the dozen or more victims of shrapnel injuries.

Only moments after the confrontation with the woman whose hair color evidently matched her temperament, Kismet once again found himself under fire for having saved the day.

"Who the hell fired that AT-4?"

The voice belonged to a man, but was no less strident. Kismet straightened from his labors, turning to face a man wearing desert-pattern fatigues with a brown oak leaf sewn into the collar. He checked the nametape over the man's right breast pocket before answering. "I did, Major Harp."

The officer gaped at him in disbelief, momentarily losing his voice. It was evident from his manner that the man had expected to find one of the soldiers under his command responsible for what must have seemed like a reckless act. "Who the hell are you?"

"Nick Kismet." He extended his hand ingenuously.

"A goddamned civilian?"

Kismet lowered his hand with a sigh. "I guess so."

"I don't know who you think you are, but this is not some playground where you can come live out your Rambo fantasies." Kismet got the impression that Harp had used this speech before, practicing and refining his imprecations for maximum effect. The rant continued unchecked. "This is a goddamned war zone, mister. You civilians are to keep your goddamned heads down. I will not have my soldiers put in harm's way because you people want snapshots for your fucking scrapbooks and war stories to impress women at cocktail parties…"

"Major!"

The torrent of rage and blasphemy instantly evaporated with that single, sharply spoken recognition of rank. Harp stiffened to attention, his eyes no longer fixed on Kismet, as the person who had called out stepped into view. Like the major, this man also wore a khaki camouflage battle dress uniform with an oak leaf on his collar, but his insignia was black: a lieutenant colonel.

The newcomer scrutinized Kismet, then turned to his subordinate. "At ease, Major."

Harp relaxed from the disciplined posture; it was evident that his fire had gone out. The colonel turned back to Kismet. "You'll have to forgive Major Harp. He doesn't understand that any man who has earned the Silver Star deserves a little respect even if he no longer wears the uniform."

Harp's eyes widened at the revelation and a flush of embarrassment crept over his sand-abraded cheeks, but he kept his silence.

Kismet raised an eyebrow. "Not very many people know about that."

"Well, I do." The lieutenant colonel took his hand and began pumping it vigorously. "Jon Buttrick, Mr. Kismet. A pleasure to meet you. And from what I've heard, we all owe you a debt of gratitude. If that car had gotten any closer, we'd be cleaning this terminal up with a bulldozer."

Kismet risked a satisfied grin. "Frankly, Colonel—"

"Call me Jon, Nick."

"Jon. Frankly, I'm glad someone appreciates that I knew what I was doing."

The officer chuckled. "I'm sure they'll all figure it out once they hear about it on CNN." He nodded to a gathering knot of reporters who circled like vultures, waiting for an opportunity to move in and tear him apart with their questions.

"Monsieur Kismet." The small dark-haired woman who had initially met him upon his arrival darted in front of Buttrick. "You'll be late for your meeting."

"My meeting," Kismet echoed, loud enough for all the journalists to hear. He could almost sense their panic as they saw him maneuver for an escape. "Thank you again for your kind words, Colonel."

The other man nodded with a knowing smile, allowing the woman to guide Kismet away from the swarm. "Hey, Nick. Listen, if you want to blow up some more stuff, do me a favor and re-up."

Kismet ignored the chuckling officer and focused intently on the woman's shoulders. She hastened directly to the spot where Kismet had left his bags, the place where he had pushed her down and shielded her with his own body. He didn't even know her name. "Mademoiselle, I don't believe we've been—"

"Marie," she replied, looking up from beneath the bulky helmet. Her smile could not quite erase his memory of the haughtiness he had earlier detected. "My name is Marie Villaneauve," she continued in English. "And I also appreciate your prompt action in my defense."

She then nodded toward the pack of reporters and videographers that had decided to chase after him. "However, I believe we are now even."

No matter where he went in the world, Saeed Tariq Al-Sharaf always made sure that he had a view of water. He preferred river frontages most of all. Rivers were the source of life, as far as he was concerned. He had grown up in a place without rivers, a place where water was procured only through physical labor, but as he matured, gaining authority and with it a measure of wealth, he had moved closer to the great river and made a solemn promise to always pitch his tent within sight of water.

Of course, he was not alone in his appreciation of an aquatic panorama. The scenic vistas he craved came with a hefty price tag, especially here where the presence of so many affluent businessmen, politicians and celebrities had inflated real estate prices by an order of magnitude. Additionally, the lease of the chateau was being handled through a proxy, a faceless law office in Geneva, and that act of representation further bumped up the expense of maintaining a view of the river.

But what a view it is, thought Saeed. *Worth every euro.*

His eyes lingered on the sun-dappled surface of the waterway, contemplating it meditatively, as if in prayer. It was as close as he came to devotion. Even when he had lived in the desert, he had flaunted the five-times daily ritual call of the *muezzin*. He accepted that there was no God but God, but held to the personal belief that Allah had put man on earth to find his own way. Religion was a tool for rallying, and if necessary manipulating, the rabble, but served no divine purpose that he could see.

The muster of the masses was now fully underway in the country of his birth. The Persians had not won the nation through conquest—that had been the work of the American devils—but in anticipation of the fall of Saddam Hussein's government, the theocratic government of Iran had sent hundreds of mullahs over the border, insinuating into the Shiite community in order to cultivate popular support for a religious government in Iraq. During his reign, Saddam had brutally quashed any number of attempts on the part of the faithful to organize, recognizing the power inherent in such zeal, but the Americans were reluctant to employ such decisive tactics in defense of their cause, and so the Shiite majority was becoming emboldened to take control of the nation.

Saeed had been following the story with great interest, even as he had followed the build-up to war and the subsequent campaign. He did not really care how the game eventually played out, but he craved information about the struggle. It was very important to know which way the wind was going to blow in order to chart his course.

He turned away from the river, his eyes slow to adjust after staring into the glare, and turned up the volume on the television set. The twenty-four-hour satellite news channel to which he kept the set tuned at all times had been broadcasting almost nothing but coverage of the war and civil unrest for several weeks. The latest developments concerned him directly. Agents from Interpol and the American Federal Bureau of Investigation had successfully recovered a great number of art treasures looted from the National Museum in Baghdad, preventing them from being dispersed in the European black market. While Saeed's interests had not been directly affected, the affair would draw unwelcome attention to what had been a largely ignored enterprise.

A flashing graphic on the screen seized his interest, the words "Breaking News", which sometimes heralded a significant change in the position of the pieces on the global game board. As he had come to expect, the new development regarded something that had just occurred in his homeland. He listened carefully to the English-language broadcast, mentally translating the foreign words as he watched.

There had been an attack at what he still thought of as the Saddam International Airport. A suicide bomber had blown himself up in an effort to bring great destruction upon the troops massed at the large facility a few kilometers outside of Baghdad. The explosion had done some structural damage and caused several injuries, but it was being reported that the only fatality resulting from the blast was the bomber himself. As if to underscore this point, the handsome journalist reporting the incident stood on the runway, with a smoking pile of debris just over his left shoulder.

"The suicide bomb attack appears to have been part of a broader strategy. An effort to disrupt a key supply route. However, that desperate mission was thwarted, not by US troops, but rather by a civilian bystander."

The screen cut to video footage of two men conversing: one a soldier in desert camouflage, the other wearing blue jeans and a khaki shirt. Judging by his appearance, Saeed would have believed the second man to be a soldier in civilian attire. He was obviously in excellent physical shape and his close-cropped hairstyle was de rigueur among American military personnel. *Probably from their CIA.*

"This man," continued the reporter in a voice-over, "an American representative of the Global Heritage Commission, part of the UN's effort to address the looting of Iraqi antiquities, happened to be in the right place at the right time, and with the right weapon, to prevent the terrorist bomber from reaching his destination.

"The man, identified as Nick Kismet, picked up a portable missile launcher, like the one seen here." The picture changed to stock footage of a US soldier carrying an anti-tank weapon, but Saeed had already stopped watching, and after a moment, thumbed the button on the remote control to mute the speaker in order to make a telephone call.

Her introduction notwithstanding, Marie Villaneauve was proving to be a tough nut to crack. As she guided Kismet through the mostly vacant terminal building she said very little, answering only a few direct questions with monosyllabic replies. He no longer sensed that she was trying to be rude, but her quiet indifference was nevertheless wearing thin.

He made one last attempt. "So you're with UNESCO?"

"*Oui.*"

Kismet admitted defeat. Small talk had never been his strong suit anyway.

Their destination lay in an unfinished wing of the airport building. The Baghdad International Airport—the metal letters affixed to the exterior walls still read "Saddam International"—had never really been used for its intended purpose. Shunned by most of the global community for decades, Iraq had failed to become a leading travel destination, even in the Arab world. The facility had however become a critical target of the US-led coalition during the month-long campaign to overthrow the brutal despot. A perfect landing zone for resupply flights, it was lightly defended and close enough to the capital city to serve as a base of operations for the final push on Baghdad. It now served as a central receiving area for both military and civilian activities, and until the earlier suicide bomb attack, was thought to be a safe haven for foreigners.

Baghdad was actually a safer place for Americans than some of the areas to the south, where Shiite activism was reaching a fever pitch. The Sunni Muslims living in the country's largest city were primarily interested in restoring their infrastructure, and the US Army engineers assisting in that effort were viewed as heroes rather than interlopers. But as the events of that morning had amply demonstrated, violence did not require a majority opinion. There were international journalists still occupying some of the hotels in the city, but most critical operations were being run from the secure environment of the airport. Likewise, the UN headquarters had been locked up and left behind two months previously, meaning that UNESCO's mission in Iraq would also have to be based at the airport.

Marie led him to a windowless door at the end of a hallway, identified only by a sheet of paper from a laser printer with the acronym of her organization in block letters, taped beside the doorpost. She turned the knob, pushing the door open, and stepped aside.

Kismet demurred. "Ladies first."

The instinctive deferment won a crooked smile from his reticent guide, and she proceeded through the door ahead of him. Once over the threshold, he eased his duffel to the floor, sensing that the long journey was nearly over.

"Hello, Nick."

Kismet whirled, instantly recognizing the voice, and all thoughts of breaching Marie Villaneauve's social defenses were put aside. "Pierre, you old bastard."

Pierre Chiron, the man who had befriended him during a visit to

France eight years before, and who had ultimately given him a job, crossed the barren room and embraced Kismet heartily. "Ah, Nick. It's always good to see you."

"I had a feeling you'd be here, though I can't imagine why." Kismet drew back, holding his old friend at arm's length, and got his first real look at the man. He didn't like what he saw.

He knew Chiron to be in his late sixties, but the UN scientist seemed to have aged at least another decade beyond his natural years. On the occasion of their last meeting, the Frenchman had been robust if slightly stooped from years of academic torpor, but he now seemed hollow, a summer leaf gone prematurely to autumn. Kismet smiled to hide his dismay.

"My God, Nick. How long has it been?"

"Not since..." He hesitated. He had not seen Chiron since Collette's funeral. "Almost six years," he amended hastily, trying to steer his comments away from the painful memories that his recollection was stirring up. "We've done a lot of good in that time."

Chiron managed a wan smile. "My many young protégés have accomplished wonders. Alas, I have done little more than sit back and take credit for it all."

Kismet was not fooled by the old man's modesty. Although he had not since paid a visit to Chiron's home or to the UNESCO headquarters—both in Paris—he had stayed in touch. Following the death of his spouse, Chiron had to all appearances thrown himself into the task of saving the UN's scientific and cultural organization. His Global Heritage Commission had been an integral part of restoring UNESCO's credibility, to the point that the United States had now committed itself to restoring its lapsed membership. Nevertheless, his desolate physical appearance bore testimony to the fact that he had not completely found solace in his work.

"Well, you've got me this far. What's next? Are we going to comb the city for looted artifacts?" Though his voice held a hint of irony, he half-expected Chiron to answer affirmatively. The collapse of the Iraqi regime had led to a period of wanton vandalism and pillaging, stripping away in a single night the treasures of the most ancient civilization on earth. Protecting those tangible links to cultures since past was part and parcel of the GHC's charter. Although Chiron had been trained as an atomic scientist, as chairman of GHC it was appropriate that he take an interest in the crisis.

Chiron shook his head sadly. "Interpol and your American FBI have already taken that task upon themselves, and with great success I might add."

"What, then? Putting the National Museum back together? I hope you didn't bring me over here just to sweep up the broken glass and build new dioramas?"

The old man stared at him silently for a moment, then glanced at Marie. "Ah, where are my manners? You've made a proper introduction to my assistant, I trust."

Kismet's eyebrows betrayed his irritation, but he otherwise kept his expression neutral. "After a fashion."

"Monsieur Kismet saved my life," intoned Marie, her voice matter-of-fact. She removed her bulky helmet, giving Kismet his first real opportunity to study her face. Her dark hair, not quite black, was styled in a modified wedge cut, longer toward the front where it curled under at her jaw on either side. Her forehead was covered by squared-off bangs, perfectly parallel to her sculpted eyebrows. The effect was decidedly contrived, too artificial for such a rugged environment. Kismet recalled his earlier appraisal. She did indeed look like a fashion model, stranded now on the wrong kind of runway.

Chiron burst into laughter. "Did he indeed? He has a habit of doing that." He laughed again. Though smile lines cracked his face, the humor seemed to erase years of despair. "Yes, I heard some shooting. Was that you, Nick?"

"Old habits die hard."

"Well you both look no worse for wear. Come, let's settle down." He gestured toward one of the unfinished walls where several foam shipping containers had been arranged into makeshift furniture. "Have you eaten?"

"On the plane. I don't know if that qualifies as food."

"Alas, it's better than what I have to offer." Chiron held up a brown plastic bag about the size of a book. "Meals, Ready to Eat, or so they say. I like the fruit candies, but..." He shook his head sadly.

Kismet didn't think his old friend could afford to miss any meals. He opened his duffel bag, rooting around inside for a heavily wrapped parcel. "When I realized you might be here, I took a chance. I think you'll be pleased."

He opened the package, revealing a bottle of red wine along with a baguette and a wheel of Brie. Chiron's eyes lit up. Kismet turned to Marie. "I imagine you're getting pretty sick of MREs, too. Join us?"

For a moment, he thought she would accept the invitation. She even took a step toward the improvised settee, an eager smile blossoming on her painted lips. Then, unexpectedly, the smile wilted. "I'm sure you two have a great deal to discuss. Regrettably, I shall have to decline."

Kismet nodded, unsurprised by her decision. He sensed Chiron's disappointment, but did not entirely share the sentiment. "Another time, perhaps. Though I'll warn you, the fare might not be as palatable."

She nodded, and then backed away, her helmet tucked under one arm. When she was gone, he turned to Chiron. "Where did you find the ice queen?"

The Frenchman pretended not to hear the question. He held up the bottle, displaying the label with mock contempt. "Sonoma Valley? I mistook you for a civilized man."

"It gets worse," Kismet replied ruefully. "I didn't bring any glasses."

Chiron lifted his drink, tilting the ceramic coffee mug toward the younger man. "To Collette," he declared in a solemn voice.

The corner of Kismet's mouth twitched in anxious surprise, but he raised his own cup in salute. "To Collette."

The sun was settling into the western sky, but the air remained warm as an arid wind blew in from the south. After scrounging the porcelain cups, the two men had made their way onto the flat roof of the terminal in order to enjoy the imported repast as they contemplated the end of the day. It was a scene that harkened back to the summer Kismet had spent in Paris, a guest in the Chiron household.

Pierre's wife had doted on him, welcoming him as the child she would never have, and Kismet, whose biological mother had vanished from his life before his earliest memory, eagerly embraced the attention of a maternal figure. It had proven to be a brief, but mutually satisfying relationship. Meanwhile, Chiron had helped him scour the UNESCO archives for any clues that would lead him to resolve the mystery of what had happened one fateful night in 1991: Kismet's first journey into the desert. Though never fully understanding what it was the young man sought, the scientist and diplomat had enjoyed the role of mentor. More than once, the two men had gathered, along with Collette, on the veranda to watch the sunset. Her conspicuous absence was now a painful reminder of what had happened in the years that followed.

Chiron sighed. "I do miss her, Nick."

Kismet nodded uncertainly, but said nothing.

The other man stared into his cup, swirling the dark contents as if looking for an omen in the dregs. "Do you think she is with God?"

The question caught him off guard. He knew Pierre to be a staunch secularist, at best an agnostic. The issue of faith had been broached almost from the start of their acquaintance; two men of uncertain beliefs, meeting on the threshold of a place revered by the devout, had presented a noteworthy contrast.

"If He's out there, I've no doubt she's with Him."

"If." Chiron laughed, then drained the contents of the mug. "The great unanswered question. She never had any doubt though. Not even at the end."

Kismet looked at his own cup, averting his eyes from the older man. The Frenchman's turn of speech reminded him of the morose rambling of a drunkard. He made no attempt to fill the uncomfortable void, but silently hoped the other man would change the subject. Chiron was not finished.

"You think a lot about God when you get to be my age. Always wondering if you made the right choices."

"I imagine that's only natural."

Chiron chuckled again, but there was a bitter note in the words that followed. "What a game this is. Blind, we must choose a path through the maze and follow it to the end. Only then are our eyes opened, and the wisdom or foolishness of our choices becomes manifest. I don't know about you, but I hardly think that's fair."

"That's where faith comes in. You and I aren't believers, so we can never really understand why someone might choose a life wholly guided by their religious beliefs. But to the true believer, it must seem like the only choice." It was more than Kismet had wanted to say on the subject and he immediately regretted having let the other man draw him out. Still, nothing he had said was a revelation. They had exchanged similar words on more than one occasion. The difference this time was the import Chiron seemed to place on the subject.

"Ah, yes. Faith. Jesus' disciples asked for more faith. Do you know that what he told them? 'If you have faith as a grain of a mustard seed, you shall say to this mountain: Remove from hence hither, and it shall remove; and nothing shall be impossible to you'." He moved close, so that Kismet could not avoid direct eye contact. "How can that be, Nick? You either have faith, or you do not, correct? How can you quantify faith?"

"I have no idea." He moved back a step, then sat on the brick parapet, his back now against the sunset. "Christ, Pierre, you didn't drag me halfway around the world to debate philosophy, did you? We could have done that in Paris."

"My apologies. I recall a time when you enjoyed our discussions."

The reproof lacked the weight of sincerity, but Kismet still chose a conciliatory tone. "Chalk it up to jet lag. Maybe tomorrow, over coffee…"

"No, you are right. There is a time and place for this, and it is not now. It is rude of me to distract you from the real reason I have summoned you. There is important work for us here, and to be quite honest, I need your help.

"As you may have heard, many of the early reports about the pillage of the museums were exaggerated. In some cases, the relics had been stored away by the staff in anticipation of the coming war. A great many other pieces were returned by thieves whose consciences caught up with them. A few pieces made it out and are already showing up on the European black market."

"But you said that Interpol had that covered."

"Indeed they do, and I've no interest in duplicating their efforts. However, I have been monitoring their investigation and discovered some rather disturbing inconsistencies.

"There is a secret list of art treasures being circulated among illicit collectors. Interpol has access to it, but does not wish this information to become public. I have seen the list. Some of the items that are being made available do not appear to have come from the catalogue of Iraq's national museum."

Suddenly Kismet understood. "You're thinking grave robbers?"

Chiron nodded. "It is a crime in the eyes of Allah to steal, but to dig something up from the ground and sell it to buy bread for your family? Where is the crime in that?"

"How much are we talking about? Could it just be one guy who got lucky and found a trove, or is this an organized effort?"

"That is what I hope to determine." He tipped the bottle toward his cup, half-filling it. "A significant historical find would be a great boon to the people of this country—to the whole world. It would remind them that this place is the source of civilization. A timely distraction both from the war and the memories of oppression."

"Where do we start?" Wheels were already turning in Kismet's head, the earlier conversation thankfully forgotten.

Chiron refilled Kismet's cup, decanting the last of the Pinot Noir from the bottle. "There is a man at the museum who has…ah, we shall say that he has demonstrated divided loyalties. He is one of the assistant curators, devoted to the cause of history, but a pragmatist. I suspect he may be trading with a rival organization to the one we are seeking, but his indiscretions are not our concern at present. I believe he will be able to put us on the path. Getting to him in order to conduct an interview however has proven difficult. The city is a very dangerous place."

The last piece fell into place. "Oh. I guess that's where I come in."

"You have experience in this environment. That is unique among our organization. My people are scientists, academics. Furthermore, I suspect that our search will lead us into the wilderness, where our lives may be placed in further jeopardy."

"So I'm the hired muscle." He made the statement without a hint of accusation.

"If you like. There are other considerations, some of them personal."

"Such as?"

Chiron leaned on the short wall next to him, the weariness once more in evidence. "You are like a son to me, Nick. I can't think of anyone I would rather have with me. That being said, you are also an American, whereas I—not only am I French, but also a representative of the United Nations. As you might well imagine, neither of these factors have endeared me to the military authorities."

Kismet nodded, comprehending. Despite repeated position statements to the effect that France remained an ally of the United States and that the UN was both a legitimate and important presence in the process of building world peace and security, popular sentiment among Americans, both citizens and soldiers, remained decidedly isolationist. The French government's vocal opposition to US foreign policy in the days preceding the war had severely widened that rift, so much so that certain reactionaries had pushed to rename "French Fries" and "French Toast" in congressional cafeterias. It had been no coincidence that the bottle of wine Kismet had purchased before leaving New York had been from California; many retailers had pulled French wines from their shelves.

Meanwhile, the perception of an impotent United Nations had only been reinforced by that body's inability to maintain concerted opposition to the ruthless dictator of Iraq. To make matters worse, immediately following the unquestioned victory of coalition forces, the UN had demanded a significant role in the rebuilding of that devastated nation. For many Americans who were already questioning the relevance of the UN, this only added insult to injury.

A lifetime of travel and association with men like Chiron had taught Kismet not to paint the world in the broad strokes of nationalism. To be sure, political differences among nations could not be ignored, just as religious, economic and tribal distinctions sometimes led to unbridgeable gulfs between individuals, but Kismet preferred to make that determination only after giving a person a chance to demonstrate where their loyalties lay. As for the United Nations…well, perhaps it was deserving of some of the criticism heaped upon it, but Kismet could not escape the fact of where his paychecks originated.

Chiron let out his breath with a sigh. "And…."

"There's more?"

The older man turned to face him, his expression unusually grave. "The artifacts, Nick. They date from the Babylonian dynasty—seventh century BC—but they are not of Babylonian origin. They are the treasures of Nebuchadnezzar's conquest. Do you know what that means?"

Kismet felt his breath catch in his throat. He knew exactly what it meant.

THREE

A column of olive drab Heavy Motorized Multi-Wheeled Vehicles (HMMWV), known as Humvees in the argot of the common soldier, departed from the airport at 0915 local time. Each of the military transports was identified by a series of stenciled letters painted on the front and rear bumpers. These four were numbered in sequence, from D-42 through D-46. Delta four-six was the vehicle reserved for the platoon leader but today it carried the mission commander—Lt. Col. Jonathan Buttrick—along with two other soldiers. Bringing up the rear was a resupply vehicle, different only from the others with respects to its cargo and passenger complement. This Humvee carried only a driver and an assistant, along with five twenty-liter jerrycans of diesel. The second Humvee in the convoy likewise was crewed by two soldiers, but carried also two VIP passengers.

Kismet had experienced an odd moment of déjà vu upon climbing into the military vehicle. The wide-bodied conveyance had just been coming into its own twelve years earlier, and while he had ridden in them on numerous occasions prior to the first war against Iraq, he had not been in one since. Although the design had been modified for civilian use, proving very popular as an urban utility vehicle especially among wealthy celebrities, Kismet still thought of it primarily as an engine of war. The fact that he was now wearing Kevlar armor only served to reinforce this impression. While his actions the previous day owed a great deal to his military training, that had been instinctual. Voluntarily getting into the Humvee had required a conscious decision, and was therefore just a little bit disconcerting. Once inside, the stale smells of sweat and mildew proved almost overpowering. It was an unwelcome transition from what had occurred the night before.

Locating Buttrick in the sprawling, chaotic complex had been a difficult task, but once accomplished, securing a squad of infantry soldiers to serve as an escort proved virtually painless. Despite Chiron's fear that support for a United Nations mission would be in short supply, the accommodating officer had looked upon the request as good public relations. Nevertheless, Kismet wondered if someone like Major Harp would have been as quick to send the request up the chain of command. Afterward, Kismet had headed back to the GHC office to pass along the good news.

He had found Marie sitting silently in the sparsely furnished office, reviewing maps of the city. "Where is Pierre?"

She raised a finger to her meticulously painted lips, then pointed to a dark corner where lay a shapeless cloth mass: a sleeping bag, presumably with Chiron inside. "He was tired," she whispered.

Kismet could tell she was being diplomatic. Chiron had been inebriated at their parting—too much wine, drunk too fast—and had likely passed out the moment he lay down. For his own part, the Pinot Noir had left him with a mild headache. He nodded deferentially, then went to find some water.

"Monsieur...Nick."

Mildly surprised that she had initiated communication, he had turned. "Yes?"

She had crossed the room silently and now stood only a step away. Her expression had changed somehow—nothing more than a relaxing of her disdainful jaw line—but the effect was irresistible. "Did you save any wine for me?"

Although he had not, the ice was nonetheless broken. They had stayed up longer than Kismet intended, talking about their respective tasks with the Global Heritage Commission and how they had each met up with Pierre Chiron. The discussion had then turned to a shared concern regarding the older man's mental status. Marie had not known him prior to Collette's death and therefore was unaware of the severe change that his unresolved grief had brought about, but his decline even in the brief time she had known him was impossible to ignore.

Eventually, the conversation had faltered. Kismet's initial reticence had been swept away by her charm, all the more so because he had not anticipated being attracted to her, but there was a limit to what could be accomplished in a single evening. She was curious about his motives, about his personal stake in uncovering the source of the black market artifacts, and that was something he was not prepared to reveal. Even Chiron, the man who had been like a second father to him, barely knew the half. As she probed his defenses, he had begged off, once more citing the cumulative effects of jet lag, and bade her goodnight. Only a dozen paces separated their sleeping areas, and while nothing more was said, he remained acutely aware of her nearness until fatigue finally overcame him.

Reflecting on the pleasantness of the night before was a welcome distraction from the brief journey into the city. The anxiety of the soldiers escorting them was a constant reminder that they were heading into a potentially hostile area. Each of the soldiers carried an M4 carbine along with an assortment of other personal weapons but the Humvee turrets, which were capable of supporting numerous heavy weapon systems, remained sealed. Kismet understood the logic behind this decision. Openly displayed .50 caliber machine guns would have sent the wrong message in a city where the US military was trying to project a benevolent presence. It was a command-level decision, not necessarily supported by the soldiers on the ground, who felt rather like they were being sent into a potentially dangerous situation with one hand tied behind their backs.

Kismet was also armed, though the handgun in his waist pack—a lightweight Glock 19, semi-automatic pistol—was hardly the weapon of choice for a combat zone. In addition to the gun he carried a *kukri* knife, likewise secured in the small nylon pack he wore around his waist. The heavy chopping knife, with its distinctive boomerang-shaped thirty-centimeter-long blade, was a tangible link to the events that had changed his life twelve years previously. The blade had been offered as a token of respect, but before that night had ended, Kismet had been forced to use the *kukri* as a weapon of last resort. It remained a treasured memento of that ill-fated mission, though no less utilitarian.

To distinguish themselves from combatants, the UN personnel wore white flak jackets and helmet covers, prominently displaying the letters of their organization. A similarly adorned banner was draped across the rear of each Humvee, hopefully reinforcing the message to the local populace that their excursion into the city had only peaceable motives.

The convoy moved at a safe but deliberate pace of eighty kilometers per hour, along highways that were virtually empty. In a modern city of six million souls, the lack of automobile traffic was vaguely disturbing, but Baghdad was still recovering from the brief siege that had heralded the end of a dictatorship. Certain parts of the city were still without electricity and running water, and there were reports of gasoline shortages and long lines—even riots—at refueling stations.

Navigating by means of a GPS system, the lead vehicle in the column charted a decisive course toward the city. Their route took them along the main highway within sight of several palatial complexes, some of which were now only shattered memories of their former opulence. As the road drew parallel with a westward curving segment of the Tigris River, the convoy threaded between the Sujud Palace and the military parade grounds, both of which bore testimony to heavy bombing and ground battle. Kismet did not strain for a better look. He loathed the idea of playing ghoulish tourist.

The journey progressed uneventfully, but the comfort level inside the Humvee bottomed out rapidly. The Lexan windows remained closed as a protective measure, bottling up the musty odor which emanated from the cracked upholstery. To make matters worse, the driver informed them that he would be running the vehicle's heater in order to dissipate the rising engine temperature. The interior quickly became a claustrophobic hot-box.

"A pity Marie couldn't join us," mused Chiron, raising his voice to be heard over the incessant roar of the engine. It was the first comment the older man had made on the subject—the first thing he had said all morning really, except for a few brief utterances in preparation for departure.

"She didn't strike me as the rugged, adventurous type. I'd say she's lucky to have stayed behind." Kismet then threw a sidelong glance in the other man's direction. "I thought that it was your decision."

Chiron smiled cryptically. "I found a pretext with which to discourage her from joining us, but I did so for your sake."

"I don't understand."

"Nick, it's been clear to me from the start that whatever this thing that drives you, it is a deeply personal matter." He leaned over the upraised platform covering the drive shaft and lowered his voice to a stage whisper. "You've kept it secret even from me. What you haven't told me only fires my curiosity. Shall I review?

"You are sent on a clandestine meeting in the desert with a defector. The man seems to have information about you, and believes you will be interested in a very precious relic, unearthed in the ruins of ancient Babylon. What was that relic? Never mind. I suspect I don't want to know.

"Then your meeting is violently interrupted by a man who also claims to have knowledge about you. Both men believed that you will have an interest in whatever this relic is, but you claim no particular desire to possess this, or any other artifact of the ancient world.

"I have tried to offer whatever help I can. And I have let you keep your secrets. It is clear that the beginning of this labyrinth begins with a discovery here, in the sands of Iraq—the ruins of ancient Babylonia—and perhaps by returning to the source, we will be able to find the thread of Theseus and a solution to this mystery."

"Theseus." Kismet echoed the word in a distant voice, his mind elsewhere. He knew he ought to trust Chiron. The Frenchman had certainly demonstrated uncompromising fealty, without demanding a full disclosure of his own personal agenda.

"Pardon?"

"You mentioned Theseus—the warrior in Greek mythology who survived the labyrinth designed by Daedelus and slew the Minotaur. It made me think of something." He drew in a deep, contemplative breath. "The truth of the matter is that I've never shared all the details of my search because most of it is just too unbelievable."

"I think I can keep an open mind."

"I told you about the men who attacked us that night and about their leader. What I didn't tell you was his name. He seemed more than eager to share it at the time: Ulrich Hauser."

"Ah, a German perhaps?"

"He told me that he was not part of any nation's army, but he and his men obviously had military training. He told me something else. When I asked who he was—not just his name, but the reason behind his actions—he said: 'We are the chains of God, sealing Pandora's box for the preservation of mankind. We are Prometheus, guiding the destiny of the world until humanity is ready to ascend Olympus'. I've never forgotten those words."

"Ah, thus the association with my mention of a figure from Greek myth. Prometheus, the Titan who stole fire from the gods and gave it to mankind. But what's the connection to these 'chains of God'? If memory serves, Zeus chained Prometheus to a mountain, where he was tormented until Hercules set him free. I don't recall anything about his sealing up Pandora's box; in fact, Pandora was created as Zeus' retribution for the theft of fire."

"I didn't say I knew what it meant," confessed Kismet. "From the context, and from some bits and pieces I've put together over the years, I've come to suspect that they might be some kind of mystery cult."

The convoy exited from the main highway, entering the city streets, and the driver's assistant relayed the message that they would be arriving momentarily. Kismet nodded in acknowledgment.

"A modern mystery cult." Chiron was quick to return to their conversation. "The Pandora's box reference could indicate their belief that mankind is unready for some secret knowledge that only they possess."

"I told you it was hard to believe." He feigned a chuckle, trying to conceal his discomfort with the subject.

"And this artifact? It would have had great significance to them? And to the world?"

Kismet shifted in his seat, but did not answer. The question had been rhetorical anyway.

Chiron began ticking off facts on his fingers. "Let's see, we have a relic unearthed in Babylon, from the period of Nebuchadnezzar's conquests. It is something uniquely significant; not some potsherd or clay figurine, but a treasure that might upset the balance of the world. In his day, Nebuchadnezzar conquered most of the Middle East, even taking tribute from Egypt. Most noteworthy to moderns of course was his victory over Jerusalem. The city was razed and all of the treasures of Solomon's temple were carried off as spoil."

He paused, his gaze intensifying as he looked across the seat. "Have I found the thread, Nick?"

Kismet shrugged. "I didn't get a very good look at it, whatever it was. In any event, it's gone. It sure as hell isn't here anymore."

"Then what do we hope to learn today?"

He laughed. "I thought we were trying to protect the cultural history of Iraq."

Chiron sat back with a smug grin. "There, you see? You have secrets which even now you do not wish to share. I understand, but Marie is curious. She would ask the same questions, but demand a better answer. That is why I have left her behind."

"Pierre, I promise that one day, I will tell you everything. Right now, it's so confusing that even I don't know what to believe."

The Humvee slowed as it pulled into an almost vacant parking area, alongside a blockish two-story brick building. The ornate facade—a reproduction of a Babylonian era arched city gateway—

and prevalence of weathered statuary in the courtyard seemed confirmation enough that they had arrived at their destination: the Iraq National Museum. The spectacle presented by the edifice and the artistry that adorned it was not sufficient to draw the eye away from the damage wrought by the recent fighting. Twisted iron and shattered brick littered the museum grounds, and the walls were now scorched and pitted with bullet holes. To underscore the volatility of the situation, two M1A1 Abrams tanks were parked in front of the structure, their crews hunkered down inside the protective armored shell. The presence of US troops not only deterred potential looters, but evidently also scared off everyone else.

Kismet worked the door lever, eager to be out of the sweltering interior of the vehicle. Chiron however had more to say. "Perhaps today will be that day."

The Frenchman was the last to get out, pulling himself from the vehicle like a man twenty years older than he was. The soldiers had already fanned out around the parked convoy, and though the muzzles of their carbines were pointing at the ground, to a man they gripped their weapons purposefully.

Buttrick was quick to approach, glancing around anxiously. "Well, this is your show now, Nick. I've got to tell you, I feel kind of exposed out here."

"I wish I could tell you how long this will take, but I've really no idea."

Buttrick followed them toward the entrance, warily scanning the surrounding area for any signs of trouble. Kismet focused on the path ahead and spied two men standing beneath the Ishtar gate reproduction. The men were well dressed, but their suits had a rumpled appearance, and their facial expressions were haggard and lean. The older of the two, a distinguished-looking man in his fifties, sporting a bushy mustache shot through with gray, watched their approach nervously. The younger man stepped forward to greet them.

"I am Hussein Hamallah. Peace be upon you," he said, offering the traditional greeting in accented English. He gestured to his companion. "This is Mr. Aziz."

Kismet dredged up his own memory of the Arabic response: "*Wa aleekum is-salaam.*"

Hussein appeared pleased. "I will serve as translator on your behalf today. Please sirs, come inside."

A large open garden area greeted them just beyond the formal entrance, but it was evident even from the first glance that the museum had undergone an upheaval. Piles of debris—stone chips, broken glass, and reams of tattered paper—were everywhere. Working among the chaos were several men and women, presumably the staff of the facility, attempting to restore the repository to its former glory. Kismet felt a silent respect for those people, knowing that in all likelihood, they were laboring with only a tacit promise of reward. His own office, in the sub-basement of the American Museum of Natural History in New York City, brought him into regular contact with similarly devoted individuals, people for whom the call to educate others about culture and history was more than just a job.

Buttrick excused himself from the group and returned to the convoy to organize security, while Hussein steered the party into a corridor where a few examples of Assyrian art and history remained visible amidst the smashed display cases. They did not linger within sight of these but instead ascended a spiral staircase to the second floor. From there, Kismet and Chiron were directed into a small conference room, which aside from a uniform coating of dust on the furnishings, appeared to have missed out on the ill fortunes of war. They removed their bulky armor while Hussein hastily brushed the seats of two chairs, then gestured for the guests to sit.

Aziz remained aloof, as if debating what tack to take with the men from the Global Heritage Commission. For Kismet, who had studied law and seen his share of deposition proceedings, the man's reticence was understandable. The Iraqi curator would doubtless hold back from volunteering information, lest he accidentally incriminate himself. The burden of asking the right questions would fall to the interrogators. Addressing the older man directly, Kismet fired off a positioning shot.

"What is your function here, sir?"

The translation was almost instantaneous, and Aziz rattled off a response. "Until this war, I was restoring the palace of Ashurbanipal. Now, I do what I can for the museum."

"Your efforts are greatly appreciated," supplied Chiron, diplomatically. "Hopefully, the rich history of your nation will soon be restored to a place of dignity, for all the world to discover."

"*Inshallah*," murmured Aziz. God willing.

"We are pleased that many of the relics thought lost in the looting have already been accounted for."

"Yes. The situation could have been much worse."

Kismet decided to move in. "Has the looting stopped?"

The curator blinked at him, then turned to his assistant. "Mr. Aziz does not understand your question. Do you refer to the looting in the city, or to the museum?"

"The museum, of course. Are items still being stolen and sold on the black market?"

"No. We have inventoried all that remains. It is accounted for." The answer was unequivocal, but Aziz's certainty came as no surprise.

"What about other relics? Relics from archaeological sites that perhaps haven't been catalogued yet?"

Aziz's lip twitched. "There are rumors of men finding the treasures of the ancients and selling them illegally. If I knew more, I would immediately contact the authorities."

Chiron jumped in, his tone conciliatory. "We know, of course, that you have no part in this criminal activity, Mr. Aziz. However, it is these rumors that interest us. Anything you could tell us would be greatly appreciated."

Kismet struggled to hide his dismay. His old mentor had just tipped their hand to the Iraqi curator, virtually promising the man immunity from further action as well as implying that his cooperation would be rewarded. In a culture where bargaining was almost an art form, a basic rule of negotiation was that the first person to make an offer lost the advantage. Aziz would now be able to dictate the terms of the exchange. He could tell that the Iraqi sensed victory as well by a subtle shift in the man's posture.

"Do you know Samir Al-Azir?"

Aziz had been on the verge of speaking when Kismet blurted out the name. He paused long enough for Hussein to make the translation, but it was evident that he had understood the question. The Iraqi curator barely concealed a frown as he replied.

"This name means nothing," explained Hussein. Kismet could not tell if the young man was translating Aziz's words or elucidating at his own discretion.

Samir Al-Azir; the name given to Kismet by the defector he had met in the desert during the fateful mission in the hours prior to the war known as Desert Storm. Kismet knew that there must be more to the man's name—the defector had supplied a proper name and a family designation, yet had withheld his surname—but there was nothing else to go on. Samir Al-Azir was the end of the thread Chiron had mentioned. If he failed to pick it up here, a singular opportunity to unriddle the maze of his life might be lost.

"He was an engineer working for the government twelve years ago. He was working on the restoration of Babylon."

"The restoration of that ancient city has been going on for more than twenty years. Thousands of men have been involved. You can't expect me to remember one particular man."

"Don't you?" Kismet's voice held a tone of accusation. He was trying to regain control of the situation by putting the curator back on the defensive. "He uncovered a wealth of artifacts from the Babylonian dynasty. I can't believe such an important discovery would have gone unnoticed."

Hussein rattled off the Arabic equivalent, then turned to Kismet before the older man could reply. "Please sir, you must understand. What you are asking... It would be like asking you if you know Joe from New York."

Kismet's stare never left Aziz. The other man continued to squirm uncomfortably as he uttered another denial.

"I don't believe you." Kismet understood enough that he did not need to wait for an interpretation before pressing his argument. "I think you know exactly who I am talking about, and what he discovered. I think you've been illegally selling other artifacts from that same dig. And I think you had better start telling us everything you know about Samir Al-Azir and what he found at Babylon."

The accusation hung in the air like a static charge as Hussein reluctantly converted the demand into his native language. Before Aziz could reply, a trilling noise broke the silence. Mildly startled, Kismet turned to Chiron, but the Frenchman only shrugged. It was Aziz who eventually responded to the electronic tone, drawing from his breast pocket a familiar-looking object: a Qualcomm portable telephone handset. He opened the oblong device and began speaking in a low voice. After a brief exchange, he rose and excused himself via Hussein.

As Aziz stepped across the threshold of the conference room,

Kismet turned his attention to the young translator. It was evident to Kismet that Aziz was concealing information, but Hussein seemed truly in the dark respecting his superior's activities. "Where did you learn English?"

After a moment of distrustful incomprehension, the young man smiled. "Oxford. I studied abroad in my youth."

Kismet smiled at the implication that Hussein had somehow left his immaturity behind during his instructional years. "You speak it very well. How long have you been working with Mr. Aziz?"

"I have been at the museum for three years, but not exclusively with Mr. Aziz. I translate for many among the staff and assist visiting dignitaries, such as your honored selves."

Kismet nodded slowly. It was doubtful that Hussein would be privy to any dark secrets. Men like Aziz rarely entrusted such matters to their subordinates. He decided to try a different tack. "I wasn't aware that phone service had been restored."

Hussein raised an eyebrow, then cast a glance over his shoulder toward the exit where he had last seen Aziz. "It has in some places. But that phone does not require a local connection."

"It's a satellite phone, isn't it?" Kismet already knew the answer. The unusual antenna configuration of the Qualcomm GSP1600 marked it as a device designed to do more than simply interface with the local cellular network. In an age where most cell phones were miniaturized to the point that they might easily be concealed in a closed hand, the bulky handset and long antenna extension had given Aziz's phone away as a receiver capable of picking up transmissions beamed to the Globalstar satellite network. With a sat-phone, you could take a call from almost anywhere in the world. "That's a pretty expensive piece of hardware."

Hussein immediately went on the defensive. "We maintain a large repository of knowledge about the ancient world. Our patrons in Europe want us to be able to share information with universities and scientists around the world. When the threat of war began to loom, they arranged for this technology to be put at our disposal."

Kismet nodded slowly. "And there's been a lot of communication since?"

"Many scholars are concerned about the looting and damage to priceless antiquities. They call to express their support for our efforts to restore the collection."

"Then we are all working toward the same goal," intoned Chiron.

For once, Kismet was grateful to the older man for his saccharine observation. He had no desire to keep Hussein on guard. If anything, he needed the young translator in a more cooperative frame of mind. "Have you been to any of the major dig sites?"

The young man remained wary. "I have been to all of them."

"I spent some time in the ruins of Ur, Tall al Muqayyar."

"Near An Nasiriyah. Yes, I have been there."

"This is a wonderful country to live in if you are a lover of history," Chiron remarked. His expression of vague disinterest belied the conviction in his tone, but the sentiment was evidently something the young assistant curator could grasp. Hussein broke into a broad smile.

"It's all here," he answered, an enthusiastic boy discovering the world for the first time and eager to share. "The birthplace of civilization, the oldest forms of writing, the oldest laws. The father of all faiths, Ibraim, was born here and his descendants—the twelve tribes of Arabia—remain to this day. Alexander the Great walked here, as did the Christian Saint Peter. History begins here."

"You've barely scratched the surface, my boy. God himself has walked here. In the oldest writings, His presence is felt. The Garden of Eden was here, at the headwaters of the river Euphrates."

"Yes!" Hussein clapped his hands together emphatically. "And He spoke to Ibraim and called him out of Chaldea. Exactly. No matter what your faith, you cannot escape the fact that God has made His will known in this place."

Kismet glanced at Chiron, trying to determine if the sudden oration on the religious significance of the region was part of some broader plan to gain the younger man's trust. If it was, the Frenchman hid it well.

"I wonder what's keeping Aziz?" he ventured, looking for a way to put the conversation back on track. Hussein started to rise, eager to be of service, but Kismet forestalled him. "No, I'll go. I wouldn't mind a chance to stretch my legs. I'll yell if I get lost."

He moved past the long table toward the doorway Aziz had exited through. As he turned the knob, he listened for the sound of the man's voice. "Mr. Aziz?"

The door opened into an office half the size of the conference room. It was difficult to say what purpose the room had served prior to the chaos following the war. Now it was an impromptu storeroom cluttered with paper and boxes. Another doorway on the opposite wall exited the room and Kismet picked his way carefully though the litter, intent on locating their reluctant host.

The next room appeared to be a gallery set aside for seasonal exhibits, but like the storeroom, it now housed only rubble. Piles of broken statuary and brick were heaped in the corner, while empty display cases with smashed-out glass windows lined both long walls. At the far end of the hall, Kismet saw Aziz talking animatedly to a shorter individual dressed in the long garments of a Bedouin. The man's face was almost completely covered by a swath of fabric from his turban.

Kismet stopped short, mildly embarrassed at the interruption. "I'm sorry. I didn't realize you were—"

Both men turned abruptly at the sound of his voice. Aziz wore a guilty expression, as if caught in an indiscreet moment, but the robed figure showed no such hesitancy. He thrust a hand into the folds of his garment and whipped out a long, tubular object. In the instant of time it took Kismet to recognize that it was a pistol, outfitted with a sound and flash suppressor, the man aimed and fired.

Aziz took two rounds in the chest at close range before Kismet could raise a hand in protest. The groan that escaped from the curator's lips as he sank to his knees was far louder than the noise of the fatal shots. Then, a third shot bored a red cavity, no thicker than a pencil, in the center of Aziz's forehead to silence him forever.

FOUR

Kismet's initial shock wore off in the instant the killer administered the *coup de grace*. He threw himself sideways, ducking behind the solid base of a shattered display case, and thrust a hand into the nylon pack belted around his waist. The small pack was designed around a breakaway holster, secured with Velcro, which contained his Glock 19 semi-automatic handgun. He ripped it free of its stays and balled his fist around the grip as he chambered a round. His finger tightened on the trigger. With his left hand steadying the barrel, he rolled into the open, bringing the gun to bear on the place where he had seen the assassin a moment before, dreading the inevitable return fire.

The hall was empty.

He caught a glimpse of the killer's loose robes, fluttering through the doorway like a bird taking to flight, and decisively gave chase. After crossing the hall, he vaulted over the still-twitching form of Aziz, and was just in time to see the assassin's back disappear into a gallery to his right. With the pistol outstretched before him, he gave chase.

The gallery into which he ran seemed to abruptly transition him four millennia into the past. The room was like a darkened chamber in an ancient temple keep. One wall was devoted entirely to a sculpted alabaster relief featuring figures with curly, square-cut beards. Even in the mere seconds in which Kismet had to identify the objects in the gallery, he had no difficulty recognizing the signature of the Akkadian civilization, the second great culture to arise in Mesopotamia.

Yet here too, the hand of war had dealt a blow. Many of the artifacts had been vandalized, smashed by looters with no rational motive. Kismet had read news reports concerning one noteworthy sculpture, a bronze bust of the great Akkadian king Sargon, that had been taken by an opportunist hoping to score a small fortune in the international antiquities trade. Though the head had been recovered, it would be some time before such a valuable relic would again be displayed openly. Hundreds of other pieces—cuneiform tablets dating back to the time of Hammurabi, alabaster lions and gryphons, bronze artworks from the dawn of metallurgy—were now likewise secreted away from public view.

He caught sight of the robed figure dashing through the middle of the gallery, intent on reaching the far exit. He was gaining on the man, his longer strides closing the distance, but the assassin held the advantage of knowing where he was going. If Kismet lost visual contact, even for a moment, the pursuit would be over. He raised the gun, sighting down the barrel on the fleeing killer. "Stop!"

The assassin did not look back, but the shouted warning triggered a spontaneous response. He dove forward, making a fluid transition into a somersault that momentarily removed him from Kismet's sight picture. As the man came up, he pivoted on his leading foot, turning away from the headlong course toward the far end of the room.

Kismet's finger tightened on the trigger, but he could not bring himself to fire. The adrenaline surging through his veins was not quite strong enough to override a deep-seated inhibition against causing inadvertent harm to innocents. He knew well the limitation of his ability with the firearm—he was out of practice. Although the basic knowledge of how to shoot was something never quite forgotten, it was a skill that lost its edge over time, and it had been a long time since he had fired the weapon, even on a shooting range. Using the anti-tank rocket the day before had been simple by comparison; the AT-4 was a sledgehammer compared to the nine millimeter projectiles from the Glock, which would require near surgical precision to be effective. He might have scored a hit on the darting figure, but it seemed just as likely that his round would go astray, striking and further damaging one of the Old Babylonian artifacts, or worse, wounding an unsuspecting museum worker. The escaping assassin, while never realizing that he was not nearly in as much danger as he might have believed, took advantage of Kismet's internal struggle to widen the gap between them, and slipped out of the Akkadian gallery.

Recognizing that the gun would only be a liability in his chase, he jammed the weapon back into the waist pack as he ran through the hall and put on a burst of speed as soon as it was secure. There had been no hesitation in his decision to chase after the killer; it had been an immediate reaction to what he had witnessed. Yet now, as his brain went into overdrive, he began to see the ultimate goal of his pursuit. The killer had silenced Aziz, locking away whatever knowledge the curator possessed that might have aided Kismet in his search for answers. That pre-emptive strike might forever throw him from the path if he failed to bring the assassin to heel.

Another corner separated the relics of Old Babylonia and Akkad from the earliest civilization in the region, and perhaps the world: Sumeria. With his hands now free and his purpose set, Kismet sprinted through a maze of displays featuring potsherds and clay tablets, restored to their proper place by virtue of being relatively valueless.

The assassin, never once looking back, seemed to hesitate as if uncertain about which route of egress to follow. Only as his pursuer's footsteps became audible did he think to take evasive action, but the opportunity to escape had already passed. Kismet dove forward, arms extended, and tackled the fleeing killer.

Both men tumbled uncontrollably, caroming between the upright display cases. Kismet folded his arms around the assassin's legs, immobilizing him, but in the corner of his eye, he saw one of the openly presented relics tremble with the force of impact. A female figurine, arms raised to balance a large water container on her head, wobbled like a bowling pin atop a squarish pylon directly above where the two combatants lay sprawled.

Kismet breathed a curse as he realized what he would have to do. Releasing the grip of his right arm, he thrust his hand up and snatched the sculpture away from the inevitable attraction of gravity. Even as his hand closed protectively around the statue's legs, the assassin seized the advantage. He flexed his knee, then drove his leg straight out like a piston, solidly connecting with the side of Kismet's head.

A haze of bright blue momentarily eclipsed his view of the world. He felt the killer squirming out of his weakened grasp and made a belated but vain attempt to redouble his efforts. As gently as possible, he laid the figurine aside and brought his hands up defensively. Kismet knew he could physically overpower the smaller man, but his foe still possessed a gun and had showed no hesitation in dispatching Aziz. His ears were ringing from the first blow and through a haze of stars, he could just make out the other man, rising to his feet, legs spread in a defensive stance.

The killer moved like lightning, spinning on one foot and bringing the other around in a kick aimed at Kismet's head. A raised arm deflected most of the powerful assault, but Kismet felt a stab of pain just below his elbow. He tried to grab the outstretched leg as it rebounded away, but was too slow. His opponent twisted out of his reach, leaping and rolling like an acrobat.

The evasive maneuver took the lithe killer sideways, away from the center of the room and off course for a hasty exit. Kismet moved to flank the man, forcing him back to the edge of the gallery. The man paused as he realized his mistake, drawing to a stop in front of the balcony wall that overlooked the garden courtyard below. He spun around and his eyes, the only part of his face not covered by the turban and veil, locked for a moment with Kismet's. There was nothing human in the gaze. Just the cold, tactical stare of a killing machine, surveying a battlefield. In that instant, Kismet realized that if he failed to quickly subdue his opponent, the violence would escalate to a fatal conclusion.

He raised his hands, palms down in a steadying gesture, and took a slow step forward as if attempting to negotiate. The move was a feint. As soon as he sensed that his opponent had taken the bait, Kismet sprang forward again. The assassin was fast, but he had nowhere to go. Kismet's shoulder plowed into the man's mid-section, driving him back even as the former's arms encircled him.

Kismet's cheek struck a hard object beneath the assassin's robes, the silenced pistol, but it was something soft and yielding pressing into his forehead that caused him to falter in the ferocity of his assault.

The veiled killer struggled free of his grasp and Kismet careened headlong. He managed to recover his footing and backpedaled to block the exit once more, but the assassin no longer seemed interested in escaping by that route. Instead, with robes fluttering like the scarves of a dancer, his foe whirled around and dove toward the balcony wall. Kismet gasped involuntarily as the other figure took flight.

He reached the railing just in time to see the assassin land gracefully, cat-like, on two feet. The downward momentum translated effortlessly into forward motion and the assassin moved unimpeded toward the exit, oblivious to the amazed exclamations of clueless laborers working in the garden.

"Shit." Kismet muttered the rare curse because he knew what he had to do.

With considerably less elegance than his opponent, and a good deal more trepidation, he closed his fists around the railing and vaulted over the barrier. He kept his handhold firm, describing a pendulum motion with his body, until the soles of his feet were parallel with the floor. Only then did he let go, narrowly avoiding a collision with the outward-facing balcony wall, and dropped two vertical meters to crash noisily into an unidentifiable thorn bush. The assassin reached the entrance lobby while he struggled to disentangle himself, and Kismet knew he had lost the race.

The assassin hit the double doors, blasting through them with hardly a pause, and continued through the elaborate archway. After the controlled interior lighting of the museum, the rays of the midday sun stabbed down like knives, causing the robed figure to raise a shading arm. No one took notice. What was one more traditionally dressed Arab in a nation almost exclusively populated by them? The killer slowed to a walk, staying close to the outer edge of the building, and crept along the perimeter. The soldiers, unaware of the commotion inside the museum, carried out aimless patrols around their vehicles or huddled together in small knots of conversation. Aziz's slayer saw an opening and launched into motion.

A lone infantryman stood at the rear of D-42, the refueling vehicle, idly smoking a cigarette and paying attention to little else. The assassin moved like lightning, flashing in front of the hapless soldier and striking before the young man could even register surprise. A slashing blow to his exposed throat left the soldier gasping for air, while the robed killer effortlessly ripped his carbine away.

The violent attack did not go unnoticed by the other soldiers, but the lethargy of too much heat and too little action slowed their collective response. Before a single man could lift his weapon, the assassin checked the captured M4, advanced a round, and switched the fire selector to "burst". Fire and lead erupted from the muzzle, splitting the silence with a series of rapid cracking sounds. To a man, the infantry squad hit the ground, dashing for cover as they wrestled to bring their weapons to bear, but their target had already moved on.

The assassin popped open the door to the Humvee and slipped inside with practiced familiarity. The military vehicle had a simple starter switch and was secured only by a padlocked cable looped around the steering wheel. Using the stubby barrel of the carbine as a pry-bar, the assassin broke the shackle and toggled the starter switch. The diesel fuel, already warmed by the desert sun, ignited instantly.

Kismet could barely hear the shots through the dense brick walls, but what he could make out was enough to slow his pace as he ran toward the exit. His shirt and the skin underneath had been torn to shreds during his violent extrication from the museum's interior gardens, but he gave it little thought. He was far more concerned about catching a stray bullet as he stepped outside the sheltering brick structure.

The distinctive popping sound of gunfire ceased as he reached the doors, but he continued with hasty caution, moving in a duck walk through the archway. He eased around the corner, just in time to see a lone Humvee tearing out of the parking area and onto the street. The pandemonium that lingered in its wake was explanation enough as to what had just occurred. The lone assassin had somehow stolen the vehicle under the noses of the infantrymen and was escaping.

Colonel Buttrick was already marshaling his troops for the pursuit, but every passing second put the fleeing Humvee further away. Before Kismet could cross half the distance to the parking area, the first of the three transports took off in a spray of sand and gravel, while three soldiers, now standing in a firing line, continued to pump short bursts from their carbines at the rapidly diminishing target vehicle. If the bullets found their mark, they were insufficient to slow the assassin.

A second Humvee pulled away close on the heels of the first and Kismet saw the third give a slight tremor as its gears were engaged. Desperate to reach that last remaining vehicle, he sprinted ahead, no longer concerned about the exchange of weapons fire.

He was not sure what exactly he hoped to accomplish. Catching up to Aziz's killer seemed a remote possibility at best, but that individual was the only person remaining who could answer the question burning in Kismet's mind: Why had Aziz been silenced?

The death of the curator had been eerily familiar. The killer had controlled the situation, yet upon discovery, Aziz had become the target, not Kismet. The phone call had evidently been a ruse to separate the Iraqi from his inquisitors, yet for what purpose? Had he been marked for death all along? What secret had died on his lips?

Kismet knew from experience that secrets worth killing for were the kind of secrets that most needed to be revealed, and presently the assassin was his only link to that secret. If the soldiers succeeded in overrunning the fleeing Humvee, they would probably follow the time-honored progression of shooting before questioning. Perhaps that fact, more than anything else, spurred him onward as he drew closer to his last opportunity to join the chase.

As he closed to within ten meters, the Humvee's rear tires began to turn. A scattershot of gravel blasted into his face as the driver punched the accelerator a little too eagerly, and Kismet involuntarily looked away for a moment. Three more steps, in less than a second, brought him to the place where, only a moment before, the Humvee had sat idle. Now there was only a toxic cloud of diesel exhaust. Still running, he thrust out both hands, blindly groping for the vehicle as he blinked away the sand and fumes.

The fingers of his right hand bounced off the hardened aluminum exterior of the rear hatch, momentarily catching on the fabric of the white United Nations banner rigged across the back end of the vehicle. His left hand closed on something more substantial: the driver's side antenna mount. He reflexively closed his fingers, gripping the coiled spring of metal as he might a lifeline.

The Humvee lurched forward and Kismet was abruptly yanked along with it. A stabbing pain shot from his elbow to his shoulder as his full weight suddenly depended from that lone extremity, but he did not let go. He made a futile effort to run behind the vehicle. There was no hope of keeping pace with the racing transport, but Kismet reckoned he only needed to get his feet under him long enough to propel himself up and onto the rear hatch. If he failed to do that, nothing else would matter.

For a moment or two, he succeeded. Pouring on a burst of speed, he actually managed to run along behind the Humvee, easing the strain on his left arm incrementally. He could feel the ground vanishing beneath his toes, moving faster than his legs could propel him, and knew that he would only get one chance. With two more bounding steps, he threw his right hand forward, groping for anything that might give him a second secure point of contact.

Once more, his reaching fingers found no purchase. The smooth exterior of the vehicle was free of latches and other protuberances. With half a meter of ground clearance, the designers had not even bothered with collision bumpers. The rear of the vehicle was a featureless metal wall, rising vertically above nothingness before sloping forward at a forty-five degree angle. He once more found himself clutching the flimsy UN banner as he was yanked forward off his feet.

Miraculously, the flag did not tear as his weight pulled the fabric taut. The sudden shock was absorbed by the rubber bungee cords that stretched from grommets at each corner of the strip. As he lost his footing, Kismet swung forward and his face slammed into the vehicle. The impact was not hard enough to knock him loose from his precarious handhold, but it proved a thankful distraction from the jarring blows that now traveled up from his feet as they dangled and scraped along the rough macadam roadway. The heavy leather of his boots afforded a measure of protection, but that would not last. His footwear was being methodically sanded away by friction from the relentless forward movement.

The Humvee's speed was impossible to judge, but Kismet knew intuitively that he was now moving too fast to safely let go. He could not give up in his quest to gain a perch on the vehicle even if he chose to do so. If the impact did not kill him, the drop onto the pavement would scour the flesh from his bones. Though his left arm now burned with exertion and the pain of torn ligaments, he summoned every ounce of will power that remained and channeled it into a single pull.

His muscles bunched under the tattered remains of his shirt. To avoid losing what little progress he had made, he jammed his right arm deep under the UN flag until he could feel the fabric cutting into his armpit. Though his progress seemed marginal, he found that by flexing his knees, he could lift his feet away from the constant scraping punishment, if only for brief moments.

Nothing else existed in his world but the task of hauling himself onto the back of the Humvee. The streets of Baghdad flashed by unnoticed, and even the pursuit of the assassin now seemed a secondary concern. Kismet counted twenty ragged breaths before trying once more to lift himself higher, but his effort collapsed after only a moment, yielding almost no reward. Gritting his teeth, he tried again.

Lt. Col. Jonathan Buttrick pushed the accelerator pedal to the floorboard, intent on closing the gap between his own vehicle and the rest of his command. He had no idea what had happened inside the museum, much less the identity of the robed malcontent who had opened fire on his men and stolen the resupply vehicle, nor did he care. The enemy had struck a blow on his watch, and that was intolerable.

One of his men, the driver of the stolen Humvee, was down, possibly dead from a crushing blow to cricoid cartilage. Buttrick had only glimpsed the man's fall, hands ineffectually clutching his throat as he collapsed beside the vehicle, but his blue pallor was explanation enough; the man was suffocating. He knew the medics might be able to save the man with an emergency field tracheotomy, but it would be messy. Buttrick clung to the image of the gasping soldier in order to fuel his resolve.

"Where the fuck are we?" he growled.

The sergeant in the seat beside him was frantically checking his city map against the GPS locator. "We're coming up on the Shuhada Bridge over the Tigris."

Buttrick's mind ran through possible strategies. The bridge would be an excellent place to catch their prey, but only with outside help. "Get on the horn and see if anyone's patrolling on the other side. Maybe we can scare up a roadblock."

"Yes, sir." The sergeant's fingers closed on the radio handset before his superior finished speaking.

Neither man was aware of Kismet's life and death struggle, less than three meters away, nor could they have possibly known that his fingers were at that very instant clenched around the base of the radio antenna.

The military radio had the capacity to send and receive coded information on a shifting cycle of frequency modulation wavelengths. Yet, beneath all the computerized circuitry, it operated on principles that had not changed in over a century. At its core, the device converted the sounds of the human voice into bursts of electricity, which then traveled along copper wire to the antenna, and it was only there that the electrical pulse became a radio wave. The antenna was essentially an electromagnet, disrupting the local magnetic field with measured bursts of energy that could be gathered out of the air and deciphered only by a correctly tuned receiver unit. Depending on the power of the transmitter and the length of the antenna, it was possible for those signals to reach out over hundreds of kilometers, or even into space. Despite quantum leaps in technology, long-distance communications still relied on that simple conversion of electricity into magnetism.

When the soldier in the passenger seat of the Humvee depressed the switch, even before speaking, an electrical circuit closed. A pulse of electricity, amplified by a system of transistors and capacitors, raced from the small box secured to the dashboard, along an insulated coaxial cable, to the rear antenna mount, where it burst into the atmosphere in an invisible lightning bolt.

And like lightning, it would blast anyone unlucky enough to be

touching the antenna at that instant.

FIVE

Two things saved Kismet. Two factors, which by their random and coincidental nature, could only be described as pure luck.

Unaware of the impending radio transmission, and only faintly cognizant that such a surge could erupt from the antenna, Kismet had but one goal: to reach just a little higher. His knees slipped ineffectually against the metal shell of the vehicle in a struggle to find purchase and relieve, if only for a moment, the burning fatigue in his arms. His right elbow was tucked under the UN banner strung across the back end of the Humvee but he didn't trust the thin fabric to hold his weight. His left arm however, bruised at the elbow during the struggle at the museum and on fire with lactic acid buildup, could hold on no longer. His fingers, though rigid like claws, began to uncurl, involuntarily slipping away from the spring-coil at the base of the antenna. The failure of his grip saved his life.

Though grounded by the glancing contact of his feet with the roadway, his fingers were barely touching the antenna. Had the transmission occurred mere seconds earlier, the fierceness of his grip would have held him locked in place as the current poured through his body, but the severity of the shock was greatly minimized due to the marginal contact between Kismet and the antenna. Even so, the surge slapped his hand like a blow from a baseball bat.

The shock seized every muscle in his body, instantaneously firing all the nerve endings in a numbing jolt. The kinetic release knocked his hand away, and would have easily thrown him aside like a rag doll had his right arm not been entangled in the UN flag. Therein lay the second bit of luck to which Kismet would owe his life: The fabric held up under the sudden weight of his collapse.

Hung up in the banner and stunned by the electrical discharge, Kismet dangled behind the racing Humvee like a fish caught by the gills in a net. His feet trailed helplessly along the roadway as the vehicle pulled onto the Shuhada Bridge.

The call for assistance reached several listening ears. A two-man patrol cruising in the vicinity of the now defunct Baath party headquarters, just north of the city's transportation hub, immediately turned toward the 14th July Highway, racing to intercept the fugitive vehicle. Further away, a Sikorsky UH-60A Black Hawk helicopter was diverted from its landing at the Baghdad International Airport and sent to provide aerial surveillance. Its estimated time to contact was less than three minutes. All over the city, R/T operators began relaying the urgent call for help to their commanding officers, who in turn began weighing Buttrick's urgent needs against their own respective assignments. More than a few of these hastily dispatched squads of soldiers to the target area, but even the closest contingent had no chance of reaching the bridge before the chase moved beyond, onto the west bank of the Tigris River. Despite their tardiness, it was reasonable to assume that the crew aboard the Black Hawk would guide the reinforcements, via radio transmissions, through the urban area in order to trap the commandeered Humvee.

In the pandemonium of pursuit, it never occurred to any of them that the assassin was also listening.

Kismet was gradually roused from his stunned condition by the incessant hammering of his feet against the deck of the bridge. The memory of the electrical shock was already fading. The discharge had done no permanent damage. A lingering numbness in his extremities was all that remained. In every other way however, his situation continued to be dire.

Cautiously twisting his torso, he brought his left hand around, gripping the corner of the banner in order to relieve the cutting pressure under his right arm. There was no choice now but to trust the flag to bear his weight. Nevertheless, gaining a more dependable perch remained imperative.

With deliberate slowness, he raised his right leg, hooking his heel under the bungee cord that secured the lower right corner of the banner. The rubber band provided a surprisingly stable foothold, allowing him to wrestle his arm free. After flexing his fingers for a moment to restore circulation, he reached back to his waist pack, fumbling until his fingers closed around the carved wooden grip of his *kukri*.

Kismet drew the heavy blade from its sheath and in a single practiced motion brought it around in an overhand chopping motion. The curved edge of the knife struck true but the blade rebounded from the aluminum shell, nearly twisting out of his fatigued grip. Disheartened by the failure, he braced himself against the anticipated recoil and tried again.

His attack against the vehicle's metal skin failed to do more than make a few dents, but the incessant hammering alerted the occupants of the vehicle to their unexpected passenger. Kismet, lost in a single-minded effort to chop out a secure handhold, was oblivious to the shouted offers of assistance, originating from the open turret atop the Humvee. When the sergeant's voice finally broke through, he could only stare dumbly at the outstretched hand.

"Take it!"

Methodically sheathing his knife, Kismet leaned in close and reached up. Surrendering himself to the other man's grip, he allowed the soldier to draw him up onto the flat roof. Only there did he take note of the pursuit. From this vantage, he could make out the other vehicles in the convoy as they raced single file across the bridge. The Humvee piloted by Aziz's killer had a lead of only a few seconds, but it was enough. As he watched, the vehicle shot past the end of the span and down the rampart. A few moments later, it made a hard right turn on the banked exit onto a divided highway. The driver made no effort to slow down for the turn, allowing the wheels to drift across the outside lane until they rebounded from the concrete abutment. The large tires left a streak of black, but were otherwise undamaged as the Humvee bounced back into the left-hand lane. The heavy suspension shuddered violently but the driver never lost control.

"You okay?" the sergeant shouted in his ear.

Kismet nodded, gripping the edge of the turret with both hands to show that he was secure.

"Better get inside. This is going to be one rough ride." With that, the sergeant ducked down into the vehicle, settling into the front passenger seat. Kismet waited until he was clear, then heaved himself headfirst through the opening.

Despite the noise of the diesel engine, he thought that it seemed much quieter in the Humvee's interior, at least until Buttrick addressed him.

"Kismet!" The urgency of the crisis had evidently superceded their first name basis. "What the fuck is going on?"

He fought to catch his breath. "We were interviewing one of the curators. I guess somebody didn't want him talking to us."

"Shit. Who is this guy? Local?"

"I don't think so." He mentally reviewed what he did know about the escaping killer. The initial crime had borne the earmarks of a professional hit, but what he had witnessed thereafter suggested the kind of training available only in the world of international espionage. Kismet had one more salient bit of information regarding the assassin, but decided to play his cards close to the vest and refrained from supplementing his claim of ignorance.

"Well whoever he is, he can sure drive. The American people paid good money for that vehicle. I'd hate to have to destroy it, but this guy isn't giving me much choice."

"You would also be destroying our only chance to get some answers." He could sense the colonel's disapproval in the silence that followed. "I guess if that's what it takes."

The Humvee left the bridge, following in the trail blazed by the other three. Kismet gripped the seat in order to keep from being tossed around the interior as the vehicle went off-road. The other two pursuing vehicles were visible, but he could not discern the one that led the chase. Buttrick's co-pilot maintained communication with the other soldiers in the command, verifying that the quarry was still in sight, and took updates from the other forces moving in to close the trap.

The driver of the captured Humvee did not relent, red-lining the transport's engine and refusing to yield to pedestrians or other vehicles. In order to prevent the gap between them from widening, Buttrick and the other drivers were forced to implement a similar strategy.

At a major interchange near Tala'a Square, a car driven by a local civilian screeched to a stop, narrowly missing the stolen Humvee as it plowed through heedless of other traffic. The irate driver blasted an angry, sustained note with his horn before applying the accelerator. The soldier in the leading pursuit vehicle—designation D-44—intently focused on his prey, reacted too late. The front end of his Humvee crushed the fender panels of the smaller car and the heavy truck tires rolled up onto its hood, snapping the chassis and demolishing the engine block. The military vehicle scraped over the wreckage, wreaking further ruin on the already devastated vehicle, then bounced down once more onto the pavement. The encounter had lasted only a heartbeat, but it was a moment added to the assassin's lead.

Other cars, speeding into the intersection from each direction, scattered to avoid becoming caught in a pile-up. Several of these took to the sidewalk in a last-ditch effort to avoid a collision with the wrecked car or the rest of the convoy as it charged past the scene of ruin. Buttrick clenched his teeth in a fierce grimace as he glanced down at the shattered civilian vehicle, but he said nothing.

The chase continued along a main boulevard, known locally as Hayfa Street, heading north and west. To their left, the Tigris followed a meandering path, weaving into view before turning away at a right angle. With the river effectively blocking one avenue of escape, it seemed inevitable that they would eventually trap the fleeing assassin. Buttrick began directing his reinforcements to close in ahead of them and stage a roadblock at the foot of the Al Azamiyah Bridge. On the straight thoroughfare, Kismet had an unobstructed view of the entire progression. Their prey dodged in and out of the moderately heavy civilian traffic, as did the other two vehicles. With nearly half a kilometer between Buttrick's vehicle and the assassin's, it was difficult for Kismet to differentiate the almost identical vehicles. Unable to add anything to the pursuit, he resigned himself to the role of spectator.

A voice crackled from the radio speaker. "Delta Four-Six, this is Bravo Two-Five. We are leaving the rail yard and proceeding onto Hayfa Street ahead of you. Do you want us to block the road? Over."

Buttrick glanced at the map, then shook his head. "We'll pass them before they can get in position. Have them block the highway leading to the Sarafiya Bridge, just in case. Then they can join us in closing the trap."

His commands were relayed by the sergeant and a moment later, the Humvee, which had identified itself as B-25, broke across the road in the barely visible distance, crossing the intersection well ahead of the chase and came to a stop in the middle of the cross street.

The stolen Humvee suddenly cut hard to the left, sweeping across both lanes of traffic on a perpendicular approach toward the edge of the road. A collision with the concrete barrier seemed inevitable, but when the front end of the vehicle reached the steeply sloped obstacle, the elevated front end passed over its upper limit, allowing the tires to make contact. The rear wheels continued to supply forward momentum, while the front tires ascended the near vertical hump of cement and stone.

Instantly, the Humvee launched into the air. The rear wheels finished their journey, striking the barricade to give a final burst of impetus as the vehicle leaped skyward and sailed over the highway divider in a short parabolic arc.

The rear tires touched down first, seeming to lightly kiss the pavement, but the contact was enough to snap the front end down violently, creating a ripple of energy that bounced the Humvee across both lanes toward the far edge of the road. Traffic on the highway was light enough that no unlucky souls happened to be in the landing area, but the drivers of several approaching cars instinctively jammed their brakes, skidding out of control to collide with one another. The pile-up began to cascade behind them as the captured Humvee hit the barrier on the far left, lifting once more into the air.

At almost the same moment, the turret gunner on Bravo 25 overcame his disbelief and squeezed the butterfly trigger of his Browning fifty-caliber machine gun. A noisy stream of ammunition began pouring after the renegade vehicle. A few of the rounds found their mark, punching enormous holes in the rear of the stolen truck, but most went wide as evidenced by the tracer rounds that sizzled well past the Humvee and smacked into parked railway freight cars hundreds of meters beyond. The noise and light show was enough to cause the war-weary motorists on the lane ahead of the convoy to stop short and duck their heads.

"Damn it!" Buttrick raged. "Tell them to hold fire. There goes our roadblock."

Before the sergeant was able to key the message, Delta 44 broke to the left. Inspired by the success of the assassin's jump and intent on maintaining the pursuit, the young soldier driving the lead chase vehicle drove head-on into the concrete barrier. Buttrick muttered a disbelieving oath as the Humvee lofted over the divider and touched down successfully.

The sergeant sent out a frantic call to the forces deploying near the bridge to abandon that location. Meanwhile, the assassin's vehicle kicked up a column of dust as it continued across an open field toward an obvious destination, the rail yard, with the daredevil soldier in the lead Humvee close behind.

The driver of the second Humvee—D-43—seemed less enthusiastic about making the airborne transition across the opposite lanes and off of the highway, but he knew what had to be done and did not ease off of the accelerator once committed to the jump. Buttrick began swinging to the far right of the road in order to begin his approach along the same path.

Delta 43 cleared the barricade easily, but as the rear tires hit the short wall, there was an audible snapping noise. One of the struts on the right rear wheel broke, causing it to cant outward at a forty-five degree angle. As the rear tires banged down on the pavement, the wheel on the right was no longer supplying power in a straight line. The back end turned an impossibly tight circle, pivoting on the undamaged left wheel and spun around beneath the still elevated front end. The Humvee corkscrewed in the middle of the highway and flipped onto its back with a sickening crunch.

At that instant, unaware of the second vehicle's demise, Buttrick began his charge toward the barricade. Like the three others before, the last Humvee in the column hit the concrete divider and launched skyward. The jump was flawless, but the wreck of the D-43 lay like a turtle on its back directly in his landing zone. Because there was nothing else to do, Buttrick held the steering wheel steady as they crashed down toward its exposed underbelly.

Delta 43 was still turning counter-clockwise circles on the macadam as D-46 dropped from the sky. The two vehicles almost missed each other. Half a second earlier or later and the two Humvees would have been parallel. Instead, the left side of Buttrick's vehicle caught the outstretched front end of D-43 as it swung around through another revolution. Delta 46 tilted sharply to the right and when the wheels on that side made contact with the pavement, the angle was enough to pull the Humvee over.

Kismet had planted his feet squarely on the floorboards and gripped either side of the driver's backrest in anticipation of the jump, but nothing had prepared him for the violence of the landing. As Delta 46 began its roll, the doors flew open and Colonel Buttrick, overwhelmed by centrifugal force, was ripped from his seat as the Humvee rolled onto its right side. The roll continued, and the twisting Humvee moved forward and sideways at the same time, missing the stunned officer by mere inches. An instant later, the open doors were crushed as it turned onto its left side. Kismet felt the almost irresistible tug of G-forces wrenching him toward the opening, and for a heartbeat, he saw nothing but dusty pavement. His grip failed and he slammed face first onto the roadway as the vehicle turned again, coming to a rest on its tires.

Kismet lay stunned for a long moment before daring to open his eyes. He instinctively struggled to his knees, and was mildly surprised that his body complied with only a minimum of complaint. Despite the initial violence of the wreck, he had managed to remain in the protective confines of the Humvee until most of its energy was expended. The force with which he had hit the roadway was no worse than tripping and falling onto a hard surface.

No better either, he thought darkly as he pushed to his feet.

A few steps away, Buttrick and the sergeant were also coming around. A figure in combat camouflage snaked from the overturned D-43 and hurried over to assist their fallen comrades. Though shaken, the soldiers inside that Humvee appeared to be uninjured. Kismet absently wondered if they had been foresighted enough to buckle their seatbelts before engaging in the ludicrous pursuit. No one in Buttrick's vehicle had taken that precaution, and to a man they had been yanked from their seats.

Delta 46 sat idle a few meters away.

Kismet stared at the crumpled, but relatively intact Humvee as though trying to divine its purpose. The engine had evidently stalled, but for all the outward damage—the missing doors and crushed fender panels—the vehicle appeared operational.

Still trying to determine the significance of the Humvee's presence, Kismet saw movement in the corner of his eye and looked out across the field. Beyond the second concrete barricade, the stolen resupply vehicle was struggling to maintain its lead. Its left rear tire—perforated by a few lucky shots from Bravo 25's machine gun—was coming apart. Huge chunks of black rubber were thrown out in its wake, directly in the path of the remaining chase vehicle. Though the Humvee was equipped with a run-flat rim, essentially a hard rubber tire inside the inflated outer tire, which allowed it to remain operational in exactly such a circumstance, the reduced wheel diameter cut its top speed nearly in half, especially on the loose sandy surface. Delta 44 was going to win the chase.

Kismet glanced back at the dazed survivors of the crash, then looked again at the vehicle from which he had been thrown. Responding to an undefined impulse, he began walking toward the wounded Humvee.

"Kismet?"

He heard Buttrick's croaked inquiry, but elected to ignore it. Instead, he quickened his pace, reaching the doorless vehicle in a few steps, and slid behind the steering wheel. He searched for only a moment to locate the starter switch, and turned it all the way to the right.

A triumphant grin crossed his mouth as the engine rattled to life. Still in gear, he had only to depress the accelerator and Delta 46 was back in the chase.

Buttrick was shouting for him to stop but Kismet, full of purpose, paid no heed. He brought the vehicle around in a wide turn, taking it nearly to the center divider before turning the front end toward the outside of the road, where a second unbroken string of concrete barricades stood as a guard rail. Almost as an afterthought he pulled the seatbelt taut across his lap and locked it in place before stomping the accelerator pedal to the floor.

Though he had already endured one such jump, the perspective from the driver's seat was different somehow. He was a little closer to the action and further from the pivot point of the rear wheels, but the real dissimilarity lay in the act of initiating a nearly suicidal assault on the barrier. As a passenger, all he had to do was hang on. Although the approach seemed to take forever, it was over in an instant. The front end was violently knocked upward and the rest of the Humvee followed. The landing on the loose soil beyond the road was less forceful than the first and Kismet easily maintained control.

He quickly located the chase by the enormous cloud of dust. Both vehicles were traveling in a straight line toward the city's main rail yard. The Humvee driven by the assassin became visible as it made an abrupt right-hand turn, peeling off from what would otherwise have been a collision course with a line of empty freight cars, and began traveling parallel to the rail spur. Realizing he had an opportunity to intercept, Kismet angled toward a point ahead of their quarry while Delta 44 swung into line directly behind, continuing the relentless advance.

Kismet gripped the wheel breathlessly. His bid to flank the assassin had only one fatal flaw: The artificial barrier posed by the rail cars ended well short of the intercept point, butjust beyond the last car, at the point where spur entered onto the main track, a second train was moving through the rail yard at a deliberate but unstoppable pace. Once that train passed the intersection, it would close the door of escape.

The assassin evidently saw this as well. With a desperate burst of speed, Delta 42 charged ahead. As it did, the run-flat rim on the left rear tire began to come apart, scattering large pieces of rubber across the gravel near the rail bed. The vehicle swerved uncertainly, but somehow the driver managed to maintain control as it approached the end of the idle train.

Kismet saw what was about to happen but was powerless to prevent it. The assassin swerved across the spur, the vehicle fishtailing uncertainly as it bounced over the iron rails, but straightened as it crossed the mainline a whisper ahead of the advancing locomotive. The driver of D-44, once more suffering from tunnel vision, never looked away from his goal.

Kismet made an instinctive grab for the radio handset, impotently shouting: "Break off!"

The message was never received.

The train was only traveling about twenty-five kilometers per hour but its mass was relentless. It hit the Humvee broadside, nearly bisecting the vehicle, and drove it forward along the tracks. The horrifying scene was lost from view as the locomotive pushed the wreckage beyond the parked train on the branching track, but there was no mistaking the eruption of black smoke as the diesel fuel tank, warmed by the desert sun and compressed by the crushing weight of the train, reached its flashpoint and exploded.

Kismet, still shouting a warning that would never be heeded, stomped on the brake pedal, bringing the Humvee to a halt a few meters from the rolling line of rail cars. The pursuit seemed to be over.

Fired by the same impulse that had motivated him to chase after the assassin in the first place, Kismet refused to admit defeat. Flooring the throttle once more, he veered out into the open area for several seconds before coming around in a wide turn that brought him parallel to the incoming train. He eased back on the accelerator, matching the pace of the rail cars, and tried to put the pieces of his plan into coherent order.

He knew that Delta 42 was nearly on its last gasp. Once the ruined tire fell completely apart, the assassin would be forced to continue on foot. All Kismet had to do was get to the other side of the moving train and that meant he was going to have to abandon his Humvee and transfer to the train. As long as D-46 was traveling at the same speed as the rail cars, he would at least have a chance of making the transition.

He looked around for something to hold the accelerator pedal down, but found nothing. Everything not bolted in place had been thrown clear during the earlier rollover. His eyes then settled on the radio unit. While it was secured in place, the clamping bolts were easily loosed, and a moment later he pulled it free of its mount. The weight of the back-up battery inside the oblong metal box made it ideal for what he had in mind. He removed his foot from the pedal and replaced it with the radio.

That minor success was overshadowed by the fact that he was now running out of road. His course alongside the moving train was soon going to bring him to the spur where the idle freight cars were parked. He would have to make his move quickly or not at all.

The train loomed above the passenger side door and the metal rungs of an access ladder were visible beyond the opening, but Kismet did not relish the idea of trying to squirm across the interior of his vehicle in the seconds that remained. He instead sprang for the open turret hatch in the center of the Humvee's roof and thrust himself through the opening in a single decisive jump. The driverless vehicle maintained course and speed, but he knew there was no time for delay.

His objective now seemed much further away than before. Though he was relatively close to the rolling train, there remained a distance of almost two meters between the edge of the Humvee's roof and the rungs of the ladder. To make matters worse, the train was slowing; the engineer had thrown the brakes in a futile effort to prevent the collision with Delta 44 and the juggernaut was still steadily decelerating. The ladder Kismet was so focused on reaching was gradually falling behind him.

Throwing caution to the wind he stepped back, then took a running leap toward the train. An instant later, he found himself hanging from the rungs on the side of a tanker car. He wasn't sure of how he had completed the leap, but there was no time to waste figuring it out or congratulating himself on making it look easy. With a deep breath, he started ascending the ladder.

Delta 46 continued to roll alongside the train, gradually pulling ahead in its race to oblivion. A heartbeat later it plowed into the parked freight cars and annihilated itself. The Humvee came apart in a spray of metal, plastic and rubber, pelting the moving train with almost unrecognizable pieces of debris. Kismet ducked reflexively as a chunk of olive drab fiberglass struck near his extended hand.

His arms were still burning from the exertion of his crazed ride on the back of the ill-fated vehicle and he felt the fatigue rapidly building to the point of failure. After heaving himself onto the catwalk that framed the oval cylinder of the tank car, it was a struggle to get to his feet. From this vantage, he could see all but a few shadowy corners of the labyrinthine rail yard. The assassin's vehicle was limping along parallel to the moving train, taking refuge in its behemoth shadow, the driver perhaps assuming that the chase was over. Kismet saw clearly that path that would take his foe to freedom, but wondered if the way out was as obvious at ground level. Shaking the fatigue from his arms, he took off at a sprint.

Running along the top of the moving train was disconcerting. Though he poured all his remaining energy into the effort, he felt like he was losing ground with every step. His progress along the top of the tanker remained unimpeded, but the simple truth of the matter was that the train was still taking him in the wrong direction at a pace nearly equal to his own.

At the end of the tank car, he made a relatively simple leap over the intervening distance, onto the next cylindrical body. Though mindful of the moving surface beneath him, he nevertheless went sprawling as soon as his feet touched down. Fortunately, the opposing forces of motion were in line and he did not slip from the narrow metal walkway, but another moment of advantage had gone to the fleeing killer. Kismet scrambled up and took off again.

By the time he reached the far end of that second rail car, the train had slowed almost to a full stop. His next leap was far less dramatic, and as he ran along the top of yet another tank car, the movement beneath him ceased altogether. Fatigue from his aerobic effort was settling into his legs and chest, but he pressed on, prompted to still greater exertion by the fact that he was finally getting somewhere. However Delta 42 was slowing, hampered by the ruined tire and the driver's uncertainty about how to negotiate the maze of train cars parked on spur lines at every turn. He closed the distance on the Humvee in what seemed like only a few seconds, then continued ahead along two more rail cars before turning to face the killer.

He moved out to the edge of the catwalk, calculating the effort required to cross the distance and fixing in his mind the exact moment at which he would have to jump. There would be only one opportunity for him to make the crossing—no false starts, no second-guessing. Yet his earlier successes now filled him with confidence, overriding that instinctive fear of falling. As the Humvee crept closer, he drew in a deep breath, then let it out.

Suddenly his world seemed to collapse inward. Blood, rushing to nourish and repair his exhausted extremities, seemed to have been shunted away from his brain, and darkness began closing in around the periphery of his vision. He felt an overwhelming need to vomit.

The Humvee was nearly below him. It was now or never; Kismet had no choice but to make a leap of faith.

The transition from the top of the train car onto the moving hood of the vehicle was not so much a jump as a controlled fall. Kismet made no effort to keep to his feet as he slammed into the molded fiberglass cover, but instead redirected the momentum of his drop into a sprawl across the broad windshield.

Through the dark haze occluding his vision, he could not make out the assassin's reaction to the sudden assault, but he was not expecting a hospitable welcome. He had not forgotten that the killer was armed with a silenced pistol, but there was a much simpler way for repelling boarders against which Kismet would have little defense. His earlier misadventure had revealed just how difficult it would be to cling to the smooth shell of the vehicle.

The Humvee immediately began to swerve back and forth, but Kismet was ready. Blindly grasping the top mounted windshield wiper arms, he held on as the vehicle bucked beneath him. The driver's attempt seemed half-hearted. The lost rear tire was proving more troublesome than expected, and after only a couple attempts, the Humvee's path straightened once more. Kismet did not wait to see what would happen next. He scrambled onto the roof of the vehicle, removing himself from the killer's line of sight.

The momentary dizzy spell seemed to relent as he resumed moving. It was the rest, not the exertion, that had compromised his blood pressure. He did not find this realization especially encouraging. He knew the effect would only worsen as the struggle continued, eventually reaching a point where he would simply collapse. It wouldn't do at all to finally capture his foe and then pass out before commencing the interrogation.

The Humvee shifted to the left beneath him, not in an attempt to shake him loose, but simply a turn leading them one step closer to the edge of the maze. As the platform beneath him stabilized once more, Kismet turned his attention to the hatch covering the turret. The sheets of metal were secured from within by several snap-down clamps. He contemplated trying to use the *kukri* to pry it open, but rejected that plan. His forced entry would likely be so noisy that the assassin would be waiting to dispatch him with a gunshot as soon as he tried to pass through. He would have to find a better solution.

Spread-eagled prone on the roof and still fiercely gripping the driver's side windshield wiper pivot with his right hand, he drew the gun from his waist pack and wormed toward the left side of the car. He ducked down long enough to look in through the window then pulled back quickly in case the assassin was waiting with gun drawn. Seeing no evidence that such was the case, he reached down with the gun and hammered on the pane.

"Stop now!" He repeated his order twice more, shouting each time and punctuating his words with taps on the plastic surface.

His demand was ignored. Delta 42 continued limping across the rail yard, angling toward the gaps between parked trains and scraping over the metal tracks. Like a table with one short leg, the entire vehicle wobbled uncertainly as it moved, dropping down on the chewed-up remains of the rear wheel then rebounding onto the three good tires. But then, as the path out of the maze became apparent, the driver did something that seemed completely counter-intuitive. The Humvee began to accelerate.

He was forced to stow the gun once more and hold on with both hands as the vehicle picked up speed. The last set of tracks fell behind as it pulled onto a graveled road, and as the engine poured more and more power into the three good wheels, the vehicle seemed to stabilize. Kismet on the other hand, began to feel more and more uncertain as their velocity increased, and a glance into the hot wind blasting against his face supplied more than adequate reason for concern. The road on which they were now hurtling forward ended in a locked gate.

Reason dictated that the driver was bluffing. Surely no sane person would charge such an obstacle headlong. Yet, as the barrier drew nearer, Kismet became more certain of the assassin's intentions. When the Humvee hit the simple iron gate, the sudden stop would catapult him forward, hurling him from his precarious perch and launching him like a missile. It was conceivable that he might survive with only a few broken bones, but the odds did not favor that outcome. The only safe choice was to abandon the vehicle.

With only seconds remaining before the collision, he scooted headfirst toward the sloping rear hatch of the Humvee, and reached down to the familiar United Nations banner that had adorned each vehicle in the ill-fated convoy. From this perspective, the damage wrought by Bravo 25's machine gun was evident. A series of ragged holes marred the smooth shell of the vehicle and had punched through the white flag in several places. A dark stain—diesel fuel from the resupply cans—was spreading like blood from some of the wounds.

Kismet grasped the damaged banner with both hands, then allowed his weight to fall sideways. His feet came around in a broad arc and abruptly all of his mass was depending from the torn flag as his boots dragged along the gravel roadway.

"This seems familiar," he muttered through clenched teeth. Dismissing the irony of his situation, Kismet braced himself for what was about to happen, and let go.

The impact was much worse than he had expected. His chest slammed into the ground, driving the air from his lungs even as inertia continued to propel him along behind the doomed Humvee. The grainy pebbles that covered the roadway were more forgiving than a paved surface, but nonetheless stripped the skin from his palms and elbows. It was, he imagined, like being pulled across a cheese grater. He made a belated effort to roll in order to reduce the burn of friction, but all this seemed to do was spread the pain around evenly.

He did not see the collision, but there was no mistaking the sickening crunch of metal on metal. Kismet's agonizing tumble ended about ten meters from the rear of the Humvee. The vehicle was still quaking on its springs from the shock of hitting the barrier.

That the driver had been willing to flirt with suicide in an effort to knock him loose from his perch seemed too ludicrous to consider, yet there was no refuting the obvious outcome. Nevertheless, it stood to reason that the assassin would have taken steps to survive the crash, and it was this assumption that motivated Kismet to haul himself erect and draw his weapon.

He advanced with due caution, feeling acutely the pain of his exertions in every muscle and joint as he crept forward, staying low. He expected the assassin to appear at any moment, brandishing a gun, but there was no sign of activity on board the Humvee. He raised his head level with the windows for a second, then quickly ducked down again.

The vehicle was abandoned. Kismet looked in again, more assertively to verify what that initial glance had revealed. There was no sign of Aziz's murderer behind the wheel.

The collision had crumpled the hood and grill of the vehicle, and a plume of superheated steam rose from the ruptured remains of the radiator. However, aside from what was mostly cosmetic damage, the Humvee had weathered the crash quite well. The cheap padlock securing the gate had snapped, allowing the single iron I-beam to burst open on its hinge, transferring some of the kinetic energy away from the vehicle. Nevertheless, the occupant of the vehicle would have been subjected to a violent burst of force, certainly enough to stun, if not kill.

Kismet backed away quickly, realizing that the assassin had in all likelihood abandoned the doomed troop mover just as he had. He turned a quick circle, making sure that the killer had not somehow flanked him, then hastened to the other side of the wreck.

The passenger side door was gone, ripped off its hinges by the force of the collision, and thrown well beyond the gateway. Kismet drew the obvious conclusion: The door had been open at the moment of impact. He scanned ahead, seeing for the first time that beyond the gate, the service road connected with a paved street and the city proper. After a momentary survey, he detected movement, and recognized the retreating back of the killer, now well over a hundred meters away.

He took off running before he could even consider the alternatives. It galled him to have been so close to capturing his foe, only to suffer such a setback. The first steps were sheer hell, but his determination carried him through, and once he hit his stride, the pain seemed to recede, but the pounding in his skull returned with a vengeance and as he sprinted toward the street, dark shadows gathered in his vision.

He knew on a clinical level what was happening. He was getting dehydrated. The outpouring of energy in pursuit of the killer beneath the brutal desert sun had sapped his finite reserves. The adrenaline that fired him through one bruising encounter after another was no substitute for the most basic element of life: water. He only hoped the assassin was feeling it as well.

A horn blast and screeching tires alerted him to the peril he had completely ignored. Though traffic in the city was light, it was by no means nonexistent, and he had wandered into the middle of the Arbataash Tammuz or 14th July Street, one of the busiest thoroughfares in this section of the city. He reached the center of the divided road without mishap, and paused there to wait for a clearing. After so many close calls, this minor brush with fate hardly fazed him.

Despite the delay, he was gaining on the assassin. His longer legs gave him a definite advantage but his stamina was not without limits. He waited for an opening in traffic, and then darted toward the far edge of the road, vaulting the concrete barrier to continue across the barren expanse.

Aziz's murderer had nowhere to hide in the open vastness. Acres of dusty nothingness stretched in every direction. The tableau was broken only by an occasional warehouse or shipping container storage yard. The assassin however seemed to be angling toward a construction site, with tall columns of steel and masonry springing out of the sand like a stricken forest. Kismet focused the flagging strength of his will power into a final burst of speed.

As he neared the incipient structure, its overwhelming scope became apparent. The upright columns, arranged in pairs around the perimeter, delineated an area as large as a football stadium. A great deal of excavation had been done, literally carving the site out from the desert floor, but the building work was yet in its infancy. He had no idea what purpose it would serve when, or if, it was completed. All he saw now was a chaotic maze in which his foe might seek refuge.

At the edge of the site, the assassin made a misstep, tripping over a piece of re-bar and sprawling headlong. Kismet seized the opportunity, and before the robed figure could rise, closed the gap and pounced.

The assassin struggled from his grip, kicking at his outstretched arms and backpedaling away. After enduring so much, Kismet was not about to be thrown off now. Shrugging off the ineffectual blows, he charged forward again, leaping from a crouch at his enemy's mid-section.

His arms closed on air. Somehow, the assassin had ducked beneath him, rolling across the ground and springing up lightly, even as Kismet committed to the futile assault. This time the trained killer made no attempt to flee.

As Kismet struggled to rise, he felt something strike the back of his knees. The assassin had gone on the offensive, knocking his feet from beneath him with a low sweeping kick. This was followed immediately by a flurry of punches aimed at his face and torso. Some of the blows he blocked, and those that made contact were not especially forceful, but the overall effect of the assault was cumulative. He felt like a piece of steak being tenderized by repeated hammer blows.

Rejecting the innate impulse to protect himself, he lashed out into the heart of the storm. His fist caught the assassin on the cheek. Though a swath of fabric—the killer's veil—muted the intensity of the contact, the insistent attack ceased as the robed figure pitched backward. Kismet's follow-up was sluggish; he was at the limit of his strength and resolve. Sensing this, his opponent sprang lightly erect and ran at him.

The charge was abruptly aborted as Kismet brandished his pistol, aiming directly at the other person's face. The assassin froze and for a long moment, both simply stood their ground, panting with exhaustion. Finally, Kismet broke the relative silence. "That's better. Now, let's talk about a few things."

The assassin took a tentative step backward, but Kismet gestured with the Glock, asserting control. "You know I'll do it."

"I don't think you do."

The assassin's voice was low, intentionally unrecognizable, but even that short declaration served to establish certain facts about the killer's identity. The words were delivered in English—confident, unaccented, idiomatic English. Despite the conscious effort at disguise, there was something faintly familiar about the voice. Kismet tried to keep his foe talking.

"Believe me, I will. It's the least I can do for the soldiers you killed today."

He could almost sense the mocking laughter behind the veil. "You know I could have killed you, back at the museum."

Kismet felt a chilly whisper of déjà vu. When he spoke, he felt he was reciting the words from a script burned in his memory. "Why didn't you?"

He knew exactly what the assassin was going to say, or at least the substance, but his expectations were proven wrong. Instead of speaking, the assassin remained silent for several seconds, then abruptly flashed into motion.

Kismet squeezed the trigger reflexively, snapping off a shot that pierced the air where an instant before the assassin's laughing eyes had been. He missed by a hair's breadth and immediately began tracking the movement with the barrel of the pistol, but the assassin remained a moment ahead of his impulse to fire. The Glock barked several times in succession, but the bullets zipped ineffectually past their target. He stopped firing when his foe ducked around an enormous stack of unused masonry blocks, and resumed the foot chase with the gun still locked in his right hand.

As he approached the corner around which his quarry had disappeared, he was able to distinguish a strident cry in Arabic. The words were simple enough for him to translate. It was a cry for help. While the tone was several octaves above the low voice the assassin had used, Kismet had no doubt that the same person was now summoning help, perhaps from the workers on the site. Underneath the shouted words however, there was a strange humming noise, like a building electrical current.

Ready for anything, Kismet raised the Glock and rounded the corner.

A sea of faces gazed back at him. Hundreds, possibly thousands of men, young and old, armed with crude signs demanding that the United States leave their country, as well as sticks, stones and at least a few AK-47 assault rifles, stood their ground directly ahead of Kismet. To a man, they were barefoot. The assassin had already vanished into the throng, blending chameleon-like into the surroundings, which left him alone to face the wrath of the mob.

It dawned on Kismet right then that the construction site in which he now stood was not a stadium or high-rise office complex, but rather the Al-Rahman mosque, which upon completion would be the second largest in the country and certainly one of the largest houses of worship on the planet. Not only was his presence an affront to the collective political will of the group before him, he was also insulting their faith by standing on holy ground.

No one moved for a long, eternal moment. Then, from somewhere in the back of the crowd, a shout went up, demanding that the blood of the infidel be shed. The tide turned and the outraged sea roared toward him like a tsunami.

SIX

At nine o'clock that morning, roughly fifteen minutes before Kismet and Chiron had set out with their escort to interview Mr. Aziz at the Baghdad Museum, a very different sort of meeting was taking place not far from the route chosen by Colonel Buttrick. The assemblage was open to any male resident of the city, but implicit in the invitation was the message that those who chose to attend ought to have a deep belief that there was no God but God—Allah in the local parlance—and an abiding faith in the guidance of the *imams*, the spiritual heirs to the Prophet Mohammed. The meeting—a protest rally—was for, of, and by the Shiite citizens of the city, which accounted for roughly half its population. Baghdad was a melting pot where many members of that majority sect, displaced by the pogroms of Saddam Hussein during his twenty-six years in power, had ultimately relocated, living and working alongside the more secularly minded Sunnis.

There were a few among the crowd who were not Arabs, nor even citizens of Iraq, but were in fact Persian agitators, bent on stirring the sleeping giant that was the Shiite majority in Iraq to forcibly oust the United States' occupying forces and establish a theocracy. Their simple message resonated with a people too long oppressed, who looked upon the foreigners in their midst as merely the latest form of subjugation.

Nearly three thousand men had gathered in front of the Parliament building, not far from the Sujud palace and the military parade grounds, outwardly carrying signs, American flags and effigies, the latter items to be consigned to flames when the watchful eye of the news media turned their way. But under their robes, they carried weapons. For the most part, these consisted of knives and cudgels. A few however had laid their hands on Russian-made assault rifles and sidearms abandoned by the defeated Iraqi military forces. While there was no particular plan to make use of these articles of destruction, the rabble were ready for the call to arms; ready and willing.

Shortly after the four Humvees had passed by unsuspectingly, the crowd had commenced a march to the Al Rahman mosque, a distance of just over two kilometers. The raw skeleton of the massive Islamic temple had become a powerful symbol to these people. Because it was incomplete, not yet bedecked with gaudiness like the extravagant Umm al-Ma'arik or "Mother of All Battles" mosque which stood more as a testament to the former president than to God, it represented the potential of the Shia to shape their own destiny, albeit with a gentle nudge from their fellow believers to the east.

The center of the mosque site was an open circle, more than one hundred meters across, where no work had yet been done. In fact, very little would be done in this area at least until the construction reached the final stages, following the erection of a glorious gilt dome. For now though, the area served as an impromptu amphitheater where a number of honored speakers whipped the already fervid crowds into a religious frenzy.

It was no coincidence that brought the assassin to this place. The rally was an ideal place to blend in and escape the searching eyes of the US military. Had Kismet realized that his foe had intentionally led him to this place, he would have greeted the notion with a degree of irony. There was a very good reason why the crowd spread out across the mosque site was exclusively male. The Quran did not permit members of the fairer sex to attend such a gathering.

Therein lay the one piece of information concerning Aziz's murderer about which Kismet had no doubts. It was the secret he had, for no rational reason, held back in his discussion with Buttrick. In the initial moments of the chase, when they had grappled at the museum, he had felt breasts. The cold-blooded, highly trained assassin was a woman.

At just that instant however, the assassin's gender, or for that matter, the inequality of the local religious teachings was the last thing on Nick Kismet's mind.

He instinctively brought his gun to bear, waving it in a broad arc before him in hopes of intimidating the crowd. It was a foolish effort, he realized. In the zeal of the moment, a collective sense of invulnerability had come over the protestors. To be sure, each man had applied the simple logic of the odds—there were far more of them than bullets in his gun, but the charge was deflected somewhat. The human surge seemed to run into an invisible barrier three meters from where he stood, wrapping around him to either side while maintaining that minimum safe distance. In the space of a heartbeat, he was surrounded.

Realizing his mistake too late, Kismet turned to flee. Although they had outflanked him, the mob was at its weakest point where they had filled in at his rear. The human wall was a thin line no more than two men deep. He swung his pistol in their direction and fired.

The shot was intentionally high. The last thing he wanted to do was compound an already dire situation by killing someone. If he crossed that line, the crowd would settle for nothing less than dismembering him. As it was, the sound of the discharge fanned the flames of wrath, but for those directly in the line of fire, the warning shots had the desired effect. The men dropped in a panic, weakening the line as he charged.

In that moment of sublime pandemonium, Kismet reckoned his chances of escape were about even. Despite the overwhelming force of numbers, the crowd was a cumbersome entity, limited by the strength and speed of its leading edge. Those in the middle had to rely on guidance from their comrades and sometimes the lines of communication were slow and unreliable. The seeds of a plan sprouted as he closed in on the skirmish line. All he had to do was get past them and he would have the advantage.

At the moment of contact, he attempted to vault over the cowering defenders. His focus was narrowed to the three of four men who actually had a chance of stopping him. One man, older than his companions and more wary, was practically on his hands and knees. Kismet leaped over the man's bent back, and was a step closer to freedom.

Suddenly his world spun around. Instead of open sky, he found himself staring at the desert floor and before he could even begin to comprehend what had happened, the wind was driven from his lungs as his torso slammed into the ground. Someone, perhaps the old man, had snared his ankle, ripping him out of the air in mid-leap.

The protest marchers swarmed over him like warrior ants, tearing blindly at his extremities. The gun discharged several times, although he made no deliberate effort to pull the trigger, and cries of pain and rage went up from the dog pile. The Glock was torn from his fingers a moment later, even as blows began raining down upon him.

In that frantic moment, adrenaline took over. The instinctive need to survive—to flee and fight—directed his hands and feet in a way that his conscious mind could not fathom. He began to kick and punch and gouge, twisting like a dynamo, inflicting close-quarters damage that slowly accumulated to the point where his attackers were forced back, if only to arm's length. As they fell away, Kismet's fingers closed on the haft of his *kukri* and he wrenched it free from its scabbard, waving it menacingly. The large steel blade intimidated the mob in a way his firearm could not. It held promise of slashing wounds and lost limbs, rather than the almost intangible threat of a bullet hole.

There was blood on the sand. Some of it was his, but at least two of the men had suffered gunshot wounds and lay motionless on the ground. Others bore the marks of Kismet's adrenaline-fueled counterattack with bloody noses and split lips, but he knew that whatever traumas he had managed to inflict were reflected and magnified on his own body. Rivulets of warm fluid were dripping from his chin, and somehow he knew it wasn't perspiration.

He feinted experimentally with the *kukri*, driving once more at what he perceived to be the weakest point. As he did, one youth broke toward him, screaming a war cry. Kismet whirled to face him, slashed blindly and the blade found flesh. There was a crunch of steel on bone as the heavy knife lopped off a hand, and the battle yell became a howl of agony.

Kismet did not waste time surveying the damage. The youth had broken ranks to attack him, leaving a hole in the perimeter of the assault. Still slashing the *kukri* before him, he charged toward the gap. A few brave fingers snagged his clothing as he pushed through, but none were able to stop him. In a moment he was through.

As the mob began to realize that their prey had eluded the pinchers and was now escaping, their rage grew to blinding proportions. Men pushed forward, heedless of those ahead of them, and dozens were crushed or trampled in the surge. The crowd seemed to fragment beyond that point, with individuals breaking loose and sprinting after Kismet, while most remained caught in the snarl. Notwithstanding this, their strength of numbers remained.

Kismet wove through the obstacles of the construction site, more intent on staying in motion than reaching any particular goal. The task before him seemed overwhelming; he had to find refuge in an unfamiliar city where virtually everyone wanted him dead.

For a moment, he thought about trying to cross back through the rail yard in order to rendezvous with Buttrick and his soldiers. He immediately dismissed that idea. All it would accomplish would be to bring the rage of the masses down on those men as well. Instead he stayed on a straight course, veering left or right only when an obstacle presented itself.

He ducked his head reflexively when he heard the familiar crack of his own gun being discharged. The distinctive sound of the nine millimeter pistol repeated two more times, but none of the rounds found their mark, and after the third concussion, the gun fell silent. It was only a momentary reprieve. Kismet knew there were other guns among the crowd.

He reached the edge of the construction site, slipped through an inexplicable stand of trees, and once more onto the barren brown desert floor. The *kukri* in his right fist seemed like an anchor, weighing him down and making each step that much harder, but the crimson stain on its edge was compelling testimony to its usefulness. Besides, the thought of throwing it away was abhorrent. He had once believed he would die with the blade in his hand; now it seemed another such opportunity for that fate had arrived.

He dared not look back. There was no need to verify the fact that the mob was at his heels. He was more concerned about what lay directly ahead—a lot of nothing. There was nowhere to hide, no safe place where he would be granted refuge. This was an endurance race, and he would lose only when he could run no more.

So he ran.

Nothing else existed but to keep moving. Time was measured by the pounding of his heart in his ears, synchronized to the rhythm of his footsteps—four strides per beat. He could hear nothing else. His field of vision likewise was narrowing, focusing in on a fixed object: a high-rise structure directly ahead and perhaps five kilometers in the distance. He had no idea what the building was and there was no way he would ever reach it, but it was something tangible that he could move toward. He was barely aware of the darkness closing in at the edge of his vision.

The crowd could not match his pace. Their collective motivation to rend his limbs was not as fierce as his will to survive. Barefoot and exhausted from the long march, many were content to fade into the background, allowing their brothers and neighbors the thrill of the kill. A few score surged ahead, breaking away from the mob and sprinting with all their might after the fleeing figure. Unconsciously, the men separated into two packs, forming wedges behind the fastest runners. As they narrowed the gap, each leader angled away from the distinctive pattern of Kismet's footprints, swerving into a parallel course that would enable them to cut off and overwhelm him. Through the pounding and the darkness, he almost failed to notice.

One young man, wielding a rudimentary carving knife whetted so frequently that it was a mere sliver of steel, charged prematurely. He dived at an angle, the wooden grips of the knife squeezed tight in his right fist, and stabbed at the center of Kismet's back. The blade snagged in the already ragged fabric, and as he felt the first twinge of pain, Kismet twisted away. The attack had thrown the running youth off balance, and as the knife was torn from his grip, he sprawled forward onto the sand. The man closest behind tried to leap over his fallen comrade but mistimed his jump, tripping on an outstretched leg and likewise ending up prone on the desert floor.

Aware now that his enemies were within striking distance, Kismet slashed back blindly with the *kukri*, sweeping the blade like a scythe in order to clear the area directly to his right. He then made a sharp turn in that direction, creating further confusion among his pursuers and the left-hand wedge inadvertently collided with the other group in their eagerness to adjust course. Before they could orient on his new vector, Kismet wove back in the other direction.

The mosque was now well behind him, along with most of the protestors. A distance equivalent to two football fields separated Kismet from the place where he had, for a moment at least, brought Aziz's murderer to heel. The featureless arid plain was grudgingly giving way to urban growth and he could discern streets ahead and a handful of commercial structures rising up before him.

A distant crack of thunder signaled that one of his pursuers, possibly with the main body of the crowd, had finally realized that bullets travel farther and faster than human feet. The Kalashnikov assault rifle chattered for only a moment before falling silent. The shooter had discharged the entire magazine with a single fully automatic burst, but a moment later, other guns joined in a thunderous symphony. Kismet saw a few puffs of dust where bullets struck ahead of him. The soldier he had once been knew that the men were simply wasting ammunition. Although the unrelenting stream of lead seemed intimidating, the explosive discharge of gases from the muzzle of the AK-47 typically caused the weapon to buck and pull up, sending most of the rounds off into space. Still, there was always a chance that one of those randomly fired projectiles would find him.

He dismissed that possibility, not because it was unlikely but because there was nothing he could do about it. Dissociating from the dire circumstances, he returned his gaze to the high-rise tower. It seemed no closer now than when he had begun, but in the back of his mind, he decided he would visit the skyscraper and see what the city looked like from its highest vantage.

A different sort of noise overpowered the cacophony of gunfire, a deep, rhythmic pulse that resonated in his chest and even throbbed at his fingertips. He tried to fit this puzzle piece into the tapestry of his flight but it simply didn't belong.

That was when he heard the voice from heaven.

The assassin wasted no time separating herself from the crowd. She well knew the fate she would suffer if her gender were discovered by the mob, to say nothing of her ethnicity. Fortunately, the masses were focused elsewhere.

On the margin of the gathering there was little movement and rampant speculation. She overheard some of the men relaying gossip passed back from the front. Rumor had it that a squad of US Marines had attacked the holy men leading the rally and killed several young men with their bayonets. She smiled behind her veil and kept moving.

At the eastern edge of the mosque grounds, she found a flatbed truck, still loaded with steel re-bar. The uniform layer of dust accumulated on the vehicle suggested that it had been some time since anyone had reported for work at the job site. After checking that nobody was paying her any special attention, she climbed up onto the bed, then pulled herself onto the roof of the cab.

Though only about three meters above the desert floor, she had a clear view of what was fast becoming a riot. Kismet was a barely visible speck, followed by several more insect-like shapes, scurrying across the sand. Behind them, a single dark mass, gradually resolving into individual entities. She greeted the scene with satisfaction. Kismet had chased her across half the city and very nearly killed her. It was nice to see him on the receiving end for a change.

Her smug expression fell a moment later as a dark shape hove into view above the crowd. She knew immediately what it was. During her wild ride through the city streets, she had monitored several transmissions between the motorized forces and the crew of a Black Hawk helicopter. The military aircraft had been following the developments on the ground, waiting for an opportunity to move in and rescue Kismet. She shook her head in resignation and took out her phone.

Saeed picked up on the second ring. "Well?"

"It's done."

His relief was unmistakable. "And...ah, the other matter?"

She thought for a moment about how to phrase her report. It was no secret that the US National Security Agency employed a small army of computers to monitor every telephone call and radio transmission on the planet. Because the volume of communication was simply too great for every conversation to be analyzed, the eavesdropping programs watched for certain keywords—"bomb" for example—or specific names, at which point a recording would be made for further analysis. If one was not already the subject of scrutiny, it was a fairly simple thing to avoid detection by the careful employ of euphemisms. However, it had come as no small surprise to learn that one of the earmarked words was the name of the man who had nearly killed her. She had more than once wondered why Nick Kismet merited such special attention.

"As you instructed, I left it alone. As it turned out, the situation almost took care of itself without my help."

"How so?" Relief was instantly changed to concern.

"I took your advice and went to the meeting. He followed and attracted a lot of attention."

"Ah, I see. Well, that would be something beyond our control, wouldn't it?"

She didn't understand why the distinction mattered, but for now she was content to maintain the illusion that Saeed was calling the shots. "It doesn't matter. He's going to be leaving on his own terms."

There was another audible sigh. "A pity, but perhaps it's for the best."

"I can still take care of this."

"No. I have something else in mind. For now I want you to find out what further plans will be made. Call me again when you know more."

"Very well." She severed the connection without exchanging the customary pleasantries and replaced the phone handset in the folds of her garment. Only then did she return her gaze to the scene playing out in the distance.

The Black Hawk was hovering above a block of buildings, evidently looking for a clear area in which to set down. She squinted, trying to bring the far-off tableau into focus. Abruptly, a tendril of white smoke leapt from the center of the crowd, arcing toward the helicopter.

The smile returned to her lips. Perhaps she had been premature in reporting Kismet's escape.

The electronically amplified voice from the helicopter suffused Kismet with hope, something that had been in short supply since his initial encounter with the angry mob. But he wasn't home free yet.

"Mister Kismet! You have to find a clear area where we can set down! Keep moving, sir. We're here for you."

The voice was reassuring, although the request seemed a Herculean task. It was all he could do to stay ahead of his pursuers. Furthermore, he had no idea what lay ahead or how to go about finding a suitable landing zone. All he could do was continue moving forward and hope for the best, but knowing that he was no longer alone somehow made it bearable.

The crew of the Black Hawk did not limit themselves to encouraging words. The helicopter dropped in low over the buildings, its rotor wash stirring up a cloud of sand that occluded the view of all but those closest to Kismet. This was followed by a scattering of warning shots fired from the aft door of the aircraft. The 5.56 millimeter rounds kicked up more dust, but the noise of the shots was lost in the thunder of the rotors.

Someone on the ground recognized that the American soldiers were firing on the crowd and took the action he deemed appropriate. The young man had long dreamed of striking a blow against the godless Americans occupying his country, and a lucky discovery of a munitions cache had given him the means to do so. Hauling out the long tube of a rocket-propelled grenade launcher, he sighted in on the open door and pulled the trigger.

An eruption of fire from the back of the tube engulfed half a dozen people standing directly behind the young man. Because the launcher was pointed skyward, an explosive concussion rebounded off the ground, instantly killing the grenadier and two others. Several more people lay stunned and smoldering in a three-meter radius around the now useless weapon. The grenade however, once released, did not require its operator to continue living, and raced mindlessly toward its target.

The co-pilot spied the incoming RPG and shouted a warning. The warrant officer at the controls immediately banked the helicopter. It was a blind throw. If the projectile was aimed accurately then the maneuver would likely save them, but there was an equal chance that by moving, he was putting the aircraft directly in the path of what would otherwise have been a near miss.

While the hapless youth's inexperience with the weapon had cost him dearly, his marksmanship was intuitive. Had the Black Hawk remained at station, the grenade would have entered the open hatch and detonated inside the armored craft, killing everyone inside and probably dozens more on the ground. The flight officer's desperate move saved countless lives. The grenade missed the body of the helicopter by scant inches, but the yawing maneuver left the rotor blades completely vulnerable. The white plume of exhaust shot by the fuselage and up into the circle described by the airfoil-shaped vanes. A loud clank filled the cockpit as one of the rotor blades struck the grenade.

Miraculously, the detonator tip of the grenade failed to make contact. The edge of the rotor struck the rocket body scant millimeters from the high-explosive payload, shattering the fuze mechanism and rendering the device impotent. As the broken pieces fell back to earth, the crew of the Black Hawk exchanged incredulous glances. Then the pilot put some more air between them and the ground.

Kismet was unaware of the helicopter's brush with disaster, but there was no mistaking the sound of its retreat. A grimace crossed his lips as he threaded into an alley, then crossed a through street and continued on in a straight line. He had lost sight of his reference point—the skyscraper—but he had not deviated from his course.

The commercial area gave way to another open field, through which cut Dimashq Street, part of the route leading from the airport into the city. Kismet charged headlong toward the lanes without checking for oncoming vehicles.

He made a furtive glance to his rear. At least a score of men continued to dog his heels, and behind them perhaps a hundred more spilling from the city blocks. He couldn't fathom why the Black Hawk crew had not chosen to set down in the open area he had just crossed. He could not imagine a better LZ. But stopping and waiting for them to arrive was not an option.

There was a shriek of rubber on macadam and a strident horn blast as oncoming vehicles, unaware of his life-and-death crisis, vented their irritation as they swerved past. The mob swarmed over the barrier a moment later.

Beyond the highway lay a stand of trees—some kind of urban park—through which he dared only navigate the straightest possible course. The terrain was irregular, demanding greater exertions and more attention to every step. He stumbled mechanically through the forested area, beyond exhaustion now, beyond awareness of the pain and fatigue. His flight from the mosque had taken him across nearly three kilometers of the city. Nearly fifteen minutes of non-stop effort, while blood seeped from dozens of scrapes, lacerations and contusions; and the desert sun stripped away vital moisture, leaving him dehydrated and feverish.

He had no doubt that, one way or another, it would all be over soon.

His gaze then fell on something that, for the moment at least, defied comprehension. The first thought to cross his mind was that a spaceship was taking off from a low hill a few hundred meters away. From his perspective, the smooth shape looked like an upside down spoon lifting into the sky. Spurred on by an irrational curiosity, he almost forgot about the bloodthirsty mob at his heels as he raced toward the reddish object.

He quickly saw that the curved structure was not floating free above the ground. Rather it was supported at one end by a massive column, from which the rest of the dome cantilevered at a slight angle, giving the illusion of flight. As he drew closer, he recognized it was yet another of the gaudy monuments built by the former government, and while its purpose eluded him, it now became a critical point of focus for a very different reason: The Black Hawk had returned, and was hovering near the copper-colored dome.

Like spider's silk, a rope dropped from the underside of the helicopter and a human shape slid down onto the upraised surface where he took to one knee and readied his weapon. Kismet couldn't tell what the man was doing, but a moment later a projectile shot over his head and fell into the midst of the swarm. A cloud of white vapor erupted from the grenade—non-lethal CS gas—which left dozens among the crowd gasping and choking, and stalled the main body of the mob. The head of the monster—more than two dozen men who had managed to match Kismet's pace—was already well out of the affected area.

There was an obscene noise from the helicopter, and a simultaneous eruption of stone chips in a line to Kismet's left. A soldier aboard the Black Hawk had fired a burst from the side-mounted mini-gun. The motorized system of rotating barrels threw an astonishing number of rounds down-range, chewing through a target like a chainsaw—sounding like one too—but the gunner was still trying to minimize civilian casualties, and at some unconscious level, the crowd knew this. The pursuers simply fell into line behind Kismet without breaking stride.

The soldier on the dome now raised the butt of his carbine to his shoulder and commenced firing. Kismet could not hear the M4's report but there was an audible cry of pain behind him. The agonized cursing continued, suggesting that the shot had wounded rather than killed. In fact, the round had done nothing more than graze the man's shin, but it was enough to take him out of the chase. More similarly well-placed shots followed, but the threat of pain was only stoking the fire of rage among the mob, some of whom were also armed with automatic weapons. Sparks began to dance on the surface of the dome as one AK-47 after another was emptied at the lone soldier. The man stood his ground. Most of the wildly aimed shots missed the monument completely and those that hit were nowhere close to his position. Nevertheless, his comrades aboard the helicopter began directing their weapons at the muzzle flashes in the crowd and this time they did not hold back.

As Kismet closed to within a hundred meters of the monument, another soldier fast-roped onto the dome surface and directed the heavy line down toward the base of the structure. The helo moved in low over the center of the broad dome, until it was hovering about ten meters from its summit. The additional slack in the rope allowed the soldier to rappel down to the bottom of the arching pedestal, where he began urging Kismet onward. His right hand maintained a fierce grip on the lifeline.

Kismet hurdle-jumped a short wall, landing in what appeared to be the basin for a fountain—the water supply had been shut off at the onset of the war—and continued up a series of long concrete steps. The final distance was the hardest, requiring him to climb and zigzag a course of ramparts and stairs leading up to the monument. At one turn, he found himself staring out over the oncoming horde, while a glance to his left revealed that a dozen men were now only a few steps behind. Failing to find any reserves of energy in his body, he wrote a mental IOU and sprinted ahead.

A dark vise closed on his skull as a ringing nose deafened him to the sounds of battle. He could just make out the soldier, beckoning frantically only a few steps away, and before the curtain fell over his eyes, he threw out his left hand.

He wasn't aware of the moment where the soldier's grip closed around his wrist, nor did he feel the rope go taut as the Black Hawk ascended a few meters, drawing both men up the steep incline toward the top of the dome. The next cognizant moment found him lying supine on the crest of the curved structure, spread out like a sacrifice.

The soldier who had pulled him up knelt beside him, shouting something in his ear. Kismet nodded dumbly and rolled over, automatically sheathing his *kukri*. Had he been more alert, he might have simply discarded the weapon. It had sentimental value, but his rational mind would have judged his situation far too urgent to squander precious seconds keeping track of his equipment.

The helicopter's rotor wash tore at the ragged remains of his clothing. He was reluctant to stand up, lest the insistent wind blast him from the smooth metal surface of the dome. The Black Hawk moved off, easing the tempest, and took up a position just off the forward tip of the upraised monument. Several faces crowded around the open side door, urging the three men to make the short jump to relative safety. The soldier who had pulled Kismet up now turned to him, and shouted in his ear.

"This is easier than it looks, sir. Watch me!"

He turned away and crossed cautiously to the edge of the dome, hunched low to avoid the whirling vanes overhead, and stepped out onto the deck of the Black Hawk. From Kismet's point of view, it seemed that he had not even leapt. The soldier turned to face him, once more exhorting him to hurry.

The crowd was massing at the base of the monument, the initial attempts to scale the forty-five degree slope had been easily thwarted as the remaining soldier clubbed at outstretched hands with the plastic stock of his carbine. But as reinforcements joined the vanguard, the advantage of their overwhelming numbers now became apparent. From several points around the fulcrum of the cantilevered structure, groups of men began boosting individuals high enough to get a purchase on the hot copper surface. The infantryman, recognizing that their tactic would eventually succeed, turned away and ran toward the helicopter. Only then did Kismet realize that it was Colonel Buttrick.

"Get the fuck off this thing!"

Kismet nodded again, then scrambled to his feet, preceding the officer by a few steps. At the outer limit, the gulf between the aircraft and the dome seemed less traversable. Not trusting his weary body to make the crossing in one easy step, Kismet took a running start and hurled his weight forward at the last instant.

No less than four pairs of hands caught him as he entered the helicopter. Once his feet were planted on the deck, he turned to watch Buttrick make his move. Directly behind the colonel, the heads and shoulders of the first wave became visible. Desperate to find a vent for their anger, the mob was not relenting, even though it appeared their prey had already eluded them.

Like Kismet, Buttrick was not about to showboat the crossing. All that mattered to him was getting off the dome by the most expedient means. Hunched over, he moved at a dead run across the dome, gathering his strength for the final jump.

At that instant, the pilot saw the telltale plume of another RPG launch off in the distance. Although he knew there was still a man outside, his instinctive response occurred a millisecond ahead of rational thought. He tapped the rudder pedal with his left foot, swiveling the helicopter a few degrees on the axis of the main rotor. The grenade's trajectory brought it nowhere near the aircraft, but that momentary correction came at the worst possible moment.

Buttrick had already committed to the jump. There was no halting or redirecting his momentum. The opening in the side of the Black Hawk was no longer where he expected it to be. He managed to throw an arm around the edge of the door before slamming into the armored side of the helicopter and surrendering to gravity.

Inside, the sudden maneuver had thrown everyone off balance. The confident soldiers, unprepared for the shift, abruptly found themselves clutching for handholds. Kismet, nearest to the door, was hurled against the bulkhead, but even as he hugged the wall, trying to keep his feet, he saw Buttrick make his doomed leap from the monument. He threw out a desperate hand and somehow snared the colonel's wrist.

As Buttrick's full weight came down on the outstretched arm, Kismet was pulled to the deck. The colonel's face twisted in agony as the burden wrenched his shoulder out of joint, but Kismet did not let go. He felt the other man groping with his free hand for a purchase, but dared not release the grip of his other hand on the bulkhead, lest both of them fall. After a few seconds of scrabbling, the colonel's fingers knotted into the fabric of Kismet's shirt, easing the strain on his pinned arm.

With the platform beneath them stable once more, the soldiers hastened to assist their colonel, forming a human chain to keep one another secure. It took them only a moment to pull their leader to safety, after which the helicopter pulled away. Kismet struggled to his feet, still clinging to the bulkhead, and gazed down at the receding mass of people swarming around the monument. As the distance grew, the individual faces smeared into an indistinguishable mass.

"So that's what it looks like from up here," he mumbled.

Then he realized that everything else was growing blurry. Despite the desert heat, he began to shiver uncontrollably as his world darkened. He felt strong hands seizing his arms and body, holding him fast, but he nevertheless began falling and there was no pulling him back.

PART TWO

FINGERPRINT

SEVEN

When he awoke, his first impression was that he was back home in a cool bed, and that everything that had happened in the desert was merely a bad dream. But when he tried to rouse himself, all that he had endured returned with a vengeance. Blinding agony speared through his head and he winced involuntarily, thrashing as he reached up to hold the halves of his skull together. That was when he realized he was in water, lying naked in a makeshift basin filled with tepid liquid. Bracing himself against the expected pain, he cautiously opened his eyes.

Beyond the fact that he was laying naked in a few centimeters of water, it was difficult to discern anything. The room was dark, lit only by a sliver of light seeping in around the edges of the window blinds. Even that nominal amount of illumination felt like a spike piercing through his retinas, so he stopped looking and relaxed once more. It took him a moment to perceive that he was not alone.

"Welcome back to the land of the living."

The soft voice seemed familiar, but he did not open his eyes to identify the female speaker. "Where am I?"

"Back where you started. The airport." He sensed her moving closer. "Open your mouth."

He obliged without thinking, and abruptly found a thin probe thrust under his tongue. He clamped his teeth down to hold the thermometer in place. A moment later, a beeping sound signaled that it had completed its task. The woman removed the device.

"Well?"

"Your fever has broken," she announced, matter-of-factly. "I consider that no small accomplishment. When you arrived, your body temperature was forty degrees Celsius and you were badly dehydrated."

"Marie?" He risked opening his eyes once more, trying to bring the face of his caregiver into focus. He immediately recognized the woman, but it was not Marie Villaneauve.

"No," remarked the auburn-haired woman he had initially encountered on the plane. She looked no different than in that initial encounter, save for a butterfly tape bandaging a small cut under her left eye. "I'm Dr. Gault, and your life is in my hands, so stay put and do as I say."

I could have killed you...

Staring at her, Kismet suddenly felt vulnerable and it had nothing to do with his nakedness. She gazed down at him a moment longer, her dour expression never softening, then turned away long enough to procure a plastic bag of dextrose solution. Kismet noted a similar container, nearly drained, secured with hemostat clamps and white tape to a wall near his head. A long tube snaked from the fluid bag to his arm, where an intravenous needle had been inserted.

The first thought to cross his mind was that the woman had decided to finish the job she had started at the museum. He tried to dismiss the idea as he had no evidence to support his suspicions, but his instincts told him that this woman was not to be trusted. He had felt it first when she had abandoned him during the effort to rescue trapped soldiers during the RPG attack at the airport. She might have called herself a doctor, but she had not behaved as one. When he had determined that Aziz's killer was female, he had put her at the top of his list of suspects, even though there was nothing to substantiate that accusation.

Yet, she had saved him from heat exhaustion, hadn't she?

Your life is in my hands...

She finished changing the IV solution, then turned back to him. "I don't know what happened to you, but you seem to be a living mass of bruises. It's difficult to tell where one ends and the next begins. Were you dragged by a horse?"

"It kind of feels that way." He was ambivalent about sharing information with her. If she was the assassin he had chased, then it was conceivable that she was watching for some sign that he had recognized her. In her role as medical care provider, nobody would think twice if Kismet suffered an unexpected fatal relapse. Even if she was innocent, her unpleasant personality made him reluctant to engage in conversation. "Are my friends okay?"

"If you mean Monsieur Chiron, then the answer is that he will be all right as soon as I allow him to see you. He's been very worried."

"I'd like to see him now."

She frowned. "Well, if it were up to me, I'd make you wait until morning. I don't think you appreciate that you almost died, Mr. Kismet."

Several times, actually. He held back the comment. "Please, it's important."

She crossed her arms. "Very well. I suppose there's really nothing more for me to do. I'll come back in about fifteen minutes to remove your line. After that, you'll be on your own. I can give you some analgesics for your pain... I imagine you've got quite a headache. Other than that, you just need to stay hydrated and take it easy."

"Whatever you say, doc."

She sighed and turned toward the door. "I hope you brought along some extra clothing. I'm afraid there wasn't much left of what you were wearing."

Though it was against his better judgment, Kismet made a final bid for the last word. "Well, I guess this makes us even."

She paused, then looked back. A single arched eyebrow was just visible in the narrow beam of outside light. "I beg your pardon?"

"I saved your life. Now you've saved mine."

"You give yourself too much credit. I seem to remember that you very nearly killed me."

Kismet's lips twitched into a smile but there was no humor in his expression. "Believe me, I've thought about it."

She held his stare for a long silent moment, her eyes unreadable, then pushed through the door.

Pierre Chiron burst through almost immediately, bathing the room in light from the hallway. Kismet raised a hand to shade his eyes, then struggled to a seated position as his old friend rushed to his side. Marie was right behind him.

"Nick, we've been so worried. They say you fainted in a helicopter."

Kismet was mildly irritated by the suggestion that he had "fainted", but clarification to soothe his ego seemed superfluous. "Who was that woman?"

"Do you mean Dr. Gault?"

"I do. Why was she treating me? I would have expected to end up in an army field hospital."

Chiron appeared confused by the question. "Dr. Gault is with the International Red Cross. She's certainly capable, if that's your concern."

Marie stepped forward, proffering a blanket to Kismet for the sake of modesty. "I was here when you arrived, Nick. The soldiers seemed to think you were to blame for whatever it was that happened out there. I had them bring you to Dr. Gault in order for you to get some treatment. From what she's told us, it's a good thing I did."

"Nick," Chiron intoned. "What happened? Did you know that Mr. Aziz was murdered?"

"Someone didn't want us talking to him. I walked in on it and tried to chase after the…the guy that did it." He decided to withhold his knowledge of the assassin's gender. That tiny scrap of information was his hole card and he wasn't ready to play it yet. Not until he knew more about Dr. Gault, at any rate. Kismet pressed his palms to his eyes, trying to force the insistent pain to abate, if only long enough to continue speaking. "From there, everything went to hell. I'm sure it's already made the news by now."

Marie flashed a wry smile. "They say you started a riot."

"I wouldn't say I started it, exactly. I just sort of happened upon it."

Chiron laid a fatherly hand on his forearm. "Nick, what really happened? Who did this?"

"I-I'm not quite sure. I have some ideas." His gaze flashed between Chiron and Marie. "I don't want to speculate right now."

The old man seemed to comprehend his subtle body English. "Of course. It would serve no purpose. Besides, I'm sure your doctor wants you to rest. And perhaps eat something. Marie, be a dear and see if you can't find something for our friend to eat. Something palatable, if at all possible. I will stay with Nick and regale him with my own adventures from this afternoon."

Kismet could tell by her eyes that Marie was disappointed at being dismissed—and that she knew why—but managed a smile and nodded to Kismet. There was more emotion in her expression than he had previously seen, but to his chagrin, he couldn't will himself to entertain amorous thoughts as he watched her go.

Chiron waited until the door clicked shut behind her. "Well?"

Kismet gingerly extricated himself from the bath, careful not to dislodge the intravenous line. Despite his headache, he felt a primal need to start moving again. The basin of lukewarm water, which had doubtless been instrumental in lowering his fever and probably saving his life, now seemed merely an annoyance. He wrapped the damp blanket around his torso and faced the other man. "What time is it?"

"After nineteen hundred—7:00 p.m. that is."

He had slept almost nine hours, yet he did not feel at all rejuvenated. "A whole day lost."

"Perhaps. But you've obviously been through a great deal. Rest is the best thing for you, I imagine."

"I need to get my bag...get some fresh clothes." He spied his ragged boots on the floor nearby. He had not thought to bring alternate footwear.

"Yes. Nick, tell me what happened. Do you know who killed Mr. Aziz? Or who it was that wanted him silenced?"

"The answer to both questions is 'maybe'. I'm going to do some digging with respects to the identity of the killer. As to who's behind it..." He leaned against a table edge. "As I see it, there are two possibilities. The obvious answer is that Aziz was a black marketeer, dealing in antiquities. Either he was offed by a rival, or somebody in his own organization suspected he was cooperating with us and wanted to keep him from spilling his guts."

Chiron appeared stunned. "I had not considered that approaching him would present any sort of risk."

"Relax. If Aziz is everything I think he was, the world is probably a better place without him. However, I said there are two possibilities, and right now I'm leaning toward the alternative."

"And what is that?"

Kismet glanced at the door, wondering if Marie would return before he had finished explaining himself. "The killer said something to me—something that was very much like what Hauser told me, twelve years ago."

"And that was?"

"I asked him why he didn't kill me along with everyone else. He said that if he had killed me, my mother would have his head."

There was a gasp. "Your mother, Nick? But I thought you never knew her?"

"I didn't...I don't."

"The man that killed Aziz said this to you?"

Kismet shook his head, unintentionally aggravating the throbbing pain there. "No. Hauser said that. The...ah, guy that killed Aziz just said that he could have killed me if he had wanted to."

Chiron began mentally arranging the puzzle pieces. "So you believe that this man Hauser, or someone like him, murdered Mr. Aziz in order to prevent him from sharing information vital to your ongoing search."

"That pretty well sums it up. I was so close to finding a link to what happened that night, but someone got there ahead of me."

"What will you do now?"

"I was hoping you'd know. Was Aziz the only lead you had on these Babylonian discoveries?"

"Yes." Chiron's reply was thoughtful and Kismet could tell he wasn't being entirely forthcoming.

"You're up to something, Pierre. Tell me."

"Well, I had always recognized the possibility that Mr. Aziz would not cooperate. From the outset, I believed that we would have to go to Babylon."

Kismet was incredulous. "What, just head out there with a shovel and start digging?"

"Something like that," Chiron answered with a grin. "I may have to save that for a surprise, though. We'll go as soon as you are feeling better."

"In case you haven't been following the news, I think I've pretty much worn out my welcome. Even if Colonel Buttrick doesn't declare me *persona non grata*, I can't see him loaning us more vehicles."

"That won't be a problem. The UN inspection team left behind a small fleet of Toyota Land Cruisers."

"I heard the UN headquarters facility was looted."

"The offices at the Canal Hotel were ransacked, but the UNMOVIC team stored most of their sensitive equipment, along with some vehicles, at an industrial complex along the Hillah Road to the south. As far as I know, the location was secret and remote enough that I doubt anyone will have raided it. The only difficulty will be getting there."

Kismet sighed resignedly, wishing he knew what scheme Chiron was hatching. "Well, I'll ask Buttrick tomorrow. The worst thing he can say is: 'Go to hell'."

It had been a long time since Saeed had set foot in the part of the world populated by his own people. After more than a decade spent in self-imposed exile, he had grown quite fond of what some in the Islamic world labeled Western decadence. He had come to believe that nothing would ever pull him back to the hellish desert he so loathed. Nevertheless, here he was.

Damascus had the reputation of being the world's oldest continuously inhabited city, its recorded existence dating back more than five thousand years. Saeed understood how the Syrian capital might have justified its existence in the days when trade caravans sought refuge from the bleak desert, but could not imagine why anyone would choose to continue to remain there when the need for such an oasis had been obviated by modern technology. Whatever the reason, the city certainly seemed to be showing its age, especially in the slums on the outskirts, where people lived in houses of baked clay as they had for uncounted generations.

Damn my brother for bringing me here, he thought sourly.

He suspected that Farid was already there, hiding out somewhere to observe him surreptitiously, or perhaps simply to watch him sweat. Although he had purchased a *djellabah*—the traditional overgarment—he felt distinctly out of place. The locals had certainly noticed him A group of children had harassed him for nearly an hour before finally tiring of the game and leaving him alone. It had now grown late, but Saeed remained there sitting in the dust.

"Alms?"

Saeed did not look up. He had spied the bent form of the beggar shuffling down the street earlier and had intentionally crossed to avoid making eye contact. The mendicant had moved on, but now it seemed he had worked his way around for a second try. When he was standing directly behind Saeed, he repeated his request in a low, earnest voice, almost daring him to refuse.

Saeed's nostrils filled with the beggar's stench. "Go away, old man!"

Then a different voice issued from the tattered rags covering the wanderer's head. "What a pity that you could not even find it in your heart to observe this smallest command of the Prophet."

Saeed looked around suddenly. "Farid? Son of a whore."

"I see that you continue to disgrace our family both in deed and word." There was no trace of humor in the familiar voice. The beggar stood straighter, but his disguise remained otherwise intact. He was unrecognizable as Farid Tariq Al-Sharaf, even to his own brother.

Saeed scowled at the complaint. He had heard the substance of the comment too many times to count. "Spare me. I did not travel to this godforsaken place because I missed your berating comments."

"Indeed?" Farid sat down alongside his brother. "And I had

desired never to see you again. Yet at your request, I have made this difficult journey. So tell me, brother, why is it that you have left your palace of pleasure behind to visit me after so many years?"

"A matter of mutual concern has arisen—"

"I do not believe our concerns could possibly be mutual," Farid interjected disdainfully.

"Hear me out." Saeed took a deep breath to regain his composure. "Have you been following the news from Baghdad? There was a suicide bomb attack against the US soldiers at the airport yesterday."

"Yes." Farid spat in the dirt. "Fedayeen Saddam loyalists. I'm glad they failed."

Saeed hid his disappointment at the revelation. He had believed other forces responsible for that action. "And early this morning, there was another incident near the Monument to the Unknown Soldier."

This time he saw the reaction he had hoped for. From behind his beggar's disguise, Farid's face drew into a mask of rage. "Yes. One of the American devils blasphemed our holy place and killed several innocents. He then ran like a coward into the arms of the soldiers."

"The man responsible for that atrocity and the man who thwarted the attack at the airport are the same person."

"How do you know this?"

Saeed risked a smile. "You forget who I am, brother. I served with distinction in the Mukhabarat for many years. Gathering information is my business."

His mention of the hated Iraqi Intelligence Service triggered another expression of contempt, but Farid withheld comment on the matter, focusing instead on the issue under consideration. "So who is he?"

"His name is not important. What is important is that I can give him to you."

The old distrust returned. "And why would you do this? How does our struggle for justice against our enemies benefit you?"

"This man has long been an enemy of all that we regard as holy—"

"Please Saeed." Farid's tone and expression were sour. "You regard nothing as holy."

"An unfortunate choice of words, perhaps. But when I left the home of our parents and strayed from the teachings of the *mullahs*, I did not cease from loving our people or from hating our enemies."

"Nevertheless, I find it difficult to believe that you would leave your self-indulgent lifestyle behind, simply to take revenge on an enemy of our people."

Though he was wearying of his brother's venom, Saeed chose to answer honestly. "The truth of the matter is that this man is a direct threat to my personal interests. For some years now, I have been trading in art treasures recovered from a site near Al Hillah on behalf of our government in order to raise hard currency during the economic embargo."

"But the embargo has ended, as also has the influence of the dictator and his agents."

Saeed pretended not to notice the veiled insult. "True, but the demand for these antiquities remains. As you have pointed out, I enjoy my decadent lifestyle and this is how I support it. But the man we have been discussing works for a department of the United Nations dedicated to shutting down my operation. That's why I want him dead."

Farid smiled knowingly. "Now at last you have said something I can believe. But if you know his identity, why do you not simply kill him yourself?"

"As events have demonstrated, he is not an easy man to kill. I doubt that I could do it alone and my former comrades in the service have been scattered. I imagine many are dead or imprisoned. Moreover, my information indicates that he may be traveling to Hillah to look for the site near the ruins of Babylon. You could pass there freely with your men, whereas I might draw unwelcome attention from those who dwell there."

Farid stroked his chin thoughtfully. Saeed now saw that much of what he had mistaken for a disguise was in fact his brother's true appearance. The Shiite activist and sometimes resistance leader appeared unnaturally aged and haggard. Nevertheless, underneath a crust of desert-parched skin, his younger brother's eyes burned with the zeal of a true *mujahideen*. After several silent seconds, Farid faced him once more. "Very well. I will do your dirty work, brother. However, I must ask something of you, as well."

"I expected no less. I would be honored to contribute to your cause—"

"Your evilly acquired profits do not interest me. Rather, I wish to offer you the chance to acquit yourself of the reproach you have heaped upon our family and your own name. I want you to return with me. Stand with the warriors of God as we send this American devil back to Shaitan."

Saeed shifted nervously. "I would gladly do as you ask, but surely your men would refuse to join company with me." The argument, while probably true, was not his primary reason for demurring; there was no reason to burden his brother with the details.

Farid would not be sidetracked. "They will do as I instruct. The question is, will you?"

For a moment, all Saeed could think about was the desert, and the growing certainty that he would die there, in that awful hell to which he had vowed never to return. But if Kismet was not stopped, all that he had built would crumble anyway. When he finally gave his answer, he almost could not believe what he was saying. "I will go with you, my brother. We will fight together. Death to our enemies and the enemies of God!"

Another nine hours of sleep, aided by a cocktail of pain relievers and sedatives, wiped away most of the lingering effects of his brush with heat exhaustion, but Kismet reckoned it would be weeks before the bruises faded and the aches subsided. When he arose from his sleeping bag to dress, he found he could barely bend his joints in order to pull on his battered boots.

He made his way through the complex, following the route that had previously led him to Colonel Buttrick's office, but when he arrived, he found only the unpleasant Major Harp seated at the commander's desk. The officer regarded him with a look reserved for encounters with animal excrement.

"What do you want?"

"I need to speak with Colonel Buttrick."

Harp scowled. "He's not here. In fact, thanks to you, he's been sent home—relieved of his command."

The major's words were like a fist to his gut. "That's crazy. What happened out there wasn't his fault."

"No shit. But you aren't in the army any more, so they can't take action against the person who is responsible."

Although he sensed it would be futile, Kismet spoke in his own defense. "I know this is a hard concept for you to grasp, but have you considered that maybe you should be mad at the person we were trying to catch. You know, the bad guy?"

"Lt. Col. Buttrick failed yesterday, Kismet. He failed to apprehend or destroy the enemy, and he failed to bring all his boys home. But in my opinion, his biggest mistake was letting you talk him into going out on that fool's errand." Harp stood and leaned over the desk so that he was face to face with Kismet. "Now I know that you aren't here to ask me for any foolish favors, right?"

"I don't suppose so." Kismet sighed and turned away. At the threshold however, he paused and looked back. "Could I at least use your phone?"

"Only if you're calling your travel agent."

The phone in this case was a secure military satellite server, which allowed for voice-to-voice transfers, as well as broadband Internet capability. It was a generation ahead of the handset Aziz had employed. When Kismet placed his call, the clarity of the signal was outstanding; he might have been in the same room as the person who answered. Except it wasn't a person.

"Thank you for calling the International Red Cross and Red Crescent. To continue in English, press 'one' now...."

Kismet patiently navigated the computerized system of menus until he eventually reached a living breathing person. After identifying himself, both by name and as a representative of UNESCO, he launched into his carefully rehearsed story. "I was hoping that you could help me contact one of your relief volunteers, a female doctor. She helped me out of a rather sticky situation recently and I wanted to thank her personally, but I'm having trouble tracking her down. Her last name is 'Gault' but I'm not certain of the spelling or nationality, and I don't have a first name."

"Bitte." He could hear the sound of the young woman on the other end tapping the keyboard of her computer. "Let me look at our directory. There is a Doctor Rebecca Gault of Belgium." She spelled both names. "She regularly works with our international relief missions. Where did you say you met her?"

Kismet recognized the trap. Doubtless the woman was looking at a list of Rebecca Gault's activities, and would volunteer no more information unless he gave the right answer. He took a blind guess.

"Afghanistan."

"Oh, so it was a very recent encounter. She's only just returned. Would you like me to page her?"

"I beg your pardon?"

"She's presently here at the headquarters. If you'll hold a moment, I can page her."

"Sure." As soon as he heard the click of his transfer, he hung up. He had his answer.

Chiron was crestfallen by Kismet's announcement that there would be no further military cooperation. "Then all is lost."

His reaction seemed disproportionate to the setback. "We could hire a local driver to get us as far as the UN facility. But frankly, I'm not sure we should go on. We'll be unarmed and unsupported. If something goes wrong—if we have a breakdown or get attacked— we'll be on our own."

"Nick, we must get to Babylon. The answers are there."

Kismet remained skeptical. "I still think this is going to be like looking for a needle in a haystack."

Chiron smiled. "But you forget, we do not have to find something buried four thousand years ago. They have already done that. When you know that the needle really is in the haystack, all you need to do is search patiently."

"But there's no guarantee that the site hasn't been completely ransacked. We may find the evidence of its existence, but it could just as well turn out to be one more dead end."

Chiron shook his head emphatically. "The answers are there, at Babylon. I am sure of it."

"What answers, Pierre?" Kismet's voice took on a hard edge. "What exactly is it that you are looking for? Yesterday, when we were interviewing Aziz, you practically walked him around answering any of my questions. I thought we were after the same thing, but I'm beginning to wonder what your agenda is."

For a moment, Chiron looked as if he might continue to protest his innocence, but his expression fell before he could utter a word. "You are right. I am looking for something more. But I assure you, I had no intention of helping Mr. Aziz conceal information. If I erred in my eagerness to gain his cooperation, I sincerely apologize."

"What are you looking for?"

Chiron rose from his chair and paced around the room. "I tried to broach this subject with you earlier, when you first arrived, but you did not seem interested at the time."

Kismet recalled the subject of their conversation. "We talked about God and faith. Is that it? Is that what you're looking for? Is this some kind of vision quest?"

Chiron suddenly smiled. "That's exactly what it is, Nick. To find God, men of faith—and I suppose men of doubt, too—have always had to wander in the wilderness for a time. In my own way, I've been wandering all my life, though not really looking. But the journey to Babylon is something different.

"In the oldest holy writings, God has always had His finger on Babylon. The name of the city literally translates as 'Gate of God', and if you'll recall, that name was given at a time when most civilizations were polytheistic. The Book of Genesis in the Bible tells how men, in defiance of God, began building a tower that would reach to heaven. To thwart that purpose, God confused their languages, scattering mankind to every corner of the globe. But two thousand years later, He used King Nebuchadnezzar and his Babylonian armies to punish His errant people by razing the city of Jerusalem and exiling the survivors.

"Some of the most startling prophetic visions recorded in the Bible occurred during that time—the writings of Ezekiel and Daniel—and only a generation after the conquest of Jerusalem, God's finger literally appeared in Babylon, writing a message on the palace wall, declaring that the existing dynasty was to be swept away; a judgment that was carried out that very night."

Kismet shook his head wearily. "Pierre, I'm familiar with the Bible stories. That's just what most of them are. The Book of Daniel is a fabrication, probably written in the second century BC, so most of the information supporting your argument is questionable. But even if those writings are based on actual events—actual divine revelations—what is a trip to Babylon going to prove? You said God's finger has always been on the city. Are you looking for His fingerprint? Are you hoping to find that piece of palace wall with God's graffiti still intact after almost three thousand years?"

"That would be rather compelling testimony, don't you think?" He gave a wry smile. "Nick, I don't expect you to understand. I'm not even sure that I really do. I'm not looking for faith, not at my age.

But if there's even a chance that a god exists—that my Collette is in a better, happier place—then I have to know. One way or another, I need to have that question answered."

Suddenly Kismet did understand. Chiron was suffering from a crisis, not of faith but rather the lack thereof. The loss of his wife had opened a wound in his heart that a lifetime of skepticism had not equipped him to bear. Because he was a scientist, demanding concrete evidence in support of hypotheses, the only solution he saw was to find proof, either for the existence or non-existence of the Divine. Yet a basic tenet of faith was that it could only occur in the absence of proof. "Pierre, you aren't the first person to have these doubts, or to look for answers this way. But Babylon has been there for thousands of years; I don't think you're going to find anything that hasn't been studied and catalogued dozens of times over."

Chiron started to protest, but Kismet quickly raised a hand to forestall him. "On the other hand, I suppose it's up to God to decide when and where he wants to reveal himself, and like you said, he spends an awful lot of time out there in the desert.

"I've got my own reasons for wanting to visit those ruins. Maybe I won't find anything either, but I'll never forgive myself if I don't at least take a look."

The old man smiled triumphantly. "Then that much at least is settled. Now all we have to do is find someone to get us there."

"Actually I have an idea about that. I think it's time we enlisted some local help."

Hussein arrived early in the afternoon, driving a dilapidated Renault. Kismet and Chiron, this time accompanied by Marie, had trekked to the outermost checkpoint leading to the airport, in order to expedite the young man's arrival, and had not been waiting for long when the tired-looking compact automobile rattled to a stop. Hussein got out of the vehicle and immediately walked over to Kismet.

Although it had been Kismet's idea to contact the young scholar, he had allowed Chiron to finalize the arrangements. The two had developed a rapport in the moments leading up to the grisly discovery in the upstairs gallery of the museum, whereas Hussein's initial reaction to Kismet had verged on antipathy. The determined set of his jaw suggested his opinion had not changed.

"I am told that you tried to apprehend the man that killed my teacher, Mr. Aziz."

The statement caught Kismet off guard. What he had mistaken for hostility was really nothing more than grief at the loss of a father figure. "I'm very sorry for your loss."

Hussein nodded slowly and managed a mournful smile. "You placed yourself in great danger to avenge a man you barely knew. I should have been there for him. I owe you a great debt, Mr. Kismet."

"Why don't you call me Nick, and we'll consider it paid in full." He extended a hand, which the young man graciously accepted.

Hussein next greeted Chiron as he might a long-lost relative, who in turn introduced Marie. The young man's eyes lingered on her for an uncomfortable interval, before he finally directed them to stow their gear in the small boot. Marie and Kismet folded themselves into the rear seat, while Chiron rode shotgun.

In spite of its shabby appearance and malfunctioning exhaust system, the Renault drew far less attention than the camouflaged Humvees had on the previous day. Hussein seemed casually indifferent behind the wheel but drove like a madman, rarely observing traffic signs and never slowing for pedestrians.

Kismet made a conscious effort to relax. Still weary from the ordeal of the previous day, he did not welcome the rush of adrenaline that accompanied the wild ride. Beside him, a sun-wilted Marie held the armrest on the door with a white-knuckled grip, saying nothing.

The first part of the journey followed the road from the airport, but at Chiron's direction, they turned south, into an industrialized section of the city. The roads were empty of traffic and the warehouses and factories they passed seemed deserted. The storage facility used by the UN inspectors was housed in an anonymous-looking complex, which had survived both the bombings and the subsequent actions of the looters.

Chiron leaned over the back seat. "Marie, please call the UNMOVIC headquarters in New York. They will have the codes to disable the security system."

She uncurled her fingers from their death grip and reached into a canvas shoulder bag. Although he was aware that Chiron had access to some form of telecommunication, he was mildly surprised to see a satellite phone almost identical to the one he had seen Aziz using the previous day. He shrugged the coincidence away.

UNMOVIC, the UN Monitoring, Verification, and Inspection

Commission, had carried out an exhaustive, but ultimately futile effort to determine if the former Iraqi regime had been engaged in the development of biological and chemical weapons. The inspectors had continued looking, right up until the last moment, in hopes of providing something that would either demonstrate beyond possibility of reproach that the so-called WMDs did exist, which would unify the UN member nations in their condemnation of the regime, or prove beyond all doubt that Iraq had ceased development of nerve agents and anthrax spores, and had destroyed their stockpiles. On March 22, the warning to evacuate had been given and the inspectors had locked up their equipment and fled the country, only a few days ahead of the war.

The security system they had employed to protect their vehicles and other gear from theft and possible misuse was a basic electronic combination lock, but the inspection team had taken a further step of jury rigging a series of low-yield improvised explosive devices throughout the facility. Anyone attempting to force the door would activate the charges, destroying most of the inspection equipment and permanently disabling the vehicles. A large warning sign written in English and Arabic explained most of this, but Kismet doubted that any looters had even tried. After several minutes of explaining the situation, Marie received the disarm code, and the door was safely opened.

Kismet stepped inside cautiously, unsure of what he would find. Although the electrical lock mechanism was still working, its computer powered by a lithium battery, the overhead lights were not operable. He shined the beam of his MagLite into the darkness, revealing two rows of white Land Cruisers, adorned with the globe and olive-branch emblem of the United Nations. The keys to each vehicle depended from the ignition switch. Choosing one from the front row, he removed the security measures then slid behind the wheel.

The starter cycled repeatedly for several seconds as the gasoline was gradually drawn through a fuel line that had sat dry for nearly two months. Despite the momentary lag, Kismet was encouraged by the fact that the battery still held enough charge to fire the spark plugs, and after churning for half a minute, the fuel-air mixture ignited and the engine roared to life. He flashed a thumbs-up to his companions, then eased the vehicle through the open roll-up door.

"Maybe our luck is changing," he remarked, rejoining the group as the Land Cruiser continued idling.

"Nick, there's something I want to show you." Chiron led him back into the building, past the vehicles to an area where several pieces of equipment were stored on pallets. "Do you know what that is?"

The object to which Chiron directed his attention was a nondescript metal box, attached by wires to an electronic control unit. The box was labeled: ZOND 12 1.5 GHz.

Kismet raised an eyebrow. "Pierre, you sneaky devil. You had this planned all along, didn't you?"

"What is it?" inquired Marie, stepping out from the shadows.

"It's a ground-penetrating radar system."

"The UNMOVIC inspectors use it to look for entrances to buried bunkers and the like," Chiron explained, supplementing Kismet's simple declaration. "It can penetrate to depths of up to thirty meters, revealing buried objects, cavities, and even soil density changes."

"Meaning?"

"Meaning it can tell you when someone has dug a hole then filled it in again." Kismet grinned triumphantly. "This is the magnet that is going to help us find a needle in a haystack."

EIGHT

They were greeted at dawn by a glorious sunrise over Babylon. Their arrival the previous night had been in the waning minutes of daylight, depriving them of a chance to fully appreciate the scope of the ancient city. Drawn as they were to the only source of artificial light, emanating from the magnificent neo-Babylonian palace a short distance from the rebuilt city walls, they had eyes for little else after the brief but nonetheless arduous journey from Baghdad.

They had been spared any hostile encounters on the road, but the absence of trouble did not ease their anxiety. Every bend in the road might have concealed a party of armed paramilitary fighters or highway bandits, and there was absolutely no predicting where land mines might be buried or if even simpler measures, like nearly invisible wires strung across the road to disable their vehicle, might have been employed. Thankfully, the road from Baghdad through Al Hillah was part of a supply line, regularly patrolled by friendly forces, and despite the constant tension, the journey was without incident.

A contingent of US Marines occupied the palace, which despite its resemblance to a massive ziggurat temple was the product of modern workmanship. Unable to resist the urge to step into the shoes of the ancient Babylonian emperor Nebuchadnezzar, whose Hanging Gardens had been one of the seven wonders of the ancient world, Saddam Hussein had devoted massive amounts of money and man hours to rebuilding sections of the ruined city and erecting a palace to rival that of his historic predecessor. And like so many of the grandiose residences the deposed dictator had constructed during his quarter-century in power, it was rumored that he had never actually set foot in the complex.

The Marines greeted them cautiously, but it was evident that word of Kismet's recent misadventures had not reached them. They were permitted to set up temporary lodging with their vehicle just inside the walled compound, safe in the knowledge that armed sentries would be walking the perimeter throughout the night. Chiron woke first, gently rousing the others as the first gleams of light appeared on the horizon, backlighting the object of their quest.

The rebuilding of Babylon, commissioned in 1982, had been a

controversial topic among archaeologists and historians, chiefly because the supreme architect of the project, Saddam himself, elected to build on top of the buried ruins. Newly baked clay bricks were laid on the ancient foundations—in some cases, there was a visible line of demarcation where the older, darker bricks ended and their modern counterparts began—in keeping with the city map as established by Greek and Roman chroniclers who had witnessed the gradual decline of the city. Yet while a great deal of effort had gone into accuracy, there could be no doubting that the reproductions had covered over many centuries' worth of buried relics, which if further excavated might have shed still more light on the civilizations which had occupied the region between the Tigris and Euphrates Rivers.

The modern palace was easily within walking distance of the old city, but Kismet and the others got back into their Land Cruiser and made the short drive to a stunning reproduction of the Ishtar Gate at the north entrance to the city. The actual arched entryway, dedicated to the fertility goddess who appeared in nearly every polytheistic culture, currently resided in a museum in Berlin, but in keeping with the pattern of resurrected splendor, the copy probably conveyed a more accurate impression of the sight that would have greeted a visitor to the city, or perhaps one of Nebuchadnezzar's conquered slaves.

A large map of the city had been posted on the gate, written, curiously enough, in English. Kismet joined the others in staring at the ground plan, and gently took Chiron aside. "So where do we start looking?"

"I'm not really sure," confessed the Frenchman. He gestured to the rebuilt walls. "I was not prepared for all of this."

"There's still an ancient city hidden here. Samir Al-Azir told me that the treasures of Solomon's temple were concealed beneath the Temple of Marduk. I don't imagine even Saddam would risk the wrath of the global Muslim community by rebuilding a temple to a false god, so that's one site that is probably not covered over." He glanced at the map. The ziggurat of Marduk, chief god of ancient Babylon, had been situated at the southern end of the city, near what had at one time been a bridge over the Euphrates and the western entrance. "I hope you brought your walking shoes."

Their heaviest burden was the antenna head for the ground-penetrating radar system. Fortunately, it had been designed to be dragged over dirt and rock, so Kismet had no reservations about using it as a sled upon which to heap the rest of their supplies. He was mildly surprised when Hussein volunteered to pull the cumbersome load. Because he had been mentally prepared to accept every physical task in their expedition, the break from laborious duty came as a welcome if unexpected surprise. He was further caught off guard when Marie approached him during the walk.

"So, Nick Kismet, what is it that we are looking for?"

He gave her a sidelong glance. It was the first time she had addressed him since their departure from Baghdad, and from that moment forward, she had shrunk into the background. To all appearances, Marie Villaneauve was a rose wilting in the desert sun; never complaining, but quite obviously taxed by the harsh environment and the constant threat of violent attack. He did not find her weakness especially endearing. He preferred the company of strong and confident women, and while he did not judge or scorn Marie for her failure to cope with the hardships of their quest, he could not help wondering why she had elected to continue with them.

"I thought Pierre would have filled you in. We're trying to find a site that may have been recently looted."

She managed a wan smile, which somehow accentuated the fact that she had applied lipstick in defiance of the elements. "I know all about that, Nick. But I get the feeling that there is more to all this."

He shrugged. "Not much more. This is about the only option left to us since our contact at the museum was killed."

"And there is nothing more you seek here? I sense that Pierre is searching for something more."

"What do you mean?"

"In the days before our departure, he seemed very anxious to come here—to Babylon. He spoke of it often, and I assisted him with a great deal of scholarly research."

Kismet nodded indifferently. "We know that the artifacts probably originated here. It's no mystery that he would want to do his homework."

"Perhaps." She let her response hang for a moment, then abruptly changed the subject. "You are a hard man to kill, Nick."

The non sequitur blind-sided him and he burst out laughing. "What makes you say that?"

She smiled again, and for a moment, Kismet wondered if her helpless damsel routine wasn't merely for show. "Just an observation. The person you were chasing obviously tried very hard to kill you, as is evident by your wounds. I imagine most people would have given up long before it reached that level of risk."

"Well, I have this nasty habit of not quitting."

"And what of the person you fought with?" she asked. "What if he is similarly resolute?"

"You are thinking he'll put in another appearance?" Kismet chuckled. "I'm almost sure of it. And when that happens, we'll know we're on the right track."

She suddenly stopped walking, placing her hands on her hips. "You would knowingly place us in danger from this killer? We don't even have a single gun with which to defend ourselves."

"Relax. There are about a thousand Marines on the other side of that wall, just waiting for something to shoot. Besides, I don't think this guy wants me dead."

Her mask of umbrage slipped and she resumed walking apace. "Why do you say that?"

"You said that it looked like he tried very hard to kill me. Well, believe me, he had several chances. I suspect this killer may have been trying very hard to *not* kill me."

"I don't understand. Why would a killer not want to kill?"

"That's a very good question," sighed Kismet. "I'll tell you when I figure it out."

Dismayed by his answer, she turned her gaze forward and remained silent as they approached the ruins of the Temple of Marduk.

Saeed was tired—deathly tired. He had been on the move for nearly two days, snatching sleep at rare intervals but always in a seated position: a few hours on the flight to Damascus, a few brief naps during the long overland journey across the Syrian Desert, which were invariably interrupted either by the jarring terrain or the ideological rants of his brother. Thankfully, as the darkness grew, the latter source of irritation had diminished. Intently focused on driving without the aid of headlights, Farid had less to say as he peered into the night.

They had left their vehicle behind a few kilometers from the banks of the Euphrates, and continued on foot, marching toward the dawn and a place of concealment near the water's edge on the western shore. In the marshes near the river, the normally dry desert heat was transformed into an exhausting humidity. Saeed rubbed sweat and tiredness from his eyes, then raised a battered pair of binoculars.

"I see their vehicle," he announced. "We are not too late."

Farid made a spitting noise. "And what are we supposed to do, brother? Take on the US Marines? Even if I had an army to do so, I would not. These Americans will not leave if we attack them; they will simply send more soldiers, in greater numbers."

"I had not thought you so cautious," murmured Saeed. He chose his words carefully. Despite the tenuous bonds of blood relation, he suspected Farid would slit his throat if accused of cowardice.

Farid evidently was not offended. "There is no advantage to open warfare. We protest their presence publicly and conduct small raids to weaken their resolve. It is better to kill one man every day with a hit and run attack or a car bomb, than to launch an outright offensive. Our goal is not to kill their armies here, but to wound the hearts of their leaders in America."

"Well, you need have no fear, my brother." Another veiled insult. "I also have no desire to fight the Marines. For now, I am content to simply watch and see what they discover. If they find nothing, then we will set an ambush for them on the road. But I suspect Kismet will find what he is looking for, and that will take him well away from the safety of US forces."

"Kismet," murmured Farid, thoughtfully. "What a strange name for an infidel. Do you suppose he knows its meaning?"

"I suspect he does." Saeed was annoyed that he had let the name slip. He waited for the inevitable questions.

"It will give me great pleasure to avenge the blood of the faithful men who died at his hands. But I think his death will give you even more satisfaction than I. Why is that, my brother?"

Saeed did not lower the binoculars as he answered. "You are very astute, Farid. This man is an old enemy. Many years ago, he was captured near An Nasiriyah—he was a soldier then—and I was summoned to interrogate him. He escaped before I could learn the truth about his mission, but my investigation continued. It was that encounter that introduced me to the very profitable antiquities trade."

"God is great to give you this opportunity to avenge yourself on a lifelong enemy."

Saeed smiled. His explanation, while truthful, was not the real answer. Nevertheless, it was impossible to refute Farid's sentiment. "Indeed He is, my brother. Indeed He is."

After three hours of dragging the GPR unit across the uneven temple mound, Kismet surrendered the towing harness to Hussein then went to join Chiron in the shade. Kismet had concentrated on the foundations of the structure, which in its heyday had measured over two hundred meters in length. The young Iraqi would now focus on one of the three courtyard areas that surrounded the site. Marie had remained in the sheltered area, observing the tedious search without speaking, and did not stir as he sat down. To all appearances, she was on the verge of collapse, and although the three men in her company had repeatedly exhorted her to drink a copious amount of water, her lethargy continued. Chiron, on the other hand, seemed to be holding up well.

Kismet opened the ruggedized laptop computer, which was linked by a wireless connection to the GPR, and began analyzing the collected data. "Let's see what's under our feet."

The Zond unit consisted of two parts: the radar unit, which consisted of the antenna head and a control box and the computer. The software loaded into the computer was designed to collate the information gathered after walking a search pattern of overlapping lines, and give the illusion of seeing through the rock and soil to whatever lay beneath. To the uninitiated, there appeared to be no corollary between the rainbow colors on the monitor and the ground upon which they stood, but with just a little practice, Kismet was able to differentiate the large solid blocks, buried beneath centuries of dust, from the surrounding soil. The three-dimensional cross section allowed him to isolate certain areas and examine them from several angles. The results of his search, while fairly easy to digest, were less than encouraging.

"What does it mean?" inquired Chiron, sensing his growing frustration.

"That this whole area has been disturbed, and more than once." He pointed to several lighter areas on the display. "I can't tell when this happened. Definitely within the last century or so, and that's our whole margin for error. But the soil density is pretty much uniform. There are some larger objects: cut stone blocks and so forth, but no evidence that someone dropped an exploratory shaft."

"Maybe we're looking in the wrong place?"

Kismet shrugged. "Samir specifically said the artifacts had been located under the Esagila the Temple of Marduk."

Chiron gestured to a high mound in the distance. "Could he have meant the Tower of Babel? Or perhaps a different temple to Marduk?"

"I would be inclined to rule out Babel. The site held no special significance to the Babylonians, and unless he was actively trying to deceive me, Samir would not have made that mistake. As to another temple…" He shrugged again. "We may have to accept that we aren't going to find what we're after. They've had twenty years to completely loot this site. Maybe everything was moved out when they first excavated, and our black marketeers have just been sitting on their trove, saving it for a rainy day."

"Surely you are not ready to admit defeat so quickly?" Chiron's words were rapid and anxious. "This may be the only tangible link to the mystery that has troubled you for more than a decade. You know, Nick… You know that something was found here. You have the word of the man who died revealing this truth, and you have the testimony of your own eyes. You have seen the proof."

"Proof of what, Pierre? Proof of the existence of a historical site that needs UN protection? I think we both know that's not what we're talking about anymore."

The older man glanced quickly toward Marie, looking to see if their sharp words had roused her. She appeared to be sleeping. When he spoke again, his tone had softened. "My apologies. It would seem I find the specter of failure the most haunting ghost of all."

Kismet sighed, almost regretting what he had said, even though both men knew it to be true. "Christ, Pierre. You don't really think you're going to find some piece of rock with the words 'God was here', do you? I know it would make everything better if you could believe that Collette had gone to the Elysian Fields, but you know as well as I do that there isn't a single tangible thing on this planet that can convince you of that if you don't already have faith that it's true."

Chiron shook his head sadly. "You are right, Nick. Even now, as hungry as I am to believe, I cannot bring myself to accept that God can be found."

"Then what in hell are we doing out here in the middle of nowhere?" He meant it as a joke; a way to diffuse the gravity of their discussion, but Chiron was not ready to let it go.

"Nick, do you believe in miracles?"

Kismet considered answering once again with levity, but thought better of it. "If you mean the water-into-wine variety, I guess I'd have to say no."

"And yet so many do believe, and not just in the miracles of Jesus Christ and Moses. There are thousands, perhaps millions, of personal accounts. Everything from healing to the intervention of angels to preserve someone in a time of great danger."

"Faith is a powerful thing…"

He knew from Chiron's smile that he had inadvertently made the very point the old man was arguing. "No doubt you will say that those who believe they have been healed, did so psychosomatically, or perhaps that their maladies were imagined to begin with. Or that the reports are simply fraudulent. And you would probably be right in ninety-nine percent of the cases. But it is the one percent that fascinates me. Does an irrefutable account of a supernatural act establish the existence of the Divine?"

"Irrefutable?" Kismet countered. "That's a pretty tall order."

"Ah, you are right. I have strayed from what I meant to say." Chiron checked Marie's motionless form for any indication that she was stirring, then resumed speaking in a low voice. "Real or not, the world has been shaped by miracles, most outstandingly, those spoken of in the Holy Bible. Moses' ten plagues and the crossing of the Red Sea are images burned into our collective consciousness. More than that, they are the foundation for a system of belief that dominates our thinking four thousand years later. Think about it—more than half the world's population subscribe to one of the three forms of monotheism: Christianity, Islam or Judaism. All three worship the same God and recognize the events described in Genesis as part of true world history. The same could be said for the miracles of Jesus Christ. Without those events, do you imagine that these men would have made such an impact on history?"

Kismet recalled this facet of Chiron's personality—the philosopher. The argument had changed, but the passionate search for truth remained. For his part, the novelty of the debate had worn off. He had never really been that interested in grasping the meaning of life—his personal quest always seemed more immediate—but on warm Paris nights, over brandy and the occasional cigar, philosophical meanderings had their own unique charm. Not so in the swampy heat on the banks of the Euphrates. "So what are you saying? That those miracles had to have been real in order to have such a profound impact?"

"Maybe. Or maybe that they have become real because we need them to be."

Kismet returned a blank look, saying nothing.

"But again I have strayed," Chiron continued. "You mentioned earlier the power of faith. What if it is more than simply a neurotic, individualized response to a passionate moment? What if a person could believe something so strongly, they could actually influence the physical reality of their surroundings?"

"Like telekinesis? I tend to lump parapsychological phenomena in with miracles anyway. You're just substituting psychic power for God. So far, I haven't seen substantial proof for either."

The Frenchman raised a hand. "There is compelling evidence to suggest that psychic power does exist, Nick. I'm not talking about parlor tricks—hypnosis and spoon bending—but simple occurrences of precognition…déjà vu. Have you ever been humming a song, then turned on the radio only to discover that very song being played?"

"Coincidence." Kismet's voice lacked the weight of certainty.

"Perhaps not. We are electrical beings, and what are radio broadcast waves but electrical signals? In any case, I only ask you to hold an open mind on the subject, as it relates to the broader discussion.

"Are you familiar with the precepts of quantum physics? One of the most basic theories is that something becomes real only if it is observed, and that the observer cannot help but influence the outcome by his presence. I'm oversimplifying, but this has been proved on the subatomic level. Now, employing the inverse of the alchemistic method—as below, so above—let's apply this to the visible world. Do we influence our reality simply by experiencing it?"

"Think happy thoughts, is that it?"

"On a small scale, yes. But what about collectively? If enough people believe in something—not just wishful thinking, but ardent acceptance that something is true—does it become so?"

"Or if enough people believe in God, does He become real?" Kismet shook his head. "We could debate this forever and never prove any of it. But we sure as hell aren't going to find the answer under a ton of dirt in the middle of Babylon. Which begs the question, what in God's name are we doing here?"

"Nick, you have jumped ahead of me. I don't know if collective faith in God is enough to will Him into existence, but I have seen compelling evidence to suggest that we humans do influence the physical world, not just with our bodies, but also our minds. We are all broadcasting and receiving, every minute of every day. We exchange a torrent of low frequency electrical energy that once in a while becomes coherent—a precognitive event, a premonition—but it is always there."

Chiron paused to drink from a water bottle, giving Kismet the impression that everything he had posited was merely prelude. The old man did not disappoint. "Now, as you have asked, what does any of this have to do with our activities here?

"You know my heart, Nick. You know that I have long doubted, even in the face of Collette's belief, but it wasn't until her death that I began to desire a definitive answer. I cannot bring myself to accept the divine revelations of her church or any other. Would that I could, for then at least I would know that her belief was not in vain. Yet I realized that I had erred as a scientist by automatically refuting these belief systems. I had applied Occam's Razor to the matter, imagining that if some element of the argument for God failed, the inverse was automatically true. But as Hamlet said, there is more in heaven and on earth than is dreamt of in our philosophy.

"What I am about to tell you is by no means an original concept. It exists in one form or another in many cultures, notably in Taoism, but I arrived at my conclusions quite independently. I have come to believe that our world, perhaps our entire universe, is part of a great organic entity, and that we are its brain cells. Our thoughts and perceptions collectively become the mind of this organism, and this interaction occurs in tandem with the Telluric currents—earth's own electro-magnetic field. Now, like any force of nature—the wind or the sea—we are powerless to control this…this spirit, if you will…but we can harness it and use it to our advantage. That I believe, is what the great miracle workers have done, whether consciously or otherwise."

Kismet offered a conciliatory shrug. "Okay, it's a little wacky, but I'll take that under consideration."

"But you're still wondering: why here and now?" Chiron seemed pleased that Kismet had not dismissed the subject following his revelation, and took a moment to compose himself again before continuing. "Let me tell you another story, one pieced together from papyrus codices discovered in Egypt and presently buried in the UNESCO vaults. It's about an Egyptian high priest named Thutmosis who lived about three thousand five hundred 3,500 years ago. Thutmosis was well-versed in all the mystic arts of the ancients, and by that I mean the chicanery used to convince the general public that gods were real and very much involved in the affairs of men. We imagine that we understand how Egypt's magic-practicing priests used sleight of hand, smoke and mirrors, to deceive the masses, but we don't know the half. These men, of whom Thutmosis was likely the last, were able to tap into the global spirit I have been describing. Now, this was no simple task. There is evidence to support the idea that the pyramids were erected for the sole purpose of channeling these currents of energy. Or it may have been the other way around. Perhaps it was this power—geomancy or earth magic—that enabled them to move the massive blocks that formed those monuments. I suspect it may have been a little of each, but in any case, the foundation for Thutmosis' power was laid millennia before his birth.

"Thutmosis was highly intelligent and very popular among the upper echelons of Egyptian society, but the ruling class and especially the Pharaoh became fearful. To discredit him, they circulated a rumor that he was a foundling, cast up on the shores of the Nile and likely the bastard offspring of slaves. As the rumor began to take on a life of its own, Thutmosis twisted it to his own advantage and began looking for support among that lowest of classes, ultimately fomenting a slave rebellion that shook the ruling dynasty to pieces. But this was no mere popular revolt. Thutmosis convinced the slaves that he was the messenger of a god more powerful than those of the Egyptians, and to prove it he performed fantastic acts of magic such as transforming his staff into a snake or changing water into blood—"

Kismet raised a hand to interrupt. "Okay, I've seen this movie. You're telling me that Moses wasn't a Hebrew, but an Egyptian priest? That's a pretty bold assertion."

"And it would be very inflammatory if revealed today. Now you understand why the ancient records which tell of these things have been suppressed by UNESCO. However, it matters little. Thutmosis, or Moses if you prefer, quickly won the hearts of the slaves. Through a clever combination of magic tricks and actual manipulation of the Telluric currents, he convinced them that an unnamed God had chosen them to be His holy people. As their collective faith grew, so did Moses' power, culminating in a series of fantastic plagues that devastated Egypt.

"As the revolt gained strength however, Moses realized that the framework for this new belief system would not be sustainable if he remained in Egypt. There was too much evidence laying around to expose his secret. Additionally, there remained the possibility that another priest might use the same machinery of magic to overpower him and cast down his new God. Or perhaps he simply got so caught up in the role of demagogue that he lost the ability to distinguish reality; maybe the God he had invented actually began speaking to him. In any event, he decided that his supporters—a new nation of them—should set forth on an expedition to capture the fertile lands of Palestine. This exodus from Egypt culminated in the most fantastic display of his power yet: the parting of the Red Sea.

"Now as you may know, Biblical scholars who can't quite bring themselves to believe in the power of God have opined that a coincidental volcanic eruption on the Greek island of Thera may have cleared the sea floor temporarily, allowing this nation of people a few hours in which to make the crossing. It is a plausible explanation, but a little too convenient...unless Moses himself triggered those geological events in order to part the sea."

Chiron paused and waited for Kismet to weigh in. "Okay, it might have happened that way. I'm familiar with some of the fringe theories about pyramid power and ancient Egyptian science as magic, so I know you're not just making all this up. But what does it have to do with us?"

"If you will for the moment accept that this version of events is more or less true, then ask yourself this question. How did Thutmosis defeat the other priests who were also tapped into the Telluric energies? And how did he sustain his own connection to this power once removed from close proximity to the pyramids?"

Kismet shook his head. "I don't know. In the movie, I think he used a stick."

"The wizard's staff? The magic wand?" Chiron chuckled, but his eyes were serious. "That's exactly how he did it. The Staff of Moses was no mere shepherd's rod. The Midrash Rabbah, an oral argument expounding on the Torah, has a great deal to say about the Staff of Moses. It is said to be made of pure sapphire, weighing hundreds of kilograms—too heavy in fact for a man to lift without God's power. According to Rabbinic tradition, the Staff was given to Adam by God following his expulsion from Paradise, and was passed down through a succession of holy men until it came into the possession of Jethro, one of Pharaoh's advisors, who lived in the land of Midian. Jethro incidentally became Moses' father-in-law. However, I suspect this story was merely a clever invention by Moses himself to conceal the Egyptian origins of the Staff. It is my belief that the Staff was fashioned by Egyptian priests as a key to unlock the energies channeled by the pyramids, and that Moses wrested control of this talisman from them, ultimately turning their greatest weapon against them."

Kismet finally understood. "So that's what we're looking for? Moses' magic stick?"

Chiron raised a hand. "Is it so hard to believe? At some point the Bible stories do begin to agree with recorded history. The people who named themselves Israelites—descendants of Jacob—did conquer Palestine and establish a kingdom that endured until Roman times. More than that, they established a belief system unique in their time—a religion where there existed only one true God. Some factual incident inspired these accounts. I think that classifies it as more than just a bedtime story."

Kismet rubbed the sweat from his eyes, trying to hide his exasperation. Philosophical discussions notwithstanding, he could not escape the fact that Chiron had somehow shanghaied him into a war zone for the sake of a treasure hunt. "What makes you so certain that it ended up here?"

"Ah, there's another story. The Bible does not speak of the disposition of the Staff. In fact, every effort is made in the writings attributed to Moses to minimize its significance. I suspect that he did not want his own acolytes figuring out how to steal the power and seize control, so he couched much of the knowledge inside the rites of the Levitic priesthood. The design of the priestly vestments and the architecture of the holy tent of meeting are consistent with theoretical mechanisms for modulating the earth's magnetic energy. The fabled Ark of the Covenant is perhaps the best example of such a device."

Kismet made a sour face at the reference, but he did not comment.

"In any event, the Staff's fate is unknown. Some traditions hold that Moses placed it inside the Ark. Others believe that it returned to God. One thing is certain, with the passing of Moses, the frequency and magnitude of miracles began to diminish. The Bible tells how Joshua stopped the sun in its tracks and threw down the walls of Jericho, but remember that he was in the company of priests hand-selected by Moses. It is also quite likely that some of these events—stopping the sun, for instance—were embellished to establish Joshua's legitimacy.

"I tend to believe that the Staff remained in the care of those priests, even though they gradually lost touch with the knowledge of how to use it. As the traditions of their new religion deepened and victory in their wars brought an end to the need for uncanny power, the priests forgot how to utilize the awesome resource that lay at their fingertips. In fact, according to the Bible, the Ark was put into storage until the time of King David.

"I believe that David may have commenced the search to relearn the mysteries that Moses brought out of Egypt, handing them down to his son Solomon, who in turn used this newfound wisdom to acquire extraordinary wealth for his nation and to build a permanent structure which, like the pyramids, would channel the earth's energies. Evidently his quest for knowledge offended some of the true believers. The Book of Kings records that Solomon left the God of his forefathers. Doubtless he realized the truth that Moses had so cleverly concealed. God was not a wizened old man in a heavenly abode, but an awesome omnipresent force that could be tapped as one might harness the wind in a sail."

Curious in spite of his skepticism, Kismet volunteered a question. "Are you saying that he found the Staff?"

"Quite likely. Or else he learned how to make one for himself. The alchemists believe that he found or made a 'Key', also sometimes referred to as the Philosopher's Stone, with which, among other things, he could transmute base metals into gold. Since Moses' Staff was a whole crystal of sapphire, no doubt a singular occurrence in nature, I'm inclined to believe that he located that original Staff or was given it by his father. But once again, the knowledge fell into disuse as the next generation, spoiled and self-satisfied, saw no reason to continue the pursuit of wisdom. There are a few noteworthy incidents recorded in the Bible that, if true, would suggest that the power was still there to be used: the miracles of Elijah and Elisha; the defeat of an Assyrian army numbering nearly two hundred thousand. For the most part however, the power and certainly the Staff—or Solomon Key—was once more hidden away. When Nebuchadnezzar successfully overthrew Jerusalem, casting down her walls and carrying everything away as spoil, he no doubt took the Staff and likely the Ark of the Covenant along with all of the other temple treasures.

"I suspect that Nebuchadnezzar might also have been adept in the power of geomancy, but evidently he did not recognize the significance of these items, or perhaps feared to use them, and hid them away in a vault deep beneath the ziggurat temple of the chief Babylonian deity.

"That is where you come into the story, Nick. Whatever it was that Samir Al-Azir showed you twelve years ago, it convinced you that at least the last part of my story is true. And the artifacts that have begun appearing on the world market are identical to the utensils used in Solomon's temple, as described in the Book of Kings. We both know that someone found that vault. Yet the most treasured artifacts have not reappeared on the world scene."

"Has it occurred to you maybe there's another very good reason for that? If even half of what you're suggesting is true, then this is exactly the kind of thing the Prometheus cult would be interested in." Kismet drew in a sharp breath, still wondering if it was time to tell the old man the whole story. He chose his words carefully. "I can tell you this much—at least one of the artifacts you mentioned was taken by Hauser that night."

Chiron's lips moved as if trying to form a word, but no sound was uttered.

"Pierre, I'm sorry to burst your bubble, but there's almost no way that your Staff—or Solomon Key or whatever you want to call it—is still here. If someone had tried to fence it, the Prometheus gang would have pounced on them in about two seconds."

After the impassioned argument, Chiron seemed to deflate a little, but he stood his ground. "But if we could find the vault, at least that would give us a starting point, and perhaps we would find some clue to guide us on our way."

"It's a long shot. Honestly, Pierre, what difference would it make? It's not going to prove your theory, and even if it did, how is that going to… How will it ease your sorrow at losing Collette? I don't think the answer's here, at least not the one you're really looking for."

"So that's it? You're giving up after only a few hours of searching?"

"Pierre…" Kismet sighed, shaking his head in frustration. "If you had been up front about this, I probably would never have even started looking. A magic Staff? We don't belong here, Pierre. It's time to go home."

Chiron opened his mouth as if to continue protesting, but Kismet did not linger. He rose and headed across the ruin to where Hussein was laboring, pausing only long enough to switch the computer off. The brightly colored display abruptly winked into nothingness; a fitting metaphor for Chiron's quest and its abrupt end.

From a window on the fourth story of Saddam Hussein's Babylonian palace, the woman calling herself Dr. Rebecca Gault watched the distant figures from the GHC expedition through a pair of 7 X 50 binoculars. The magnification was not good enough to allow her to pick out facial features at this distance, but it was easy enough to determine the identity of each person.

Rebecca, along with her team, had trailed Kismet and the others from Baghdad, finding overnight lodging in Al Hillah to avoid discovery, and ended their travels in the early hours of morning. They had taken a station in the palace complex, content for now, at least, to simply observe. She had little doubt that the search upon which Kismet had embarked would not be quickly resolved. That was why she found the scene unfolding in the circular view-field of the binoculars so disturbing.

After only a few hours of dragging the ruins, the expedition appeared to be packing up and leaving. When there could not longer be any doubt as to their intent, she lowered the glasses. This was one eventuality they had not anticipated. On an impulse she took out her phone, but paused without entering a numeric sequence.

It wasn't her place to determine their next course of action. Her controller was even more dedicated to the success of their expedition than she. He would know what to do and he would call with the next move. For now, she and her team needed only to stay out of sight. Putting the phone away, she resumed her surveillance.

NINE

Although centuries had passed since her fall, the ancient city of Babylon continued to suffer from what seemed like a divinely sent plague: mosquitoes. The marshy banks of the Euphrates teemed with enormous blood-sucking insects, and as the evening shadows began to cool the bricks of the palace, a great buzzing cloud settled in as well. Because looters had smashed every window in the massive edifice, there remained no overall defense against the swarm. The Marines not actively engaged in their duties sought refuge inside tents, which they had pitched in the interior rooms, or in the closed environs of their vehicles. Insect repellant compounds were effective, but in the face of such a constant attack, it made more sense to simply limit exposure.

Kismet found the small sacrifice of blood preferable to the company of his associates. Since his decision to suspend the survey of the Esagila, Chiron had been alternately contemptuous and desperate, insisting that the truth was there to be found, while Hussein seemed torn between his respect for the old man and the unarguable certainty that Kismet had made the right decision. Marie merely acted irritated that they had endured so much difficulty for no apparent reason, but she at least had not burdened him with reproachful stares. In any case, he was enjoying the seclusion of the open third floor terrace, and as the sky darkened, a slight breeze fluttered across the balcony, driving even the mosquitoes away. Stretching out on the bare marble floor, Kismet closed his eyes and enjoyed the rare moment of peace.

"You made the right decision."

The voice intruding on his solitude belonged to Marie, and while he did not open his eyes or rise to greet her, he could tell by the sound of footsteps that she was alone. "I know," was his simple reply.

Her steps grew louder with her approach and when she stopped, it wasn't difficult to conclude that she had lowered herself to sit beside him. "I have a confession to make. I was eavesdropping this afternoon."

Kismet slowly opened his eyes. For some reason, his heart had begun beating faster.

"There's obviously a great deal more to you then I had first believed, Nick Kismet."

"I wouldn't go that far," he replied, guardedly. "But there are a few things I prefer to keep private."

"Forgive me. I did not mean to intrude. In fact, I only came here to assure you that I am in full agreement with your decision. I heard what Pierre said…what he's looking for. It's crazy. He's put us all in grave danger for the sake of…of a Bible story."

"Pierre is a complicated man. I may not agree with what he's done, but I understand it." He wasn't sure why he felt the need to defend the old man, but the words poured forth unbidden.

"Perhaps. But the Staff of Moses? It's ridiculous."

"Probably."

"Don't tell me you believed him?"

Kismet finally sat up and looked at her. "I don't have all the answers, and I don't believe anyone else does either. But a whole lot of people in the world believe that Moses was a real person, looked a lot like Charlton Heston, and used his stick to part the Red Sea. Who am I to say it didn't happen that way?"

"You know that's not what Pierre was saying."

He thought her argument strange. She wasn't refuting the basic story, but rather Chiron's elaborate interpretation. "No, Pierre believes in a slightly different version of events but either way, his belief that the Staff might be hidden here somewhere is not without merit."

She fixed him with a deliberate stare. "So you do think it's here? Or that it was?"

"I didn't say that either. I don't know."

"I don't understand. If you thought it might yet be found, why did you turn away?"

He frowned, and then jumped to his feet. The pleasant solitude was gone, and suddenly the idea of sitting still was anathema. He paced over to the balustrade and gazed out over the dark river. Directly below was an elaborately tiled courtyard with a large square swimming pool, partially drained since the occupation and overgrown with dark moss so that it now resembled a deliberately built mosquito fen. Kismet worked loose a piece of mortar from between the tiles and flicked it out toward the pool as he answered. "Because it was all wrong. I don't know, maybe I was just mad at Pierre for dragging me out here under false pretenses. I'm no treasure hunter."

She joined him at the railing, standing close enough that their elbows were touching. "But that's not what you said out there. You said that if it had been there, it was almost certainly gone... Wait a minute. I remember now. You said something about a cult of Prometheus? Who are they?"

"Just one more unanswered question. And one of those things I mentioned that I prefer to keep to myself."

"But Pierre knows about it." Her tone was insistent. Her curiosity, now aroused, would not be satisfied with a brush-off. "He used it to get you out here. What's the connection?"

"I don't know. To be perfectly honest, all I know is what you probably overheard. There may or may not be a group of people out there with a particular interest in artifacts with religious significance. I'd like to find them, and there's reason to believe that they may have already discovered what we were looking for." Despite the deepening twilight, Kismet found that he could see the ruins of the temple in the distance off to his left. "Only we couldn't prove it today."

"So if it can't be proved, what does it mean? That this treasure vault doesn't really exist? Or that is was never really discovered?"

"Well, no. All we really determined was that there has been no significant change in the soil around the temple mound to a depth of thirty meters. If the vault exists there, it must be deeper than that. And if Saddam's engineers found it, they must have gone in by a different route—" His fingers abruptly tightened on the railing. "Damn!"

His sudden exclamation caught her off guard and she jumped back a step, breaking the subtle physical contact. "I'm sorry—"

He shook his head, self-deprecatorily. "I can't believe I didn't see it."

"What? What are you talking about?"

He drew in a deep breath, willing himself to relax. "I first learned about this from a man who was involved in the project to rebuild the old city. He claimed to have been there when a discovery was made at the Marduk temple. But there hasn't been any work done there."

"So he lied?"

Kismet shook his head. "No. Don't you see? He wasn't working on the temple site at all when he made his discovery. He was doing something else…some kind of excavation that inadvertently uncovered the vault. It had to have been deep, because we didn't detect any sort of cavity, but somewhere under that ruin is a tunnel leading to a secret chamber underneath the Esagila."

"Then where's the entrance?"

"That's what we have to figure out. We assumed that after the discovery, the engineers simply filled in the hole, but if the discovery of the vault was incidental, then the excavation was an end in itself."

Marie blinked uncomprehending. "What end?"

"We'll know that when we find the entrance." He peered once more into the darkness, as if doing so might reveal what hours of patient surveying had not. "It would have to be very well hidden. The UNMOVIC team scoured this place for underground bunkers and buried weapons caches."

"Could he have used the rebuilt ruins to conceal the excavation?"

"Maybe, but that wouldn't really permit free access to the tunnel." Kismet shook his head, as if to clear away cobwebs. "Let's try to think about this logically. We know there's a tunnel down there. We know that it runs under the ruins of the temple and that it's very deep. We also know that Saddam managed to build it in complete secrecy and a thorough search of the area didn't uncover it. So, where didn't the UN inspectors look?"

"In the river?" Marie ventured.

Kismet's gaze involuntarily swung toward the ribbon of water passing below their vantage. "I don't know. This whole country has been under satellite surveillance for most of the last decade. I doubt an undertaking on that scale would have gone unnoticed. Still, you may have something there. The inspectors probably wouldn't have looked in submerged areas, so water would be an excellent camouflage…"

As his words trailed off, they both looked down at the courtyard three stories below. The square basin of the swimming pool was a shadowy void in the ornate terrazzo floor. Marie spoke first. "Surely not."

"Only one way to find out." Kismet spun on his heel and raced into the palace.

He had no difficulty navigating the corridors back to the ornate stairway and quickly descended to the main floor. He could hear Marie's footsteps tapping out a rhythm but no one else seemed to be moving in the main hall of the palace. She caught up with him a few moments later as a shortage of choices forced him to rein in his eagerness.

"What's wrong?" she asked as she reached his side.

"That pool was just off this wall, right?" He gestured toward a broad expanse, decorated with antique swords and a gaudy mural which looked as though it might have been inspired by a pulp fantasy novel from the 1920s.

"I think so." She glanced back up the stairs to see if the descent had somehow turned them around. "Yes, that's where it is."

"Well, it looks like we can't get there from here."

Her gaze swung back to the wall and she instantly understood. Its entire breadth was solid. There were no doors or windows to the outside. "Perhaps you have to go through one of the adjoining rooms."

"I don't think so." The apparent setback had not blunted his enthusiasm. "Something tells me that we're not supposed to be able to find that pool."

"I'm not sure I follow you."

"It's like a secret room. From the outside, say with satellite reconnaissance or a flyby, you would see an ordinary swimming pool. Nothing too suspicious about that. But there's always a chance that a closer inspection will reveal its true purpose, so it was designed to be inaccessible from within the palace. My guess is that we'll have the same trouble outside. I'd even bet that it doesn't appear on the floor plan."

"So how do we reach it?"

He scratched his chin thoughtfully. "Well, there has to be some way to get to it, but I'm in favor of the direct approach."

"Which is?"

He flashed a grin, then headed back up the stairs, returning to the balcony. In the moments since their departure, the night sky had deepened to the extent that the floor of the courtyard below was no longer clearly discernible. He nevertheless peered down into the darkness, leaning out over the balustrade to get a better look at what lay directly below. After a moment, he turned to Marie. "I'll be right back."

Without further explanation, he climbed up onto the stone railing and lowered himself out into the open. His initial moment of bravado faltered as the gravity of the situation quite literally asserted itself, but he forced away the instinctive reaction and surrendered himself to the drop. By first dangling from the lip of the balcony, he was able to reduce the distance between his feet and the terrace below to just over four meters. At nearly twice his own height, it was not an insignificant distance. The drop he had taken from a similar overlook at the museum had been only three meters and the landing surface had been softer, if somewhat thornier. Still, that leap had been in extremis, whereas this occasion allowed for a more cautious approach. Steeling his courage, he let go.

He flexed his knees before landing and threw himself forward into a roll as soon as his feet made contact. A twinge of pain shot through his lower extremities, followed by a more pronounced hurt in his shoulder as he slammed onto the hard tile surface. Mindful that he was being observed—and by a woman for whom he could not deny a certain attraction—he jumped to his feet, disdaining the multiple aches that were starting to flare up all over his battered body.

"Are you okay?" Marie whispered her question, although there seemed to be no reason for stealth.

"Piece of cake," he called back.

"Should I come down?"

Something about the question struck him as odd. His brief experience in Marie's company had not conveyed the impression of a woman who embraced difficulty. After a day of languishing in the semi-tropical environment that pervaded the ruins, her sudden interest struck him as out of character. She now seemed almost eager to jump off the balcony into the darkness. "No," he answered, certain his concerns were unfounded. "Wait up there for me. I won't be a minute, and besides, I might need your help to get out of here."

The slick terrazzo mosaic reflected gleams of moonlight, but not enough to show any detail. To better investigate the courtyard, Kismet took out his MagLite and pierced the veil of darkness. His earlier assumption, namely that the pool area was completely isolated from the house, was quickly proved correct. There were several faux windows lining the wall that bordered the courtyard, but a close inspection showed bare masonry under the dark glass. He continued along the perimeter of the pool deck, looking for other points of egress. A three-meter-high wall, topped with wrought-iron spears, surrounded the pool on the remaining three sides, but on one corner near the palace, the wall was interrupted by an arched gateway. An iron barrier, like a portcullis, stretched across the opening and was secured by a heavy chain and padlock.

"I guess he didn't want anyone crashing his pool parties," called Kismet, quickly detailing the results of his initial survey. "I'm going to check out the pool now."

He played his light toward the murky reservoir. It was impossible to distinguish the bottom through the accumulation of moss and algae, but given the relative smallness of the square basin, Kismet concluded that it was probably no more than two meters deep and currently half-filled. The muck covering the surface offered no further clue as to how the pool might conceal an entrance to his hypothetical tunnel, but the smooth walls, though discolored, caught his eye. Unlike the ornate mosaic work on the pool deck, the vertical concrete faces were strictly utilitarian, finished only with a coat of white sealant, now almost uniformly stained by rings of dead algae and numerous irregular dark streaks that looked curiously like tire skid marks. The pool's period of disrepair seemed to go back further than the start of hostilities.

Kismet noted that the corners were set at right angles. Most swimming pools utilized rounded corners with smooth seamless joints. It stood to reason that the bottom of the pool was likewise squared at the corners and Kismet tried to draw a mental picture of what it might look like when empty. He was now certain that the swimming pool concealed the entrance to a subterranean passageway, but there remained one more crucial piece of the puzzle: a means of opening that secret door.

Stepping away from the edge, he returned the beam to the outer perimeter and began scrutinizing the walls and the false windows for some sort of control mechanism, but nothing seemed out of the ordinary. He was not overly disturbed by the lack of discovery; the efforts at concealing the doorway would have been poorly served if the doorknob were so obvious to spot.

Marie seemed to understand what he was looking for. "Perhaps it uses a remote control unit, like a garage door opener."

He pondered the suggestion. "Think about this from their point of view. Radio signals can be detected and intercepted. For that matter, any kind of electrically operated system would be detectable.

They would have tried to eliminate any elements that might attract unwanted attention."

"What does that leave us?"

"A simple mechanical system." He glanced back at the pool. "Or hydraulics."

Although he had looked past them several times, the four decorative statues guarding the corners of the basin seized his attention. The life-sized stone carvings—two lions and two water buffalo—were incongruous with the general decor of the area. Though it was easy to dismiss their presence as one more example of Saddam's eclectic sense of style, Kismet decided to take a closer look.

The nearest lion's torso straddled a single stone tile, roughly two meters in length. The rectangular surface appeared to have been laid as a pedestal for the sculpture, but none of the lion's feet were touching it. Kismet knelt and shined his light around the edges of the tile and found that the slab was not held in place by mortar. Inspired by this discovery, he set down the flashlight and used both hands to give the statue a shove.

With surprisingly little resistance, the stone lion moved. Like the slab it guarded, the statue was not anchored in place. Kismet pushed from different angles until all four of the figure's feet were on the rectangular tile.

Nothing happened.

"We're missing something," he declared after a moment of waiting. "But I think we're on the right track."

"What makes you think that?" asked Marie from the darkness above.

"This lion has Teflon pads under its feet. It was designed to be moved around without damaging the tile beneath. I think the four statues are counter-weights. If I can figure out the correct sequence, it should open the door."

"But where is the door?"

"It's in the pool...under the water." He briefly illuminated the other statues, lingering on the horned likenesses of the water buffalo. "Could it be that simple?"

He returned the lion to its original position, then moved to the next sculpted figure, a representation of the domesticated river bovine once common in the marshes of southern Mesopotamia before dam construction dried up the swamps. Kismet was not surprised to see that the buffalo's feet were already positioned on a similar stone tile. After a moment's exertion, he shifted the statue away from the slab.

From deep beneath his feet, there was a groaning noise and a faint tremor. The rectangular stone seemed to waver in the beam of his flashlight, but there was no dramatic movement and after a few seconds the noise from below ceased. Encouraged nonetheless, Kismet crossed to the opposite corner where the remaining water buffalo was stationed, and likewise pushed it from its perch.

The groaning resumed instantly, followed a moment later by the sound of rushing water. Kismet checked the level of the pool and was not surprised to see that it had been completely drained in a matter of seconds. As the last few drops vanished into drains located along the perimeter of the pool bottom, the groaning noise changed into the scrape of stone sliding against stone. The stone on which the water buffalo statues now stood abruptly rose into the air, revealing that the slabs were merely the caps to twin pillars of concrete. As the columns rose from the deck, the bottom of the pool rose also. Movement ceased only when it drew level with the edge of the pool.

"It's a hydraulic lift," declared Kismet, a hint of amazement creeping into his voice. "They built an elevator in the swimming pool."

"An elevator to what?" inquired Marie. "How do you make it go back down?"

"I'm betting it's as simple as moving the lion statues onto the trigger tiles." He moved to test this theory.

"You didn't answer my first question," she complained. "Where does it go?"

He tried to answer in between grunts of exertion as he moved the statues. "To our mysterious tunnel. Whoever built this made it big enough to handle a truck. My guess is that it was supposed to be some kind of bunker; a last redoubt, designed to hide the remnants of the high command, along with a representative number of vehicles and tanks, until the immediate threat had passed."

"We're more than a kilometer from the temple ruin. Are you saying the tunnel is that extensive?"

"I guess it would have to be." He gave the last remaining lion a final push, and as the legs of the sculpted feline came to rest on the stone, the supporting slab began to sink. At the same time, the pool deck fell away, sliding back down to its original position. The pedestals for the water buffalo statues also receded into the pool deck, but stopped as soon as they were flush with the mosaic surface. The pool bottom kept going.

In the beam of the MagLite, Kismet could distinguish the catch basins in the walls to which the pool water had been shunted. Doubtless, the architect had designed the pool to be emptied or refilled on a moment's notice. He found himself once more in awe of the engineering achievement.

The descent of the surreptitious elevator continued unchecked, dropping to a depth of ten fathoms—nearly twenty meters—into the darkness below. The shaft had been reinforced with concrete, maintaining the illusion of a swimming pool, albeit one that was ridiculously deep. When it finally stopped, Kismet could not tell if there was a means of continuing on.

He walked back to stand below Marie on the balcony. "I'm going to play with this for a minute to see if I can bring it back up. Go get Pierre and tell him what we found."

"You're not thinking of going in tonight, are you?"

"Why not? It's time something went our way for a change." As she turned away, he remembered one more thing. "And bring a rope!"

Marie hastened away, oblivious to the human form concealed in the shadows that had listened to every word of their conversation.

Saeed and his brother had remained concealed until well after the fall of night, long after Kismet and the others had withdrawn from the temple site. The hasty retreat was disturbing, for while he knew that the UNESCO team would find nothing of consequence in the ruins, he had expected them to invest several days, perhaps even weeks, before admitting defeat. The swiftness with which they concluded their operation made him wonder what Kismet had discovered, but he dared not contact his informant for fear of exposing her presence. So, he and Farid waited in the sweltering heat as the sun finished its journey across the sky.

They had only begun the trek back to Farid's vehicle when the satellite phone receiver trilled, signaling the call he had been so eagerly awaiting. He answered immediately. "Yes?"

"Our mutual friend is very efficient. He has discovered untapped reservoirs of ingenuity."

The double-speak wasn't too hard to unriddle. 'Reservoir' surely referred to the hidden lift in the swimming pool. Saeed had known of it since its creation, but he was one of a privileged few. That Kismet had so quickly located it verged on the miraculous. "I understand. When you follow him in his voyage of discovery, we will no longer be able to communicate in this way. However, I will meet you along the way."

"You know of another way in?"

"I do. But that need not concern you. Do nothing to arouse suspicion. This matter will soon be resolved." He ended the conversation with typical abruptness then turned to Farid. "Kismet has found the tunnel entrance."

"What? You mean it is inside the palace?"

"Fear not, my brother. That is but one entrance of many. When he begins to comprehend what he has found, he will make his way to the ultimate destination. That is where we will meet him. Now it is time to gather your men. We have a long journey ahead of us."

As the concealed elevator bearing Nick Kismet and his companions slowly receded into the unseen depths, Rebecca emerged from her hiding place. Her simple civilian attire had been replaced by a utilitarian black combat uniform and her mane of fiery copper was concealed beneath a matching knit watch cap. Almost invisible against her dark clothing was a compact Steyr TMP machine-pistol.

She moved stealthily to the balcony rail, unsure of how long it would take to remove the descending group from her line of sight. She risked a quick look, ducking back before her brain could completely process the information gathered by her eyes. Her caution was unnecessary. Kismet and the others were nowhere to be seen. She raised a hand from her weapon and made a "come along" gesture.

Immediately, seven similarly clad figures stepped from various hiding places and wordlessly moved to join her. One man drew to within a few centimeters of her face in order to hear her whispered orders. "Chance and Jacques will stay here to guard our rear and maintain contact with our recovery team."

The man nodded then moved back to relay the orders in a whisper while Rebecca climbed over the railing. Kismet's group had left behind a fixed rope which, under his guidance, each person had used to rappel down to the pool deck three stories below. She had watched with great interest as Kismet coaxed and cajoled the reluctant woman and the older Chiron, eventually convincing them of the inherent safety in what he was asking them to do. Rebecca now coiled several lengths of that same rope around her torso, then effortlessly abseilled down to the terrazzo surface below.

There was a faint grating sound emanating from the depths of the shaft. The platform was still making its ponderous descent. Rebecca stayed well away from the edge until the vibrations ceased, and then held back a few minutes more. She had been told that the objective was not immediately accessible from the shaft, so there was no harm in allowing their quarry to get a head start. Better that than to reveal their own presence by activating the noisy lift.

The remaining members of her team descended in order, joining her on the pool deck. In a subdued voice, she directed each of them to stand beside the statues and wait for her cue to begin the complicated sequence of shuffling that would bring the lift back to the surface. She had surreptitiously observed Kismet's experiments with the sculpted animals, noting the exact pattern of movements required to raise or lower the device.

One of the men made a faint tisking noise to get her attention. She could see that he was holding something, but in the darkness it was impossible to discern what the object was. She moved closer to get a better look.

It was a crude sign—a permanent ink marker on a sheet of paper—with a brief message. Her first impulse was to believe that Kismet had somehow become aware of her presence and left the message behind to mock her. She read the words a second time:

"Gone after the White Rabbit. Back soon! Alice and the gang."

The message was in English, flippant in tone, but vague. Kismet's handiwork, she reckoned, but not for her eyes. Doubtless, he expected the Marines to find his ropes and the blank hole where the swimming pool had been, and had left the message as a clever way of letting them know who it was that uncovered this mystery. She crumpled the sign in her fist and stuffed it into one of her deep cargo pockets.

Exactly five minutes after the elevator platform completed its descent, she gave the signal for her men to begin moving the statues.

As soon as the pool bottom was level with the deck, she and five selected members of the team moved out onto the concrete slab. The remaining men—Jacques and Chance—shifted the lion statues into place and commenced yet another drop into the dark shaft. One of the men began unspooling a thin antenna wire that would serve as their communications link to the surface.

Rebecca watched as the gossamer strand paid out in generous curlicues overhead. As the walls began to rise up on all sides, the implications of what she and her team were doing finally hit home. The smooth concrete shaft resembled nothing less than a tomb, and while she would never reveal even a hint of the trepidation she now felt to her subordinates, she was keenly aware that their lives hung by that single thread-like strand of metal.

Pure, unrefined darkness swelled around them and still they descended. When they finally stopped, it took a supreme effort of will to take that blind step away from the platform. She took out a flashlight, capped with a red lens, and shined it up the shaft, signaling for their comrades to return the elevator to its original state, effectively sealing them in.

As the platform removed their final link with the world above, her fingers unconsciously found the crumpled page in her pocket. She once more curled her fist around the message and decided that Kismet had gotten it all wrong. This wasn't a magical doorway into Wonderland. More apropos would have been the words of Orpheus.

Abandon all hope, ye who enter here...

The inscription above the gates of Hell.

The darkness swallowed them whole. Kismet's MagLite was insignificant against the overwhelming totality of the subterranean night. There was a larger lantern in the supplies Hussein had packed, but it seemed pointless to use up that resource when there was nothing in particular to look at. They had settled instead for yellow Cyalume sticks—plastic tubes filled with a phosphorescent substance that would shine for hours once activated. The chemical light source did not afford much in the way of illumination, but was useful for keeping the group together.

From his position at the front of the line, Kismet could not see the handheld light sticks, but he could hear the distinctive sounds of his companions' footsteps. In the absence of visual cues, he was soon able to distinguish the differing styles of footwear and the particular rhythms of each person's stride. The tapping of their feet on stone was the only sound in the dark womb of the earth; hardly a word had been spoken since their arrival.

The tunnel began immediately at the bottom of the shaft and cut due east through the bedrock at a gentle slope. Compared to the claustrophobic confines of most caverns and mine shafts, the passage through the rock was immense, rising several stories overhead to a smooth arched ceiling. With the exception of an occasional buttress to reinforce the walls or roof, the tunnel was unremarkably uniform. It was a long hallway stretching on indefinitely without doors or junctions. As Kismet had earlier suggested, the corridor was easily large enough to accommodate a military vehicle. He surmised that most of those who found their way to this place made the journey with the assistance of motorized transport.

The slope of the tunnel soon leveled out. Kismet was keeping a careful pace count, reconciling the distance traveled in the subterranean passage with the actual separation between the palace and the temple ruins. There was no question that the tunnel's vector would intersect that point, and he had little doubt that they would find the treasure vault when they reached that critical junction. Despite his earlier dismissal of Chiron's agenda, there was no denying the excitement he felt as he pushed forward.

"We're getting close," he said, breaking the unintentional silence. His words echoed hollowly, ricocheting indefinitely from one wall to the other. The effect was anything but reassuring. To counter the ominous cloud of dread, he turned his flashlight beam against the walls, scanning for any irregularities. As diligent as he was in his search, he almost missed the opening.

The architects of the passage had used crushed rock from the excavation to plaster over a semicircular section of wall, rising from the floor to just above Kismet's knees. There was only a faint seam delineating the patch from solid rock and an almost indistinguishable color difference. He knelt beside the cemented wall and probed it with his fingertips.

"This is it," he said, unable to hide the eagerness in his tone.

Rather than wait for Hussein to sort through the gear for an excavating tool, he drew his *kukri* and used its iron-capped pommel to hammer at the facade. The rest of the group crowded around, barely giving him room to swing. He passed his light to Marie and resumed the assault with both hands.

The improvised plaster crumbled after only a few blows, revealing a web of chicken wire. Pieces of the patch dropped through into the void beyond and rattled against a solid surface almost instantaneously. He banged the knife hilt against it a few more times, then used his feet to smash through the mesh. The entire facade vanished into the darkness beyond.

Kismet tossed his chem-light into the opening and followed its journey with his eyes. The glowing stick dropped a few meters, illuminating a series of perfectly parallel lines for only an instant before rebounding and disappearing from view. He took back his flashlight then cautiously poked his head through the hole. There was a faint odor underneath the generic mustiness that pervaded the tunnel. It was a repugnant smell but diluted to the point that it was impossible to identify. He wrinkled his nose, then pulled back from the opening.

"It's a stairway," he reported. "It looks like they just barely intersected it during the excavation. If they had deviated by a few degrees, they would have missed it altogether."

"Where does it go?" Chiron asked.

"Up and down. Beyond that, who can say? The treads are carved from solid rock and don't show any wear whatsoever. If this is an ancient tunnel, then it was hardly ever used."

"We must be over a hundred meters below the surface." Marie now added her voice to the chorus. "I can't believe the Babylonians would have dug so deep."

"The ruins of the city also lie beneath the surface," Hussein supplied. "Perhaps it was not so far for them to dig."

"I think we also need to consider what it was that Nebuchadnezzar sought to conceal." Chiron's comment must have seemed cryptic to the young Iraqi, but Kismet understood and agreed.

"It would have been an ambitious project, but we're talking about the architect of the Hanging Gardens. And Nebuchadnezzar certainly had the resources to pull it off. Ruthless dictators never have a shortage of cheap labor."

Hussein nodded gravely, but did not comment.

"So it is your belief that this stairway ascends to the Esagila,"

Marie persisted. "Why then did we not find the other end of it when we searched the ruins?"

"Judging by the condition of those stairs, I'd say that the shaft was sealed up during the time of Nebuchadnezzar himself. He must have piled enough rock on top of the opening to keep it hidden through thousands of years of looting."

"And archaeology," added Hussein with a grin.

"Never mind where it goes up," Chiron interjected. "What we want lies in the other direction."

"For once, I can't fault your logic." Kismet stuck his head and shoulders through once more. "It's a little bit of a drop. Do we have any more rope?"

"We left all of it tied to the balcony," Hussein answered guiltily.

"A fine bunch of Boy Scouts we'd make." His quip earned only blank stares and he thought better of elaborating. "Well, if somebody stays behind to pull us back, we can probably boost one another high enough to reach this opening. The last one down is going have to jump pretty high."

Hussein's expression fell as he realized that he would be the one to remain while the others pushed deeper into the unknown, but he nevertheless volunteered to serve as the anchor. "Perhaps you will find a ladder down there, so I can join you," he offered with a weak smile.

Kismet gave him a nod of gratitude. "How about you, Pierre? Want to sit out this round of rugged adventure and daring acrobatics?"

The Frenchman's face revealed his inner turmoil, but his answer was unequivocal. "I have not come so far to be turned aside at the very threshold of discovery."

"I was afraid of that," Kismet murmured. He repositioned so that he could enter the portal feet first in a reverse belly-crawl. "I'll wait below to help you through."

As his thighs scraped over the rough edge, he felt the familiar sensation of losing control. With his legs dangling over nothingness—worse, dangling into the darkness of an ancient crypt underneath millions of tons of earth—he felt the urge to scramble for a safer position. It was an instinctual response and easy enough to sublimate. Nevertheless, as his torso slid deeper into the hole, his anxiety increased proportionately until at last, he was dangling above the stairway, secured only by his fingertips on the flat surface to the tunnel floor.

Marie leaned in and illuminated the stairwell with Kismet's flashlight. It would be a tricky drop. The stairs were uniform, but the treads were shallow, providing only about a hand's breadth of surface upon which to light. Even the slightest deviation might cause him to pitch headlong down the stairwell.

To compensate, Kismet kicked his legs, working up to a gentle pendulum motion, and at the optimum moment he let go. The momentum of his swing carried his body up the stairs, and even though his feet slipped uncertainly on the short steps, his controlled fall was less painful than a chaotic slide into the depths.

The rotten smell was stronger now that he was fully immersed in the environment, and he saw the first evidence that the original unsealing of the ancient vault had exposed it to contemporary vermin. A fine layer of dust covered the stairs along with heaps of rodent excrement, petrified with the passage of time. He quickly brushed off and shouted for Marie to descend.

The petite Frenchwoman eased through the opening and the dim artificial light from above was momentarily eclipsed by her body. Kismet felt another wave of irrational fear as darkness enveloped him, but he shook it off. As her feet dropped toward him, he hugged her legs to his chest, relieving the strain from her arms. "I've got you. Let go slowly and I'll do the rest."

She hesitated for only a moment before Kismet felt her weight shift fully against his body. It was then a simple thing to deposit her on the step beside him. She gazed back up at the illuminated opening and shook her head in despair. "Are you certain we can get back up there?"

"Piece of cake," he replied, with more conviction than he felt, then turned his attention to the hole as well. "All right, Pierre. Your turn."

Chiron's approach was predictably more tentative. Kismet could hear Hussein patiently explaining how he ought to position himself, but the Frenchman seemed bent on scooting through the hole from a seated position. His focus on the older man's plight prevented him from hearing Marie's soft footsteps as she commenced descending, but when he reached up to take hold of Chiron's ankles he caught the subtle movement in the corner of his eye.

"Marie!"

His shout caught her by surprise and she turned to face him with a guilty expression. Her chagrin turned to surprise and horror however as she lost her balance and wavered backward over the decline. Forgetting Chiron, Kismet impulsively reached out for her frantically waving hands, but his fingers closed on nothing. Marie gave a shriek and tumbled down the stairs.

TEN

Kismet dashed after her, shouting her name, but the steps were so steep that he could not match the runaway rate of her fall. She vanished into the darkness before he could take three strides, and each subsequent foot forward dropped him deeper into the absolute subterranean night.

Marie's cries of surprise were quickly replaced by less strident grunts of pain, which punctuated the thudding of her body against the stone. These noises were abruptly replaced by a sound like the breaking of tree branches. *Or bones*, thought Kismet.

"Marie?"

There was a low groan then the sound repeated. "I'm all right," she finally said, with far less misery than he would have expected. "I've landed in something...I'm not sure what it is."

"I'll be right there." He backtracked to the opening, where Chiron was scrambling out of the opening, and called for Hussein to throw down the flashlight. Thus armed, he stabbed the beam of light into the depths and charged after his fallen companion. Yet while he was bracing himself for the discovery of Marie's broken form at the end of the flight, he was completely unprepared for the sight that awaited him at the bottom of the stairwell.

His initial impression was of zebra stripes: a haphazard pattern of light and dark which either reflected his light at oblique angles or swallowed it whole. Yet there was no mistaking the unique spherical shapes, each uniformly marked by a pair of smaller craters, that were scattered throughout the endless web of shadows: human skulls.

Marie's fall and subsequent movements had left her partially submerged in the skeletal sea. As her eyes focused on the area revealed by Kismet's light, she lost any semblance of control. However, her hysterical attempt to flee only shifted the interlocking puzzle of bones, opening a chasm that drew her deeper into the charnel embrace.

The bones were everywhere, stripped clean of flesh and gleaming white. Beyond the area where Marie had landed, the arrangement was more orderly. The corpses had been stacked in tight rows and heaped several layers deep. The descending stairs continued out into the midst of the vaulted ossuary, completely obscuring the floor.

"Hold still!" shouted Kismet, wading into the jumble. At the first crunch of bone beneath his boots, he felt an otherworldly chill; there were unhappy ghosts here.

He tried to think of it like quicksand. It was certainly swallowing Marie down like a quagmire and her frantic thrashing was only exacerbating the situation. He shouted another unheeded exhortation for her to be still, then cautiously stretched himself horizontally over the skeletal bed. For a moment, the bones shifted beneath his weight, opening a rift to snare him, and he could feel thousands of fleshless fingers closing around him to pull him under. The urge to break free and scramble to safety was almost overwhelming, but he forced himself to remain motionless, with his arms and legs spread-eagled. Despite the initial settling, the bony lattice bore his weight. Buoyed by the minor success, he began rolling with deliberate slowness toward her.

Though her panic had left her deeply mired in the ossuary, Marie had regained a degree of self-control. She continued trying to extricate herself, but with more deliberation and less hysterics. When Kismet was close enough to extend a hand, she simply took hold without succumbing to the drowning victim's impulse to drag her rescuer under.

"Good." He tried to inject a note of optimism into his tone. "Now, carefully pull yourself toward me. Focus on trying to stretch yourself out. It's just like swimming."

She gave a nod then cautiously brought her other hand up to grasp his wrist. The skeletons beneath him shifted again and he felt Marie's grip tighten as both of them settled deeper. Neither of them moved, patiently hoping the network would stabilize before swallowing them completely, and after a moment it did.

"Okay, let's try that again." Kismet could barely get the words out. Trepidation and exertion had conspired to rob him of his breath and left his throat so tight that his voice had to struggle to reach his lips.

Marie resumed pulling and this time the bones merely groaned in annoyance. She released her grip on his hand and extended incrementally up his forearm. In this fashion, she worked her way toward him, hand over hand as if climbing a rope. She managed to draw her torso up from the embrace of the long since departed occupants of the chamber and lay flat atop the surface, until only her legs remained caught in the snare.

She was close enough now to grasp his shoulder and her fingers knotted in the fabric of his shirt. He nodded encouragingly. "Good. I'm going to start rolling back toward the stairs. Do the same, but don't let go."

He waited for an affirmative reply then slowly twisted away from her. As his right cheek lighted on the irregular surface, he spied a subtle movement in the shadows. A careful turn of his wrist pointed the flashlight that way and Kismet realized with a start that he and Marie were not the only living creatures in the mass tomb. A shiny black scorpion, as long as his hand, was silently stalking them.

"Marie, don't move a muscle." He tried to keep the panic out of his voice, but there was a faint quaver in his undertone.

Marie did not ask for more information, but as the venomous arachnid drew closer, she began to utter a low wail. The tip of the scorpion's tail, pregnant with a toxin that could paralyze or even kill, wavered in her direction. Kismet grimaced, but with the creature's attention thus diverted, he saw his opening. Using the small flashlight like a club, he struck the scorpion a glancing blow that launched it several meters across the bone pile.

"Nick!" Marie's voice was growing frantic again.

"It's okay. There was a scorpion, but I took care of it."

"It?" Her voice was incredulous. "What about them?"

He gingerly raised his head and peered over her supine form. In the broad circle of illumination cast by his MagLite, he saw the reason for her anxiety. An army of vermin was emerging from the bones, swarming toward them with a collective goal. There were more scorpions in their midst, along with enormous cockroaches, centipedes and dozens of other scavenger and predatory insect species.

It was easy to imagine what had happened. Once upon a time, when the bones had belonged to recently deceased slaves and prisoners, a few insects had found their way into the chamber. Trapped though they were, there was a seemingly endless feast of flesh, sustaining not only the insect and arachnid populations, but likely larger vermin such as mice and rats. The supply was not infinite however, as food began to dwindle in the closed environment, its denizens adapted to a new diet, devouring one another as occasion arose. No doubt, the scorpion's deadly sting had moved it to the top of the food chain, but now that fresh meat had been delivered, there was no longer reason for anyone to go hungry.

Kismet turned back to roll the remaining distance to safety, then froze. Dozens more insects, spiders and scorpions had materialized and were relentlessly advancing from every direction. Before he could even begin to think about a way of hastily quitting the tomb, he espied movement on his own person. An enormous black scorpion had emerged from a nearby cavity and made its way stealthily onto his trouser leg. He could just make out its shiny carapace and the curl of its venomous tail as it scuttled along his thigh, moving higher in search of a place to plant its sting. Then he felt something tickling the back of his hand.

He flicked his eyes downward and saw a second multi-appendaged creature meticulously working its way toward the glowing lens of the MagLite. The scorpion's pincer feet were lightly gripping the skin of his hand, securing itself with each step forward.

Kismet's familiarity with the scuttling crab-like creature was limited. The only thing he was certain about was that he didn't want them crawling all over him. He knew that not all members of the animal kingdom relied upon sight to stalk and locate prey. Some used sound, smell or even the ability to detect changes in body temperature. He did not even know if the stings of this particular species would prove fatal, but only that he didn't want to find out.

There was another tickle in his hair and he barely restrained himself from reaching up to scratch the sudden itch. It occurred to him that the scorpions might have been drawn to motion, in which case the heaving of his chest as he fought to control the adrenaline coursing through his veins was like a brass band announcing his presence. He carefully sucked in another deep breath, holding it so that no movement would betray him. His heart continued to pound against the walls of his chest cavity, but slowed in response to his cautious breathing. The scorpion continued meandering along his scalp and onto his forehead.

In spite of the chill in the subterranean air, Kismet could feel perspiration leak from his pores, pooling wherever the scorpion gripped his skin. The creature stopped abruptly as if curious about this subtle change in its environment, or perhaps sensitive to the pheromones of panic that his body was pumping out in each drop of sweat. Its tail curled and flexed slowly over his left eye, and despite a furious impulse to blink, Kismet remained motionless. The scorpion on his hand meanwhile settled near the end of the flashlight, drawn to the unfamiliar warmth and light, but at the same time tentative in its approach, while the one on his leg continued its journey seemingly unaware of the living body upon which it traveled.

His foot twitched as the urge to flee overcame his intentional paralysis. The nearest arachnid paused as it detected the movement then quickly reversed, intent upon confronting this new prey. With surprising speed, it darted along the seam of his pant leg and gripped the sole of his boot with its front pinchers. Even through the thick leather, Kismet could feel the repeated thrusts of the stinger against his foot. Acting on an impulse, he brought his feet together in an abrupt, violent motion, to grind the creature beneath his heel. There was a satisfying crunch as the black exoskeleton was crushed, ending the attack.

He felt the grip of the scorpion on his face tighten as it detected the movement at his opposite extremity. Its tail stiffened and extended defensively, ready to strike if threatened by the fate that had befallen its brother. Kismet wiggled his foot again, trying to draw the creature away from his unprotected skin, but its reaction was slow and methodical. The poisonous tail gradually relaxed, curling back over its body, and the scorpion took a step onto his cheek.

Kismet's lungs were burning with a breath held for too long, but he dared not even let it out in a subtle exhalation. The menacing arachnid would surely detect the movement and plant its sting on his exposed face. He felt his throat tightening with the urge to exhale and draw a fresh breath, but he willed the impulse away and continued moving his foot to draw the creature away. The scorpion responded, moving from his cheek onto his throat and over the flap of his collar. Kismet slowly exhaled in relief as the pincher claws at last broke contact with his unprotected skin.

He could not see Marie beside him and heard no sound to indicate whether she was similarly overrun by the scaly denizens of the ossuary. He took her silence as a good sign, but if she was not currently plagued, it would only be a matter of time before she too felt the pinch of scorpion appendages on her skin or in her hair. When that happened, he had no doubt that she would erupt in a screaming fit that would bring them all down on her.

"Marie." He let the words out in a low whisper through clenched teeth. "On the count of three, we're going to get out of here as fast as we can, got it?"

There was a guttural affirmative. He could hear her better now, breathing rapidly, panicked.

"It doesn't have to look pretty," he continued. "We just have to move. Do you see where the stairs are? That's as far as we have to go."

"Got it."

"Okay. Take a deep breath." He took his own advice, filling his lungs with the odious atmosphere of the crypt, then exhaled half of it. "One…two…three!"

On the final number, he threw the MagLite with a snap of the wrist. The scorpion on his hand had no time to attack, but was flung away as the flashlight arced through the air. There was a scattering of random rays into various nooks of the chamber as the light rattled down onto the mesh of skeletons. Upon landing, the heavy aluminum tube slipped into a crevice between the bones and continued its journey, noisily rattling through the layered remains and casting an eerie shadow show on the ceiling of the vast hall.

Kismet and Marie paid no attention to the MagLite's final moments. They were already scrambling to avoid joining the ranks of the permanent occupants. Just as he had suggested, their hasty attempt to reach the staircase was not a study in graceful movement. The bones shifted and broke beneath them, dropping them deeper into the quagmire, but the impetus driving them granted a nearly superhuman strength. Much like a run through deep snow, Kismet's legs scattered the remains with each step, hooking the interlaced bones with his feet and thrusting them out of the way as he plowed forward. Behind him, Marie was having similar success.

The sacrifice of the flashlight had limited their ability to navigate by sight. The MagLite's rays were indistinct behind the curtain of bone, forcing them to follow a path marked only in their memories. In the frenzy to escape, Kismet could only hope that they stayed on course. Then the sudden darkness yielded an almost insignificant bit of luck.

Their eyes were drawn to a slightly elevated point only a short distance away. In the back of his mind, Kismet recognized it as the Cyalume stick he had initially dropped into the stairwell. It had rolled down several steps before coming to rest near the base of the flight.

Though its yellow light provided scant illumination, it shone like a beacon, guiding them to safety.

Kismet's feet abruptly hit something solid—stone treads buried beneath a covering of skeletons—and he redoubled his efforts. As he emerged from the mire, he swung his arms out, caught hold of Marie's wrist, and yanked her from the bony embrace of the ossuary, but their flight did not end there. Pausing only long enough to scoop up the light-stick, Kismet led the way up the steep staircase. The crunching noise of their footsteps suggested that simply escaping the mass grave had not ended their encounter with the venomous denizens of the chamber.

A second beacon materialized in the darkness ahead; a single shaft of brilliant light stabbing down from above. Kismet gave an audible sigh of relief as they stepped into the cone of illumination cast by the powerful lantern Hussein had activated in order to guide them back. Both he and Marie sagged onto the steps beneath the protective aegis of overhead light, catching their breath and letting the adrenaline drain from their extremities.

"Nick? What happened?"

Kismet took several more deep breaths before looking up to answer Chiron. "Marie fell."

The short statement did not begin to explain what they had seen and experienced in the chamber below, but Kismet found that as he tried to put it into words, he kept sticking on that initial point: Why had Marie fallen? Why had she even attempted to descend the dark stairway alone?

"Did you find anything?"

Kismet looked up again. "What we found…no, there's nothing down there. Get us out of here and I'll tell you all about it."

He dragged himself erect then proffered a hand to Marie. Shelving his doubts, he focused on the more immediate problem of how to escape the tunnel shaft. The well-lit opening where Hussein and Chiron waited was a good three meters from the stair tread directly below. The narrow steps were a precarious platform from which to attempt an ascent, and even more so for what Kismet had in mind. His gaze flickered between the opening and the steps, trying to gauge the optimal location from which to boost Marie high enough for the others to pull her clear. He finally settled on a position that placed him sideways beneath the opening, squatting on one leg while the other was extended downward as a brace.

"All right, let's get you out of here."

She made no effort to hide her relief. Despite the awkwardness of using a living stepladder, she gripped his shoulder and planted her foot on his thigh. Her balance did not waver as she lifted herself from the stairs then reached up to take Hussein's hand, leaving Kismet to wonder how she had fallen in the first place. She seemed as footsure as a tightrope walker. After only a few seconds, her weight lifted and she rose through the hole. There was a moment of darkness as her body eclipsed the bright lantern and Kismet was once more alone in the stairwell.

When the light returned, he began looking around to plan his own exfiltration, but something was different. As he stood and brought his extended leg back up, he both heard and felt a crunch beneath his boot soles. The brilliance of the lantern had compromised his ability to see into the shadowy crenellated recesses of the steps, but he was sure of one thing: There had been nothing on the bare stone moments before. He knew without looking what had caused the sound and hastened up several steps as a pure reflex. Just as quickly, dark menacing shapes began to materialize under the rays of the lantern. The multi-appendaged swarm had followed them from the ossuary. The scorpions, as kings of their food chain, once more led the charge, but behind them were species of arachnids and insects too numerous and diverse to identify.

Kismet backed up the stairwell, instinctively withdrawing from the creeping menace. His head was now level with the opening and he could see the faces of his companions, staring down in horrified disbelief as the miniature army overwhelmed the area where he and Marie had rested only moments before. Drawing a deep breath, he flexed his legs and thrust himself toward the opening.

His fingertips grazed the edge of the hole and in a single instant, bloated out of proportion by the rush of adrenaline, he knew that his hold would fail. He would rebound from the overhang and plunge headlong into the swarm. But then, as his weight came down and his fingers slipped against the stone, Hussein seized his forearms with an iron grip.

He hung there like an offering, arms extended over his head while his feet dangled above the squirming mass. Hussein's hold seemed to be failing—he could feel his wrists slipping through the young man's hands—but it was just an illusion. With Marie and Chiron lending their support, the Iraqi scholar hauled Kismet's upper body through the hole in a single heave.

Hussein did not immediately let go, even though his ferocious pull had caused him to lose his footing and fall backward. His eyes reflected his determination—he would not let go until Kismet's feet were once more on solid ground—but his grin was a triumphant assertion of victory. Kismet returned the smile with a grateful nod, but in that instant, Hussein's expression changed to a mask of sheer terror.

A single black scorpion scuttled along Kismet's right arm and darted toward the exposed flesh of the young Iraqi's hand. Hussein instinctively let go of Kismet, shaking his hand to thwart the attack, but it was already too late. The creature's pincers closed around his fingers and it jabbed forward with its tail, planting its sting.

Kismet immediately began sliding back through the hole. His hands curled into claws, fingertips scratching against the smooth rock for a purchase, but the forces of gravity and inertia were allied against him. As his chest scraped over the stone lip, the buttons popped from his shirt like a burst from a machine gun.

And then he stopped.

Nothing he had done in the brief struggle had arrested his fall. At the last possible instant, Marie had leapt into motion, bracing her feet against the tunnel wall and knotting her fingers in the fabric of his shirt. The strain of halting his slide and simply holding him was evident in the bunched muscles of her jaw line, and Kismet knew that without more assistance, her efforts would merely serve to postpone the inevitable.

Hussein wailed in agony, unable to shake the scorpion free. In desperation, he slammed his fist against the wall, crushing the relentless arachnid even as it stung him again. Through the pain, he remembered his friend's peril and hastened to relieve Marie. Kismet could see bright red welts erupting like tiny volcanoes on the back of the young man's right hand and blood streaming from the wounds caused by the scissor-like claws. Only when he and Marie had nearly succeeded in drawing Kismet back from the brink, did Chiron shake off his languor and lend a hand.

As soon as Kismet's knees touched the stone, he rasped: "I'm good. Let go." His first concern was to make sure that the scorpion that had stung Hussein was a solitary hitchhiker—it was—then he rushed to help the young scholar.

Hussein's hand had swollen like a balloon. The stings had darkened and spread to form a single grotesque bruise. Kismet searched his memory for the first-aid treatment for venomous bites, but his ability to offer aid was limited by the scant medical supplies they had brought along. He activated two instant cold-compresses and bound these to the affected area with a loose wrapping of bandages. Beyond the initial pain and surprise of the attack, the swelling seemed to be the only ill effect from the toxin.

Chiron watched as Kismet finished ministering to the young man, then broke his silence. "Nick, what did you find down there?"

Kismet gave him a sharp look. He had never known the Frenchman to be so single minded, and had in fact always thought of him as a compassionate figure. His apparent disregard for Hussein's misery seemed out of character. "Nothing. Whatever was down there was completely looted when this tunnel was cut."

"Nothing?"

"Bones," Marie intoned. "Nothing but bones."

"The vault has been turned into a mass grave," explained Kismet. "There are hundreds of skeletons down there. Maybe thousands."

"Babylonian slaves?" wondered Chiron.

Kismet felt profoundly uncomfortable with the older man's eagerness for all the gruesome details. "Not Babylonian and not ancient, but slaves nonetheless: Saddam's workforce. After they excavated this tunnel, he had them all slaughtered to keep its existence secret."

Marie shuddered involuntarily, but offered nothing more. Despite his suffering, Hussein was also keenly attentive, his expression revealing that he was all too familiar with atrocities of the sort Kismet was describing.

"Perhaps we have been looking for the wrong treasure chamber," Chiron mused.

"It makes no difference now. We have to get Hussein back to the surface."

"He can go back alone. Or with Marie. We need to find out where this tunnel leads."

Kismet stared in disbelief at his old mentor, but before he could begin to formulate a contrary argument, Hussein interjected. "I am able to continue. The sting of this creature—it is not fatal."

"If Hussein can go on," voiced Marie, "I vote to continue our search as well. I also would like to know where this tunnel leads."

As the lone dissenting voice, Kismet fought back an urge to rage at his associates. "It doesn't matter. There's no reason to continue. Whatever we hoped to find is long gone. If Saddam's engineers found some kind of treasure trove, they would have moved it—" he fixed a stern gaze on Chiron, "—or destroyed anything of religious significance."

"Nick." Chiron's tone was passionate and pleading. "We're here. We've come so far… You have brought us this far. Don't you want to see where this path leads?"

Kismet sensed his friend was talking about more than just the tunnel. He stared back silently for a moment, then glanced once more at the wounded Iraqi. "Hussein, are you sure you can make it?"

In spite of the cool air in the tunnel, the young man's forehead was beaded with droplets of perspiration and his face showed a distressing pallor, but he nevertheless nodded eagerly. Kismet drew in a breath and exhaled with a defeated sigh. "Well, I suppose it has to lead somewhere. I just hope we don't run into any of the former tenants."

After a few moments spent gathering and inventorying the remaining supplies, the small party began advancing once more along the tunnel route. Although they progressed in much the same manner as before, Kismet was now more keenly aware of the separation of each member of the party. The space that divided them as they moved was more than simply a physical interval. Alone with his or her thoughts, each person walked silently more than a meter from the next, and Kismet found himself wondering what occupied the minds of his companions.

Chiron's obsession with finding the trove, and specifically the Staff of Moses, was most troubling, but at least it was something he could understand. In his own way, Kismet was also searching for the answer to a question that was much bigger than anything he could put into words. He didn't for a moment believe that the old man would find something definitive—the fingerprint of God, written large in the desert sand—but in a quest for faith, sometimes the search itself was the goal.

Marie's motivations were less easy to read. Initially, it had been easy to dismiss her attendance as peripheral, a titillating presence in the right environment, but a deadly distraction in the midst of life and death hardships. Yet, there had been a few moments when her behavior seemed out of character with that impression, not the least example of which was her eagerness to push ahead into the treasure vault. And her simple declaration of interest in discovering what lay at the end of the tunnel bespoke a deeper personal investment in their quest than a simple wish to support her employer.

Under the pretense of checking his physical condition, Kismet diverted the lantern's broad cone of light away from the tunnel to briefly illuminate Hussein's face. The young man's movements were labored, as was his breathing, and his countenance betrayed the ongoing war his body was fighting against the toxins in his bloodstream, but he flashed a determined smile and managed to straighten his posture.

Kismet had no reason to doubt that Hussein's intentions were anything beyond the obvious. The young scholar, like most people his age, was interested in adventure and discovery. In that, they were not so different, though Kismet could remember a time in his own life when subterranean passageways and ancient ruins held no significance for him. In fact, it had not been until that fateful night in the desert that he had begun looking into the mysteries of the past, and even then only as means to solving a more immediate enigma. The depth of his knowledge of history was incidental to a quest rooted solely in the present.

As he continued to tread the trail of his thoughts, he found Marie at his side. "Nick, a question if you please. You said that anything of religious significance would be destroyed. Is that the goal of the Prometheus group? To destroy that which might reinforce religious faith?"

He tried in vain to read her expression; she floated like a wraith in the darkness beside him. He resisted the urge to play the light on her face as he had Hussein's. "I don't know for sure. In any case, that's not what I meant. There's reason to believe that Saddam Hussein would have ordered the destruction of certain relics—artifacts from the Temple of Solomon and perhaps even the Staff Pierre is seeking—out of fear that the Israeli government might risk war in order to recover them."

"How can you know this?"

Kismet gave a vague shrug. "It's not so farfetched. The Taliban government of Afghanistan destroyed several stone carvings of Buddha because they believed it to be the will of God."

"But Saddam Hussein has never been devoutly religious. He would view such relics merely as antiquities to be prized or sold." She took a step forward so that her face was partially bathed in light, her expression stern. "And you did not answer my question. Is this something that Samir Al-Azir told you?"

He made no attempt to hide his dismay, but lowered his voice in an unspoken plea for her to use discretion. "So you really were eavesdropping. But the answer is yes. That's what he told me."

"And had he been so ordered? I am wondering what he found that could have been so inflammatory."

"Marie." Kismet's voice took on a forceful edge. "Drop it."

"I think I have as much right to know as Pierre," she continued defiantly, but dropped her tone to a whisper. "And you may be sure that I will demand an explanation when this is finished."

Kismet breathed a relieved sigh at her temporary retreat from the subject. Between Chiron's probing and Marie's spying, he had inadvertently revealed more about his encounter with Samir Al-Azir than at any other time in his life. He had kept the details of what had happened that night secret with a passion that bordered on mania for the simple reason that he wasn't really sure who he could trust. His attempts to regulate how much of the tale he would reveal were proving futile. Each revelation led to more questions and to deductions that were startlingly accurate.

Nothing more was said on the subject and a few minutes later the discussion was forgotten as the group reached the terminus of the tunnel. There was an abrupt transition from the smooth, symmetrical tube through which they had walked into a vast cavern hewn by nature but reinforced by human engineers. The discovery of the cave must have been a serendipitous event for the excavators of the tunnel, who had evidently chosen it as the place to begin the next phase of the project. As Kismet played the light into the recesses of the grotto, he saw what the tunnel had been leading up to.

The cavern had become a subterranean warehouse. Vehicles and medium-sized shipping containers lined the nearby wall, while several neat rows of pallets, each loaded with various crates and cardboard boxes, occupied the middle. Three crude shacks had been erected along on the far edge of the area, but their doors were secured with padlocks. These discoveries however were insignificant alongside the one other feature of the cavern that was also the work of men. Commencing at the center of the underground chamber and cutting across the floor at a forty-five-degree angle when viewed from the mouth of the tunnel were two parallel rails of iron, which disappeared into a second passage bored into solid rock.

"I'll be damned," whispered Kismet. "They built a subway."

The group advanced with cautious curiosity to stand at the railhead. A gunmetal gray control box stood adjacent to the enormous shock-absorbing bumper which established the absolute end of the line. Kismet played the light over the green and red switches, absently noting the almost uniform layer of dust on the operator's panel. "No one's been down here in a while. I'd say this facility was abandoned weeks—maybe months—before the start of the war."

"Can you tell where it leads?" Chiron inquired.

Kismet shook his head. "Hussein?"

The young scholar shuffled forward, and after a momentary assessment, leaned over the panel and blew across its surface. A cloud of dust lifted from the neglected control buttons, the motes dancing eerily in the artificial brilliance of the electric lantern. When the air cleared, he surveyed the tableau. Behind him, Kismet could now clearly distinguish the delicate Arabic script which marked several of the buttons and LED indicators, as well as a numeric ten-key push button pad. The letters were incomprehensible to him, but the universal numerals required no translation.

"These are simply controls for summoning and operating the tram," Hussein explained after a moment. "It does not indicate what the final destination is, or how far away."

"It would have to be a significant distance to warrant construction of a train," intoned Chiron. "Otherwise they would have simply continued to utilize trucks."

Kismet stepped away from the group, playing the beam once more onto the tracks. Still curious about the control box, Chiron directed Marie to break out two Cyalume sticks and a few moments later, the area around the dull metal panel was bathed in a surreal yellow glow. In the stillness, their conversation echoed tinnily from the cavern walls.

"Is it still operational?" Marie asked.

"The power indicator light is off," Hussein explained.

Kismet's eyes followed the parallel rails to the point where they disappeared into the tunnel. The unreadable darkness offered no clues to the train's opposite terminus, but for the first time since discovering the railway, he noticed the overhead wires which were suspended at intervals from the ceiling of the excavated passageway. The lines appeared to be uninsulated power lines, designed, he surmised, to deliver non-stop energy to a trolley car. If Hussein's assessment was correct, those lines were presently dead. Without being able to utilize the railway, the feasibility of continuing the underground journey was in doubt, an outcome that was by no means unwelcome to Kismet. Especially since the disastrous foray into the desolate treasure vault beneath the Esagila, he had come to believe that no more answers would be found in the tunnel, and did not share Chiron's enthusiasm for pursuing the search literally to the last dead end. A disapproving scowl crossed his face as his old mentor's next question reverberated through the cave.

"Is there any way to turn it on?"

Hussein's answer was not audible and Kismet did not turn back to see if the injured scholar was attempting to follow through on Chiron's request. Despite his reticence, Kismet could not help but be curious about what clandestine operations or discoveries had been so important as to motivate the former Iraqi dictator to undertake such a colossal construction project. He was mildly surprised to find himself speculating about the destination of the railway and wondering if perhaps other palaces concealed similar entrances. Perhaps Saddam Hussein had built an elaborate, nationwide subway system in order to move swiftly and secretly through his domain.

His eyes followed the power line out of the tunnel and through the air to one of the upright stanchions which reached out over the tracks, suspending the line at a constant height. The design was similar to mass transit street cars in many cities, though notably different than the third rail system used by the New York transit authority, with which Kismet was more familiar.

His gaze was then drawn to a smaller brown wire which ran the length of the main line. It was basic sixteen-gauge, two-conductor stranded wire, often called "speaker wire" because of its use in home audio systems. Kismet knew it wasn't good for much else. Cheap and thinly insulated, the copper strands could only conduct a very low voltage current. He followed the wire along its path, wondering if it was part of some kind of intercom system. There was only one other application he could think of that did not involve the transmission of electrical impulses for purposes of sound amplification; stranded wire was also used for triggering blasting caps.

"Hussein, wait—"

His admonition came a moment too late. Even as he shouted, he heard the click of a circuit breaker being thrown on the main panel, but the expected detonation did not occur. His relief was short-lived. In the relative silence that followed his warning, there was a faint, modulated tone, oscillating at intervals of exactly one second.

It was a countdown.

ELEVEN

Kismet muscled past the paralyzed forms of his companions and scanned the control board. Directly above the numeric keypad, an LED display ticked off the seconds remaining until whatever ugly surprise hard-wired into the security system was revealed, with what he now had little doubt would be explosive consequences.

24...23...22...

A thirty-second countdown, he realized. But thirty seconds—now twenty—to do what?

"Run!" he rasped. "Get out of here, now!"

As he moved to heed his own advice, he saw Hussein and Marie following suit. Chiron however hesitated, then leaned over the control board, his gnarled fingers hovering above the buttons. Kismet half-turned and shouted over his shoulder.

"Pierre, leave it! It's wired to blow!"

"I can't." The old man's voice was pleading. "I've come too far. There's got to be a way to turn it off."

"Damn it." Kismet's rage was mostly self-directed. He knew that he wasn't going to surrender Chiron to his fate, and that meant he was going to have to figure out a way to defuse the bomb or die trying. He wheeled around and came up to the platform alongside the other man. The count was down to eighteen seconds. "Don't touch anything."

He located the wire strand where it disappeared into the control box. One hard yank on the wire might be enough to rip it free of the timed trigger. Or it might complete the circuit and blow the detonators. In fifteen seconds, it would cease to matter.

He looked at the dust-covered ten-key buttons again. Their significance was now obvious. Anyone attempting to summon the train would first have to enter a security code. Failure to do so would quite literally bring down the roof. "Impossible," he muttered, reaching for the wire. "There must be millions of combinations."

He stopped again. 12...11...

On an impulse, he leaned close to the numeric keypad and blew away the fine coating of dust. About half of the numbers remained partially obscured by an accumulation of particles adhering to a film of skin oils. Curiously, these buttons—seven, four, one, and zero, along with the asterisk and pound symbol—formed an L-shape. The significance of this was not lost on Kismet. These six characters alone had been used whenever anyone wished to disarm the security system.

9…8…

"Hussein! What was Saddam's birthday?"

"What?" The young man's voice was faint, whether because of distance or the venom-induced illness, he could not say. "Twenty-eight, April. 1937."

Kismet shook his head. "That's not it. Any other important dates in April, January, July—"

"Fourteen, July! The revolution!"

4…3…

He quickly punched the asterisk, followed by 1, 4, 0, 7 and then the pound sign. The beeping tone abruptly changed to a long single note then fell silent. The numeric countdown likewise ceased.

Kismet sagged against the console, his extremities feeling numb from the surge of adrenaline. When he could breathe again, he looked over at an ashen Chiron, and enunciating slowly and clearly as he might with a wayward child, said: "Don't touch anything."

It was nearly fifteen minutes before they heard a distant screeching sound of metal on metal issuing from the tunnel. There was a faint breeze as air was pushed ahead of the arriving mass, and a few moments later, a single flatbed rail car rolled out of the darkness and coasted to a halt against the bumpers. Perhaps owing to their most recent brush with disaster, no one approached the car until Kismet made the first move.

The flatbed was little more than a freight platform. The motors were situated near the wheels and the only part of the vehicle that rose above the flat surface was a metal tower that reached up to make contact with the power lines. There were no creature comforts, nor did there appear to be any means of regulating speed or direction.

"It's all controlled from the main console," Kismet deduced aloud. "There's probably a computer in there to automatically slow it down when it gets to the end of the line."

"Dare we get aboard and see where it leads?" asked Chiron.

"Since you've probably already determined to do that, I guess there's no reason not to. Go ahead and climb on. I'll get it started and run over to join you. Hopefully, there's another control panel at the other end."

"What if there's not?" inquired Marie. "Should someone remain behind?"

Before he could weigh in, Chiron once again exercised his veto. "I don't think that's wise. Look what happened when we separated before. We should remain together. I trust that Nick is right. Logically, there must be a second set of controls."

Kismet did not find his mentor's vote of confidence especially gratifying, but the older man's certitude seemed vaguely inappropriate. He felt a shiver of déjà vu and wondered once more what Chiron was really up to. "Well, if I'm not, it will be a long walk back. All aboard, everyone. Last call for the Helltown Express."

Once Hussein, as the last member of the group save Kismet himself, had ascended the platform and secured one of the heavy nylon freight slings anchored around the perimeter, Kismet pressed the green button to activate the rail car motor. After a momentary delay, in which Kismet was unsure if he had selected the wrong control, the vehicle began to roll away from the bumper. Though it moved slowly, Kismet had to sprint to catch the car before it was once more swallowed up by the tunnel. He could feel its velocity increasing as the darkness swelled all around.

They activated several chem-lights to illuminate the journey but there was very little to see. Except for the overhead lines suspended at regular intervals, there was nothing but roughly worked black stone. The tunnel was a long, straight passage driving through the earth's crust. The narrow dimensions of the tube reflected the noise of the motors and wheels in an endless cacophony that was comparable to a torture session with fingernails on a chalkboard, but amplified to monstrous proportions. Conversation was impossible, and Kismet was left alone with his thoughts which, given the circumstances, were not the best of company.

The featureless tunnel ended abruptly, much as it had begun, and the rail car rolled out into an open chamber similar to the depot at the opposite terminus. Before anyone could react to the sudden arrival, the car screeched to a halt.

Kismet jumped down first, eager to scout the area for further traps. A control panel was situated near the bumper assembly but the security keypad was conspicuously absent, as was the wire strand that might indicate that it was linked to an explosive device. As his companions moved closer, he expanded the scope of his survey.

The chamber in which they now found themselves was much smaller than the first and hewn into a rough rectangle. Although there were several pallets and containers near the tracks, most of the area was vacant. The walls parallel to the train's approach were broken with stainless steel doorways—two on either side—bolted into the coarse stone and sealed with a thick seam of epoxy. At the end of the chamber opposite the tunnel entrance, a second cylindrical passage, large enough to permit only pedestrian traffic, led into the dark beyond. Kismet withheld comment, but gestured to the nearest framed opening.

At Chiron's nod of assent, he began walking toward the doorway, but when he had crossed only half the distance, a torturous noise— metal shrieking against metal—caused him to start. He whirled toward the source of the familiar sound and was chagrined to discover that Chiron had held back. Only Marie and Hussein had followed along behind him while the Frenchman had gravitated toward the control panel. In that moment, he caught a glimpse of the rail car as it vanished into the tunnel.

"Damn it, Pierre. I told you not to touch anything."

Chiron evinced guilt with a grimace. "I was looking for the overhead lights."

Kismet shook his head in frustration as he reached the other man's side. He toggled the switch that Chiron had used to activate the rail system, but nothing happened. The noise of the car on the tracks continued to diminish as it progressed away from the chamber. "Must be an automatic sequence. We'll have to wait until it gets to the other end before we can call it back. At least I hope it works that way. Otherwise, we'll have quite a walk."

"Time enough to do some exploring," replied Chiron with a wan smile.

"I suppose so," Kismet conceded. "But I don't think we're going to find what you're after in here. This looks like it might have been some kind of research facility."

"Have a little faith, Nick." Chiron gave his shoulder a paternal squeeze then moved toward the others.

"Faith?" Kismet's repetition was barely audible and if Chiron heard, he gave no indication. Instead, the Frenchman took the lead, moving purposefully toward the opening, and Kismet had to sprint to head him off. "Pierre, remember. Don't touch anything. If this was, as I suspect, some kind of weapons lab, not only will it probably be wired to a fail-safe, but there might also be some nasty things laying about."

Chiron raised his hands by way of reply, but the meaning of the gesture was uncertain. Kismet shook his head again, then moved through the open portal. The lintel of the steel doorway concealed an overhead panel designed to drop like the blade of a guillotine and seal the chamber beyond. The thickness of the steel panel, a good thirty centimeters, was more than a little unnerving. Whether it was meant to keep something out or prevent something from escaping, Kismet knew he did not want to be caught on the wrong side of that door if it closed.

There proved to be little reason to continue beyond the threshold. The chamber was impassible, almost completely filled with a haphazard arrangement of metal vats. Some of the enormous containers were secured to the floor along the perimeter, but most had simply been shoved in hastily. Kismet instantly recognized the tanks and divined their diabolical purpose.

"Well, either we've stumbled upon Saddam's answer to Anheuser-Busch…" He trailed off in response to the blank looks he was receiving from his comrades. "They're fermenters," he explained. "A sealed environment where bacterial cultures can thrive and propagate. You use them in the final stage of brewing beer."

Chiron nodded in dawning comprehension. "Ah, of course. Dual-use technology."

"Exactly. You can also grow and harvest any number of bacteriological strains. Anthrax comes to mind."

"Then this is a bio-weapons laboratory," Marie gasped. "This is what UNMOVIC was looking for: proof of an ongoing program for weapons of mass destruction."

Kismet glanced around again. "I'm not sure 'laboratory' is the right word. It doesn't look like any of the equipment has ever been used. More likely this is the hole they shoved everything into so that the inspectors wouldn't find anything."

"Still, this would qualify as…what is your expression? A smoking gun, *n'est pas?*"

"That's not for us to say," reproved Chiron, but his tone and expression were distracted, as though the discovery was inconveniently timed. "But rest assured, we will report this to the correct agency. Come, let us continue looking. If they were using this place to hide secrets, then we may yet find the object of *our* search."

The Frenchman again led the charge, forcing Kismet to hasten to catch up. The second opening, like the first, was equipped with an emergency gate. Beyond the doorway however, the scene was markedly different. The enclosure seemed to be a general storage area, and was cluttered with wooden crates and hard plastic shipping containers. The cartons rose before them like a wall, almost completely blocking access to the room beyond. Many of the boxes were stamped with stenciled Cyrillic characters, but a few were easier to decipher, with descriptions written in French, German and English. Without exception, the painted letters indicated the contents of the containers to be military munitions. A random inspection revealed only packing dunnage. "Just empty boxes," Kismet observed. "Either this stuff was passed on to army units before the war, or it's being stockpiled somewhere else by insurgents."

"But why keep these?" inquired Hussein, gesturing with his bandaged hand at the pile of containers.

"I'd say this was their answer to throwing it away."

"If I may," Chiron interjected. "There may be another explanation. Camouflage."

"You think there's something behind all this refuse?" Kismet sighed and resignedly began shifting the cartons out of the way. It was painfully clear that the French scientist would not be satisfied until he had explored every possibility. Nevertheless, the stacked containers did look a little like a facade, set up to give the illusion that the space beyond was entirely filled up, and he wasn't surprised at all when, after clearing three vertical layers out of the way, he revealed another laboratory workspace. He continued digging at the barrier until the opening was large enough for them to pass through single file.

The space that Kismet now thought of as "Laboratory Two" appeared to have nothing at all to do with the development of biological weapons. Rather, it looked more like a machine shop, with drill presses and metalworking lathes, and a large supply of metal ingots. He picked up one experimentally and found it to be lighter than expected. "Aluminum?" he speculated aloud. No one answered.

A large worktable occupied the center of the area, and spread out across its surface were the pieces to some kind of device. Kismet studied the fragments, trying to imagine what they would look like if assembled. A spherical casing in the middle of the puzzle gave it away.

He sucked in his breath suddenly and glanced at his companions. Both Marie and Hussein seemed only mildly curious about the items on the tabletop. He sensed no recognition from either of them. Chiron had given the device only a cursory glance before continuing his explorations, but Kismet wasn't fooled. Chiron knew what it was. He had to know.

There were three hard plastic containers, each about half the size of a coffin, stacked at the end of the table. One was open, but the cavity inside was filled with packing foam, cut out to cradle a torpedo-shaped object. The exterior was marked with the seal of the French Ministry of Defense and what seemed to be an identification code: CER 880412. The other two cases were similarly labeled, though with a different six-digit code. Extruded plastic seals, resembling tiny yellow padlocks, were threaded through the clasps. These containers had never been opened.

Kismet nonchalantly moved closer to Chiron, who was presently examining the contents of a workbench. He kept his voice low. "There's something over here you need to see."

"The detonators?" Chiron seemed to understand the need for discretion. "I saw. Do not worry, my friend. They are not armed."

"How can you tell?"

"Many years ago, my government foolishly agreed to exchange certain technologies for oil leases. It was their belief that the Iraqis would never be able to successfully reverse engineer the devices or refine the nuclear fuel to make them operational." He gave a half-hearted smile. "In this at least, it would seem they were correct. Saddam Hussein's nuclear program never got off the ground."

Kismet realized that the object Chiron was inspecting was a partially assembled version of the same item that lay exploded on the table. But unlike the latter, this device seemed rougher at the edges. This fourth atomic detonator had been manufactured here in Laboratory Two, rather than in the *Centre d'Etudes du Ripault.*

Because he was a nuclear scientist, Chiron's grasp of the intricacies both of atomic weapons and the politics of exchanging such technologies far outstripped Kismet's, and the latter had no reason to question his old mentor's appraisal. Nevertheless, the idea that he was looking at a nuclear bomb, or rather the detonator—the component that used a shaped charge of plastic explosives to bombard a core of plutonium with neutrons, thereby triggering a catastrophic fission reaction—was just a little unnerving.

Chiron turned away from the workbench. "This isn't the relic we seek. Let's continue looking, shall we?"

Their counter-clockwise circuit of the laboratory complex moved, not to the third such stainless steel room, but to a tunnel situated at the end of the rectangular cavern opposite where they had entered. After the artificial symmetry of the first two rooms, the passage through which they now moved seemed wholly organic, as if carved out by the forces of nature. It was in fact more likely that the original dimensions of a naturally occurring fissure had been improved with excavating tools and explosives. Yet the workers had not seen fit to work the walls smooth or bore the tunnel in a straight line. It wended back and forth, ascending steeply for more than one hundred meters, before emerging into a larger open chamber.

Kismet flicked off his flashlight and waited for the others to catch up before announcing: "I think we just found the back door to this place."

The opening, through which indirect daylight was streaming in, was situated more than twenty meters off the cavern floor. It was large enough to fly a helicopter through, which apparently was exactly what someone had done. At the bottom of the chamber, hibernating like a tired old dragon, was a Russian-made Mi-25, NATO designation HIND D. A combination of gunship and transport, the Hind had gained recognition during the Soviet occupation of Afghanistan in the 1980s. Beneath a five-bladed rotor, the Hind's fuselage was aerodynamically thin, like the body of an insect, with stubby outriggers on either side—the wings of the wasp—supporting multiple weapons platforms.

The helicopter appeared to have been well maintained and kept ready for action. Only a thin layer of dust had accumulated on its exterior. Nearby, several drums of aviation fuel were arranged in a neat formation. Kismet slid back the door and briefly inspected the fuselage. "This was somebody's 'Plan B'. They kept it ready to go right up until the end."

Marie offered the only response. "I wonder why it was never used?"

"Like everything else down here, what was the point? There was no way one helicopter, or some incomplete weapons research or a stockpile of munitions, would have made an iota of difference." Kismet turned away from the Hind and rejoined his companions. "And it's not going to do us much good either."

They returned back down the passage and moved toward the third stainless steel laboratory. Of the three they had so far encountered, this one seemed to most resemble the sobriquet Kismet had applied to the facilities. The neatly ordered space was equipped with stainless steel tables, computer terminals attached to gas chromatographs, centrifuges and autoclaves, and racks of glass beakers and test tubes. There was even a glass alembic, looking like a prop from an old mad scientist movie, on one of the tables. Additionally, there were two sealed glass chambers with airlocks and glove ports, and a bank of empty cages large enough to hold a variety of animals. The back wall was arrayed with shelves and cabinets storing glass and plastic containers of various chemical compounds. There was nothing resembling an archaeological discovery—no holy relics. Kismet turned to Chiron. "Well, let's look behind door number four."

But Chiron was not there.

"Pierre?"

There was a sudden rasp of metal, then the guillotine gate slammed shut with a forcefulness that sent a tremor through the room, shattering several glass containers. Marie shrieked reflexively and rushed to the solid barrier, along with a stunned Hussein. Kismet hastened to join them and peered through the narrow view port.

"Pierre, I told you—"

Chiron stood just beyond the doorway, his finger still on the large red button that had activated the emergency measures, which had sealed the lab. He raised his eyes slowly to the window and spoke. Although the thick glass completely muted his voice, Kismet had no trouble reading his lips. *I'm sorry, Nick.* Then he turned away.

Kismet felt numb. Marie and Hussein began frantically searching for some means to open the door, but Kismet was looking for something else: comprehension. Try as he might, his mind could not put the pieces together. The man he thought of as one of his closest friends had intentionally trapped him inside a chemical weapons lab, deep underground, and he couldn't think of a single reason why.

And then he noticed something else about their situation that forced him to leave off wrestling with the riddle of Chiron's actions. "It's getting hot in here."

When Pierre Chiron hit the switch, he did more than simply lock his companions inside Laboratory Three. The large red button controlled a fail-safe mechanism designed to protect the rest of the facility from an accidental release of biological or chemical contaminants. Under normal operating conditions, each of the four laboratories would have been monitored by an officer from the Republican Guard with a single order: At the first hint of danger—if a researcher dropped a test tube or if a Rhesus monkey, whether infected or not, escaped its cage—he was to hit the button.

Rihab Taha al-Azawi al-Tikriti, the scientist known to Iraqis as 'Doctor Germ', had designed both the laboratories and the fail-safe mechanisms with grim efficiency. The door was composed of a thick panel of lead, sandwiched between equally dense sheets of steel, and was held in place only by two stubby bolts. When the system was triggered, a tiny explosive charge would blast the bolts out of their recesses, allowing the gate to drop. There was no device in place to raise the barrier, which was nearly as heavy as a railroad car. Once a laboratory was deemed compromised, there was no reason for anyone to ever enter it again.

Between the steel walls and floor of the laboratory, and the solid stone of the cavern, there were several bands of granular magnesium. The same impulse that blew the door bolts also ignited these strips of flammable metal, causing them to burn with a brilliant white intensity. By the time the fuel supply was exhausted, the temperature inside the laboratory would approach sixteen-hundred 1600 degrees Celsius, at which point the stainless steel would become molten and collapse, releasing the final measure: an almost equivalent volume of sand and rock suspended above the laboratory that would drop down and completely bury the thoroughly sanitized remains of the laboratory.

Anyone unlucky enough to be caught in the laboratory would of course be completely incinerated long before the catastrophic denouement.

PART THREE

EXODUS

TWELVE

Rebecca Gault jumped down from the moving rail car as soon as it entered the laboratory complex, dropped into a tactical crouch and brought her machine pistol to the high ready. Her team imitated her actions and before the tram could bump to a halt, they had formed a defensive perimeter and were scanning for possible targets. The holographic reflex sight on Rebecca's weapon illuminated the center of Pierre Chiron's chest with a red dot. There was no one else visible in the spacious cavern. The scientist was seated on a bulky object, covered with a large nylon sack bearing the seal of the United Nations and UNESCO. It looked eerily like a body bag. Without lowering the gun, she rose to her full height and advanced on him.

"Where are they?" she asked in their shared tongue.

Chiron gestured toward Laboratory Two. "I think you'll be pleased. Two of them are still in their shipping containers. The third was disassembled for research, but all the important parts are there."

"That's not what I meant."

"Oh." The old man winced guiltily, but straightened, assuming a supercilious air. "That's not your concern. You won't be bothered. Have your men load this onto the tram."

She regarded him with barely concealed distaste, but two members of the team hastened forward, following his orders without her verbal direction. There was no question of who was really in charge. The heavy parcel was hefted onto the rail car bed.

"What is that?"

"That also is not your concern." Chiron gave a sigh, and then softened his tone. "Suffice it to say, I found what I was looking for. Now, let's finish this business and be away from here."

Rebecca nodded and secured her weapon. In the corner of her eye, she saw the scientist following her, but made no effort to acknowledge him. Her reaction to the man was not based on any sort of personal dislike. She barely knew him. Instead, she was troubled by the fact that he was there at all, right in the middle of a very delicate and important mission. The situation was further complicated by the fact that he was, nominally, at least, in charge.

The complicity of the French government in sustaining the

hegemony of Saddam Hussein was arguably no worse than that of any other Western nation. Even the United States had turned a blind eye to the internal atrocities and human rights abuses of the Baathist dictator in order to cultivate an ally first against the growing Soviet influence in the region, then against the perceived danger posed by Iran. The French government in the mid-1980s had gone a step further by loaning the war-beleaguered nation three nuclear detonators in exchange for future oil leases. Because the deal did not include the plutonium cores necessary to arm the weapons, nor the technology to process that element, it seemed akin to giving a child a gun with not only the bullets but also the firing pin removed. It was perhaps not the wisest thing to do, but certainly posed no imminent threat.

In fact, no peril had arisen from the transaction. Saddam had not produced a nuclear weapon for use against Iran, Israel, or the allied nations during the first Gulf War. With the eyes of the world upon him, the dictator could not openly pursue nuclear refinement technologies. But the weapons now posed a new sort of risk to the French government. If the inspectors from the International Atomic Energy Agency found the detonators, it would be scandalously embarrassing to the French government. And now that victory in the war to oust Saddam ensured that every corner of the country would be scoured for anything relating to weapons research, such a discovery seemed inevitable.

But help had come from an unexpected source. An atomic scientist and UN official named Pierre Chiron, who had always been a thorn in the side of the Defense Ministry for his opposition to ongoing testing of France's nuclear arsenal, had approached his long-time nemeses with a conciliatory offer. He believed he could locate the missing detonators, and with help from a commando team, secure or destroy them. The matter was given over to the *Direction Generale de la Securite Exterieure* (General Directorate for External Security) who in turn handed the assignment to one of their top field officers: the woman who now called herself Rebecca Gault.

Rebecca immediately recognized the shipping containers. The numbers stenciled on each were identical to codes she had been given, but that was only the first step toward verification. She leaned close to the scattered pieces until her eyes fell on twin hemispheres, the disassembled halves of the primary detonator. The primary was essentially a conventional bomb: a layer of plastique, held in place by interlocking hexagons of solid titanium. However, the detonation alone would not be enough to initiate a critical reaction. Between the explosives and the solid plutonium core was a layer of neutron rich beryllium. In the instant of the blast, the metal skin of the ball would focus the energy inward, driving the neutrons into the core, where they would shatter the reactive plutonium atoms to trigger a runaway fission reaction. Without the core, the primary was still a dangerous explosive device, albeit one of relatively low yield, but plastique was relatively stable. She felt no trepidation as she lifted one of the hemispheres and turned it over. Each hexagonal plate was stamped with a unique serial number, verifying what she already knew to be true: This was unquestionably one of the detonators from the Ripault research center.

She broke the seals on the remaining cases and repeated the process with both detonators. "Mission accomplished," she announced. She spent another two minutes packing blocks of Semtex from her combat pouch around the detonators. Into each square of the pliable explosive compound, she carefully inserted a three-volt blasting cap, all of which were linked together with spliced sections of speaker wire. When she was done, she walked backwards, spooling out the wire as she went, to link up with her comrades outside the laboratory.

In the time it had taken for her to authenticate the three nuclear devices, her team had set charges throughout the facility. She added her wire to the web, and connected them all to a single electronic timer. "Half an hour should be enough time for us to reach the surface again." She directed her words to Chiron. "You will be returning with us?"

He nodded.

Rebecca bit her lip. She didn't care what fate had befallen the scientist's companions, or at least that's what she kept telling herself. But she couldn't bring herself to believe that the old dodderer had coldly killed them, which suggested that they were probably still alive somewhere, perhaps bound and gagged. It was Chiron's intention to leave them here to be buried alive when the charges they had planted eventually went off.

Oh, well. It's on his head.

His worst nightmare had come true. He was in the desert, surrounded by his enemies, and he was going to die here.

Saeed sighed wistfully and closed his eyes, trying to remember his villa on the French Riviera, but the memory was an elusive chimera. The gravity of his present situation was too strong for the magic of daydreams.

It had been a long night. After leaving their hiding place on the banks of the Euphrates, he and Farid had rendezvoused with a dozen of his brother's most trusted compatriots. To a man, they despised Saeed. No doubt they had heard of his earlier life as an intelligence agent and minion of the hated dictator. But their hatred of the new enemy, the American invaders, was greater, and the old proverb held true: The enemy of their enemy was now their friend. Saeed had given them a target for their rage, and so he was to be tolerated, if only temporarily.

The desert crossing was no easy matter. Their destination lay far to the south, in the empty reaches of the Arabian desert. Saeed had never been there, but knew the longitude and latitude of the place well enough to plot the course on a map. Out here in the wilderness however, maps had little value. Every few kilometers, it was necessary to stop and check their heading against a compass reading, but even at that, they might be off by a few crucial degrees, which over the course of an all-night journey might translate into a navigational disaster.

To make matters worse, they had to steer an elaborate zig-zagging course in order to avoid what Saeed could only assume to be the probable reach of coalition patrols. As they cruised along, without the benefit of headlights, each man knew that at any moment they might be strafed by an Apache gun ship or obliterated by a TOW missile. Farid's militants were philosophical. *Inshallah*—God willing—*we will survive.* Saeed could not share their ambivalence toward danger and was forced to put his faith in his own uncertain skills.

Whether by the grace of Allah, or his own abilities, Saeed led them true. As the sun began creeping over the horizon, they arrived at a rocky plateau, which rose from the sand like an island. Leaving behind the vehicles, they commenced a three-kilometer trek to a fissure that split the sandstone formation like a canyon. Yet, in spite of having survived the gauntlet, and the nearness of their destination, Saeed's dread was multiplying like a virus; it was as if the desert was eating him alive.

He would feel better once Nick Kismet was dead.

"What now, brother?" inquired Farid, gazing over the lip into the chasm.

"There should be an opening in the wall. It is quite large, but impossible to see from the air."

Farid squinted into the shadows. Through their sun-blasted eyes, it was difficult to differentiate anything in the darkness below. "I think I see it. But we have no rope."

"This entrance was accessible only by helicopter," Saeed volunteered.

His brother threw him a contemptuous glance. "We also have no helicopter."

He began unwinding his *kefiya*, the traditional head covering which he wore like a turban for added protection from the scorching sun. His confederates, as if telepathically linked, did the same, and when knotted together, the woven scarves formed a cord about eight meters long.

Saeed regarded the improvised rope dubiously. "Will that hold a man's weight?"

"Will it hold? Is it long enough?" Farid shrugged. "*Inshallah*, my brother."

One end was tied around the stock of an AK-47, which was in turn braced by two of the now bareheaded desert fighters. Farid led the way, easing his wiry form over the edge to begin his descent. In a matter of seconds, he was low enough to swing inside a barely visible recess. One by one, the militants followed suit, until only Saeed and the two men holding the belay were left. One of them addressed him with barely veiled scorn. "You must go also."

Saeed blinked. "I am unarmed."

"Then keep your head down if there is shooting," laughed the other man.

Resignedly, Saeed dropped to a prone position and lowered himself into the fissure. It was pleasantly cool in the shadows, but this gave him little comfort. He felt his adrenaline spike as his feet lost contact with the solid surface and his full weight depended from the tenuous grip of his hands on the equally uncertain rope of head cloths. He started involuntarily as a hand gripped his belt, but it was only Farid, pulling him onto the ledge where he and the others stood.

Saeed blinked rapidly to adjust his vision to the new environment. The fissure in the otherwise solid wall was immense, spreading from the relatively small corner where they stood to a maximum height of twenty meters. It was indeed large enough to fly a helicopter through, if the pilot of that aircraft was either very skilled or completely insane.

As the sunspots gradually faded from his vision, he was able to more clearly distinguish what lay on the other side of the opening. The Mi-25, its rotor blades looking like an enormous asterisk, sat patiently on the floor of the enormous cavern. "Another long drop, brother. And we have no more *kefiyas*."

Farid sneered at him, then leaned out into the fissure, gave a short whistle and caught the Kalashnikov rifle as it fell through the air. "Now we do."

Saeed's eyes widened in disbelief. "Now how will we get out of here? This is reckless, Farid."

"Reckless? This was your plan, brother." Farid chuckled at his sibling's obvious anxiety. "It is time for you to show some faith. You may go first."

Another belay was quickly established, two more men culled from their fighting force in order to secure the line. Saeed rode the wave of his rising ire as he dropped to his hands and knees and started down into the cave.

Suddenly, from deep within rock, there came the unmistakable thump of an explosion, and in that instant the cloth rope slipped through his fingers.

Kismet looked frantically around the laboratory, searching for anything that might postpone or commute the unexpected death sentence. In the space of only a few minutes, it had grown as hot as a sauna in the metal enclosure. Everything in the lab seemed to be made of stainless steel and as such was conducting the heat as effectively as a griddle on a stovetop. Heat radiated from every surface until the air itself roiled like a liquid.

Hussein and Marie seemed to be dancing in place, shifting rapidly from one foot to the other as the floor seared right through the soles of their shoes. Kismet realized mordantly that he was also hopping back and forth, but it wasn't enough. It felt as if his boots were going to burst into flame. Then he spied something that would offer at least a few moments of respite. "This way!"

He knocked over the rack of specimen cages so that it was spread out like a mattress frame. Because the cages were also metal, it would only be a matter of time before they also grew red hot, but the flow of air under the wire mesh would give them a few minutes of relief. Marie followed Hussein onto the makeshift platform. "Nick, what's happening?"

"Some kind of self-destruct." He wiped a hand across his forehead, flinging away beads of sweat which landed on the floor and evaporated with a hiss. "It must have been activated when he closed the door."

"When who closed the door? Pierre?"

"It must have been an accident," he lied, none too convincingly. It wasn't an accident. *Why, Pierre?*

No time to worry about that.

In the back of the lab, several chemical containers had been jolted from their shelves by the impact of the door slamming shut. The respective contents of those jars and bottles were now beginning to smolder on the floor, evaporating or burning outright, and releasing an acrid miasma that made the superheated air even more difficult to breathe. Kismet's eyes stung as he stared at the chaos, looking for inspiration.

"Stay here. I've got an idea." He jumped back onto the floor and ran into the heart of the chemical cloud. His boot soles left black footprints on the metal floor as the rubber began liquefying on contact, and when he tried to stop in front of the storage cabinets, it was like hitting an oil slick. His feet shot out from under him and he hit the floor on his tailbone.

Everything he touched seemed to be on fire, burning right through the fabric of his jeans and scorching his hands when he tried to get back to his feet. He gritted his teeth against the pain and struggled erect, trying to focus his attention on the labels of the remaining bottles.

For a moment, he was suffused with hope. There were several substances which could be combined to form highly reactive or explosive compounds. He grabbed a glass jug of iodine and another of clear ammonia, and hastened back to the cage. He spent only a few seconds there, just long enough to see that Hussein, already compromised from his scorpion sting, was now on the verge of passing out, while Marie could only watch in disbelief. Then he was moving again, running for the door. That was when his enthusiasm wilted.

His plan had been to blow the door with an explosive chemical cocktail, but he now saw the futility of that scheme. The door was about thirty centimeters thick—twelve inches of metal. The force required to blast through it, even if it were possible, would almost certainly kill anyone inside the lab. He jogged in place in front of the solid barrier, looking for a better answer. That was when he saw her.

"Son of a bitch!"

Although her copper-colored hair was concealed by a black watch cap, he had no difficulty recognizing the woman who had called herself Dr. Rebecca Gault, framed in the glass viewport. As shocked as he was by her presence, he was not one bit surprised by her attire. She wore black combat fatigues and looked like she belonged on a SWAT team. After his call to the International Red Cross, he had justly assumed her to be some kind of intelligence operative, probably with the DGSE, one of the world's most ruthless espionage agencies, but he could not have imagined that her mission would coincide with his own. Then again, he would not in his wildest dreams have believed that Pierre Chiron would trap him inside a gigantic pizza oven.

As he watched, Rebecca activated the tram from the control board, and then sprinted to catch the car as it accelerated from the complex. She was pulled aboard by her comrades, and at that instant, Kismet caught a final glimpse of his former mentor, sitting sphinx-like on the flatbed.

He realized painfully that he had stopped moving his feet, and that his boot soles were nearly gone. He rocked back onto his heels, where there was a little more insulation remaining, and tore his attention away from the now empty window. The interval had brought him no closer to a solution. If he couldn't go through the door, what did that leave?

The walls? The floor?

The door might have been a foot thick, but the floor almost certainly was not. The fact that the stainless steel had grown so warm, so quickly suggested that it was relatively thin, with some kind of burner unit underneath. It was a slim hope, but if nothing else, it was something to do in the last remaining seconds of his life.

He set the jugs on the floor and removed the stopper from each so that the expansion of the contents would not cause them to burst. Nevertheless, it was like putting a kettle of water on a stove. Within seconds, a stinging vapor cloud began to boil off the ammonia. Kismet was too busy to notice.

Holding his *kukri* in a two-handed grip, he chopped down at a section of the floor near the corner where the door met the wall. The impact rang through the steel blade and vibrated in his hands, but there was a dimple in the floor at the point of contact. He changed his grip and tried a different technique, stabbing downward with all his weight behind the blow. The tip of the *kukri* pierced the sheet steel to a depth of nearly three centimeters.

Yes!

He worked the blade back and forth. While the metal was nowhere near molten, it seemed softer somehow, almost brittle. He twisted the knife and forced it deeper until it abruptly peeled back like a piece of tin foil.

A blinding white light burst through the hole and Kismet drew back involuntarily, He had punched through right on top of a blazing strip of magnesium. But the initial shock of the revelation was quickly swept away by the deeper implication of what he had discovered: There was a hollow space under the floor.

He shoved the bottle of ammonia into the void, then quickly decanted the iodine into it. The jug overflowed, spilling the remainder of the iodine down the outside of the glass where it either dripped down into the fire or sizzled away to nothing on the floor, leaving behind a rust-colored residue. As soon as the bottle was empty, he sprinted back toward his companions.

"Get down!"

They stared at him in disbelief. Was he actually suggesting that they trade their temporary island for the infernal touch of the steel floor? He didn't pause to explain, but leaped onto the cages and swept them off, one in each arm.

To yield the maximum explosive energy, iodine crystals, distilled from the liquid solution of which the element composes only about four percent, would need to steep in pure ammonia for a full day, yielding a brown sludge known as NI-3—nitrogen tri-iodine—one of the most volatile substances known to man. As long as it remained moist, buffered by the liquid ammonia, it would be relatively safe, but once the crystals dried out, any sort of impact would trigger a tremendous blast. Kismet did not have the time to harvest the crystals or slow brew the NI-3, but he was gambling on the extreme temperatures within the laboratory to expedite the process. If he was right, the liquid would boil away within a few seconds, and when the heat cracked the glass jug, with a little bit of luck, it would blow a hole in the corner big enough for them to escape.

If he was wrong....

The next thing he remembered was laying on the scorching floor, struggling to draw a breath. His ears were ringing and he felt as though he had just been hit by a truck. The imperative need to get away from the heat stimulated him to action before he could fully grasp what had happened, but it took only a glance to see that a dramatic change had occurred in the lab. Everything not bolted down had been blasted to the rear of the enclosure and every piece of glass that had survived the thunderous closing of the door had been pulverized. More importantly though, a section of the floor and lower wall had bulged outward, opening a narrow crack to the outside.

His companions were also just beginning to recover from the concussion, unconsciously writhing on the burning hot surface. Kismet pulled them up, and without waiting for their full cooperation, began dragging them toward the door. Marie regained her senses first, and upon realizing that escape was actually possible, lent herself to the effort of pulling the dazed Hussein across the lab. It was a ten-second journey through hell.

Stripes of red metal, where the steel was closest to the magnesium fires, outlined the walls and floor like the ribs of some terrifying dragon, viewed from within its belly. The heat was staggering, sucking their will and vital energy, and turning the very air they breathed into a poisonous wind that seared their lungs, but somehow, they made it.

"You first," croaked Kismet.

Marie looked as though she might demur or protest that Hussein should be the first out, but the logic of his request was unassailable. As the smallest member of the trio, she was guaranteed salvation in a situation where every second mattered. She clenched her teeth against the expected agony of contact with the edge of the doorframe and the portion of the wall that had bulged outward, and then plunged through the gap. A moment later, her blistered hand appeared beseechingly in the opening. "Send him through!"

Kismet bustled the still unresponsive Iraqi toward the hole, but it was plainly obvious that he was not going to pass through as easily. He gripped Hussein's shirt and started shoving. Marie was exerting all her strength from the other side, but Hussein seemed to be wedged in place. He redoubled his efforts, shouting at the top of his lungs for Marie to pull.

Hussein's shirt, and the flesh beneath it, tore free of the metal spur that had held him in place. He emitted a harsh cry, suddenly coming alert, and then was gone, pulled through the hole in Marie's grasp. Kismet didn't wait for encouragement. He plunged head first into the opening, his arms extended above his head like a diver, and pushed off with his feet. By wriggling his shoulders, he was able to squirm through the narrow gap, but it was nevertheless like escaping from a fiery womb. The torn metal sheets and the crumbled rock of the cavern wall formed a rough circle that tore through his shirt and dug long furrows into his flesh, but through it all, he felt Marie's grip, stronger than he would have imagined, around his wrists, drawing him relentlessly on. As soon as his upper body was clear, he pulled free of her grip and scrambled clear of the hole.

It was like diving into a mountain lake. He hungrily gasped fresh air into his tortured lungs, and as he lay on his back, all he could do was savor the touch of cool stone against his skin. Marie huddled at his side. Her hands were bright red and blistered from second-degree contact burns, and her face was similarly suffused with scarlet beneath a cap of lank, distressed hair, but she appeared otherwise intact. Hussein, though on his feet, did not appear to be doing quite that well. His gaze was unfocused as he meandered away from the blasted laboratory. Kismet tried to call to him but his starved lungs refused to yield the breath necessary to utter a sound. Looking into Marie's grateful eyes, he decided that it could probably wait a few minutes. After the hellish struggle to survive the laboratory, his relief at being alive overwhelmed even his desire to comprehend Chiron's betrayal. That too could wait, at least until they were done rejoicing.

Suddenly a noise like a string of firecrackers bursting in rapid succession rattled between the walls, and he knew the celebration was over. Marie gasped in alarm and instinctively pressed close to the wall of the cavern, intuiting that the sound was indeed gunfire. The young Iraqi stood frozen in place out in the open, neither looking nor moving in any purposeful way, but Kismet noticed that he had his hands pressed to his abdomen in a vain attempt to staunch a deluge of crimson. Then another burst erupted from the unseen sniper's weapon, and nearly tore Hussein Hamallah in half.

THIRTEEN

For a fleeting instant, he thought that Rebecca must have left some of her force behind to ensure that no one would escape to tell the tale of Chiron's vile betrayal. But the throaty roar of an AK-47 was an unmistakable sound, and he figured Rebecca and her cohorts for something with a little more finesse. Who did that leave?

The shots had come from the direction of the tunnel leading to the cavern where the helicopter was hangared, but from his vantage, the mouth of that passage was eclipsed by a protruding section of cavern wall. If he could not see the shooter, then it stood to reason…

"Stay here," he whispered. "I'll try to draw their fire."

Before Marie could protest, he was on his feet and sprinting for the center of the chamber, not far from where Hussein lay spread-eagled like a sacrifice. He had barely gone three steps when the assault rifle roared again, only this time it was in concert with a second. He was vaguely aware of the 7.62millimeter rounds drilling through the still air all around. The snipers were firing fully automatic, the spray and pray technique. There was a skill to leading a target, and he was betting his life that these shooters had skipped that lesson. Still, all it took was one lucky shot. He dove the last two meters like a baseball player stealing second, and hunkered down behind the control box for the tram.

He barely had time to catch his breath when the first of several rounds punched clear through the thin metal frame and exited dangerously close to where he was crouching. Twisting around, he scrambled for the more substantial cover of the bumper at the end of the tracks. The heavy steel frame rang with each impact, but the rounds did not penetrate.

When a break in the assault came, he risked a quick look around the edge of his shield. There were three of them now, Arab men wearing ragged civilian clothes, and curiously bareheaded. He couldn't begin to guess how they had discovered the complex. Maybe they were loyalist insurgents, checking a known resupply base, or maybe they were local hoodlums, hired by Rebecca or Chiron to eliminate all witnesses to their treachery. He didn't have time to wrestle with the question, but filed it away behind a curtain, along with the overwhelming sense of guilt at having brought young

Hussein to his ignominious demise.

The shooters saw him a moment later and unleashed another volley. That was all the motivation he needed. He burst from behind the bumper and sprinted for the opposite side of the complex, toward the open maw of Laboratory Two. They chased him with bullets, and it wasn't until the lead started blasting into the stacked munitions containers that he realized just how close they were coming. Then he was gone, vanished into the maze of crates that had camouflaged the lab where Saddam's scientists had labored to develop a nuclear weapon.

The barrage ceased almost immediately and the gunmen began warily advancing. Kismet did not try to monitor their approach. If they even caught a glimpse of him, his only plan would fail. One of the Arabs unleashed a short, random burst into the lab, but his comrades chastised him, telling him not to waste his ammunition shooting at shadows, or at least that was Kismet's best approximation. He could hear their steps, their breathing, and the sound of crates being moved as the men pressed deeper into the lab.

There was a loud bang as one of the shipping containers was upended only a few steps away from where Kismet was concealed. Too close. They were checking the crates to see if he was hiding in one.

Maybe this wasn't such a good idea.

The men stayed close together, careful not to flag each other with their weapons, but keeping vigil in different directions. One of them kept checking to their rear to make sure that they had not already passed by their prey. They knew enough not to separate, dashing Kismet's hopes of subduing one and seizing his weapon.

The trio left the cluster of empty boxes behind and pressed deeper into the lab. When they reached the table with the detonators, the leader of the group stopped so suddenly he almost dropped his rifle.

Kismet made his move. From his perch, prone and pressed flat atop the wall of stacked crates, he rolled toward the exit. But as his weight shifted, the box beneath him slid and all the cartons, like some toddler's creation with building blocks, crashed outward. Kismet hit the stone floor hard enough to knock the wind from his lungs. He gasped for air, surrounded by the chaos his movements had triggered. The three gunmen were staring right at him.

The leader moved first, swinging the muzzle of his Kalashnikov toward Kismet. Breathing or not, he knew he had to move. As he ducked, bullets started shredding the wood and plastic containers that were now his only source of concealment. Packing foam showered down like confetti, but while none of the rounds found his flesh, a shard of wood lodged in the ravaged fabric of his shirt and pierced the skin of his back.

He caught a breath, which was a good thing, and reached the right doorpost of the lab. The gunmen were randomly spraying the area, but most of their fire was concentrated on the center of the jumbled cartons. Kismet spied his goal and waited for a break in fire. When the gunmen on his right paused to reload, Kismet sprang up.

"Nice knowing you, fellows." He slammed his hand against the red button.

There was a crack as the stays were blown out of the way, followed by an ear-splitting shriek. The large metal guillotine gate dropped so quickly that Kismet jumped back, startled. The heavy panel smashed into the cluttered crates, blasting them to splinters as it fell relentlessly, unstoppably downward.

And then it stopped.

There was about half a meter of space above the groove in the floor, where the panel ought to have firmly settled after its brief one-way journey, and the bottom of the door itself. The smashed debris of the crates, though individually flimsy, were in concert just enough to hold open the door.

Kismet breathed an oath as he stared in disbelief at the opening. He swore again as a rifle muzzle peeked out from beneath the barrier and swung in his direction. But instead of ducking away from the weapon, he leaped forward. His foot stamped down on the exposed end of the gun, and the force of the blow rolled the front sight post at the business end of the weapon, causing it to twist in the man's grip just as the trigger was pulled.

It was like stepping on a live wire. Flame jetted from the barrel as an explosion of gases and solid projectiles exploded into the stone floor. The close proximity of the discharge caused the weapon to slam back into the gunman's forehead and Kismet almost stumbled again, but caught himself when the weapon fell silent. He immediately snatched the rifle up, shifting his grip from the scorching hot barrel to the wooden stock, and then put it to his shoulder. As he did, another AK-47 peeked out from under the door.

Kismet fanned the trigger, unleashing a burst at the opening. One of the bullets might have hit its target, but the rest found something even luckier. The lead projectiles smashed into the fragments that were bracing the doors, perforating them just enough that the constant pressure of the door caused them to finally explode outward. The door crunched down the remaining distance, decapitating the Kalashnikov and trapping the three gunmen inside a laboratory that was already starting to grow uncomfortably warm.

Kismet sagged against the steel barrier and let the muzzle of his captured rifle drop. Marie wasn't where he had left her, but a movement in the shadows near the doorway to Laboratory Four, the only one in the complex he had not actually seen, caught his attention. Why was she moving? He took a step in that direction, but a burst of gunfire from the tunnel mouth drove him back.

"Damn it!" *How many more of these guys are there?*

He didn't linger where he was. No sooner was the oath past his lips than he was running for the opening to Laboratory One. After all that had happened since Chiron's betrayal, the sight of the fermentation tanks was strangely welcoming. He hastened behind the foremost one and with a great heave, rolled it over on its side. The noise of the hollow metal receptacle hitting the floor reverberated like a gong throughout the complex. *Guess they'll know where I am now.*

He stood alongside the fermenter, near the double-thickness of metal that formed its base, and rolled it forward like an enormous wheel, out into the open. Rifle fire instantly hammered into the tank. The bullets punched right through its wall and slammed against the interior surface hard enough to create bulging dents in the exterior. A few of the rounds went completely through, missing Kismet by scant centimeters. As a shield, the fermentation tank left a lot to be desired. He decided to give his enemies something else to worry about. With one hand still turning the base, he held the AK-47 high and fired a burst left then right. Over the thunderous din he heard a shriek of agony, and knew that at least one effort to flank his position had been thwarted.

Protected behind the gradually crumbling mobile wall of aluminum, he traversed the open area to where Marie was concealed. From the moment he made eye contact with her, she began flashing hand signals to warn him of further advancements, and each time he turned them back with a barrage from the captured rifle. Nevertheless, his defensive response was chewing through his very limited supply of ammunition. Then he saw something that took him completely by surprise. Marie raised her hand and pointed, and a jet of flame leaped from her fingertip.

She's got a gun?

Marie snapped off several carefully aimed shots, laying down enough covering fire for him to finish the crossing. Up close, he saw that her weapon was a small .25 caliber automatic, easily enough concealed. Maybe that was why he hadn't seen it. It was standard operating protocol for GHC personnel to be armed in a potentially hostile environment, but the sight of her with the firearm struck him as odd.

Still, she couldn't have picked a better moment to come out of her shell, he thought. He jerked a thumb toward Laboratory Four. "Anything useful in there?"

"It's mostly storage." She leaned out for a split-second, and then ducked back as another volley of automatic rifle fire hammered into the fermenter. "But I did find this."

In her hands was a misshapen gray cube. "Semtex?"

She nodded. "I cut this from a larger piece. This whole place has been wired."

He rolled the block between his fingers. With enough time and the right material, it might be possible to fashion some kind of weapon from the chunk of polymer-bonded high explosives. The problem with Semtex, and most other plasticized blasting agents, was that they were too safe. The only effective way to set them off was with det cord or a blasting cap. He stuffed the cube in his pocket. Maybe it would come in handy later. "We've got to get out of here. It's a sure bet we'll run out of ammo before they do."

"The trolley is gone."

"Pierre and his new friends took it." He ignored her inquisitive look. "It'll be a good half hour before it comes back, provided they don't sabotage it at the other end. That's too long to wait."

"So what can we do?"

He gave her a grim smile. "Plan B."

When the fermentation tank began rolling again, trundling toward the center of the complex near the controls for the tram, the five surviving gunmen unleashed a brutal assault. While three of them maintained a withering barrage directly onto the aluminum tank, virtually shredding it in the process, two of their confederates circled wide in order to catch their prey from the side. One of them fell from a single rifle shot, but the other took cover behind the control panel and waited for the tank to get a little closer.

But Kismet and Marie were no longer using the tank as a shield. Crouched in the shadows inside the lab, they waited until the attention of their foes was firmly fixed on the rolling barrier before making their move. Kismet had taken the sniper shot that killed one of the flanking team because the man was about to discover their deception. None of the others noticed that the shot had not come from behind the fermenter.

They made it as far as the door to Laboratory Three, the crucible where Chiron's betrayal had nearly proved fatal, before the militants noticed them. With no effective cover, Kismet chose the best possible defense. "Run!"

Bullets exploded against the cavern walls and showered them with chips of stone. Kismet felt something small and hard smack into his thigh, probably a ricochet, but kept moving in spite of the dull ache that began spreading from the point of impact. Then they reached the tunnel to the helicopter hangar and left the battle behind. The respite was brief.

As they reached the top of the passage, Marie's arm snapped up alongside him, the pistol seeming like a natural extension of her hand, and squeezed off two shots. Kismet's eyes had only just registered the presence of yet another Arab gunman standing in their path, when two red flowers blossomed on his chest. A third shot drilled a hole between his eyes before Kismet could bring his rifle up.

Kismet stared in stunned disbelief as the gunman dropped to his knees and pitched forward. Then the concussion of automatic rifle fire, accompanied by an eruption of stone chips from the wall behind him, returned his focus to the urgency of their situation. He sprawled forward, unconsciously pulling Marie down as well, and began crawling toward the parked helicopter.

He hadn't seen the second shooter in his initial survey of the spacious cavern, but there were a lot of places to hide and the shots had ceased as soon as he dived for cover. "Where is he?"

Marie shook her head as she ejected the magazine from her pistol and fed in a full one. "I didn't see. But the rest of them will be coming up the tunnel soon."

Kismet's only reply was a grimace. He glanced around, looking for the unseen sniper, but his gaze fell on something else instead. "I've got an idea. Cover me."

He half-expected her to protest, but she gave a terse nod and rolled into a prone firing position, with the pistol locked in a two-handed grip. On that tacit signal, Kismet rose to a crouch and dashed toward the rows of drums off to the left. When the gunman opened fire, peppering the wall behind the fuel dump with 7.62 millimeter rounds, he dropped again.

"Maybe this wasn't such a hot idea," he murmured. But then he heard the distinctive pop of Marie's pistol over the roar of the AK-47. The latter weapon fell silent first.

Without waiting for further prompting, he tipped one of the drums onto its side and commenced rolling it toward the mouth of the tunnel. Marie was on her feet again, with her back pressed against the Hind-D and her pistol at the ready. "Got him."

Kismet withheld praise, focusing instead on the task at hand. He shoulder-slung his captured AK and drew his *kukri*. Using the heavy blade like a can opener, he hacked into the drum lid, cutting several triangular holes that immediately began to spew hi-grade petroleum. As the noxious fumes assaulted his mucous membranes, he pulled the lump of Semtex from his pocket and pressed it into one of the holes, then gave the drum a kick that sent it rumbling down the tunnel. The container traveled only as far as the first bend in the passage—about twenty meters—before coming to rest against the wall, but it continued to vomit jet fuel onto the sloping passage.

"Stand back!" He unlimbered the Kalashnikov and held its muzzle close to the pool of flammable liquid. A short pull on the trigger was all it took to ignite the substance, and with a whoosh, the entire passage filled with flame. For just a moment, he thought he could hear screams echoing up from the depths, but decided it was just his imagination.

Suddenly, the ground heaved under his feet and simultaneously, a pillar of smoke and dust exploded from the tunnel opening. The burning trail of jet fuel was snuffed out like a candle flame. Kismet was back on his feet in an instant, running for the side hatch of the helicopter. He threw open the door and turned to admonish Marie to get in, but the words died in his throat. The Frenchwoman seemed to be aiming her pistol right at him…

No. Someone behind me? In the helo?

When she did not fire, he took a sideways step, bringing his own weapon up as he turned. A robed figure, swathed in a *kefiya* wrapped Bedouin-style around both head and neck, stood in the opening, his hands raised in surrender. Kismet's finger tightened on the trigger instinctively, but he checked his fire. The man was unarmed and seemed to pose no threat. And there was something familiar about his eyes…

Kismet reversed the rifle in his hands and stabbed the wooden stock of the weapon into the man's abdomen. As the Arab doubled over, he followed through with a butt-stroke to the back of the turbaned head. The stranger collapsed onto the stone floor beneath the extended rotor blades and did not move. With a greater degree of caution, Kismet quickly checked the interior of the Hind gun ship before encouraging Marie to join him inside. The mystery of the unarmed Arab stowaway would have to be left behind with him.

As he settled into the pilot's seat in the lower cockpit, surrounded by banks of switches, gauges and indicator lights, the enormity of the final phase of his audacious escape plan finally hit him. The control panels were marked in Cyrillic characters, with Arabic equivalents painted in white alongside, but even though Kismet had a good grasp of Russian and a decent comprehension of the predominant language of the Iraqi people, the labels might as well have been written in ancient Sumerian cuneiform. He sensed that Marie was right behind him, silently goading him to take action, and clenched his fists to steel his nerve. Starting from the right, he began flipping switches—all of them. One by one, different systems of the aircraft became active and corresponding indicators on the panel began to glow. One of the toggles caused an audible grinding sound to vibrate through the fuselage before flipping back to the "off" position.

He eyed the lever to the side of his chair. It was actually two controls in one. By raising or lowering it, much like the hand brake in an automobile, he could adjust the pitch of the rotor blades, but it was also a twist throttle control. He tried the starter switch again, this time opening the throttle gently as he did. The grinding noise repeated, then turned into a steady vibration. Above his head, the main rotor began to turn, ever so slowly. Kismet risked a triumphant grin in Marie's direction, then continued flipping the remaining switches.

"It's fortunate that you know how to fly this thing," she commented.

Kismet gave a chuckle as he feathered the throttle. "That may be overstating my abilities."

He could tell by her long silence that she was wrestling with his comment, perhaps trying to determine if there was some idiomatic trick at work or a joke so thickly disguised as to elude her sense of humor. When she finally spoke again, it was with the caution of someone entering a minefield. "You have flown a helicopter?"

The five blades of the rotor assembly were now whipping by too fast to be seen by the naked eye, further disturbing the smoke and dust in the air of the cavern.

"Sort of," he confessed, trying not to burden her with his inadequacy as a pilot. "This one is a little different than…well, what I'm used to."

The awful truth of the matter was that he did not know how to fly a helicopter. But for one brief and ultimately cataclysmic experience, he had never sat in the pilot's chair. Nevertheless, he had spent many hours in the sky and had always made it a point to pay close attention to what the flight crews did. He knew the controls by heart, and had a pretty good idea when to be aggressive and when to use a light touch.

He checked the RPM gauge; it was climbing steadily, but was still well away from the red zone. The roar of the engine and the rapid thump of the rotors beating the air filled the small cabin with a deep cacophony. He increased the throttle a little more, then eased up on the collective. The craft wobbled beneath him as the rotor vanes began pushing air, seemingly lightening the helicopter. He added a little more pitch, then continued gently adding more throttle until the Hind began to rise.

Now was the most critical moment. In the close quarters of the cavern, the slightest mistake might send the helicopter careening into the walls. He kept one hand on the cyclic—the control stick between his knees that tilted the rotor assembly to provide directional movement—and pushed the throttle a little further.

He felt a surge of adrenaline as the nose dipped, but before he could do anything to correct the problem, the Hind leveled out, hovering about five meters above the stone surface. Kismet glanced out the side window. Indirect daylight continued to pour in through the spacious opening more than fifteen meters above and to his left. With his confidence growing, Kismet experimented with the rudder pedals and succeeded in swiveling the aircraft on its rotor axis so that its nose was pointed directly at the wall below the opening. He then raised the pitch a little more, and the Hind gently ascended toward the roof of the cavern.

He threw Marie another grin, realizing only then that she had been holding her breath and gripping the back of his headrest. "This isn't so hard after all."

Then everything began moving, and no matter how he moved the controls, he couldn't stop the chaos.

FOURTEEN

No one remained alive in the laboratory complex. The survivors of the gun battle had, to a man, been caught in the conflagration in the tunnel or crushed by the ensuing blast of jet fuel and plastic explosives. But their fate had been kinder than that suffered by Farid and his one remaining companion, trapped in Laboratory Two. The steadily rising temperature in the lab had killed them in a matter of minutes, but viewed through the window of a man prematurely experiencing hell, it must have seemed an eternity.

When the temperature reached a relatively low forty-two degrees Celsius, the enzymes essential to their continued existence began to denaturalize and brain death followed swiftly. By this time, neither of the men were conscious. Their body moisture had been completely leeched away, leading first to delirium, and then stupor. Both the joy of discovering fully functional nuclear detonators, and the terror of realizing that they were going to be cooked alive, faded into darkness as the men collapsed on the searing hot floor and thought no more. The temperature continued to climb.

Gradually, the combustible materials in the lab began to darken and smolder. The wooden crates burned without igniting, while the foam packing material and plastic cartons liquefied, releasing clots of acrid black smoke. And then, without warning, it was all swept away.

Although more than fifteen minutes remained on the timer that would activate the Semtex charges left behind by the French commandos, the increasing temperature in Laboratory Two, where Rebecca had placed an unusually large amount of the Czech-produced explosive, had been steadily conducting energy, in the form of heat, through the thin insulation that surrounded the detonator wire. Finally, it was enough to trigger the blasting cap and ignite the Semtex.

A massive explosion blasted the heavy door clear across the main complex and into the opposing wall. In that same instant, the rest of the charges planted throughout the facility went off simultaneously. In the space of a single second, an explosive force equal to a hundred kilograms of TNT, was released in the relatively confined environment of the cavern system. All that energy had to go somewhere. The shock wave splintered the stone walls of the cavern, turning the smallest fissures into gaping faults. The ceiling crumbled inward, and the earth began to move.

In a rush of comprehension, Kismet realized what was happening and what he had to do. With a smooth efficiency that belied his lack of expertise, he raised the collective and pushed forward on the cyclic control. The Mi-25 seemed to leap through the open mouth of the tunnel, passing over the motionless body of the sniper Marie had dispatched on his perch high above the floor.

Suddenly, their way was blocked by a wall of shivering stone, rushing ever closer. Kismet reflexively pulled back on the stick, and the helicopter abruptly lurched backward and rose out of the canyon, into the blazing early morning sun. He centered the cyclic stick and leveled the craft into a hover above the bare plateau, more to steady his nerves than anything else.

Two bare-headed men were struggling to stand as the surface on which they stood crumbled away into the narrow crevasse from which the Hind had just emerged. There was no one else in sight. Kismet left them to their fate and turned his attention to the horizon. The featureless desert spread out as far as the eye could see, in every direction.

"Where are we?" Marie was almost shouting in his ear to be heard.

He glanced at the control panel, identifying something that looked like a compass, but other than their immediate orientation, it offered little enlightenment. He had no clue how to make use of the aircraft's avionics package or any of its other systems. "We can't be too far from Babylon." He searched his memory of the region's geography. "If we head northeast, we're bound to intersect the Euphrates at some point."

Marie's nod of encouragement was all he needed. He brought the Hind onto the desired heading and accelerated across the desert. Confronted by the stillness of the wasteland and wrapped in the cloak of ambient noise from the jet engines, he was finally able to process the flood of revelations that had turned his perception of reality upside-down. Now that the danger was finally past, he could try to begin to make sense of Chiron's betrayal and everything else he had witnessed from that point forward.

One hundred and fifty miles to the south, a similarly imponderable mystery was being contemplated. A senior airman of the United States Air Force, operating the radar station aboard an E-3 Sentry Airborne Warning and Control System (AWACS) stared in disbelief at the blip which had abruptly appeared on her screen. A few swift keystrokes verified that the object illuminated by pulses of Doppler radar was indeed an aircraft and that it was not returning the standard "friendly" signal. The airman squinted at the screen a moment longer, waiting for the computer to give a more conclusive identification, and when it finally returned that there was an eighty-two percent likelihood that the contact was a Russian-made Mil gun ship, from the family of helicopters bearing the NATO designation "HIND", she spoke a phrase that had gone almost unheard during the preceding weeks of war: "We have a bogey!"

Saeed didn't want to open his eyes; didn't want to see the horror of his own premature burial. He was alive, no question about that, and was having no difficulty breathing. Aside from a scattering of bruises—some from falling debris but the most painful delivered courtesy of Kismet's rifle butt—he sensed no dire injury, but that fact gave him little comfort. It was only a matter of time before he suffocated or perished from dehydration.

Strangely, when he wept, his tears were for his brother. Unfettered emotion poured from his breast. He had lived a lifetime of conflict with his own flesh and blood, and at the end, had twisted Farid's deepest convictions to suit his own selfish ends. He was as guilty as the man whose actions had directly ended his brother's life. The only solace he found in his dark tomb was that he and Farid would share this unmarked grave.

But then daylight fell upon his exposed face, rousing him from his despair with a golden warmth that felt like nothing less than the grace of God, and Saeed Tariq, filled with a new, divine purpose, opened his eyes.

They struck so quickly that Kismet almost jumped out of his chair. Two USAF F-16 Fighting Falcons thundering across the sky at Mach Three had approached from his six and done a precursory fly-by that felt close enough to scrape the paint from the Hind. He recovered his wits just in time to steady the stick as the combined jet wash of the two fighter planes buffeted the helicopter and momentarily sucked the air from its intakes.

"What the hell?" The fighters were mere specks against the azure backdrop, trailing a filament of smoke that gradually curled around as the two warplanes lined up for another pass. In classic wing formation, the two jets swung to the right and approached from Kismet's three o'clock.

"Look!" Marie shrieked, stabbing a finger at the instrument panel. A large warning light was flashing, and although Kismet could make no sense of the markings, its ominous urgency was as plain as day. *Missile lock!*

Kismet looked frantically around the cockpit for a radio, wasting precious seconds in the futile search. The communications system was right in front of him, but without the headset and microphone, which were integrated into the pilot's helmet, the device was useless.

"Incoming missile!" Marie screamed again. "Do something!"

He nodded. "I'll put us down."

A look of desperation twisted her glamorous countenance, then she abruptly turned away. Kismet let her go, focusing his attention on trying to get the Hind down onto the desert floor where they might, with a little luck, be able to abandon the aircraft before the missile turned it into a flaming ball of scrap. He pulled the cyclic back in order to hover, then cut the pitch to reduce lift until the helicopter started to plummet.

With a lurch that threw Kismet against the cylindrical side windscreen, the Hind abruptly turned into the path of the F-16s and shot forward. He tried to regain control, but the sticks and pedals fought his steady pressure, behaving as if the aircraft were being controlled remotely…or by another pilot.

Marie?

He could barely hear her over the din of the engines, but once he realized where she was, he understood. Marie had climbed into the second cockpit, situated just above his own, and had commandeered control of the craft utilizing the redundant flight systems.

"Damn it," he raged. Her hysteria was going to get them killed surer than any missile.

Only she wasn't hysterical. Kismet stopped fighting the controls and watched with a mixture of horror and amazement as the Mi-25 raced headlong into the path of a supersonic missile. Suddenly a new noise joined the tumult. From either side of the helicopter, 12.7 millimeter rounds, every fifth one a green tracer, shot ahead of the helicopter from a pair of wing-mounted four-barreled Gatling guns.

Thousands of rounds spewed across the sky, forming a virtual veil of metal between the helicopter and the incoming AIM-9 Sidewinder missile. The projectile abruptly went out of control, venting exhaust from a pair of holes that had pierced the rocket body clear through. The Sidewinder corkscrewed wildly for a moment, then suddenly exploded well away from any of the aircraft.

A second missile was released an instant before both jets, now directly in the path of the Hind's guns, peeled off and climbed skyward. The Sidewinder acquired them instantly, its thermal sensors fixing on the helicopter's jet exhaust, but it was a tenuous lock. The Hind was equipped with passive countermeasures to mask its infrared signature and reduce its vulnerability to heat-seeking weapons, but it was still the hottest thing in the sky.

Kismet could only watch in horror as a dark speck trailing a finger of flame and smoke raced toward them. Abruptly, the nose of the helicopter swung up as if to follow the F-16s, and he lost sight of the missile. There was a roar from the side of the aircraft, louder than any gunshot, and for a moment, he was sure that it had struck, but then a ball of bright light shot out ahead of the Hind, leaping skyward as if to chase down the jet fighters.

Kismet was stunned. Marie had just unleashed one of the helicopter's anti-tank rockets at the Air Force jets. Desperate though their situation was, no possible good could come of engaging the other aircraft. Not only was it unthinkable to Kismet that they should fire on American pilots, but the Hind was hopelessly outmatched. The 9M17 Skorpion missile—NATO designation AT-2 SWATTER—was a radio-controlled, operator-guided rocket designed to destroy mobile ground targets, which meant that a human operator had to keep the enemy lined up in cross-hairs that were integrated into his helmet visor until the projectile made contact. And because the best defense against the Swatter was evasion, it was of necessity a slow-moving weapon, which allowed the operator to make continual corrections. There was no way the missile would ever get close to a supersonic aircraft. All it would do was piss them off.

Then something unexpected happened. From below the

helicopter, a streak of light like a thunderbolt blasted the Skorpion missile from the sky. The shockwave of the Sidewinder blowing apart the anti-tank rocket hammered the Hind and showered the windscreen with twisted bits of metal, but did no real damage. The Russian-made aircraft sailed through the debris cloud like a surfer pushing through a wave.

Kismet abandoned all thought of trying to wrestle control of the helicopter from Marie. He couldn't imagine how she came to have such an intimate understanding of combat aviation, and didn't care to question her on the subject. It was enough that she had kept them alive this long. He leaned forward in the cockpit, craning his head around to locate the F-16s.

The Hind reached the apex of its climb and heeled over, rolling into a shallow dive. Marie cut back the throttle and in the relative quiet, Kismet heard her shouting his name. He cautiously unbuckled his safety restraints and pulled himself out of the lower cockpit. Marie looked away from the desperate task at hand only long enough to thrust an oblong plastic object into his hands. It was a Qualcomm satellite telephone. Kismet didn't need to be told what to do.

He dropped back into the cockpit and buckled in before activating the phone. It took him a moment to figure out how to access the menu of previously called numbers, but when he found it, a long list of contacts scrolled down the liquid crystal display. Several of the most recent, made within the last two days, were to the same number, which was odd because he couldn't remember having seen her make or receive any calls. He muttered the digits twice, committing them to memory, then continued searching until he found a call made almost forty-eight hours previously to the UNMOVIC headquarters in New York. He selected the number and hit the send button.

On the instrument panel, the "missile warning" light began flashing again as the F-16s focused radar beams on their slippery prey. Kismet imagined that the pilots' amazement at Marie's evasive tactics was equal to his own. No doubt they had expected a very short and uneventful engagement. He and Marie had been lucky that the first volley had employed Sidewinder missiles; heat-seekers were easier to elude than—

The light went solid, and he knew that their luck had run out.

"You have reached the United Nations—" He hit '0' to cut off the automated receptionist. There was a click followed by an electronic trill.

The Hind abruptly plunged earthward as Marie pulled out all the stops, but Kismet knew it wouldn't be enough. The constant radar signal could only mean one thing: They were being hunted by radar-guided missile, likely an AIM-120 Slammer Advanced Medium Range Air to Air Missile (AMRAAM), one of the most relentless aerial combat weapons in the modern arsenal. Faster even than the planes that carried it, the AMRAAM could be guided by the pilot for greatest efficiency or allowed to follow its internal targeting system. There were a few defenses against the AMRAAM, such as radar scattering chaff or nap of the earth flying, but the odds favored the hound over the fox.

Marie had taken the helicopter down almost to the level of the desert floor. Its rotors were stirring up a blinding whirlwind of sand in which arcs of static electricity danced like capering elemental demons. The missile lock warning did not flicker.

"United Nations. How may I direct your call?"

When he opened his mouth to answer, he was struck by the sheer ridiculousness of the request he was about to make. He had little doubt that the operator would simply hang up on an imagined prankster. *Oh well, it was a fool's gambit anyway.* "This is Nick Kismet with UNESCO. I am in the desert west of Al Hillah, Iraq in a captured helicopter, taking friendly fire. I need to contact coalition air command immediately. This is a matter of life and death."

The long pause at the other end was, he decided, a good sign.

Although it was impossible to see the projectile screaming after the Hind at Mach 4, Marie was nevertheless able to chart its approach on the helicopter's active radar screen, a system which she had known how to activate. The AMRAAM did not have to actually make contact with its prey in order to destroy it. Rather it was the shock wave from the detonation of its forty pound high-explosive warhead at close proximity to the target that did the real damage. The AIM-120 needed only to get within about thirty meters to swat the helicopter out of the sky.

The radar showed only smooth desert in all directions. There would be no ducking behind a rock outcropping at the last instant to shield them from the blast. She pulled back on the cyclic, lifting skyward for a moment, just long enough to deploy a small grenade from a rear-facing launcher before diving toward the ground once more. The following blip on the radar screen abruptly vanished in what looked like a miniature snowstorm; the radio waves from the radar dome had been deflected away from the receiver by a shower of metallic chaff particles. Her triumph was short lived. The missile burst from the haze and resumed the chase, closing on them like a sports car chasing down a runner. Marie watched it get closer...closer...and enter the kill zone.

She whipped the Hind sideways and increased pitch and throttle simultaneously so that the helicopter shifted in three dimensions away from the flight path of the Slammer. The warhead detonated at that instant, creating an expanding sphere of force as hard as concrete that pushed a wall of shrapnel toward the retreating aircraft. The underside of the Hind was hammered by a spray of debris, but only a few of the pieces actually pierced its armor. The shock wave was far more destructive.

"What was—" The operator's inquiry was cut off as the sat phone flew from Kismet's grasp and shattered against a bulkhead. Flailing for a handhold and slammed against his restraints, he barely noticed.

And then the helicopter leveled out and dived back down toward the dunes. Marie was still in control and they were still alive. *But three missiles! Even my luck's not that good.*

Another light started blinking on the control panel, alongside a gauge which measured remaining fuel in pounds. The needle registered below the lowest mark. Shrapnel from the missile blast had evidently ripped through a fuel tank and the resulting hemorrhage had splashed their entire reserve supply across the desert sand. Before this fact could fully register, Kismet saw the missile-warning blink on again. All he could do was sit back and wait for the inevitable.

But Marie was not ready to give up. As a second AMRAAM drew close, she hauled back on the cyclic, executing a heavy-G turn that would have made the fighter pilots green with either envy or nausea. The Hind's nose thrust skyward as it started to climb...and then everything went to hell.

The Mil helicopters of the Hind family had served the Russian military and its export partners well for more than twenty years and were virtually the equal of their western counterparts the Boeing AH-

64 Apache and the Sikorsky UH-60 Blackhawk. But there was one design flaw which had plagued the helicopter in hostile engagements, most notably in Afghanistan where warriors of the Mujahideen had managed to hold their own in a decade-long war of attrition against the superior technology of the Soviet superpower: The Hind had a nasty habit of cutting off its own tail.

When Marie threw the helicopter into its sharp climb, the rotor assembly tilted back to the furthest extreme so that the rotor vanes were whipping over the tail boom with mere millimeters to spare. But the G-forces changed that. The entire aircraft flexed, as if the helicopter was trying to climb a literal hill, and in that instant, the deadly arc of the main rotor passed *through* the tail boom. A horrific shudder vibrated through the craft, accompanied by an ear-splitting shriek of rending metal, and then the fuselage, no longer stabilized by the sideways turning blades of the rudder, began to whip violently around beneath the rotors. Kismet felt as though his eyes were being ripped from his skull. He was pinned against the web belts that held him in place, unable to do anything to relieve the pressure of the centrifuge. But he could tell they were falling and the AMRAAM was still chasing them.

Marie's desperate maneuver had bought them a few more seconds. The missile's momentum had carried it past the aircraft without detonating, and although it never lost its lock, the projectile had to travel several kilometers in order to swing around and home in on the stricken Hind.

Somehow, Marie managed to boost the throttle in tandem with the jet engines, pushing the helicopter's thrust until its airspeed was more than seventy knots. For just a moment, the Mi-25 leveled out and control was regained. The force of onrushing air against the fuselage straightened their attitude like a weathervane in a stiff wind. It was the only appropriate response to the loss of a tail rotor, but it didn't allow for a lot of maneuverability. About all they could do was stay aloft until the AMRAAM caught them.

The needle on the instrument panel registered their rapid descent. Marie was trying to put the helicopter down. Maybe there was still a chance. But then the turbines coughed and fell silent. The last of the fuel had been consumed. Although the rotors continued to turn, grinding out their considerable momentum, they were nevertheless powering down. Kismet could feel the fuselage begin to twist with the torque and all of a sudden it was gyrating again. The Hind auto-rotated, unable to sustain lift, but plummeted more like a feather than a stone. Kismet mentally braced himself for impact. There was nothing he could do to prepare physically.

When it finally came, the crash seemed almost anti-climactic. Marie had retracted the landing gear before beginning the aerobatic evasive maneuvers, but had deployed the wheels to help stabilize the craft once the rudder was gone. The shock absorbers in the struts absorbed most of the impact and the sand helped dissipate the rest. Still, gravity remained a force to be reckoned with, and when the Hind slammed into the desert floor, the force crumpled the fuselage and pounded down on its occupants like a pile driver. Still, Kismet reckoned it no worse than the five static line parachute jumps he had made to earn his Airborne wings as an ROTC cadet. Incredibly, they had survived a helicopter crash.

But before either of them could make a move to extricate themselves from the ill-fated craft, a second impact blasted against them, followed by a shock wave, and then darkness.

FIFTEEN

It was impossible to tell if he had lost consciousness. The last thing he remembered was the darkness and it remained the only constant. He blinked—no change—then reached out to see if his hands encountered anything. After a few moments of searching, he found the cyclic stick, right where it ought to be.

Well, that's a good sign. But why is it so dark in here?

More probing revealed that he was still strapped in to his chair, and that it was tilted over until it was nearly horizontal; the helicopter had come to rest on its left side. It took some more doing, but he managed to locate his *kukri* and sever the straps, at which point he fell against the interior bulkhead.

"Marie?" The sound of his voice in the benighted silence was a little unnerving. "Can you hear me? Are you all right?"

"I...I am not hurt." Her words sounded as cautious as he felt. "At least. I believe I am uninjured."

He followed the sound of her voice, crawling along the canted wall until he could hear the sound of her breathing. As he drew closer, he remembered that he still had some of the Cyalume sticks in his waist pack. "I'm going to give us some light. Cover your eyes for a moment."

In the pale green glow of the chem-light, he saw her, suspended in the flight chair like a prisoner enduring some kind of grisly torture. He cut her free and eased her onto the bulkhead. Beyond the bubble windows of her cockpit, there was a dull gray nothingness.

"What happened?"

Kismet moved closer to the Perspex windscreen. "I think we got buried somehow. Maybe we hit a soft dune and it collapsed over us. Or maybe that last missile hit close enough to make the sand behave like a liquid."

"Buried?" Marie echoed hollowly.

"We're lucky it didn't pulverize us." He turned to her and smiled reassuringly. "Hey, you saved us. You picked a hell of a good time to come out of your shell."

But his intended encouragement had the wrong effect. She gazed at him for a moment, an emerald moistness gathering at the corners of her eyes, then burst into uncontrollable sobs. Kismet held her tightly, grateful that she had managed to delay her breakdown as long as she had.

Things got better once Kismet succeeded in opening one of the door panels. He chose the one on the left, what was now the bottom surface of the helicopter, correctly reasoning that there would be no external pressure weighing against it, nor a deluge of suffocating sand as soon as it was drawn back. With the coarse desert earth thus revealed, he set to work digging with the blade of his Gurkha knife. It was a tedious and frustrating task. They scooped sand by the handful into the interior of the aircraft, but the hole kept refilling itself as more grains collapsed in from the sides.

"So why didn't you tell me you could fly that helicopter?" he inquired, offhandedly. He didn't want Marie to know the desperation that he now felt. If he couldn't dig them out, the Hind would be their tomb.

"You seemed to know what you were doing," she answered, almost sheepishly. "I didn't want to interfere."

"I'm glad you did. But where did you learn to fly like that? That was combat flying. Don't try to tell me you learned that at some weekend flight school."

She gave a wan smile, looking almost sickly in the glow of the chem-light. "I was in the military as a young woman."

"Forgive me for saying it, but you don't seem the type."

"It was required."

Kismet paused in his labors to ponder this. France had a policy of compulsive military service dating back almost a century, but it applied almost exclusively to males of eligible age. In recent years, the policy had been changed to promote other forms of civil service in order to professionalize the armed forces, and additionally to include females as well, but the years of Marie's service must surely have predated that. "I thought the law applied only to men."

She blinked at him. "Forgive me, I misspoke. What I meant was that it was necessary for me to serve in the military in order to reach other goals. I showed an aptitude for aviation and was trained as a helicopter pilot. I hated it."

He nodded slowly and resumed digging, but now that Marie had regained a degree of composure, she took her turn asking questions. "Nick, what happened back there?"

It was the question he had been dreading; answering it would mean accepting some very difficult truths. "Pierre… I don't know why, but he shut us in that lab."

"Deliberately?"

Kismet nodded. "Maybe he didn't know about the self-destruct, but he shut us in and made no effort to help us get out."

"And where did he go afterward?"

"We were followed by another group. I think they might have been spies or an elite commando force. Pierre was working with them all along." He stopped speaking as the gravity of what he was saying finally hit home. "He played me for a fool. All that talk about religious artifacts was a diversion to keep me interested, so that I would lead them to what they were really after."

"And what was that?"

No harm in telling her. "French-made nuclear detonators."

She let out a gasp. "There were nuclear weapons in there?"

"They weren't armed. Pierre seemed to know all about the deal the French government made with Iraq years ago. Nuke technology for oil leases. I guess they were afraid someone would find out what they had done."

"Did they take the detonators with them?"

It was an odd question, enough so that Kismet stopped digging. "It didn't look like it. I think they just wanted to destroy them."

She seemed satisfied with that. "And what of the second group? The men that killed Hussein?"

"Insurgents. I'm sure there are quite a few high-level officers who know about that place still on the loose. Maybe they were hoping to find a weapons cache or something."

She nodded again and at that instant the sand where Kismet was digging suddenly fell away, disappearing into a newly opened funnel. There was a gleam of daylight beyond. Heartened, he jumped down into the hole and made an abrupt transition into the desert heat. Shading his eyes with a hand, he looked back to find that the gap had already been covered over with sliding sand. Part of the main rotor shaft—the blades evidently broken off during the crash—extended from the side of a massive sand dune, but that was the only sign that a helicopter had gone down in the desert. The Hind was completely buried.

"Marie!" He climbed back up the hill searching for the hole. As if to answer his summons, the Frenchwoman abruptly burst from the wall in front of him and tumbled down the slope. He tried to catch her, but the uncertain terrain upon which he stood crumbled away and they both rolled to the bottom of the gully entangled like lovers. Kismet felt her shaking in his arms and thought she was crying again. It took him a moment to realize that she was laughing.

He joined her mirth for more than a minute, but when their peals of gaiety gradually stopped echoing through the dune canyons, the oppressive reality of their new peril settled in. The desert was perhaps not as hot a furnace as the one from which they had escaped in Laboratory Three, but its death sentence was no less immutable. The sun was only beginning its climb into the eastern sky, and already the temperature was soaring. To make matters worse, they were both severely dehydrated from their earlier ordeal and had no means of replenishing their bodily reserves. Kismet sat back on the simmering sand and began reviewing their options. It was a short list.

"As I see it, we have two choices. We can continue north on foot and pray that we find water before we collapse. Or we can stay here and hope that someone sends a group out to investigate our helicopter."

"How likely is that?"

He rubbed his chin thoughtfully. "If I were calling the shots, I'd want to know who was flying a gunship across the desert. Remember, Saddam, his sons, and most of his generals are still on the run. But that helo is hidden pretty well. They may already have flown over and not seen it. If that's the case, then we'll die for sure if we stay."

Marie gazed across a landscape shimmering with convection waves. "We've come so far, survived so much. It cannot end like this. I say we take our chances in the wilderness."

Her determination, however naïve, was inspirational. But the oppressive mid-morning sun quickly prompted a compromise. They would seek the shelter of the crashed helicopter until dusk, making the desert trek in the cool of evening. They spent the better part of an hour in excavating a passage back into the buried aircraft, after which Kismet began ransacking the Hind in search of anything that might improve their odds of survival. Unfortunately, the Iraqis had not provisioned the aircraft for the eventuality of a crash in the desert. There were no water cans or foodstuffs to be found, nor any extra garments or blankets to ward off exposure. A first-aid kit yielded a roll of gauze bandages and a Mylar film space blanket, but that was the extent of their supplies. Anything else would be the product of salvage and ingenuity.

There was enough fabric in the seat cushions to fashion a pair of rudimentary turbans, and after swathing one of these around his head, Kismet ventured once more into the open. Reckoning that their most immediate need was water, he began fashioning a solar still to reclaim a few precious drops of moisture out of the air. He began by digging a shallow pit, which he covered with the space blanket. The reflective film was a poor choice for what he wanted—a piece of clear plastic would have been ideal—but he had to work with what he had. Like a miniature greenhouse, the Mylar helped create a super-heated pocket of air, which in turn caused condensation to form on the inside of the blanket. A small weight tied in the center helped the dew-like droplets to run down into a receptacle, in this case the empty plastic box which had held the first-aid kit, but the yield was pitifully small. There was barely enough water after two hours to moisten their parched lips.

Aside from that, they did little else during that long day. It had been more than twenty-four hours since either of them had slept, and the trials they had faced leading up to their escape into the wasteland had left them fatigued beyond the limits of human endurance, but even rest in the oven-like confines of their shelter was exhausting. Finally, when neither of them could stand inaction any longer, they struck out across the dunes. Huddled beneath the foil-like space blanket to ward off the worst of the sun's wrath, they commenced trekking in the waning hours of the afternoon.

No words were exchanged during that forced march—no complaints were made, nor any encouragement given. Marie had evidently found a reserve of heretofore untapped energy and kept up with Kismet without any cajoling, but that pace was barely a crawl. Not only was their speed pitiful, but to ensure that they were not wandering in circles, Kismet had to make frequent pauses to check their heading. Without a compass, or even a trustworthy wristwatch, he had to use the shadow stick method; he would place his knife upright in the sand and mark the tip of the shadow. Ten minutes later, he would check again, and a line drawn between the two gave a fairly accurate east to west reference. It was tedious and time consuming, but it was at least a guarantee that they were still moving toward their goal.

By nightfall, Kismet was reeling from the effects of dehydration. Having only just recovered from heat exhaustion, he knew that he was particularly at risk for a second bout, and this time it would undoubtedly prove fatal. As the heat of day boiled away into space following dusk, he could feel the fever raging within his flesh. Still he marched on.

Without the shadows to guide him, he looked instead to the stars. Celestial navigation at least could be performed while in motion. Their rate of progress nevertheless continued to slow. Pressed together with the Mylar blanket pulled tight around their shoulders, they moved at a shuffle, each trusting the other to stay upright. Ultimately, neither one could recall who fell first. They collapsed together, shivering against the cold and embracing like lovers, and waited for the end to come.

For the second time in a week, Kismet awoke with an intravenous needle in his arm and a solution of saline flowing into his veins. The bedside manner of his savior in this instance could not compare to that of the ersatz Dr. Rebecca Gault. Even without opening his eyes, he knew that he was in a vehicle; the noise of the engine and the vibration of the tires jouncing over the rough desert terrain was unmistakable. Suddenly remembering that he was in a war zone, he tried to sit up, but succeeded only in banging his head against an obstruction.

"Easy on, mate." A reassuring hand gripped his shoulder.

The words were in English, spoken with a British accent, which at least relieved his worst concerns. It was dark in the vehicle's interior and he could not distinguish the face behind the voice. "Marie?" he croaked.

"The lass is in bad shape, but no worse than you." There was a chuckle. "The devil must be on your arse, because it's a sure thing you two escaped from hell."

"How did you find us?"

A second voice, more sophisticated than the first and with a slightly different inflection, issued from the darkness. "Your message eventually got through to CENTCOM, but that put everyone in a bit of a spot. The Yanks didn't want to admit that they had just shot down a pair of UN envoys and they dragged their heels organizing a response. I think they were hoping you'd expire out here and save them some embarrassment."

"Then I guess I'm lucky Her Majesty's soldiers were a little more decisive."

An uncomfortable silence followed, as if the unseen conversants were waiting for the comment to be forgotten before moving on. "We knew approximately where you went down, but had a devil of a time finding the site. Eventually we crossed your trail and followed behind until we found you."

"Well, it hardly seems adequate, but thanks."

"Anytime, Lieutenant Kismet."

The word, pronounced "lef-tenant" caught him off guard. "I'm not—"

"Oh, I know you gave up your commission. But you still carry one of our knives, and that makes you one of us."

"You're Gurkhas?" Comprehension dawned. There was an old axiom about the loyalty of the Gurkhas; once you earned it, it never failed. Now at least he knew why the soldiers had not been willing to let the awkward situation simply vanish in the desert sands.

"Captain Christopher Sabian-Hyde, formerly of the Sixth Queen Elizabeth's Own Gurkha Rifles. I was a wet behind the ears ensign— Second Lieutenant—back in '92, as I believe you were also. You were leading my platoon out there, Kismet."

For a fleeting moment, he relived that awful mission. Of the soldiers who had gone into the desert with him that fateful night, only one other man had survived. "It wasn't my call."

Sabian-Hyde made a dismissive grunt. "You misunderstand. That was our finest hour since World War II. My only regret is that I wasn't out there with you."

"Believe me, I'd have traded places with you in a heartbeat."

"I imagine so." He sensed the officer smiling in the darkness. "Water under the bridge. We all get our chance for glory. It seems mine has finally come."

It was only when they arrived at the British command post outside of Basra that the enormity of Sabian-Hyde's decision to mount a rescue operation hit home for Kismet. The southern city, nominally pacified by more than a brigade of British soldiers, remained a hotbed of insurgent activity. Dozens of Her Majesty's fighters had fallen in one of the longest battles of the war, many to battlefield ruses such as faked surrenders or ambulances hiding ambush parties of Fedayeen paramilitaries. The small force of infantrymen that had slipped away to locate the crashed helicopter had been drawn from the ranks of those rotating back from the front lines for a brief respite. These battle-weary veterans had traveled more than three hundred kilometers across the wilderness to find a man who their superiors preferred to simply let perish. Had the unsanctioned venture ended in disaster, the onus would have rested heaviest upon Captain Sabian-Hyde.

The British camp stood in stark contrast to the American operation at the Baghdad airport. Not only had the month of hard fighting to capture and occupy the critical oil export hub taken its toll on men and equipment, but the British Army was notoriously underprovisioned to begin with. It had been counted a major coup when a large cache of combat boots meant for Iraqi regular army units had been seized and distributed to British soldiers whose own standard issue footwear was literally falling apart in the harsh conditions. Unfortunately for Kismet, there was not a spare stitch of clothing in the camp to replace his own tattered and scorched garments.

The former Gurkha officer found them again in the field hospital where a surgeon was bandaging their many wounds and continuing to infuse them with fluids, analgesics and antibiotics. Kismet's physical condition elicited a sympathetic grimace. "Where will you go now?"

Marie had asked him the same question and unlike the British officer, she was in possession of all the facts. *Well, maybe not all the facts*, he thought. He wanted to say simply that his next destination was home, but deep down he knew absenting himself from the war would not give him peace from the questions that ate at him like a malaise. The specter of Chiron, standing on the other side of the steel door with his finger on the fail-safe button, haunted him whenever he closed his eyes. There was only one way to exorcize that ghost, only one place where he would find answers. "Paris."

Sabian-Hyde nodded. "I wish I were going with you. There's a convoy bound for Kuwait City leaving in an hour. I can get you on it."

"I appreciate that."

"From there, you'll be on your own." He gave Kismet another

appraising glance. "I hope you brought your charge card."

Because she was the executive assistant to the director of the Global Heritage Commission, Marie was able to access a special discretionary account and arrange a wire transfer at the National Bank of Kuwait. She purchased two one-way first-class fares on a direct flight to Paris the following afternoon, and had enough cash left over for food, accommodations and new clothes. She also acquired some disturbing information. "Pierre is back in Europe," she announced after leaving the bank manager's office. "He used the account to charter a helicopter flight from Hillah to Baghdad, then flew to Geneva."

Kismet did not vocalize the curse that was on his lips. Chiron hadn't wasted any time getting out of Iraq. "Was he alone?"

"It's hard to say. All I know is how much he spent and where. I could find out more by contacting the office."

He shook his head. "Not yet. I don't know what his game is, but I don't want to spook him."

A short taxi ride brought them to the Sheraton Kuwait Hotel and Towers where, despite a dour reception from the concierge, they were able to get clothes, rooms and food, in that order. Kismet purchased a powder-blue cotton summer suit with a subtle silk tie and a pair of lightweight huarache sandals. The airy shoes were a pleasant relief from the boots, which despite protecting him through so many trials, were beyond any hope of recovery. A brief shower, while welcome, was an excruciating reminder of how much punishment he had endured, and when he gazed at his reflection in the mirror, it was a haggard wraith who stared back.

But if his own appearance came as a surprise, then Marie's transformation was nothing less than miraculous. Her simple red satin cocktail dress accentuated the femininity that Kismet had initially counted a liability. Away from the war zone and its practical necessities, the woman that she was had re-emerged. She had lost weight and her cheeks were ruddy from exposure, but somehow she made it all look good. As they left her room, she gave him an impulsive hug.

By some unspoken agreement, their conversation never touched on the events they had recently experienced, nor did they discuss what lay ahead. Rather, they made small talk about likes and dislikes, favorite books and hobbies, anything and everything, so long as it had nothing to do with the matter weighing most heavily on their hearts. When their dessert was cleared away, they agreed that it was easily the best meal they had ever eaten, though in fact neither of them could remember now what the main course had been. Arm in arm, they left the restaurant and made their way back to the rooms.

Kismet was not surprised at all when Marie took his hands, stared up into his eyes and whispered, "I don't want to be alone tonight."

But much later, when she lay sleeping nestled against his body, his mind wandered over all the pieces of the puzzle that just didn't quite fit, and he found himself wondering if he really knew who she was.

PART FOUR

CURTAINS

SIXTEEN

He spied them as they entered the terminal building and quickly ducked into a place of concealment until they passed. "Nick Kismet," he whispered, staring at the receding figures. "There is a God."

He began to follow, maintaining a casual pace so as not to attract unnecessary attention. The pair moved with no particular haste into the duty-free area. He found a telephone kiosk where he could continue his surveillance and waited for them to emerge. As he waited, he considered what his next move would be.

The woman—he didn't know who she was, and didn't really care—was Caucasian, but had dressed in an elegant but modest dress with a matching head scarf, and from a distance was almost indistinguishable from the handful of Arab women who also roamed the vast facility. Kismet's attire was similarly nondescript. He wore a simple suit and might have passed for a visiting oilman or journalist, but for the bandages swathing his hands.

After browsing the duty-free shops but making no purchases, the pair moved back toward the heart of the airport complex. Their unnoticed observer followed, gradually closing the distance as contemplation fanned his smoldering rage into a blaze of indignation.

They purchased food from one of the concessions and moved to a table in the center of the seating area, as if intentionally seeking the protection of open space. He bought a soft drink and took a seat in the corner, facing the departure gates, with his back to them. Their voices were sometimes audible, and while he couldn't make out their conversation, one word emerged from the ambient hum: Paris.

Leaving his half-empty cup on the table, he moved into the terminal to make new travel arrangements.

The desert fell away beneath the fuselage of the Kuwait Airways Boeing 737-306, and with it, Nick Kismet felt the macabre gravity of the place loosening its grip on his soul. For a second time, this desolate place had tried to kill him, and while he had once more eluded the Reaper's grasp, he was nevertheless marked by the encounters with scars that ran much deeper than the damage to his flesh.

Chiron's treachery remained an open wound in his heart. He

could not help but revisit his memories of each and every encounter with the old Frenchman, from that first meeting on the bank of the River Gave to their reunion in the Baghdad Airport, wondering if it had all been a deception leading to this end. The Frenchman had always presented himself as a pacifist rather than a patriot. It seemed almost inconceivable that he had been some sort of agent provocateur, awaiting the orders that would lull him from clandestine sleep to commit acts of sabotage in the interests of French national security. No, it was far more likely that his motives were immediate in nature. His alliance with the DGSE had to be more a marriage of convenience than a mating of sympathetic ideologies. But how had the scientist profited from the cover-up?

He glanced at Marie, seated beside him and evidently napping, and wondered if Chiron's executive assistant held some piece of the information that would further illuminate the puzzle. For reasons other than courtesy, he decided not to rouse her.

Though he had not yet revealed it to her, he was apprehensive about confronting Chiron on French soil. He had little doubt that the authorization for the mission to destroy the detonators had come from the highest levels of government. Eliminating any witnesses to existence of those weapons and their fate would be imperative to national security. There was a very real possibility that the DGSE would simply make Kismet and Marie disappear.

As the flight crew began the drink service in the steerage class, Kismet rose and made his way toward the commode, more out of a desire to keep moving than any real need to use the facilities. A week of living on little more than adrenaline had left him almost perpetually on edge. If the claustrophobic confines of the plane, with its dry recycled air and pervasive humming machinery, offered little solace, the tiny restroom, barely bigger than a coffin, promised none at all. Nevertheless, he moved inside and gently eased the bi-fold doors closed.

Suddenly the door burst open and someone pushed inside. The intruder's shoulder slammed into his back and forced him against the bulkhead. The commode platform struck him just below the knees and knocked his feet out from beneath him. Before Kismet could move, a hand snaked over his shoulder and snared his right wrist. His arm was pulled up across his throat and his assailant's forearm pressed into the back of his neck to form an almost unbreakable chokehold. Kismet rammed backward with his left elbow, but the blow glanced ineffectually against the man's torso, while the pressure against his airway doubled. Dark spots started to swim across his vision. The unseen attacker had, with almost minimal effort, rendered him completely helpless.

Then, mercifully, the death grip relaxed, if only by the merest fraction. He felt hot breath on his neck, and through the ringing in his ears, heard a voice low and harsh. "Give me one reason why I shouldn't kill you."

Through his growing panic, Kismet felt a pang of disbelief. He recognized the voice; he knew the attacker. From the corner of his eye, he could just make out the image of the man who held him, reflected in the stainless steel mirror mounted above the lavatory. Despite the civilian attire, he had no difficulty identifying the man. "Buttrick?"

"Good men died because of you, Kismet," rasped the Colonel. "Those boys would still be alive if I hadn't let you talk me into that damn fool mission. They were my responsibility, but their blood is on your hands."

"You know that's not true." He barely had the breath to form the words.

There was an interminable silence, as if Buttrick was weighing the merit of his argument, then the pressure returned. "Not good enough."

"Wait!" Kismet's plea was choked, but a moment later Buttrick relented again, allowing him to speak. "We're after the same thing: the person who's really to blame for what happened. Believe me, I've got a lot more reason to want revenge than you. But if that's not good enough, then how's this: Let me go, or you'll spend the rest of your life singing soprano."

Buttrick glanced down and saw a weapon—a polycarbonate knife—pressed into his groin. The composite of man-made polymers and glass fibers was marketed and sold as a letter opener but had been designed with a somewhat more nefarious purpose in mind: the non-metallic blade was invisible to airport metal detectors. Though he had been compelled to check both his *kukri* and his sturdy Emerson CQC7 folding knife with his luggage, Kismet always kept the polycarbonate knife clipped to his waistband whenever he traveled by air. Until this moment, he had in fact never used it for anything more illicit than opening his mail. He pushed the blade just hard enough for the other man to feel the point through the fabric of his trousers.

But Buttrick did not immediately relent. "Are you saying that you know who was behind the attack at the museum?"

"Yes. I can't tell you everything. Hell, I don't even know all of it myself. But if you want to find the people responsible, then you'll have to trust me."

Buttrick resignedly let go of Kismet's wrist and took a step back. The two men regarded each other warily for a moment until, as if by some telepathic signal, they both started to laugh. Kismet lowered the blade and leaned against the counter. "Maybe we should finish this conversation somewhere else. If we stay in here much longer, people will talk."

The debacle that had culminated in the riot at Iraq's Tomb of the Unknown Soldier had left Lt. Col. Jonathan Buttrick with a separated right shoulder, two loose teeth, an unknown number of fractured ribs, and more bruises than he could possibly count. The physical injuries would heal in time, but the wound to his career as a military officer was mortal. Despite the unpredictable vagaries of war and the inescapable truth that combat leads to losses of both men and equipment, the United States Army always demanded an accounting, and a summary review of that day's events faulted Buttrick for the loss of three soldiers, the destruction of four HMMWVs, an incalculable amount of damage to civilian property, and a diplomatic black eye that would not quickly fade. Pending further action, the injured officer was ordered to return Stateside to join the rear detachment of his battalion, knowing full well that his premature retirement would follow as a matter of course.

It was understandable, therefore, that Buttrick upon glimpsing Kismet, the perceived cause of all his woes, could think of nothing but payback. Deep down, however, he knew better. Kismet had done nothing more than ask for a ride to a particular location. The blame for everything that followed fell squarely upon the enemy. But until he confronted Kismet, it had never occurred to him that the persons responsible had nothing to do with the war currently being prosecuted in Iraq.

Buttrick took the keys from the car rental agent and moved

toward a waiting silver Mercedes E220 CDI. It was a nicer ride than he would normally have chosen, but since Kismet was picking up the tab, there seemed no reason not to indulge. He slid behind the wheel and started the engine. His right shoulder still ached, but the Mercedes had an automatic transmission and cruise control, so it practically drove itself. He pulled away from the rental lot and wended back toward the "arrivals" area of Terminal 1 at the Charles De Gaulle International Airport. Kismet and Marie were waiting on the sidewalk with their luggage.

As Kismet stowed their bags in the trunk, Buttrick appraised the woman. She had removed her head covering, allowing her dark hair to fall free and frame her angular face. Kismet had made introductions on the plane, where Buttrick had found the woman to be aloof, almost unlikable. But he couldn't deny that she was a feast for the eyes. Leave it to Kismet to find a woman like that in the middle of a war zone. He shook his head. "Lucky bastard."

Kismet rode shotgun while Marie had the back seat to herself. Driving through the Parisian streets was a right Buttrick had demanded at the outset, though of the three, he was least familiar with the French capital city. For some reason, he just didn't trust Kismet behind the wheel.

Marie guided them along the major thoroughfares between the airport and the UNESCO headquarters complex on Place de Fontenoy. The Fontenoy complex consisted of four structures of varying design, ranging from the outlandish Y-shaped main building to the almost mundane four-story cube where the Global Heritage Commission offices were located. Construction of the scientific and cultural agency's headquarters had commenced in the 1950s and despite the political infighting that had led to the United States' withdrawal in the 1980s, few could debate that the physical presence of UNESCO was a marvelous testament to the spirit of humanity. Elaborate works of art decorated the grounds, including magnificent sculptures and paintings on the walls of the various structures. Kismet had always been captivated by one in particular: a mural, measuring almost thirty meters square, of dark red on plaster by Mexico's Rufino Tamayo entitled *Prometheus Bringing Fire to Mankind*.

Leaving the Mercedes parked on the street, the trio made their way along the broad Piazza into the complex. Off to the right, The Symbolic Globe, an enormous illuminated spherical sculpture situated above the six sunken patios collectively identified as Building Four, glowed like a beacon, but their destination lay in the other direction. Passing under the elevated structure of the main building, they moved to the secure entrance of Building Three. Marie signed in at the desk and used her key card to access the elevator.

Chiron's office looked like a museum exhibit: a lifeless facsimile of a workspace. Though relatively small, the room was well appointed, with deep burgundy carpet and cherry wood bookcases on either side. A matching desk was situated at the far end of the room, facing a picture window that looked out across the city. The unmistakable spire of the Eiffel Tower, limned in electric lights, was almost perfectly centered in the frame. The arrangement struck Kismet as odd. A person entering the office would have immediately found himself looking at the back of Chiron's chair with the Tower rising from the backrest. It had been a while since he had visited the headquarters of his organization, but he had no memory of the office. The glare of the interior lights on the windowpane obliterated the view and Kismet struck it from his mind as he pushed the chair away and sat at his former mentor's desk.

"So what are we looking for?" inquired Buttrick. The Army officer was casually examining titles in the bookcase.

Marie had asked a similar question during the convoy ride to Kuwait City, and Kismet had given her the same answer he now gave his new ally. "I'll know when I find it." Of course, Buttrick didn't know about the nuclear detonators or the French mission to destroy them, only that Chiron had left Kismet and Marie to die in the desert, so he hastily added: "Look for anything that doesn't seem to fit."

The drawers of the magnificent desk held neatly sorted documents and a scattering of supplies, but like the room itself, seemed almost staged. It made sense that the Frenchman would have put everything in order prior to leaving for Iraq; he would not have known in advance how long he would be away. Still, something about the tableau struck him as wrong. The room bore the signs of routine cleaning—the surfaces were dust free and the carpet showed a pattern of straight lines from careful vacuuming—but otherwise there was no indication that anyone had been in the room for some time. *It's like he's ready to turn over the key. Or...*

Marie appeared in the doorway. "I checked the security logs. He hasn't come here yet."

Kismet stood. "He isn't going to. Whatever Pierre is up to, he's done here. And so are we."

On the slopes of Montmartre, Pierre Chiron looked out across the glittering city. His gaze was riveted upon a point less than five kilometers distant. Behind him, a navy blue Volkswagen Caravelle minibus stood in stark contrast to the chiseled marble grave markers that decorated the Cimetière du Montmartre. The brilliant white dome of the Basilique du Sacré Coeur rose from the crest of the hill like a second moon, reaching for the night sky.

If Chiron had appeared frail to Kismet on the occasion of their reunion, then he was positively a ghost of his former self now. He was thin, having eaten almost nothing since escaping the crumbling tunnels beneath the Babylonian palace, and his flesh was pallid, as if the sun had bleached rather than bronzed his skin. The hollowness in his eyes had deepened, partly because of his lack of appetite, partly because of the hunger in his soul. After a moment of contemplating his final objective, he turned away and moved into the cemetery.

Collette was here, or rather, all that remained of her. He had laid her to rest in the sanctified ground, not to honor her dying wishes or the tenets of her faith, but because his family owned a plot and, should things go wrong this night, his arrangements for his own disposition stipulated that he should be laid here as well, once more at her side. Not that it mattered.

Ashes to ashes…

There was no afterlife, no heaven in which he would find a place in her arms. She was not gazing down upon him, longing for that much delayed rendezvous. She was simply gone.

And if I'm wrong?

But he wasn't wrong. Because if he was, she would have reached out to him and stayed his hand at the moment in which he had taken the life of the man they both had thought of as their son. If the God to whom she had prayed even in the final hours of her life really existed, He would have sent her, as He sent the angel to Abraham to rescue Isaac from the slaughtering knife. No, there was no longer any doubt in his mind. The entity behind the veil of heaven was no omnipotent, omniscient benefactor, but only a hazy amalgam of humanity's unconscious superstitions, given life by the awesome unrecognized power of the planet's magnetic field.

Chiron had been raised in a house divided. His mother, like the woman he had eventually taken as his wife, was a devout believer, while his father, nominally a Roman Catholic, had been a man devoted to secular wisdom. Following the end of the German occupation, the elder Chiron had pushed his son to pursue a life of culture and learning, and the young man's fascination with both the unrealized potential of atomic power and its horrifying utilization as a weapon, had given him the focus to become both a nuclear scientist and outspoken opponent of weapons proliferation. He now realized that, in his own way, he had been searching for faith as surely as the women in his life. His scriptures were the equations of Einstein, Fermi and Oppenheimer, and in those cryptic texts, he had found the power of God.

And yet, for all that he knew this to be true, here he was at Collette's grave and standing in the shadow of the cathedral where she and thousands of others had come to pray; Sacré Coeur—the Sacred Heart.

"I'm sorry," he whispered, knowing that she would understand where further words failed him, knowing that she no longer existed save as a memory in his own fractured conscience, knowing even that his apology was not entirely directed at the ghost of his wife. He was also speaking to the presence ostensibly occupying the grand structure atop the Butte Montmartre. In that respect at least, he was heard.

"We're being followed," Kismet announced as the Mercedes raced along the Rue Royale. "I noticed him on the bridge. Everyone else is whizzing by us like we don't belong here."

Buttrick glanced in the mirror, then over his shoulder. Rather than comment, he quickly signaled and made a right turn at the next intersection. A pair of headlights, which had maintained a constant distance behind them, made a similarly hasty course change.

"Not too subtle about it," the officer observed. He made another right, onto the Rue Cambon and the trailing vehicle followed suit. "What do you want me to do?"

"I have to take a look at Pierre's flat," Kismet answered, "but there's no reason we have to let our shadow know that."

"What are you proposing?" asked Marie.

"We split up. Next time we make a turn, slow down long enough for me to jump out. There's a Metro stop not too far from Pierre's building. I should be able to get there and start searching the place in about half an hour. Meanwhile, you can take our friend back there on a scenic tour of the city. After that, go to your place, Marie, and wait for me to call."

"And what if this guy decides to do more than just tail us?"

Kismet met Buttrick's stare. "Do what you can. If I can't reach you at Marie's, I'll know something came up. Leave a message for me at UNESCO if you can."

Marie scribbled her phone number on a torn scrap of paper and gave it to him, along with a quick kiss. "Good luck."

Buttrick whipped the Mercedes left onto a narrow side street then took the first right onto an unmarked but short street and pumped the brakes. When the car slowed to a mere 20 kilometers per hour, Kismet opened the door and rolled from the passenger seat onto the pavement. The impact exacerbated latent aches in his extremities, but he pushed through the agony and scrambled for cover behind a trash receptacle. The engine of the rental car revved loudly in the confined area as Buttrick hastened away, and no sooner had the Mercedes turned the corner at the far end, when twin spots of brilliance appeared at the other. A rust-colored sedan, moving too fast for him to identify make or model, raced down the cramped street and exited onto the main thoroughfare, all within the space of a few seconds.

He lingered in the shadows of the alley a moment, searching for signs of a second trailing vehicle. Typically, intelligence and police agencies trying to maintain contact with a mobile suspect would employ as many as four different automobiles in constant radio contact, to avoid the kind of amateurish mistakes that had alerted Kismet to the presence of the tail. But with no other vehicles in evidence, he rose from his hiding place and moved in the same direction the other cars had gone.

The street opened onto the Rue de Rivoli, which ran along the northern edge of the Jardin des Tuileries. The extensive garden was just a part of the large city park which included such famous Parisian landmarks as the Arc de Triomphe and the Musée du Louvre. Traffic on the boulevard was constant and steady; if there was a backup surveillance vehicle, it had already moved on. This revelation prompted Kismet to eschew his stated plan to use the transit system in favor of a more straightforward means of transportation. He flagged down a passing taxi and in flawless French, gave the driver Chiron's address.

The building, located on an insignificant thoroughfare which connected the Rue de Richelieu and the Rue St. Roch, was just as Kismet remembered. No lights burned on the top floor of the three-story house, the floor where Pierre and Collette Chiron had lived most of their married life together in a two-bedroom apartment. Kismet had once asked why the aging couple had not retired to the country, and sensed in the answer that he had unwittingly aggravated an old wound. It had always been their intention to leave the urban environment in order to raise their children, and since fate had not deigned to grant them that fondest wish, there had been no reason to leave. Shaking off the bittersweet memory, Kismet scanned the area looking for anything out of place, then moved inside.

The interior of the apartment building was quiet. A single incandescent bulb depending from the ceiling of each landing provided the only illumination and the only evidence that the structure was in fact occupied at all. Kismet saw no indication that anyone was in the building as he crept up the stairs to Chiron's threshold.

With a grimace, he unleashed a kick to a point above the latching mechanism. The door burst inward with a noise that seemed, in the stillness, like a gunshot, but if anyone on the second floor heard, they elected not to investigate. He quickly moved inside and closed the door. After a moment of fumbled searching, he found the light switch. Even before his eyes could adjust, he knew something was wrong.

There were four of them, all dressed in black, looking very much like they had in the laboratory complex. Their guns were the same also, and without exception, were fixed on him. "Damn."

Rebecca Gault stalked forward, her gun sight never wavering. "Kismet? You're the last person I expected to see here."

Her incredulity caught him off guard. *If they're not waiting for me...?*

"I might say the same thing," he said, hiding his surprise. He looked past the barrel of the Steyr TMP nine millimeter in her hands and stared directly into her eyes. The irises were a remarkable shade of green, something he had failed to notice during their previous encounters. "I'm afraid you have me at a disadvantage."

She didn't respond, and he took a moment to glance at the door expressions of her comrades before continuing. "You've seen me naked."

Rebecca's stony mask did not slip, but when one of her men made a rude comment in their shared tongue, she silenced him with a look as lethal as a guillotine. When her gaze returned to Kismet, he saw a glimmer of humor in her eyes. "That was professional. I was your doctor."

"You're no doctor. The real Dr. Gault is still in Switzerland."

"That may be true, but I am nevertheless a physician, Monsieur Kismet." The gun came up again. "Where's Chiron?"

"What makes you think I would know? He left us to die in that hole. That was the plan all along, wasn't it, Doc? No witnesses?" He took her silence as confirmation, and it occurred to him that the death warrant was probably still in effect. Working up his best poker face, he continued. "Well I've got news for you. I've already told the UN and the US State Department. When the sun rises tomorrow, the whole world is going to know about your dirty deals with Saddam Hussein."

Rebecca's nostrils flared angrily, but she surprised him by lowering her gun again. "I'm afraid that's the least of my worries right now."

Suddenly he understood. "Pierre double-crossed you too, didn't he?"

"If you know where he is, Monsieur Kismet…" Her tone was more pleading than demanding, and that was sufficiently out of character for her that Kismet felt a whisper of uneasiness.

"What's really going on here? What's Pierre done that has you so freaked out?"

She glanced at her comrades as if uncertain what she should say in front of them, then stepped closer to him. "Seven hours ago, Pierre Chiron visited an IAEA facility in Geneva. A nuclear storage facility. After he left, a routine inspection revealed that a small amount of weapons grade plutonium was missing."

"He just walked in and took nuclear fuel?"

"His credentials allow him to conduct research. He's been there before on several occasions." She tilted her head to look up at him, to hold his gaze with her own. "He took something from the cave. He claimed it was a relic from an ancient civilization. It was the price of his cooperation. Do you know what is was?"

"Relic?" Had Pierre actually found the Staff of Moses? But then why would he need... "Plutonium. How much?"

"Enough. Six kilograms. Among other things, the facility was storing the cores from decommissioned Soviet SS-18s."

"Did you count the detonators before you blew up that weapons lab?"

"Of course. I checked their serial numbers. All three detonators were accounted for."

Kismet shook his head with a grimace. "There was another detonator. One the Iraqis were building based on the same design."

"I didn't see it."

"Of course not. Pierre had it wrapped up in a courier bag. You helped him get it out of there. And now he can arm it."

He could tell from her expression that she already knew this to be true. "You have known him longer than anyone. What will he do with it? Sell it?"

"That doesn't sound like Pierre." As soon as he said it, he realized the flaw in her statement. Though he had been acquainted with Chiron for nearly a decade, it was now very apparent that he really didn't know the man at all. "He's obviously been planning this for a while."

Rebecca nodded. "He approached the Directorate almost eight months ago."

"But he couldn't have known that our search would turn up the lab." Kismet was thinking aloud now, rather than responding to the intelligence agent's comments. He closed his eyes, trying to remember what had been said during the survey of the Esagilia. He remembered only his incredulity at Chiron's wild theories about Moses and Solomon. *But he was so sincere. If he wanted to dupe me, why would he have concocted such a wild story?* "Maybe there's something here that could tell us. Have you searched the place?"

"We made a cursory search of his papers. If he has a safe, we have not located it."

He pushed past her, heedless of the machine pistols still trained on him, and moved through the familiar environs of Chiron's flat. Little had changed since his last visit, but here too he saw the careful orderliness that had distinguished the Frenchman's office at the UNESCO headquarters. Chiron had squared everything away as if closing shop for the last time. With the decision to embark into the wilderness, he had left his old life behind forever.

Rebecca was right behind him as he entered Chiron's library. The area had always been the old man's second office, and in addition to the wealth of published knowledge lining the bookshelves, he had a personal computer equipped with a high-speed Internet connection, which at present was displaying a screen saver program with a slide show of famous paintings.

"Do you know his password?" Rebecca asked as he sat down in front of the keyboard.

He shook his head, but nevertheless tapped the spacebar to banish the screen saver and bring up the security prompt. He stared at it thoughtfully, his fingers hovering above the keys.

Rebecca took out a cell phone. "I'll send for a computer expert. We should be able to break this—"

Kismet tapped out eight letters: C-O-L-L-E-T-T-E. The password window vanished to be replaced by a graphic desktop display featuring Picasso's *Fall of Icarus*. It was, he knew, one of the large murals adorning Building Three of the Fontenoy campus. Rebecca fell silent at his shoulder and continued watching as he began randomly opening files and exploring Chiron's history of browsing the World Wide Web. A file folder titled "Geomancy" caught his eye.

"What is that?" she asked as the hard drive began whirring to locate the relevant data.

"Earth magic. It's the belief that the planet itself has power which can be tapped for…well, whatever a person wants, I suppose. The Chinese still practice a form of it today: Feng Shui. It was the driving force behind most Pagan religions as well, Wicca, Druidism, and so forth." He trailed off as the cathode ray tube began displaying lines of text. The folder marked "Geomancy" was a journal of Chiron's musings and revelations on the subject.

Before attempting to decipher and digest the information, Kismet checked his watch. Almost twenty minutes had elapsed since his separation from Marie and Buttrick. It was almost time to make contact. Then the irony of his situation hit home. He had left them in order to throw off pursuit, and in so doing had walked right into the web of the woman he most believed to be his enemy, only to forge a tacit truce in pursuit of a greater need.

But who had been following them?

"You know," he said, half turning to Rebecca. "There is something you could do for me."

With Marie's guidance, Buttrick expertly navigated the boulevards of Paris, running a gauntlet of traffic signals and fearless French drivers from one end of the city to the other. The sedan pursuing them made a valiant effort to keep up, but without even trying, Buttrick managed to lose it somewhere along the way. After another five minutes of observing the flow of traffic around them, Marie confirmed that they had lost their shadow. A few minutes after that, they pulled over in front of her apartment building.

The excitement of the chase was like a tonic to the Army officer. He had no idea who their pursuer had been and didn't really care. It had been enough for him to have an opponent against whom to pit his talent and wit. The company wasn't too bad either.

Marie had opened up more and more during their ride together, and when she finally guided him into her tastefully decorated flat, it felt as natural as a visit to an old friend. She directed him to a seat at the breakfast bar and began preparing a light snack for them to share.

"How long have you known him?" she inquired, taking a seat beside him.

"You mean Nick? We've only just met."

She raised an eyebrow in obvious surprise. "I had no idea. You two seem to have a genuine rapport."

"Well, you should have seen us earlier," he answered with a grin. "How about you?"

Marie touched her fingers to her chest in a quizzical gesture. "Me? I too have only known Nick a short time. In fact, I had only just met him at the airport when we came under attack."

It was Buttrick's turn for surprise. "I just assumed that since you both work for… You are a… I mean, together, right?"

She gave a coquettish smile. "Nick is very brave and charismatic. Given the circumstances, I suppose it was inevitable that we would…" She shook her head as if trying to dismiss a bothersome notion. "Who can say what the future holds? Nick will return to New York, I will stay here."

For some reason, Buttrick was suddenly in a very good mood, but before he could respond, Marie let her smile slip and put on a serious mask. "There is one thing that has troubled me. Nick told me that, when he was attacked that day at the museum, the assassin indicated he was under orders not to kill him. He was specifically told not to be the cause of Kismet's death. How can that be?"

The mere mention of the museum incident had instantly soured Buttrick's euphoria, but it took a moment for the precipitation from that dark cloud to actually soak in. "Hold on. Are you suggesting they were in cahoots?"

"No," she answered, earnestly. "I don't see how that could be possible. I mean if that were true, why would Nick reveal what was said? There has to be another explanation. There's something about Nick that makes him very important to his enemies. I thought you might have some insight to that."

"Do you think it could have something to do with his military service?" Wheels began turning in his head. He checked his watch. "It's still afternoon in Washington. I know someone who might be able to help. Can I use your phone?"

Although vehicle traffic to the area was restricted, Chiron managed to thread the minibus through the barricades and drove right to the edge of the structure he thought of only as "*le observatoire*". Despite the lateness of the hour, the area was crowded with tourists and it took a few moments for park security personnel and the gendarmes to reach him. As they got close, they wisely assumed defensive positions and those few equipped with handguns covered one of their comrades who cautiously approached him. Chiron rolled down his window.

"Monsieur, you must get out of the vehicle."

Chiron did not attempt subterfuge. He slowly raised his hands, openly displaying the remote. "This is the trigger for a very large explosive device. If I let go, it will detonate."

The gendarme blanched, but did not retreat. Chiron could almost see the wheels turning in his head—the blank look as he searched his memory to find the correct response for the scenario. The paralysis was contagious. Chiron knew that if he did not keep moving, if he got stalled here on the ground, it would all be for naught.

"Young man!" he snapped. "You are wasting time and endangering lives. It is not your job to negotiate with me. Evacuate the area, or the blood of all these people will be on your hands."

His words galvanized the policeman into action. The man

hastened away without comment and began conversing with his peers. Chiron kept his hands up, careful to hold the remote in their view. Beyond their perimeter, rumors were already beginning to surface and he could hear the shouts of panic welling up from the group. Even before the security guards could sound an alarm, the stampede began.

With a heavy sigh, recognizing that he was now irretrievably committed to his chosen course, Chiron opened the door and stepped out onto the pavement. He heard the young gendarme he had spoken with shouting for the others to hold their fire, but did not look to see the result. If even one of them unthinkingly loosed a shot, they would realize that the object in his hand was nothing more than the remote control unit for a television set. He had contemplated actually arming the device, but there was too much risk associated with a wireless remote. All it would take was a cell phone or garage door opener randomly hitting the same frequency to set the weapon off prematurely. There would be plenty of time to arm the detonator once he reached his ultimate goal. His bluff worked and the discipline of the gendarmes held. No shots were fired. Chiron moved to the rear of the Caravelle and opened the door.

For all the technical complexities of the device and his plans for it, the thing that had stymied him almost to the point of failure was the physical difficulty of moving the bomb the final distance. Although it was not yet armed, in order for his deception to be convincing, he could not let go of his decoy control for even a moment. He was faced with the logistical dilemma of moving the detonator, which weighed almost as much as he did, one handed. The answer had occurred to him only recently, while watching a hospital drama on television: a medical stretcher with spring-loaded collapsible wheels. It now took only a minimum of effort for him to draw the mobile gurney from the spacious interior of the minibus, and as soon as the undercarriage was exposed, the accordion-like wheel assembly deployed with the suddenness of a trap being sprung. The multi-directional rollers glided along on the concrete surface as if there was no burden at all.

Why then, thought Chiron as he began the long walk toward his destination, *does it suddenly feel like the heaviest thing in the world?*

SEVENTEEN

The suggested connection between the 1995 French atomic tests and the worldwide increase in volcanic activity was just the beginning for Chiron. He had discovered an area of science—or rather fringe science—dedicated to the study of just such a phenomenon, linked not surprisingly to the theories, both actual and suggested, of radio pioneer Nikolai Tesla. Tesla's experiments with seismology and the generation of acoustic waves, conceivably with the potential to destroy the planet, were so plausible, so inflammatory, that it was easy to gloss over the seemingly minor flaws and inconsistencies.

For a brief while, Chiron was sucked in; the link between the bombs and the period of increased volcanism seemed beyond dispute. But experimental and computer models did not support the hypothesis that an acoustic wave from the tests could have awakened slumbering mountains. Such a catastrophic harmonic could only be generated by repeated detonations of relatively small yield, not a single massive explosion. There had to be another explanation, but it would require turning his back on the exciting, but ultimately mistaken ideas put forth by the Tesla supporters. The answer occurred to him one day while he was contemplating the observatory.

"What observatory?" inquired Rebecca.

Kismet scanned the surrounding paragraphs. "That's all he says about it: '*le observatoire*'. Oh, wait… It seems to be some sort of lab for studying the earth's magnetic field." He kept reading.

When the world entered the atomic age, the governments with the bomb made the classic mistake of leaping before they looked. The full range of side effects from the weapons was not immediately understood, and it took decades of testing, which of necessity involved hundreds of detonations, before these unintended consequences came to light. One such was the EMP, or electromagnetic pulse.

Those first tests had revealed that in the instant that radioactive material went critical, it released a flux of gamma rays, which in turn produced a burst of high-energy free electrons. Trapped in the earth's magnetic field, these electrons created an oscillating current and a rapidly rising pulse of magnetism that would destroy power systems and unprotected circuitry anywhere within the visual horizon of the burst point.

Chiron, as a leading scientist in the field, knew all about the discovery of the EMP effect, yet did not immediately see how it could affect the geological makeup of the planet. But his explorations into the radical theories of fringe scientists had taught him to look for connections in unlikely places. A review of those ideas brought unexpected illumination.

Ancient man had known about the existence of the magnetic field, and had even gone so far as to lay out the supposed course of these Telluric currents. The Chinese had called them *lung-mei*, the Dragon Current, and had believed these invisible lines of force to be the *qi*, or life force of the planet itself. Pagan cultures in England had erected monoliths known universally as "Standing Stones" along what early twentieth century spiritualist Alfred Watkins dubbed "ley lines". His contemporaries further speculated on how the druids and other pre-Christian cultures might have made use of their advanced knowledge, even putting forth the theory that the Neolithic monument Stonehenge might have been erected using geomancy, perhaps even by the legendary wizard Merlin. Alternately, it was believed that Stonehenge might have been a means of focusing the earth's power with a technology indistinguishable from magic.

Kismet let out a low sigh. "I remember this. Pierre told me all about it. Only he was discussing pyramid power and the miracles of Moses."

A trilling noise from Rebecca's pocket interrupted him, and as she took the call, he resumed reading. He heard her say, "Right now? Yes… No, continue surveillance."

Chiron's writings thoroughly detailed the theories he had shared with Kismet in the ruins of Babylon, but then abruptly switched gears by jumping to the modern age. When Rebecca finished her phone conversation, he showed her the information.

"Listen to this. 'What Project Argus and its successors demonstrated is that modern man now has the capacity to permanently alter or damage the earth's magnetic field'. Project Argus? Ring any bells?"

Rebecca indicated negatively with a toss of her coppery hair.

"Those two words are in English. I wonder…" He minimized the "Geomancy" file and opened an Internet browser. Within a few moments, a search engine had returned several hits on "Project

Argus". He chose one from a reputable resource and read the information there.

"'When the US Department of Defense first conceived it, Project Argus was considered the biggest scientific experiment ever undertaken. In the Fall of 1958, the US Navy exploded three atomic bombs almost 500 kilometers above the South Atlantic Ocean, in the lower part of the Van Allen radiation belt. The Van Allen Belt, an area of intense electromagnetic activity which had only been discovered less than a decade previously, served to shield the planet from a near constant barrage of cosmic rays. Project Argus, and the subsequent EMP, created a new belt of radiation that almost completely encompassed the planet. Four years later, another DOD experiment, Project Starfish, further disrupted the Van Allen Belts, actually destroying one section completely, and created a new band of electromagnetic activity at a lower altitude'."

"It is interesting information," commented Rebecca, "but I hardly see its relevance. Chiron is out there with a live nuclear bomb, which he intends to use or sell."

"I don't think he's going to sell it. What worries me is how he plans to use it."

"You think he is going to attempt his own Project Argus?" Her tone was skeptical.

"What am I missing here?" Kismet leaned back in the chair and steepled his fingers, trying to see the pattern of the puzzle from the scattered pieces. "Pierre isn't in his right mind. No matter how ridiculous his actions might appear to us, they make perfect sense to him."

"He seemed lucid enough to me."

"He's changed since I first met him. Collette's death…" Kismet suddenly stiffened as if struck by lightning. "My God, that's it."

"What? Revenge for his wife's death? She died from an illness. There's no one to blame."

"Who do you blame when there's no one else?"

Rebecca blinked in disbelief. "God? Chiron blames God? Then he'll choose a target with religious significance."

"I don't think so," Kismet answered, shaking his head. "Pierre's beef isn't with the Church. For as long as I've known him, he's been an atheist. Collette was a practicing Roman Catholic, but Pierre never believed. Science was his religion. But he said something, just before we went into that cave, which seemed completely out of character. He claimed to be looking for proof of the existence of the Divine: God's fingerprint.

"Then he started talking about the earth's magnetic field. He was speculating that it somehow gathered psychic energy—our psychic energy—to the extent that it had become a sentient entity."

"*Lung-mei*," Rebecca whispered. "The earth's life force, not just as a force, but an actual living thing. And Pierre thinks he can... Can kill it...? With the EMP from a nuclear detonation?"

Kismet was grateful that she did not burden him with further incredulity. "We just have to figure out exactly how he plans to do it."

"Project Argus was an airburst. He might try to set it off aboard an airplane."

"Maybe. But Pierre started this research on the ground. The ley lines have to be the key to his plan. It's like Chinese acupuncture. Find a critical point and put the needle in." He scrolled the computer back to the relevant section of Chiron's journal. Crude maps showed the proposed path of the Telluric currents as they flowed across the planet's surface. There was a concentration of lines in the British Isles, but the thread also flowed in every direction, across oceans, to touch every continent. One line passed directly through Paris, but the map was too general to pinpoint the juncture. Kismet let his mind wander back to his mentor's discourse on the eve of their ill-fated subterranean journey. They had talked about miracles... the ten plagues and the exodus from Egypt... Moses' staff... "The Solomon Key!"

Rebecca was nonplused by his outburst. "Is that some sort of religious artifact?"

"Not exactly. Occult practitioners have always believed that King Solomon had some special insight into the spirit realm, and as early as the twelfth century, manuscripts purporting to contain his wisdom began to appear. Collectively, they became known as *Clavicula Salomoni*, or the Key of Solomon. But Pierre speculated that the legendary wisdom of Solomon lay in his understanding of how to manipulate the Telluric currents. He did it by building a temple. It was the structure itself that somehow channeled the energy, just like the Giza pyramids or Stonehenge. The Solomon Key has got to be a building of some kind, and I'll bet my last dollar it's this observatory he keeps talking about."

Before she could venture a question, her cell phone rang again. Kismet ignored the distraction and kept talking, not so much to share information with Rebecca as to put his thoughts in coherent form. "It would have to be tall, like a skyscraper... Incorporate metal in the frame..."

Suddenly he knew the answer. It had been staring him in the face earlier in the night. But as he saw a look of aghast horror spreading across Rebecca's countenance, he knew that she had somehow beat him to the answer. "Chiron," she rasped, barely able to speak. "He's—"

"Let me guess." There was no triumph in his tone, only bitter certainty. "The Eiffel Tower."

When it was erected as part of the World Exposition in 1889, the Tour Eiffel, stretching more than three hundred meters into the sky, was the tallest man-made structure in existence. That record endured for more than thirty years until technological advancements made possible the construction of skyscrapers like the Chrysler Building and the Empire State Building in New York City, USA. And while the Eiffel Tower had ceased to be ranked among the world's tallest structures, it remained one of the most instantly recognizable monuments on earth.

From the turret-like observatory, just a few meters below the television antenna that completed the steel tower's extraordinary skyward reach, Pierre Chiron had a spectacular view of the city. Unlike most residents of Paris, for whom it was a destination only for visiting tourists, Chiron was intimately familiar with La Tour Eiffel. He had made the vertical journey to the summit many times in the last six years and had made an exhaustive study of all available reference materials. Yet there was more to the history of the tower than what was reported in books and travel guides. There were perhaps only a handful of people alive who knew the real story, and for a brief moment, Chiron had almost joined their number.

His fleeting glimpse into the shadows that surrounded that group had left him with more questions than answers, but what little he did know drove him deeper into the mystery. He knew that the Eiffel Tower was some kind of observatory, and that it would be a focal point for some experiment connected to atomic testing. Everything else was supposition.

When in 1886 Alexandre Gustave Eiffel had submitted the plans for his entry in a competition to build a tower to celebrate French progress on the occasion of the centennial celebration of the revolution, he could not have imagined it would have anything to do with nuclear physics. Or could he? The architect, who in 1877 had designed the steel skeleton for the magnificent statue *Liberty Enlightening the World*, a gift from France to the United States of America, known universally as the Statue of Liberty, was without question a genius, but had his namesake tower been designed with an ulterior motive in mind?

Chiron had come to believe that Eiffel too had been a member of the secret society of intellectuals, and that his tower reflected advance knowledge of the coming atomic age. More than that, he believed that Eiffel, and all the others in the inner circle, had known what he now knew: The Divine Entity, worshiped by many, reviled by some, resided in the earth's magnetic field. An amalgam of charged photons and human psychic energy, God existed because of the faith of his followers and the unalterable constant of global magnetic force.

But global magnetism wasn't a constant. The charged poles were constantly shifting, changing the location of compass north. Moreover, recent experiments had shown that it was possible to obliterate the Van Allen radiation belts—the electromagnetic shroud which separated heaven from earth, and was, Chiron believed, the abode of the Entity.

They had known it—Eiffel and his co-conspirators. Perhaps knowledge of the secret went back to the dawn of civilization, to the builders of the Tower of Babel itself, who said among themselves: "Let us build a city and a tower, whose top may reach unto heaven." They had tapped into that inexhaustible source, creating miracles which could only be described as magic. But Eiffel and the others had gone a step further.

Chiron tried to recall what Kismet had said that day as they rolled along the highway toward Baghdad: *We are the Chains of God...*

The memory was suddenly painful. Unbidden, the image of the cavern and the blank wall of steel with which he—he, Pierre Chiron who had sworn an oath to watch over that young man—had entombed Nick Kismet and left him to die.

"This too, I lay at your feet," he whispered. "And you will pay."

He had manhandled the stretcher into the turret and positioned it at the exact center of the structure. Now safely out of the line of sight of any observers, he could work undisturbed. He laid aside the ersatz trigger and began removing pieces from the device itself. A globe of black metal, the plutonium core of a Russian warhead, lay innocuously beside the French-designed Iraqi detonator. The nuclear fuel was relatively safe in this form; unlike the unstable isotopes of uranium that had powered the first atomic weapons, plutonium was not neutron heavy. The greatest threat to safety was a very high risk of lung cancer if particles of the element were inhaled, but Pierre Chiron knew that cancer would not be the cause of his death.

The Eurocopter AS 565UB "Panther" roared above the city of lights like a Valkyrie charging toward an epic battlefield. Its twin Turbomeca Ariel 2C engines screamed like those mythical creatures, hungry for the flesh of dead warriors. The image was oddly appropriate; if the aircraft did not reach its destination in time, the streets of Paris would resemble the aftermath of Ragnarok—the Norse equivalent of Armageddon.

Unlike Rebecca and the other DGSE commandos, Kismet didn't have a flight helmet or even a headset to both muffle the harsh noise of the engines and keep him informed of their progress. The latter point was of little consequence. Their objective lay centered in the cockpit windscreen, stabbing heavenward and continuously sweeping the night with a blazing searchlight.

It was impossible to know if they would reach the Eiffel Tower before Chiron activated his bomb. Every soul aboard the helicopter knew that at any moment the famed monument might erupt with the brilliance of a thousand suns, erasing them and the City of Light from existence, yet here they were rushing toward ground zero.

Rebecca leaned close and shouted in his ear. "He hasn't made any demands! The police say that he has a dead-man switch. If we try to kill him, it may trigger the device!"

The words stunned Kismet. *Kill Pierre?* Despite what the old man had done to him, he had never expected that it would come down to that. He tapped the side of her helmet, indicating that he wished to answer. "You have to let me speak with him! Maybe I can talk him out of it!"

Rebecca's expression was grim and doubtful. "He tried to kill you! What makes you think he will want to listen now?"

That stopped him. Chiron was no longer a creature of reason. What could Kismet possibly say that would turn him from his meticulously thought out endgame? If he could not convince Pierre to abort his scheme, what other options were there?

He gestured for one of the commandoes to give up a headset, and at a nod from Rebecca, the man surrendered the earmuffs to Kismet. The foam insulation reduced some of the noise, but he still had to shout into the lip mic to be heard. "I've got an idea."

Rebecca stared in disbelief as he sketched out his plan, and when he had finished, shook her head. "Is that even possible?"

"It doesn't matter. All that matters is that Pierre has to believe we have done it. If we can do this, we'll take away the only reason he's up there."

No less incredulous, she shrugged in resignation. "What do you need?"

Kismet took a deep breath before answering. He knew she was right. It was a crazy, desperate plan, and there was no way to know if it would be enough to disarm Chiron. But even a bad plan was better than simply waiting for the blade to fall.

The Panther flared above the vast greenspace, two hundred meters from the base of the tower. On a normal night, the area would be thick with tourists wandering through the Champ de Mars and lovers picnicking on blankets, but tonight those crowds had been pushed back another three hundred meters beyond the helicopter's landing zone. The gendarmes controlling the scene knew only that a madman had ascended to the summit possibly with some kind of bomb, and believed five hundred meters to be an adequate margin of safety. Ghoulish spectators could rarely be persuaded to leave such a drama completely. No one on the ground could have imagined that the minimum safe distance that night would be not five hundred meters, but fifty thousand.

Rebecca and Kismet hit the ground before the Panther's wheels touched down and hastened toward a line of waiting vehicles just inside the perimeter. A dozen men stood nervously in front of the four utility trucks, each wearing workman's coveralls and molded plastic hard hats. One of the men—his hat was white instead of yellow—moved forward to greet them.

Kismet cut short the introductions and launched into a repeat of his earlier monologue. The chief engineer's eyes grew wide as he spoke, but he waited until Kismet had finished to voice his concerns. "Monsieur, what you suggest—making the tower into an enormous solenoid—even if it could be done, it might tear the tower apart."

Kismet glanced at the brightly lit grid work towering above them. It was difficult to believe anything short of an atomic bomb could bring down the ten-thousand-ton structure. But the engineer continued. "You must understand. The tower, like any steel building, is aligned with the earth's magnetic field. If you try to reverse the polarity, the tower will want to repel… It will try to flip over."

"We'll have to take that chance," Kismet declared. "It may not be the best idea, but I need to know if you can do it?"

The man frowned, then glanced back at his team. "Oui. It can be done. We need perhaps… two hours?"

"Try to do it in one. That's about how long it will take for me to climb those stairs."

The engineer shook his head as he turned away, but immediately began shouting orders to his men. Kismet started moving in the opposite direction.

"The lift is still operational," Rebecca pointed out, racing to match his brisk pace.

"Then disable it. We need to buy some time. Once Pierre knows I'm coming up, he'll hold off taking any action."

"Nick, there is something else that I need to tell you." She waited until she had his full attention, then took a deep breath. "That matter you asked me to investigate when we were back at Chiron's apartment. Your suspicions were correct."

For a moment, Kismet struggled to grasp what she was talking about. Then he remembered and swore under his breath. "I need to call her."

Buttrick almost jumped out of his skin when the telephone rang. The brief conversation with his friend at the Pentagon had not gone well and now he was… *Damn it, I'm actually afraid.* What kind of hornet's nest had he stirred up?

Nick Kismet, former 2LT in the Army Reserves, had an open file at the Defense Department, flagged for immediate action. Anyone who even attempted to look at the file came away with a big bull's eye on their back. *Who is this guy?* Buttrick wondered, not for the first time.

He allowed Marie to answer and held his breath as she spoke in French. The telephone call was not the "black spot" he had been expecting.

"Nick?" A pause. "*Mon dieu... oui...oui... Très bien.* We will meet you there."

Buttrick could barely contain himself. As soon as she returned the handset to the cradle, he asked, "Well?"

"That was Nick. We must go now."

Chiron had just finished connecting the timer mechanism to the primary when the public address speakers crackled to life. They had made several attempts to communicate with him. They used his name now, which was, he supposed, a good thing. They would know that he was no amateur, and would therefore make no hasty attempt to storm the tower and disarm him. He had been a little anxious about the helicopter that had set down to the southeast a few minutes before, but nothing had happened subsequent to its arrival.

He ignored the hum of amplified sound and began keying in the time delay sequence. *No sense in prolonging the inevitable,* he thought. Acting on a perverse impulse, he punched in one digit three times: 6:66.

"Pierre, this is Nick."

Chiron's finger hovered above the 'start' button, motionless, but every cell in his body seemed to be quivering. *Nick is alive! But that's not possible.*

He was in that instant both overjoyed and filled with despair, torn between the love of a father for a son who has been rescued from the lion's jaws and the guilt for having been the instrument of that peril.

"Pierre, I need to talk to you. I know what you are doing, and what you think... what you have to do. I'm not going to do anything but talk, but there is something you need to know before you do this."

And then, something new was added to the stir. Chiron ignored the amplified voice issuing from the speakers and directed his gaze out over the night. "You did this," he rasped, his joy turning to bile. "It's just your self-defense mechanism. You're no better than an animal."

Kismet, unaware of the imprecations, continued speaking. "The police have turned off the elevators so I'm going to have to climb the stairs. It's going to take me a while, Pierre, maybe an hour. Please let me come up. Give me an hour, Pierre. I'm on my way up now."

"You saved him, just so he could stop me." Chiron's voice was taut. The thread holding his rage in check vibrated in his throat like a piano wire tuned too tightly and ready to snap. "You could do that, but you couldn't give her what she asked for? What she begged for?"

He lowered his gaze to the number pad for the timer. His finger was still poised above the start button. He moved it back to the six and pressed the numeral once more, then without hesitation, started the countdown. "Save yourself now. If you can."

Kismet had heard Parisian tour guides tell visitors that there were 1,792 steps to the summit of the Eiffel Tower, a number that commemorated the year of the birth of the French Republic. The tower engineer he had spoken with before beginning his ascent gave the official number, starting at ground level, as 1,665. The real number was probably somewhere in-between, but by any reckoning, the task of climbing more than eighty stories worth of stairs was not for the faint—or weak—of heart.

Kismet was already weary as he topped the first flight, nearly four hundred steps, and was beginning to wonder if he had erred in deciding not to make use of the elevators. At the time, it had seemed to best way to delay Chiron from executing his mad scheme, but now he was wondering if he had the stamina to make the three-hundred-meter vertical journey. Fifteen minutes had passed since he had made his plea to Chiron for one hour, and while he had not immediately commenced the climb, he now would be hard pressed to meet that deadline.

But as he left the first level, he caught his second wind and began making steady-if-plodding progress. His conscious effort at breath control had the added benefit of helping focus his thoughts, and the enormity of what he was now marching toward no longer filled him with dread. His entire world consisted of nothing more than putting one foot ahead of the other, and before he knew it, he reached the second level, where the Jules Verne restaurant was located. Like almost every foreign visitor to Europe, Kismet had visited the tower, but he had never seen it like this, completely deserted. It was as if the world had ended, and he was the sole survivor. Shaking off the dark image, he proceeded to the locked gate that secured the stairway to the uppermost level, and opened it using a key provided by the chief engineer.

A few minutes later, a figure that had gone unnoticed by Kismet moved out of the shadowy stillness and softly padded up the stairs behind him.

EIGHTEEN

Chiron sat with sphinx-like calm at the top of the short flight up to the turret, the highest accessible point on the tower. Kismet kept a wary eye on his former mentor as he unlocked the gate at the end of the east pillar stairway, but said nothing until he was only a few meters away.

It was an awkward moment, and Kismet sensed that Chiron felt it as well. Finally, he broke the stalemate with a gesture toward the Frenchman's hands. "They said you had a dead-man switch."

Chiron glanced at his empty palms. "A necessary deception. It was the only thing that kept them back."

"Christ, Pierre, what are you doing?"

The impassive mask cracked, but Chiron kept his composure. He gave a heavy sigh. "I'm glad you made it out of Iraq. Is Marie…?"

"Marie is safe. Hussein didn't make it."

"I'm sorry," was the hoarse reply. A shadow fell over Chiron's eyes, but then he straightened, as if once more finding his resolve. "I'm sorry you made it through that, only to come to this. I have to do this, Nick, and I think you know why."

"Because of Collette?" Kismet chose his words carefully. Chiron was beyond the reach of ordinary logic. "You believe that you can strike a blow against God—against the entity you believe occupies the earth's magnetic field—because he let Collette die. Is that right, Pierre?"

Chiron gave a sad, almost embarrassed smile. "It sounds absurd when you put it that way."

"Absurd? It's obscene, Pierre. You're willing to kill two million people just because you're disappointed in a God you don't even believe in?" He shot a surreptitious glance at his wristwatch. Fifty-eight minutes had elapsed since he had given the chief engineer his task. He could only hope that the job was done.

Chiron's smile did not falter, but something behind it changed, as though his blood had turned to acid. "Two million?"

It was not the response Kismet had been expecting, and something about the way he said it made Kismet realize that he had underestimated both Chiron's resolve and the magnitude of his scheme.

Chiron continued speaking, a condemned man explaining his crimes, if not quite confessing and asking forgiveness. "Everything we know is a lien illusion created by our symbiosis with this... This thing called God. We have given Him life through generation after generation of faith, and He in turn has become a keystone to our continued existence.

"The men who built this tower understood this all too well. With it, they sought to enslave the entity, to hold God in chains and bend him to their will. But like the *banderillas* of the bullfighter, this tower is an open wound in its body. What I do here today will not simply twist the knife, it will drive the blade to the very heart of God. And when it dies..."

Kismet felt numb. He didn't know if he believed what Chiron was saying, didn't know if all of the wild speculation about God living in the Van Allen Belts held even a grain of truth. It was easy to say that, sane or not, Chiron was threatening the lives of more than a million Parisians who would be obliterated in an atomic fireball, but underlying that very real concern Kismet felt a growing dread. *What if he's right? What if the very fate of the world rests on this moment?*

"You would kill everyone on earth to avenge Collette? How can you imagine for even a second that she would want that?"

"Everyone dies, Nick. Most people live miserably short lives, filled with pain and futility. Whom do you blame for that? You think I do this because of what happened to Collette? You are mistaken. I do this to avenge every soul who has ever died wondering why their beloved Holy Father has forsaken them."

His measured tone left little room for negotiation. Chiron had become a true believer, as driven as any suicide bomber. There would be no turning him from his path. Kismet had one card left to play. He spoke very slowly, afraid that the older man would panic in the face of an ultimatum. "Pierre, I can't let you do this."

"You cannot stop it," Chiron replied, matter-of-factly. There was no defiance in his tone, only grave certainty.

"I already have. Before I came up here, I had the tower engineers start wrapping the corner pylons in copper wire. As of—" he made a show of checking his wristwatch, but paid no real attention to what the face showed, "—about five minutes ago, they started running an electrical current through that wire."

He saw comprehension in the other man's eyes, but continued

talking, hoping that the sound of his voice and the confidence he projected would be enough to disarm Chiron where reason had failed. "You see, I was paying attention when you talked about this in Babylon. I know that you think the Eiffel Tower is your Solomon Key, your magic staff to control—or destroy—the magnetic fields. So I had to come up with some way to neutralize it: magnetism. We've turned the tower into an oppositely polarized electromagnet. Right now, whatever sort of interaction this structure had with the radiation in the atmosphere has diametrically changed. I've taken away your Solomon Key. You can still hurt a lot of innocent people, but that's all. It's over, Pierre."

Chiron stared back at him like he was speaking a foreign language. But as the weight of the words settled in, he seemed to deflate. "Two million," he mumbled. "For nothing. What have I done?"

Kismet advanced on Chiron, but the latter paid no heed. Chiron buried his head in his hands and sagged onto the stairs. Kismet muscled past him and ascended into the turret. Only there, as he caught sight of the detonator, did the reality of the situation finally hit home. His employer and mentor, a person almost as close to him as his father, had assembled an atomic weapon with the sole intention of wiping out all life on earth. He bit his lip and banished the paralyzing emotional response. Rage and incredulity weren't going to help him avert this catastrophe. Only a clear head and rational thought process stood a chance of doing that. But as he reached the turret and gazed at the now completely assembled detonator, even his best attempt to remain dispassionate failed.

Bomb disposal was not something Kismet had been trained for, but he understood the principles of making and detonating most devices. Everything from a stick of dynamite, to a hand grenade, to this, a medium-yield nuclear device, worked on the basic principle of pushing an unstable chemical to its flashpoint. This was typically done through the introduction of a blasting cap—a small explosive that, when activated by a very low voltage electric charge, would trigger a cascade reaction in the larger payload. A nuclear detonator required engineering at an unparalleled level. The titanium sphere had to be machined to meet the highest tolerances, and the timing of the primary explosions had to be precise to within nanoseconds. Yet, for all the necessary exactitude, it remained a simple, electrically activated fuse. The trigger could be anything from a barometric device designed to activate at a preset altitude, to a radio-controlled detonator, but the end result would be the same: A tiny electrical charge would activate the blasting caps impregnating the plastic explosives, and a chain reaction lasting less than a tenth of a second would begin.

When Kismet saw the device moderating Chiron's bomb, his heart fell. It was nothing more complex than a kitchen timer, affixed to the metal body of the detonator with two strips of black tape, but its humble origin was deceptive. Sprouting from the back of the cheap timer were no fewer than eight wires which disappeared into the larger device and gave an implicit warning: cut the wrong wire and everything goes away. But even more shocking was the innocuous black display which methodically counted down the remaining minutes until detonation.

5:48...5:47...5:46....

"Pierre, we have to stop this thing. Tell me what to do."

Chiron shook his head without looking. "You cannot. I knew that someone might try to prevent me, so I made it impossible to disarm. Stop the timer or cut any of the wires, and it will detonate."

"Damn it." His oath was barely a whisper. If the bomb could not be turned off, what did that leave? He glanced down at the illuminated park lawn below where the aerodynamic fuselage of the Panther lay like a slumbering wasp. It was conceivable that the pilot could have the helicopter airborne in less than a minute, but then what? He could not hope to remove the bomb to an area remote enough to minimize loss of life in the very few seconds that would be left.

5:18...5:17...5:16...

A plain gray box lay next to the oblong cube-shaped bomb. On an impulse, Kismet flipped it open and found inside a variety of electrician's tools and a small rechargeable drill-driver. "What about the nuclear core, Pierre? Can I remove it without triggering a detonation?"

Because of the precise engineering requirements of such a device, even a partial disturbance of the titanium sphere surrounding the plutonium fuel would prevent it from going nuclear. It would still explode, right on time, conceivably bringing down the tower and certainly killing anyone in close proximity, but millions of lives would be saved.

Chiron did not immediately answer, so Kismet chose to recognize his silence as an implicit affirmative. If he was wrong... Well, that would only hasten the inevitable by a mere five minutes.

5:00...4:59...

He took up the handheld drill and selected a five-millimeter socket head. It was a perfect fit with the machine screws that secured the cowling over the guts of the bomb. Fixing it into the chuck of the drill, he commenced unscrewing the cover. He was so focused on the task at hand that he failed to register the significance of the declaration that broke the stillness, until in a more strident tone, the speaker repeated the threat.

"Step away, Kismet!"

4:49...4:48...4:47....

He glanced sidelong at the person who had joined Pierre on the platform below the turret. He wore the coveralls of a tower maintenance engineer, but his physical appearance gave lie to the façade that he was just another Parisian in the employ of the city. His face was a dark bronze hue that could only be gained through a combination of natural swarthiness and long hours under a desert sun, and looked like distressed leather. Capping the classic Arab countenance was a mane of black hair shot through with streaks of preternatural white, a hint of some unspeakable trauma in the man's recent past. It was his eyes however that told the tale. The muscles at the corners of each eye were bunched tight, in a perpetual squint, as though he had gazed upon the face of God and been struck blind. Kismet knew the look well. The desert sun had left its brand on his eyes too. He did not have to study the man's face for signs of familiarity. This was the same man whom he had encountered in the cavern where the Hind had been hangared. The unarmed Iraqi whom he had knocked senseless and left for dead. Kismet had almost remembered the man then, and in the days and hours that had passed, the memory had congealed into recognition. This was the man who had tortured him on that fateful night in the desert twelve years before.

"Colonel Saeed." The statement was terse, barely escaping through unconsciously clenched teeth. "Pardon me for not being more excited at this little reunion, but I've got bigger..."

The gun in Saeed's hand discharged and the sound of the report was almost simultaneous with the metallic noise of the bullet ricocheting from the side of the turret less than a meter from the opening where Kismet stood.

"I said, 'Step away'. I won't say it again."

Kismet glanced at the timer. Less than four and a half minutes remained. "I don't think you understand what's going on here, Saeed."

"Oh, I understand." A cryptic smile creased the Iraqi's otherwise pained visage. "I'm pleased that you recognize me, Kismet. That makes this easier."

"Makes what easier? Revenge? Whatever it is you think I've done, it doesn't involve the two million people who will die if you don't let me finish."

"No?" He gave a bitter chuckle. "I don't care about them. But I shall enjoy watching you suffer as that clock ticks down, knowing that you are powerless to save them."

"You'll die too."

"Yes."

Kismet lowered the drill but did not move away from the bomb. Saeed couldn't possibly know that only about four minutes remained, and revealing the urgency of the situation might only feed his suicidal resolve. "I have to confess, I didn't recognize you right away. The truth is, I hadn't thought about you in years."

Saeed's eyes narrowed as he searched the comment for some hint of an insult. "I too would have forgotten the events of that night but for one thing. I never understood why I was ordered to let you escape."

Kismet's heart seized for an instant. The unexpected admission had ripped away the stone sealing the abyss of his memories. And yet, he had already glimpsed this truth during his encounter with the masked assassin in Baghdad. He remained silent, hoping that the Iraqi would further tip his hand.

"I should have taken your life that night," Saeed continued. "No matter the consequences. My brother, in whose shadow I am unworthy to walk, would yet be alive."

"I didn't drag him into that cave," Kismet countered, affecting a surly unrepentant tone. "If anyone killed your brother, it's you."

Saeed's smile twisted into something that was not quite pure hatred. "It is true. And I will repay that debt tonight with the blood of a million souls. And yours."

"When this goes off, the world will believe only one thing: An Iraqi nuclear weapon fell into the hands of terrorists and was used against innocents. Support for the war will be universal."

"I do not care."

Kismet could see the truth of the denial in the other man's eyes. He had only one card left to play. A glance revealed that another minute had ticked away. There was still time to prevent the nuclear detonation, but the margin would be slim. "Poor Saeed. Even at the end, you're just a puppet."

The gun wavered, but the former Mukharabat officer did not answer.

"When I finally remembered you, I did a little investigative work. I learned all about your little art smuggling enterprise. I'll bet you never even realized you were working for the Israelis."

Saeed's mask cracked, revealing an even hotter rage beneath. "What are you saying?"

"That's right. Your partner in the endeavor—the person who murdered Mr. Aziz and is responsible for the deaths of several American soldiers—is an agent of the Israeli intelligence service Mossad. You've been working for your greatest enemy."

"You are lying." The gun dropped imperceptibly; Saeed had almost forgotten about it.

Almost, thought Kismet. "Think about it. You controlled the largest known source of artifacts from the dynasty of Nebuchadnezzar, the Babylonian King who sacked Jerusalem and carried off the holy relics of Solomon's Temple. Who would want that more than the Israelis? They put one of their best deep cover agents in the perfect position to help you smuggle and fence the artifacts, and in so doing, guaranteed themselves first pick. Who knows, maybe you've already given them the one holy relic that will rally faithful Jews around the globe for a final assault against their enemies."

The accusation hit Saeed like a blow, driving him back a step, but Kismet did not relent. He turned to fully face the other man, tensing his muscles in readiness as he hurled the final verbal assault. "I'm sure your brother would be proud."

As the Iraqi staggered back another step, Kismet saw his chance. But in the instant he leapt from his perch, fully intending to pounce on Saeed in order to wrestle the gun away, the other man was abruptly swept off his feet. From out of nowhere, Chiron had launched a simultaneous attack, tackling the Iraqi to the metal deck. Even before Kismet's feet touched down, the noise of a gunshot, muffled by the close proximity of bodies, punctuated the violence of the action.

Kismet landed badly twisting his right ankle and sprawled headlong, but in the grip of adrenaline, barely felt the pain. He sprang to his feet and charged at the writhing tangled shape that was Saeed and Chiron. The gun roared again, and a scarlet mist appeared for an instant in the air above them. Then Pierre Chiron, who had once attacked and defeated a similarly armed killer with only his umbrella, rolled away, clutching ineffectually at the gushing torrent of crimson that boiled from his chest.

In the instant that Kismet made his leap from the turret, a very different struggle was reaching its climax three hundred meters below. Phillipe Baudoin, the acting chief engineer stared anxiously at his wristwatch, then wiped a hand across his forehead. He had tacitly promised Kismet that the last-ditch plan to thwart the madman atop the tower would be in place in one hour. That had been sixty-three minutes ago.

He had expected that there would be delays. Experience had taught him that events rarely proceeded according to plan. Anticipation of these unpredictable but foreseeable problems had been the reason for his original two-hour estimate, but he had been confident that, if only a few things went wrong, he would be able to have the tower pylons wired ahead of the one-hour mark. True to expectations, those problems had become manifest. The supply of copper wire he had requested from the power company had to be drawn from several locations, requiring an unparalleled feat of logistical juggling. Traffic around the tower had snarled to a halt, making it difficult for the trucks to get through. The last shipment had arrived forty minutes after his request, leaving precious little time to splice and coil it around the last remaining pillar. There had been other setbacks. The team on the north pylon had inadvertently wrapped the wire in the wrong direction, and while it had not actually delayed the operation, it was typical of what Americans called Murphy's Law: Anything that can go wrong, will. Even more frustrating was the evident disappearance of one of his crew leaders. Perhaps the man had succumbed to panic or abandoned his post in a futile effort to warn loved ones. Baudoin knew the missing man, and knew him to ordinarily be of unimpeachable character, but these were not ordinary circumstances.

He had not once stopped to consider the merit of what he had been instructed to do. He had no illusions about the efficacy of depolarizing the tower in order to prevent some kind of catastrophe. Kismet had made it clear that the procedure's real value was as a psychological bargaining chip with the madman high above, and as such, it really didn't matter whether they completed the job or not, so long as Chiron believed it done. But Baudoin was driven by a different motivation. He was an engineer, a problem solver, and when he committed to a course of action, he would settle for nothing less than absolute success.

"Phillipe," crackled a voice from his walkie-talkie. It was Renny on the south pylon. He held the radio to his ear and glanced up to the sloping column where the last section of wire was being strung. The whole affair seemed like some insane Christmas decoration. "Go ahead."

"Phillipe, it is done!"

Baudoin heaved a sigh of relief and checked his watch one last time. Sixty-five minutes. "All teams get clear of the tower. I will activate the system in twenty seconds."

He continued counting audibly into the speaker as he started the gasoline generator that was spliced into a DC power converter. Although a relatively low voltage was required to create the desired electromagnetic effect, there was no escaping the simple physics. They had used more than a kilometer of copper wire, and it was going to take a lot more than a dry cell battery to make this work. His finger hovered near the switch that would start the flow of electricity into the circuit until finally the moment came. For safety's sake, he made a final visual sweep of the tower base.

All clear, he thought, and threw the switch.

A torturously loud humming noise issued from the power converter, followed by a flash of brilliant light. Baudoin did not need to smell the ozone and burnt wiring to know that something had gone wrong. The exact nature of the malfunction eluded him. Perhaps the tower's intrinsic magnetic field was greater than he had believed, or maybe he had miscalculated the resistance in the line. Whatever the cause, there was no escaping the totality of his failure. He had promised Kismet an oppositely charged electromagnet in order to thwart Chiron's plan. That wasn't going to happen.

He could only pray that Kismet had already succeeded in bluffing the madman atop the tower into relenting from his mad scheme. If not...

If not, Baudoin realized darkly, *I suppose I'll never know.*

Saeed brandished the pistol at Kismet, but he was a fraction of a second too late. Kismet's left fist wrapped around the barrel and, with a deft twist, he ripped it from the other man's grasp, but a flailing blow from Saeed knocked the gun away and sent it skittering across the platform. A second strike, directed with more force and intention, caught Kismet in the chest and redirected the momentum of his charge so that he flew over Saeed's supine form and crashed headlong. He recovered almost instantaneously, but his assailant had likewise regained his senses. Saeed struck first.

There was no hesitancy in the Iraqi's attack. His hands flew toward Kismet's throat, his fingers digging into flesh like the talons of a raptor. Kismet instinctively struck at Saeed's forearms and wrists, but his foe merely pulled himself closer to limit Kismet's range of motion. Kismet felt his pulse pounding in his veins as the stranglehold tightened. Abandoning the futile defense, he instead launched an attack of his own.

Saeed was a killer, but he wasn't a fighter. Though his victims during the long years prior to his exile were almost innumerable, they were without exception prisoners, deprived of sleep and food and tortured into submission. As an officer, he had disdained combat training, and now, faced with a battle of the most primitive kind, he had only his atavistic impulses to guide him. It was a poor substitute for skill.

Threading his hands between Saeed's forearms, Kismet gripped the lapels of the other man's garment and crossed them over to form a makeshift garrote. Ferocious though it was, Saeed's assault was ineffectual alongside Kismet's cross-collar chokehold. The Iraqi's eyes bulged, first with distress, then from the pressure of depleted blood trapped in the vasculature of his face. Realization dawned, but it was already too late; Saeed's grip on his neck simply fell away as his oxygen-starved brain ceased transmitting nervous impulses.

Kismet held on a moment longer, fearful that his foe was feigning collapse, but the foul odor of his bowels releasing signaled that the battle had indeed been to the death. For a moment, measured by the thudding of his heart in his chest and a syncopated throb of pain behind his eyeballs, he could only lie motionless on the steel deck. His memory returned in crashing waves—his tormentor was dead… Chiron was wounded… The bomb was…

"The bomb!" The words broke from his bruised larynx as he heaved Saeed's unmoving form away and scrambled to his feet. The turret, though only a few steps away, felt like the last mile of a marathon. His feet seemed mired in quicksand as he struggled up the stairs. The device, for all its potential destructiveness, gave no indication of imminent peril; it might as well have been a discarded refrigerator. The only thing that had changed since last he looked was the digital readout on the timer, and when his eyes finally focused on the black and gray liquid crystal display, his triumph over Saeed wilted.

0:05… 0:04…0:03…0:02…

"No."

0:01… 0:00.

NINETEEN

Between heaven and earth, a veil.

In the sixty years since their development, atomic weapons had only been used twice against living targets: the occupants of Hiroshima, and Nagasaki, Japan. For maximum effectiveness, those bombs, thirteen and twenty kilotons respectively, had each been detonated approximately five hundred meters above the ground. Five hundred meters, nearly a quarter of a mile, was the closest anyone had even been to the uncontrollable storm of energy released by the fission of an atom.

Although explosive yield—as reckoned in metric tons of TNT—was the yardstick by which bombs were measured, all the dynamite in the world could not duplicate the effects of even a low-yield nuclear weapon. An atom bomb did not simply release heat and kinetic energy, the forces that wreak devastation upon their intended victims. Rather, when the nuclear core reached critical mass, it became a small-scale quasi-stellar object—a miniature star on earth, which annihilated its entire mass in a single instant. The blinding flash of light, which to a distant observer seemed to precede the shock wave and firestorm by a few seconds, was in fact a burst of electromagnetic energy across the entire spectrum—X-rays, gamma rays, and light visible and invisible in a storm of photons dense enough at close range to etch shadows into stone.

It was an enduring indictment of the short sightedness of human intellect that none of the scientists involved in creating and refining the so-called "doomsday weapons" considered for an instant that the creation of a tiny temporal quasar might have a sympathetic effect, not simply on the planet, but on the cosmos itself. Realistically though, no one could possibly have known what sort of phenomena might occur at the event horizon; no one had ever been that close. Yet, the Theory of Special Relativity which had enabled those scientists to unleash the destructive power of the atom—expressed in the simple equation $E=mc^2$—ought to have enlightened them to the other effects of bringing new energy into the universe.

Any physical object accelerating toward the speed of light experienced what Einstein described as "time-dilation"; a variation in the perception of the passage of time depending on the velocity of the observer. It should have been obvious to them that in nuclear weapons, as in stars, at the event horizon where matter gives birth to energy, time has virtually no meaning.

Kismet stared at the row of zeroes for a long time before it occurred to him that perhaps something more ought to have happened. Had the bomb malfunctioned somehow? The wind had died away to nothing and the foreboding silence offered no answers.

He glanced down at Chiron. Even from several meters away, he could see that the gunshot wound was dire. A bubble of bright scarlet had risen from the center of his chest and seemed poised to erupt. *Odd that it hasn't*, he thought, morbidly. It was an arterial bleed and ought to have been spurting like a fountain so long as the old man's heart continued to pump. The explanation was brutally obvious: Chiron was already dead.

Except somehow that didn't quite seem like the right answer. His gaze shifted to the other body occupying the platform: Colonel Saeed Tariq Al-Sharaf. He did not feel the same sort of doubt regarding the fate of his old nemesis. Death hovered over the Iraqi torturer like a black aura, sucking the last vestiges of his life force into the still night. The image was so vivid that Kismet looked away, fearful that the grinning skull beneath the shadowy cowl might next turn its gaze upon him.

0:00

It was only then that he realized he had not turned his head at all. His gaze had never left the unblinking display of the countdown timer. *Then how...?*

His attention was drawn upward, to where the television aerial speared the sky, and what he saw there staggered belief.

His first thought was that he was hallucinating. In fact, he could not be literally seeing the gyrating column of energy that spiraled into the heavens for the simple reason that he was under the cover of the turret. For that matter, his eyes were still locked on the unchanging numeric display of the bomb. It was that impossibility which convinced him of the accuracy of his observations and further verified his growing suspicion that he was no longer completely in the physical world. He also realized in that instant that the nuclear device had not malfunctioned; it had detonated right on schedule.

The gyre stabbed out of the upper atmosphere and into the tower like a tornado of light. It was magnetic energy, he realized, invisible to the naked eye, but easily discernible in this frozen moment. There was no mistaking the direction of the current. The lines of force undulated down into the tower exactly as Chiron had described in his writings. And somewhere high above, something was moving in the tempest, struggling against its tether as the flames of imminent destruction licked at its back.

Oh, God. It's all true. And I failed.

The Eiffel Tower had still been polarized at the moment of detonation. Maybe the engineers had missed their deadline, or maybe Kismet's grasp of how to manipulate the geo- and electromagnetic energies had been found wanting. Whatever the reason, the end result was the same. The electromagnetic pulse from the bomb would feed back into the planetary web, just as Chiron planned, and destroy it and any sort of sentient being that dwelled therein. It was only a matter of time. It was already too late.

0:00

Rage consumed him for a long time, rage at Chiron for having conceived of such a diabolical scheme, at himself for having failed to notice the subtle signs pointing to the coming apocalypse, and even at God for not doing something more on His own behalf. Inevitably, the anger gave way to despair. Much later, when he had wrung the last drops of self-pity from his psyche, he began looking for a better answer.

He reached for the bomb, thinking that if he could carry out his original plan to remove the plutonium core, he might somehow undo the moment in which he now found himself a prisoner. Nothing happened. His physical body was completely unresponsive to the commands of his mind, or rather, the electro-chemical impulse that would instruct his limbs to move had not yet happened. Movement required time, and time was something Kismet no longer had. The only thing that could save him now was a miracle.

He once more fixed the churning heavens in his mind's eye. *Miracle. I guess that would be your department.*

But if the entity in the swirling mass of energy heard his implicit request—or if it even existed at all—it gave no indication. Nothing happened, nothing at all. The clock still read zero and time remained at a standstill.

He pondered Chiron's words, spoken only a few minutes

before—what now seemed like a lifetime ago—on the function of the tower in the schemes of the nameless conspirators who had sought to imprison the divine being. He had likened it to a knife in an open wound. Yet, the tower had only been in existence for a century. Did that somehow mean that prior to the emergence of the industrial age, God—if that was in fact what it was—had roamed freely above the terrestrial domain, doing whatever He—or It—pleased? It wasn't too hard to reconcile the tragic wars of the twentieth century to that time period…

Forget it, he thought. *Don't get lost in the spiritual debate. Focus on the problem.*

He realized with a start that he'd had the right idea all along. Depolarizing the tower was the solution, but how could he do it from this tesseract of time and space? How could he change the magnetic constant of a three hundred-meter iron structure from the confines of a frozen moment?

"How did Thutmosis defeat the other priests who were also tapped into the Telluric energies?" Chiron had asked him in the sands of Babylon. "And how did he sustain his own connection to this power once removed from close proximity to the pyramids?"

How did Moses part the Red Sea?

Kismet's answer had been flippant and skeptical: "*He used a stick*".

The Eiffel Tower was that stick, the modern equivalent of Moses' magic wand. It was the ultimate Solomon Key, built for the express purpose of manipulating the energies of the planet. But having the key was not enough. If Chiron's supposition was correct, Moses had been privy to all the secrets of Egyptian Geomancy. Nick Kismet was no sorcerer's apprentice. The most sophisticated tool in the world was little better than a hammer in the hands of an ignorant child.

Then he recalled an earlier conversation.

"*That's where faith comes in*," he had told Chiron as they contemplated sunset over Baghdad.

"Ah, yes. Faith. Jesus' disciples asked for more faith. Do you know that what he told them? 'If you have faith as a grain of a mustard seed, you shall say to this mountain: Remove from hence hither, and it shall remove; and nothing shall be impossible to you'."

Was it that simple? Did he just have to *tell* the tower—his magic staff—what to do in order to make it happen?

He could not escape the qualifier: *if you have faith*…

He did not have faith. He was a pragmatist, and his opinions and beliefs were shaped by facts—by evidence and empirical reasoning. Faith was for... Faith was for people who could believe in something without proof. The simple fact was that Kismet did not have faith even as small as the grain of a mustard seed.

Jesus' disciples asked for more faith.

He stared heavenward wondering how to phrase his request, but then it occurred to him that he already had what he needed. He had faith that an airplane would not fall from the sky because he had seen it happen. He had faith that the sun would continue to rise and set because his eyes were daily given the proof. *Faith and proof are not mutually exclusive,* he realized, grinning up at the maelstrom. *I guess I can't ask for better proof than that.*

Okay, I believe I can do this. Now what?

He reached out again, not for the bomb, but for the tower itself, and in his mind's eye, there was no impediment. His hands caressed the steel as if searching for the secret switch that would unlock a hidden doorway. And then he found it.

You owe me for this.

A shudder ran through the metal skeleton as every atom of its mass suddenly began to oppose the magnetic field of the planet itself. The transformation was instantaneous—faster even than the speed of light—and the tornado of force spiraling down from the sky abruptly reversed. Something like an eagle taking to flight shrugged out of the tempest and vanished, and at the same instant, the veil separating heaven from earth was drawn aside.

Kismet couldn't resist a satisfied smile. *Only one thing left to do now.* He turned his attention back to the spot his eyes had never left.

0:00

A shrill, electronic bleating noise filled the night, startling Kismet out of his reverie. A denial was still on his lips, but his whisper had already been caught away by the unrelenting wind. The timer continued to issue a rapid-fire series of beeps, signaling that the end of the countdown had arrived.

And that was all.

No explosion. No nuclear cataclysm to destroy the Eiffel Tower or the rest of Paris. Just a kitchen timer, trilling away cheerily as though the world had not just about ended.

He took a step back, wondering what to do next, and caught sight of Chiron. The Frenchman's hands were clutching the wound in his chest, a futile effort to stem the geyser of blood that carried away his life force with each prodigious spurt. But something about his eyes told Kismet that Chiron had finally found peace. He found himself compelled to kneel at the dying man's side.

Chiron's mouth moved, trying to form words, but there was no sound. Kismet leaned close, and the old man smiled weakly. "So much to tell you," he whispered.

Kismet felt an inexplicable rage well up. The old scientist was as good as dead, yet he felt no pity. Chiron had come within a whisper of carrying out an unimaginable atrocity—at the very least, the death of tens of thousands in a nuclear fireball, at worst, the eradication of all life on earth. "Why?"

"I had to know, Nick. She always believed, but I could not. I had to put Him to the test."

"Him? You did all this to see if God really exists?"

"Rather arrogant of me, don't you think? Challenging God to show himself and save the world?" He coughed and blood streamed between his lips. "I've certainly paid the price, don't you think? Do you suppose I'll go to Hell?"

Something in the simple question broke through Kismet's wrath. He tried to answer, but there were no words. There was nothing he could say to ease the man's passage. He shook his head, unsure of what he meant by the gesture.

Chiron managed a chuckle. "All this to see God, and instead it seems I'll meet His opposite number instead."

Kismet felt his throat tighten. "Was it worth it?"

Something changed deep in the old man's eyes, and Kismet knew his last breath was not far off. "I got my answer, Nick. He revealed himself. He used you to save His world."

Kismet decided not to waste Chiron's remaining seconds of life arguing the point.

"And now I am at peace, Nick. I know that she is with Him. She is in a place of sublime happiness. I know that now." Another gurgling breath was drawn. "Oh, Nick. She must be so proud of you. There's so much I should have told you. So much…"

Kismet reached out to take his hand, not caring if the old man misinterpreted the action as a sign of forgiveness. Maybe it was. As Pierre Chiron slipped out of the world, Kismet understood why even the condemned murderer is granted absolution. No one should die unforgiven.

He stayed there a long time with the man who had been for many years his close friend and mentor, and for a few brief hours, his greatest enemy. Later, much later, he remembered that the rest of the world was still waiting for news of its fate. He eased Chiron's cold form to the steel deck and moved to the edge of the observation deck where he waved the "all clear" to the anxious observers stationed below.

It didn't take long for Rebecca and her team to reach him at the summit. Her hard eyes were expressionless as she surveyed the aftermath of the struggle with Saeed. "What happened?"

It was too simple a query to address the events of the last few minutes. He shook his head wearily. He knew he would have to explain everything, and fully intended to do so, but there was one last bit of unfinished business to attend.

TWENTY

Every night, crowds of tourists flocked to the Butte Montmartre, both to visit the splendid Basilique du Sacré Coeur and to take in the awe-inspiring view of the city of lights. None of the vacationers there that night were aware of the crisis at the Eiffel Tower, nor would they ever know any more than that a fire had occurred at the summit of the monument and that the tower had been briefly closed to the public. They did however get a taste of the excitement when a French military helicopter descended on the lawn and shattered the quiet with the thunderous beat of its rotor blades.

Inside the basilica, a few eyebrows were raised, but the thick marble walls muffled most of the tumult. Lieutenant Colonel Jonathan Buttrick was intimately familiar with the sound, but failed to grasp its significance. He continued playing the part of the tourist, idly taking in the majesty of the elaborate depiction of Christ with arms outstretched, reputedly one of the world's largest mosaic artworks, situated above the choir. Nearly two hours had passed since Marie had received the call directing them to proceed with all haste to Montmartre, and he was itching to know why. Marie had been perfunctorily silent, but he had barely noticed. His thoughts were repeatedly drawn back to the trouble his inquiry into Kismet's past had caused.

"Nick!"

Marie's subdued cry startled Buttrick, but he whirled on his heel, searching for the man she had identified. Kismet stood framed in the entry, a grave expression on his haggard face. Buttrick didn't know the other man that well, but he knew that look. He was instantly on his guard.

Marie moved away from his side and glided toward Kismet, evidently unaware of any tension. She unhesitatingly gave him a gentle hug. "What did you learn?"

Kismet replied softly, almost too softly for Buttrick to hear. "Pierre is dead. Saeed killed him."

"Saeed? Who is that?"

Buttrick didn't know the answer to Marie's question, but thought that she had asked it a little too quickly.

"It's over, Marie. Or should I call you Miriam?"

Her demeanor reflected appropriate confusion at the statement, but neither man was fooled. Buttrick stepped closer. "What the hell's going on here?"

Before Kismet could answer, Marie's mask fell away, to be replaced by a smile that was at once both guilty and mocking. "It was the helicopter, wasn't it? That's when you figured it out."

"I think I knew all along. I knew the person who killed Aziz was a woman when we fought at the museum."

Buttrick suddenly understood, and the gravity of the revelation sent him reeling. "Museum? You...."

"I'll admit, your shrinking violet routine had me fooled. It didn't help that there was a better suspect. But when it came down to survival, your true colors came through. You produced a gun out of nowhere and started using it like you knew what you were doing. When you shot that man in the cavern where we found the helicopter, it was exactly the same way you killed Aziz: two shots to the chest, one to the head. But you let the other man live."

"He was unarmed."

"He was also your accomplice. Colonel Saeed Tariq Al-Sharaf, a former Iraqi intelligence officer who had retired to a life of luxury on the Riviera after discovering a trove of artifacts dating from the dynasty of Nebuchadnezzar, the Babylonian emperor who conquered Palestine in the sixth century BC and razed the Temple of Solomon.

"Saeed needed someone in a position of authority to grease the wheels of his black-market artifact trade, and when he was approached by Marie Villaneauve, personal assistant to the director of the GHC, he must have thought it was a gift from God." He chuckled mordantly. "I suppose in a way it was.

"Your story about learning to fly in the military set off the warning bells. France didn't have compulsory military service for females when you would have been of age, but Israel did. You should have seen Saeed's face when I told him you were a Mossad agent."

"You killed my men," Buttrick snarled. Kismet's revelations had torn away the bandages of his own guilt and the shared trust Marie had been cultivating now seemed like so much salt in the wound.

When she turned to him, her expression had shed every trace of condescension. "I never meant for that to happen, Jon."

Kismet continued. "Saeed ordered you to kill Aziz because he knew that Aziz would point us toward him. You were still playing

Saeed, hoping to get a line on where those artifacts might be stored, hoping against hope that somewhere in his treasure house, you might find the holy relics of Solomon's temple. Alive or dead, Aziz was of no consequence, so you accepted the assignment. But then I walked in and ruined everything."

"Everything that happened after that was a horrible mistake," she admitted, still directing her words to Buttrick. "I did not intend to harm anyone but the target. What happened to your men was…regrettable."

Even now, confronted with the terrible truth, Marie was still trying to win him over. Kismet saw it, too. "Just tell me one thing. You had a silenced weapon. Why didn't you just kill me and save yourself all that trouble?"

Her eyes swung to meet his gaze. "I don't know. I never understood why it was so important to him that I not harm you."

Buttrick drew in a sharp breath, and Marie realized too late that she had played into Kismet's hands. She took a step back, and then seemingly from out of nowhere, drew a small automatic pistol and aimed it at Kismet. "But I'm not following those orders any more."

Kismet's eyes flicked down to the gun, then returned to meet her stare. If he was concerned, he hid it well. "Are you sure you want to do that here? In a house of God?"

"Not my God." All subterfuge was gone. Where she had once used her appearance as a disguise, hiding behind an illusion of helplessness and sexuality, there was now a confidence that was somehow as beautiful as it was deadly.

"It's just a damn game to you," Buttrick took a menacing step toward her, oblivious to the threat of the firearm. "Life and death… Those were my boys you killed."

The weapon shifted to block his approach even as she took another step back. She was now too far away for either man to attempt to wrestle the gun away. Kismet raised his hands in a calming gesture. "Give it up, Marie. It's not too late. I can still help you."

An uncertainty crept over her expression, but her voice remained defiant. "I think you've forgotten who has the gun, Nick."

"Help her?" Buttrick gasped. "You can't be serious."

Kismet ignored him. "You still work for UNESCO. Maybe it's under false pretenses, but legally it's enough for me to protect you."

She held him with her gaze, and her tone softened. "You could do that? You could forgive?"

Kismet felt the crust of Chiron's blood on his outstretched fingertips. "I can forgive quite a bit."

Her eyes flickered between the two men as if weighing the sincerity of the offer, but then she began edging around them. A few more steps and her path to the exit would be clear.

Kismet divined her intention. "If you walk through that door, you're on your own."

"I've always been on my own." She took one more sideways step, and then turned away.

"Marie!" Kismet implored. "Is this really who you are?"

That stopped her... But only for a moment. Then she was gone.

Buttrick started after her, but Kismet placed a restraining hand in his path. "She's a killer." The officer's voice was strident, charged with pent-up rage. "You can't just let her go."

"It was her choice." He knew Buttrick couldn't possibly understand what he meant with the statement, but he couldn't quite put into words exactly what the consequences of Marie's decision would be. In spite of all the hard-won victories, he felt the burden of failure.

And when Rebecca entered the basilica a few minutes later to offer a grim but satisfied nod, he knew that this was one moment in time he would not be able to undo.

EPILOGUE

Reveal

It was raining on the day that Pierre Chiron was laid to rest alongside his wife in the Cimetière du Montmartre and the drizzling precipitation had ignited a smoldering spark of déjà vu in Nick Kismet's subconscious.

He had not thought to bring an umbrella, but thanks to the kindness of another attendee, he had been spared the heavens' outpouring during the brief graveside service. Now he was alone, facing the weather and the tempest of memories alone.

In the aftermath of the confrontation at the Eiffel Tower, Kismet had discovered that he in fact knew very little about his former mentor, and most of what he thought he knew was wrong. It had come as no little surprise that Chiron had, in the last six months of his life, expressed an interest in rediscovering the faith in which he had been baptized as an infant. Because he had resumed taking communion, there was no hesitancy on the part of Church officials in honoring his willed request to be buried with Collette in the cemetery on Montmartre. The simple fact that he had made those arrangements, even taking into account the need to give outward evidence of devotion, seemed at odds with the blasphemous events that led to his death. Had he simply been hedging his bets? Or had he believed that God—not some entity living in the radiation belts, but the Almighty Lord of Hosts—would thwart his scheme at the end, thus giving him the proof he so badly needed?

Kismet remained near the elegant coffin, studying the fresh inscription on the marble headstone. "May 11," he said aloud, and suddenly understood the source of his uneasiness. Today was the fourteenth of May, exactly eight years to the day from his first meeting with Pierre Chiron. It had been a Sunday then, and curiously, the eleventh, when Chiron had demanded and received the ultimate apotheosis, had also been a Sunday—the second Sunday of May, known traditionally in most Western lands as "Mother's Day". France remained one of the few countries to celebrate the holiday in June, leaving Kismet to wonder if Chiron had chosen the day intentionally, or if it had simply been a coincidence.

The headstone offered no insight. The bland message "Loving Husband" seemed inadequate somehow, at once too polite for a man who had very nearly destroyed Paris for love of his wife, but at the same time too cold, too unsympathetic to honor a man who had been so much more. Kismet closed his eyes, trying to remember Chiron as a friend and mentor, rather than an architect of destruction. It was a tightrope walk between extremes and his balance just wasn't that good. He touched his hand to the exterior of the coffin, as if to offer a final farewell, and then turned away. He was surprised to discover that he was not alone in making final peace with the old man.

"I'm afraid I can't quite find it in me to grieve for him," Rebecca observed from beneath the dome of her black umbrella.

"Then why are you here?" he countered.

"Actually, because I knew you would be here." She moved closer, but remained aloof in her manner. Rain continued to collect on the fabric canopy and flow down in rivulets between them. She made no offer of shelter to Kismet.

Disdaining the weather, he folded his arms across his chest. "I don't think there's any unfinished business between us. You have my pledge of silence on the matter of your stray nuclear detonators."

"If the worst had happened—if Chiron's bomb had gone off according to schedule—it would have laid the city to waste. But this place—" she gestured to the basilica in the background, "—would have survived. It is far enough from the tower that, I do believe, anyone here would have survived the blast. You sent the Mossad agent here, knowing full well what she was. She would have survived, while all the rest of us—those who knew her secret—would have perished."

"She had nothing to do with bringing that thing here. That was your doing."

The French agent blanched, unprepared for the accusation. Kismet felt a perverse satisfaction for having trumped her, but didn't have the heart to press the advantage. The truth of the matter was that he had wanted to protect Marie from Chiron's madness. Even knowing what she was, and that everything they had shared had been a lie, he could not bring himself to hate her. Especially not now.

"There is one other thing that troubles me," Rebecca said, after enduring a suitable silent penance for her ill-timed comments. "The experts who dismantled Pierre's bomb cannot find a single reason why it did not detonate. By all rights, it should have gone off right on schedule. Any thoughts on that?"

"No." He shook his head and loosened his stance in preparation to depart. "I don't know anything about bombs."

Rebecca remained at his side, unconsciously extending the umbrella to cover him as well. "Where will you go now?"

"I don't know. Home, I suppose." His reply was terse, intentionally framed to discourage her continued interest.

"I have been tasked with evaluating the intelligence gathered from Colonel Saeed's villa in Nice," she continued, oblivious to his cool manner.

"Really?"

"I am to make sure that no other embarrassing discoveries come to light."

Kismet scowled. "If that's your idea of a joke, it's a damn poor one."

"*Oui*. Yes, it was a joke, and yes, it was a poor choice of words. Forgive me, please." She continued to match his steps as they crossed toward the road where their respective vehicles were parked. "I imagine we will learn quite a lot about Saeed's trade in illicit artifacts."

That stopped him. Not the comment, but the implicit invitation.

"What do you say?" she pressed. "Are you up for a little working vacation?"

"With you? Are you serious? I don't even like you."

She made a dismissive gesture. "You don't have to like your doctor. You merely have to accept her recommendation for treatment. Besides, it's not as if you have any secrets from me."

Somehow, her fingers found their way into his. He stared in mute disbelief at their joined hands. And then, to his complete amazement, he said simply, "Why not?"

Less than two hundred meters from the final resting place of Pierre Chiron, a black-clad figure looked on from behind a gauzy veil. Her attention was so riveted upon the departing pair that she did not hear the man approach. Nevertheless, when he announced his presence by softly speaking her name, she did not give evidence of being startled. She did however react. "How dare you come here?" she hissed. "Does the truce mean nothing?"

The man regarded her with his single, steely eye. "You think too highly of yourself, madame. There is no longer anything to be gained by your execution. The truce stands. Even if it did not... Well, I have moved beyond the simple role of executioner, as was ever my right."

She shook her head contemptuously then turned away.

"You should not have interfered."

That stopped her. She turned slowly, lifting her veil to direct the full intensity of her gaze upon him. "Interfered? Are you mad? Do you know what was at stake? What Chiron sought to do?"

"We knew. It was our belief that—"

"Your belief? You would have risked everything, the future of every living thing, on your untested theory? You know the role fate has chosen for him. You know that he is to be the one."

The lupine face of the one-eyed man seemed to become more feral as he leaned close to answer. "I know," he said, enunciating acidly, "that whatever will happen must be allowed to happen, without interference. You have changed that, and in so doing, it is you who has risked everything."

Her defense wavered, as if the argument, despite its loathsome source, had merit. "I did nothing."

"You changed the password of Chiron's computer to something that he would know."

"That signifies nothing. He would have figured it out anyway."

"Perhaps. But what has been done cannot be undone. What we have lost cannot be replaced."

"You are a hypocrite. If you believe that this was in the hands of fate, then you must accept that what happened—losing control of the entity—was destined. Else you would have taken Chiron out long before this came to pass."

The man smiled, but there was no humor in his eye. "The experiment had to be seen to its conclusion, no matter the outcome."

"Then accept that what I did had negligible impact on that outcome."

"If I believed otherwise, madame, you would already be dead. But there may come a time when you will be tempted to take greater risks to protect Nick Kismet."

"You are mad. Nothing matters but the Great Work."

"See that you don't forget it, madame." He leaned closer still until she could feel his breath on her face. His words rumbled in her ear like an earthquake. "Nothing can be allowed to prevent my brother from meeting his destiny."

End

ABOUT THE AUTHOR

SEAN ELLIS is the author of several novels. He is a veteran of Operation Enduring Freedom, and has a Bachelor of Science degree in Natural Resources Policy from Oregon State University. He presently lives in Arizona where he divides his time between writing, fatherhood, adventure sports, and trying to figure out how to save the world.

Visit him online at www.seanellisthrillers.webs.com.

Made in the USA
Monee, IL
29 September 2021